Rosie Walker is a novelist who
husband Kevin, daughter Elsie and

Rosie has a Masters in Creative Wri   University of
Edinburgh and an undergraduate degree in Psychology from
Lancaster University. Her first novel, *Secrets of a Serial Killer*,
was published in 2020. *The House Fire* is her second book.

rosiejanewalker.com

facebook.com/rosiewalkerauthor
twitter.com/ciderwithrosie
instagram.com/rosiejanewalker
bookbub.com/authors/rosie-walker

Also by Rosie Walker

Secrets of a Serial Killer

THE HOUSE FIRE

ROSIE WALKER

One More Chapter
a division of HarperCollins*Publishers* Ltd
1 London Bridge Street
London SE1 9GF
www.harpercollins.co.uk

HarperCollins*Publishers*
1st Floor, Watermarque Building, Ringsend Road
Dublin 4, Ireland

This paperback edition 2022
1
First published in Great Britain by
HarperCollins*Publishers* 2022
Copyright © Rosie Walker 2022

Rosie Walker asserts the moral right to
be identified as the author of this work

A catalogue record of this book is available from the British Library

ISBN: 978-0-00-839999-3

Printed and bound in the UK using 100% Renewable Electricity
by CPI Group (UK) Ltd

MIX
Paper from
responsible sources
FSC™ C007454
FSC
www.fsc.org

This book is produced from independently certified FSC™ paper
to ensure responsible forest management.

For more information visit: www.harpercollins.co.uk/green

For Kevin and Elsie
My whole world

Prologue

The Arsonist

The first time I saw him hit her, I laughed.

Not a normal laugh, of course. It wasn't funny. This was an expulsion of noise which erupted from my mouth with the shock.

I watched through the gap in the cupboard door, from my hiding place below the stairs, huddled alongside the broom, the mop, the carpet sweeper. His punch didn't make the booming drum sound that punches make on TV, in the black and white fist fights of westerns or the Technicolor gore of primetime bar bust-ups. The sound in real life was more meaty, like someone slapping a steak onto the kitchen counter with a wet thud.

It wasn't the first time. I'd heard them before through the floorboards after they thought I was asleep. His voice raised, staccato shouts. Her voice light, pleading. 'Don't. Please don't.' And then a scuffle, a shout, a whimper. And silence.

But this was the first time I saw.

She fell to the ground like her bones had shattered, then she pushed herself across the floor, trying to get away from him. But

1

while she crawled, her hand raised to her jaw, she didn't look at him. She looked at me, where my eyes stared out at her from the shadows beneath the stairs.

She was more afraid of what I had seen than she was of him hitting her again. It mattered more to her that I saw it than that it happened. That was the scariest thing I had ever known.

He followed her gaze, saw my stare. Shrugged.

And now that I'd seen it happen once, it was like the lock opened on a canal, water pouring through; no way to stop it. He'd opened the sluice for it to happen again and again. Hiding it didn't matter anymore.

After the punch, he stood there, flexing his fingers open and closed. He rubbed his red knuckles. 'Get up.'

She barely flinched; she was so used to it.

'Don't say a word,' he howled at me. 'I don't want to hear a sound from you.'

I pulled back from my spyhole, away from her cowering form, him towering over her. But I looked once more, pressed my nose to the wood. I watched him light a match for his pipe, still standing over her.

He dropped the match, still lit. It spun as it fell through the air, the fall nearly extinguishing the flame but not quite. Then he pushed the old kerosene oil lamp off the sideboard.

He turned away, didn't watch it smash to the ground. But I did. I saw as the cheap polyester of her housecoat caught fire. I smelled the melting fibres. Embers skittered and skidded, consuming the fabric like the incoming tide rushing across the shore.

She didn't make a sound. He'd taught her not to.

She rolled away from the shattered lamp, wrapped herself with the hearthrug before her whole coat caught alight. She ran a hand down her singed hair and then she quietly, calmly walked to the kitchen to finish cooking dinner.

He sat down and puffed on his pipe, which covered the smell of burned hair and fabric.

Don't say a word, *he said to me.*

And I didn't say a word.

But silently I vowed I would kill him as soon as I knew how.

Chapter One

Jamie

J amie pans the camera slowly across the congregation to capture everyone's happy faces. She is squeezed between a wooden pew and the wall, trying not to lean against the stone and get dust on her dress. It's tough to get the right angle from here, but Spider is at the back with a fisheye lens so she hopes together they'll have enough footage for a good edit.

The minister clears her throat and the chatter fades. Someone turns the volume down on the tinny string music playing from the battery-powered stereo. Around the chapel, people shift in their seats. In the back, someone shushes their kid.

'Welcome, family, friends and loved ones of Ella and Ant. We're here today to share in the formal commitment this loving couple makes to each other, to give your love and support and to allow Ella and Ant to start their married life together surrounded by the people dearest and most important to them.'

Jamie zooms in on the altar. Mum turns around and smiles at everyone in the chapel. Her smile is huge and bright, her lipstick a perfect dusky pink. She did her own make-up, and it is flawless. Her curled hair is piled on top of her head, with little flowers dotted through it, an antique hair clip glinting in the light. Tears shine in her eyes as she looks out across everyone in the chapel.

In the front row, Cleo glowers at her feet, her dirty-blonde hair over her face, bony shoulders hunched. Jamie tries to catch her eye, to mime a smile, but Cleo doesn't look up.

Next to Cleo, her best friend Lucasz looks blank, staring into space with his mouth open. He's on a different planet half the time, that kid. Gran looks happy, at least, smiling up at Mum and Ant with tears in her eyes.

'Ella and Ant thank you for your presence here today and now ask for your blessing, encouragement and lifelong support for their decision to be married.'

Everyone falls silent, waiting. This is the moment where someone could object.

There's a quick movement in the congregation and Jamie glances over, careful not to move the camera. It's Cleo, whose cheeks are red, and her head is thrown back to frown at the ceiling.

Jamie feels a flash of fear. *Please don't ruin this for Mum.* Cleo is such a drama queen, and it's touch and go whether there'll be a blow-up today. She's been harder and harder to predict since the incident at school last year. But Jamie's not supposed to know about that.

Ant didn't help by insisting they hold the wedding today of all days. Apparently, that was the only date the minister could do because they booked at such short notice. Poor Cleo's fourteenth birthday.

Gran grabs Cleo's hand and Cleo looks back to the front of the chapel, her shoulders still tense.

Jamie turns back to watch the ceremony through the viewfinder.

Minister Mary's eyes flick from Ant to Mum and back to the iPad she's reading from. 'Before you make your vows, I ask you to remember that love – which is rooted in faith, trust and acceptance – is the foundation of an abiding and deepening relationship. Please now read the vows you have written.'

Mum and Ant turn to each other, and the minister hands them both a piece of paper. Mum's quivers in her hands, to Jamie's surprise; she didn't think Mum would be this nervous. She was excited this morning.

'I, Ella, take you, Ant, to be my husband, my best friend and partner in crime.'

The congregation titters. Jamie tries not to roll her eyes at the 'partner in crime' cliché. It's as common at weddings as Pachelbel's Canon in D. She's only filmed a handful so far, but she could play wedding cliché bingo.

Spider was surprised she wanted to video Mum's wedding, thought she would want to enjoy the day. But she likes to hide behind the camera instead of in front of it, and she needs the filming practice. Making films is Jamie's chance to prove herself. Prove she's not the total fragile failure everyone seems to think she is.

Plus, she's pretty sure Ant will offer to pay her for today, and then she can buy new equipment and get set up properly.

Mum's voice steadies as she gets more comfortable. 'I will work hard to build a lifelong home with you, a home of honesty, respect and care. It's not fashionable, but I vow to honour and obey you for all that you are and will become, taking pride in who we are, both separately and together.'

Jamie suppresses another cringe. She wonders which stock website Mum found these vows on. If only she had shared them with Jamie before the ceremony. But there wasn't time, not with the super quick engagement and making sure Cleo wasn't going to implode every five minutes.

'I promise to fill our home with love and create a sanctuary to shield you from the worries of the world. Most of all, I will love you no matter what, for richer or poorer, in sickness and in health. For ever.'

A flash of white in the edge of the camera lens: Gran, raising a tissue to dab her eyes. It must be strange to see her former daughter-in-law marry someone new. She wonders how today compares to Mum and Dad's wedding in the late Nineties.

Dad's right at the back, holding hands with Sahara. She's gorgeous, fifteen years younger than him, and has that steely look in her eyes that hints she'll push for her own wedding very soon. Today, her ordinary veneer of calm control has a slight edge to it; her mouth is set in a hard line. She keeps glancing at Dad's face as they watch the ceremony. She's probably wondering if Dad regrets the divorce; if it's weird to watch his ex-wife get married. It must be.

A rustle from the front of the chapel as Ant unfolds his own vows. He stands up straighter; turns away from Mum to face the congregation. Jamie zooms out to centre the minister in the frame, with Mum and Ant either side.

She hopes the mic is still recording, the one hooked up to Spider's phone at the front of the chapel. She glances at Spider in the back. He's switched to a zoom lens. He notices her looking and gives her a thumbs up. She grins back. She's having fun.

Ant beams at the congregation. 'I don't need these vows.' He scrunches up the paper and throws it to the ground.

Jamie wills him to turn back to Mum, to not turn this into *The Ant Show*.

There's a confused mumble through the chapel and Mum's smile falters. She looks like she's about to cry. Her body twitches, as if she wants to pick up the crumpled vows. She doesn't like mess.

The chapel is silent. No one moves. The air is heavy with tension; no one knows what will happen next.

'I spent hours trawling through the internet for sample vows, and I did write some. But they're not what I really want to say.' Ant pats his chest, over his heart, and he scans the faces of the wedding guests like a keynote speaker.

Jamie rakes a hand through her hair. This feels wrong.

'But I want to speak from the heart.' He turns to Mum, and there's a collective sigh of relief that we're going back to the expected style of vow-making. The minister straightens her spine, releasing the tension.

Jamie breathes again.

'Ella, you've changed my life.' They're facing each other now, and Ant grabs both of Mum's hands. 'Like the famous hymn goes, "I once was lost, but now am found, was blind but now I see." You found me, and helped me to find me, too. You opened my eyes to the world, and everything seems new and brighter and more beautiful with you by my side, my beautiful Ella.'

Mum looks so happy; she's glowing as she gazes at Ant, her eyes wide and shiny. Jamie feels tears prick in her eyes too.

'You saved a wretch like me, Ella,' he says. 'And I promise to save you, every day for the rest of our lives. I want to give you even a fraction of the support, steadiness and calm you have given me since the day we met. You're an amazing woman, and I will work hard for the duration of our marriage to ensure I deserve you.'

There's a smattering of applause around the chapel, and Jamie sees Cleo turn around and glare at everyone. Jamie's with Cleo on this one: if they're going to applaud Ant, they should have applauded Mum too.

Ant clears his throat. He's still not done. People start to shift in their seats.

'I know that marrying Ella isn't just marrying Ella. I'm marrying a family. So, Cleo and Jamie, where are you?' He turns and puts a hand over his eyes, shielding them from an imaginary spotlight as if he's on a theatre stage, even though they're in a gloomy chapel with only the spring light filtering through the windows.

Jamie raises a hand in a small wave. Cleo doesn't move.

'Cleo and Jamie, I vow to love you both, cherish you both and treat you as my own daughters. I'll be there for you no matter what, just as I will be there for your Mum, the lovely Ella.'

Then Ant gets a standing ovation, even though they haven't yet exchanged rings.

———————

Cleo

At the front of the church, Mum and Ant gaze into each other's eyes. There's a glint of silver at the bottom of his shirt sleeve. He's wearing a thumb ring.

'Stop fiddling.' Gran lays a hand on Cleo's arm, her skin smooth like tissue paper.

Gran's hand slides away from Cleo's arm as she goes back to fanning her face with the order of service, looking up at Mum and Ant with a small smile.

Cleo reaches each of her hands up to her armpits to yank up her new dress. Lucasz glances over at her and smirks. She elbows him in the ribs. 'Stop staring at my boobs.'

His cheeks turn red and he drops the smirk. 'Why would I want to look at your flat chest?' He rakes his fingers through his blond hair. He's borrowed his dad's shirt, too wide for his skinny torso but too short in the sleeves. He's hilarious without meaning to be.

Cleo slumps down in her seat with a sigh. She can't believe this is happening. Her throat constricts like she's trying not to laugh, or cry, or something. It's all she can do to not shake her head, scream, and shout. It would be noble to stand up. She should yell, 'I object. Don't marry this man.'

She could rescue Mum from him. They would all go back to the way it was, before Ant showed up in their lives and turned everything upside down. She'd get Mum back.

But to all the family and friends in the chapel, it wouldn't seem like a rescue. It would look like she ruined Mum's wedding. 'Typical Cleo,' they'd say. 'Such an attention seeker. Such a child.'

She looks down at her sandals and her blue-painted toenails. Mum says she's happy with him. That he treats her 'like a queen'. Cleo needs to remember that. It would mean everything to Mum if Cleo looked up right now, smiled at Ant, gave a nod.

But she can't.

She squeezes her lips together and puffs out her cheeks.

Ant turns and scans the faces of the guests. He's not smiling. He almost looks angry, like he's checking for an uninvited guest. Suddenly, he looks straight at Cleo and raises an eyebrow at her with a half-smile. A challenge. Last chance.

She tightens her arms across her chest and frowns at him.

He looks away, pretends he didn't see. But Cleo knows he did.

Gran nudges her with her elbow. 'Sit up straight,' she whispers. 'And smile.'

'It is now my honour and delight to declare you husband and wife – you may seal your vows with a kiss.'

Well, she's shown them. She didn't ruin the wedding; look how mature she is. As the congregation claps, Cleo whispers her own vow: 'I vow to get Ant out of our lives for ever.'

As soon as the ceremony is over, she pushes Lucasz out of the pew and into the aisle and runs out of the chapel even ahead of Mum and Ant. She'll get in trouble for that later, she knows it. They were supposed to wait and follow out behind the happy couple. They went through it all in an elaborate rehearsal yesterday: another excuse for Ant to stand at the front of the room and give a speech about how great he is, disguised as a speech about how great Mum is.

'"Treat you as my own daughters,"' she mimics. 'We've already got a dad. He's there in the chapel.' She kicks the head off a daffodil with such force that it lands on Lucasz's shoe five feet away. 'What a performance. He didn't mean a word of any of that.'

Lucasz is quiet, staring at the severed flower on the top of his scuffed toe.

'Don't you think, though? He's awful. It's all a big lie.' She needs to hear it's not all in her head. Sometimes it feels like she's going mad. 'Lucasz?'

He shrugs and pulls a leaf from the hedge, rubbing it between his thumb and finger. 'I know you don't like him,' he says. 'And the reasons you give make sense. He seems okay to me.' He looks up from the leaf, his forehead crinkled between his eyebrows. His eyes are big and blue, and wide open as he looks at her. He's worried he'll upset her; she can tell. Poor Lucasz.

'Everything changed when he turned up.' She sits down on the grass and leans against a smooth granite gravestone belonging to a lady called Elsie Hampson who died in 2009. The damp grass soaks through her dress and into the back of her knickers. 'You don't live with him, maybe that's why you can't see it. It's like he's wearing a mask to disguise himself as a normal human being, and then sometimes when he thinks no one's looking, the mask slips and his real monstrous face slips out. But I see his monster face all the time. And I don't understand why no one else can.'

Her throat burns, but she doesn't want anyone to see her cry. She can hear them all behind the hedge: leaving the church, throwing rice and biodegradable confetti and cheering. She's sad she's not there, standing next to Jamie and smiling for Mum on her special day. But she shoves it away; this isn't her fault. It's Ant's fault. And Mum's. If Mum wasn't marrying him, if she didn't fall for someone so obviously terrible, Cleo could celebrate with everyone like a normal person. Like a normal daughter. Like she used to be.

It's not that she doesn't want Mum to be happy. She really, really does. It's about Mum marrying a horrible person who isn't kind. Cleo wants a kind stepdad.

'Cleopatra?' It's Dad's voice.

She leaps to her feet and brushes the back of her dress to reduce the damage from sitting on the grass. Just in time, Lucasz puts his jacket around her shoulders. She gives him a grateful smile. 'You're a good friend,' she whispers. Then, aloud: 'We're here!'

Dad's head pokes around the hedge. 'Oh, here you are!' He's smiling. His big salt and pepper beard makes him look like a sea captain. She never wants him to shave it off.

'Oh, Dad,' she says, barely suppressing a sob. She runs to him and wraps her arms around him, burying her face into his tie.

'I wondered where you'd gone. You OK?'

She nods, not lifting her face from his chest. He smells of coal fires and washing powder.

'I know this is a strange day for you. Jamie too.' He puts a hand on the top of her head. 'Your mum seems happy, though. Give this guy a chance, OK? You're a tough nut to crack, I bet.'

Cleo half-laughs, her tense muscles relaxing. 'It's not that.' His shirt muffles her voice.

'Oh? What is it, then?'

She looks up at Dad's face, his crinkly eyes. 'You're our dad, not him. He can't just take over like that. Like he said in his speech.'

Dad chuckles.

'Don't laugh at me.' She tries to pull away, but he doesn't loosen his arms.

'Sorry, love.' The corner of his mouth twitches. 'There's enough love to go around, Clee. He's allowed to be your stepdad, and it doesn't take anything away from me. Okay?'

She nods reluctantly.

'Everything all right?' A breathy voice comes from behind the hedge and Sahara appears with a smile. She's got great

14

hair: wavy and bushy in the best way. And she wears bright colours all the time, like a kids' TV presenter. Today her dress is magenta and has a bright yellow handbag.

'Everything's fine, Sarah,' Cleo says, stepping away from her dad.

'Sahara.' Dad frowns at her.

Cleo half-smiles at Sahara. A semi-apology.

Dad shakes his head, disappointed. He takes Sahara's hand and they return to the gathering of chatting adults outside the chapel.

'It was a nice wedding?' Lucasz says, his voice turning up at the end like a question. 'Ant's vows were good. I can't believe he made them up on the spot.'

'I bet it all sounded sooooo romantic to everyone. They'll probably talk about it for weeks; how lovely Ant is and how lucky Mum is to marry such a *great guy*.' She kicks at more daisies and dandelions. 'But then he quotes "Amazing Grace"? Written by a slave trader. Remember? We learned about it in History last term.'

'Of course I remember.' History is Lucasz's favourite subject. 'But so what? You're just looking for things to pick on.' Lucasz gets out his phone and opens Pokémon Go, scanning to see if there are any creatures in the graveyard. 'He used lyrics he thought were nice.'

She grabs his phone and sticks it down the front of her dress in her bra where Lucasz would never reach for it.

He bursts out laughing and holds out his hand for his phone. 'Come on, give it back.'

'What about the rest of the speech though? A bit self-obsessed, wasn't it? All about Ant and how great he is, nothing about Mum.'

Lucasz stares at her blankly. This is his 'shutting down'

face. Lucasz's blue screen of death. She might be stubborn sometimes, but when Lucasz refuses to engage, she can't get through to him. He's out.

'Fine.' She slaps his mobile into his hand, just as Jamie emerges from around the hedge. She's got confetti in her curls, and she's laughing.

She's holding hands with Spider, her beardy boyfriend. As soon as she sees Cleo, the smile drops and her face clouds with anger. 'Cleo!'

'Uh-oh. I'm in trouble.'

Jamie

'You okay?' Jamie asks the two teenagers, who are skulking around by the drystone wall, poking at the hedge. The graveyard looks beautiful in the sunshine, daffodils bobbing and big white clouds sailing past against the blue sky.

Lucasz looks chilly in his shirtsleeves. He's given Cleo his jacket, and it reaches almost down to her knees. He's too kind for his own good. He hugs his arms around himself, and Jamie feels a pang of sympathy for this poor boy whose arms are too long for his body.

'Fine, thanks, Jamie.' Cleo's voice is as fake as the smile Jamie's forced onto her face. 'Just looking for some Pokémon.'

Cleo nods at her friend and, like a performing seal, he holds up his phone as if that's proof.

'OK. Well, take a break from Pokémon for a second, please – it's time for photographs. We need the family in front of the chapel.'

'Does that include you?' Cleo asks. She looks dishevelled already, her hair sticking up at the front. Her lipstick has smudged at the corners of her mouth, making her look slightly deranged.

'Yes, including me.' Jamie hands her a tissue. 'Wipe your mouth, your lipstick needs attention. Why wouldn't it include me?'

Cleo waves a hand. 'Oh, you know. Thought you might be too important and busy filming to be in a photograph.'

She won't rise to the bait.

'Spider's taking the family shots.' She smiles at him, but he's flicking through footage on his DSLR, not paying attention.

She reaches out to fix Cleo's hair but Cleo pulls away, smoothing her own hair so roughly that it sticks to her head, flat and greasy-looking.

'Wait, Cleo. Let me just…' She tries to ruffle the roots of Cleo's mousy waves, working fast before Cleo breaks away again. Was Jamie this much hard work as a teenager? She doesn't think so. 'There. Now you're ready for the picture.'

'I don't want to be in a picture with him.'

Jamie pretends to review some pictures on her camera. Pretends this argument doesn't matter to her. It's the only way with Cleo. 'I know you don't. And that's fine. But this is for Mum, okay?' She tries to sound casual, keeping her voice steady and even. 'This is Mum's day and it doesn't matter how you feel.'

Cleo's mouth falls open. 'It's *my* day too. My birthday.'

Jamie puts a hand on Cleo's shoulder, tries to steady her. 'I know. It's not fair.' She still doesn't understand why the wedding needed to be on this particular day. 'Ant doesn't have kids. Maybe he doesn't understand about these things.'

Cleo pulls up her dress. 'I can't believe Mum didn't stick up for me.'

Poor Cleo.

'There are 364 other days she could have got married. Or she could have not married him at all, that would have been even better.'

'How about we have an un-birthday for you next week? Me and you, we'll go for manicures and then to the cinema together and pretend it's still your birthday. My treat.'

She smiles a little now. 'Can Lucasz come?'

Lucasz raises his eyebrows, looking startled, like a pheasant about to be hit by a car. 'Lucasz can come to the cinema, yes. And I'll even buy us popcorn on my staff discount. But don't worry, we won't make you get a manicure.'

'Ant gets manicures,' mumbles Cleo.

'What?' Jamie asks.

Cleo shakes her head to say never mind.

'Okay, but for now, come and get in some photos. For Mum. Not for Ant. If you don't come, you will hurt Mum.'

Cleo slumps, the fight gone from her body for now.

Jamie slides Lucasz's jacket from Cleo's shoulders, and he takes it back gratefully. Then she sees the muddy stain on the back of Cleo's dress. 'Oh God, what have you done to the dress? Mum will kill you.'

She shrugs and glances at Spider. 'Just make sure my bum isn't in the picture, please?'

Spider salutes her. 'Aye-aye, Captain.'

Cleo and Lucasz wander towards the chapel, but Jamie hangs back, reaching out for Spider's hand. 'Wait a sec,' she whispers and pulls him towards her. He looks so striking in his red tartan kilt with a matching waistcoat.

He turns, a big smile on his face, and steps towards her,

cupping the back of her head for a kiss. 'Wait, it wasn't that,' she says, and kisses him once before placing a hand to his chest. She hates to push him away, but this is important.

'We got the money.'

His eyes widen. 'All of it?'

She nods. 'Ant said to consider it a wedding gift, on his own wedding day.'

Spider raises his arms in the air and takes a deep breath, about to crow with glee.

'Shhuushhhh.' She presses a finger to his lips. 'We can't tell Cleo. She'd go mental if she knew. But yes, thanks to my new stepdad, Project HouseFire is a go.'

Chapter Two

Cleo

'Your mum looks happy, doesn't she?' Gran whispers, pointing to where Ant has pulled Mum into a photo with his family: his foster parents Anne and Fred, his siblings and all their kids.

'You've grown since the last time I saw you.' Gran tucks Cleo's hair behind her ear, and Cleo tries not to shrug her off. Gran keeps trying to hold her hand or put her arm around her, and it's exhausting.

Cleo's face aches from fake smiling.

'It's been too long since I last came up to see you all. It's a long drive for an old lady, all the way from Surrey. You should come down on the train sometime.'

Cleo nods. 'That'll be an adventure.' And she'll be able to get away from the honeymooners for a few days if Mum'll let her.

Gran beams.

They've finished the big shots and moved on to smaller

groups: Mum, Jamie, and Cleo, then Mum and Ant with her best friend Tina and Ant's only friend Gaz, who is missing a tooth. Cleo untucks the hair from behind her ear. 'Are we done yet? This has been going on for hours.'

Finally, Spider takes Mum and Ant into the graveyard to get some couple photos, and the rest of the wedding guests are free to travel to the pub for the reception. Everyone wanders down the lane to their cars, but Cleo hangs back and signals to Lucasz to stay with her.

'Oh my God, Cleo, what happened to your dress?' someone shrieks.

It's Sahara, her own dress immaculate and bright.

'Nothing.' Cleo closes her eyes, takes a breath, and opens them again. 'It got wet in the grass, that's all.'

Sahara pats the back of Cleo's dress. 'You two need to get in the car. Your dad's waiting to drive to the reception. Your gran's gasping for a cup of tea.'

Lucasz nods and takes a step forward, but Cleo puts a hand on his arm.

'Actually, we're going to walk.'

Lucasz looks at her, confused.

She's about to explain when Jamie rounds the hedge, fiddling with lenses, a camera bag slung across her body. 'Whose car are you going in?' Jamie asks. 'There's space with me and Spider when he finishes the photos.'

Cleo laughs. 'Thanks, but I'm not getting in that death trap.' She nods towards Spider's van, an ancient Corsa, older than Spider himself. 'We'll walk. It's not far. And it'll dry out my dress.' She nods at Sahara, who winks at her.

'Can't you just keep your dress clean and get in a bloody car like everyone else?'

'Frankly, sister, no, I can't. This plan is better for everyone.'

Jamie raises both her hands in exasperation.

'We'll walk through the woods. When we get to the reception, my dress will be dry, and I will be on my best behaviour after burning loads of energy on the walk.'

'How long is the walk, anyway?'

Sahara's already got it on her iPhone. 'Google Maps says 45 minutes on the road, so I reckon they'll be about an hour if they go through the woods.'

Cleo looks at her watch. 'The reception starts in an hour and a half. We've got time, see? I just want a break from all the people. All the socialising.'

Jamie takes a step towards her. 'You're being ridiculous.'

'It's my *birthday*.'

Jamie can't argue with that.

They run through the woods, Cleo holding her dress above her knees with one hand and carrying her sandals in the other. It feels good to leave the wedding behind them, to shove it away for a few minutes and pretend it didn't happen. The ground is damp and covered in pine needles; she must pay attention to her feet, so she doesn't stub her toe on a tree root or stand on a sharp stone.

'Stop! Stop!' she gasps, breathless with running and rebellion. She's in that weird in-between mood where she could laugh hysterically or burst into tears, and she can't control which.

She stops and leans against a tree. Lucasz, far ahead, turns back. His cheeks are flushed pink and he's grinning. 'You OK?' he calls.

'My dress is falling down. I don't have enough hands to

hold my sandals, keep the bottom of my dress out of the mud and hoick it up all the time to stop my boobs popping out.'

'What boobs?'

She whacks him on the arm. 'Wasn't funny the first time.'

He holds out a hand and she gives him her sandals to carry.

They head in the vague direction of the village, taking detours when the trees get too thick. Soon, they're so deep in the wood that shafts of sunlight filter through the leaves. She stops and looks around. 'It's like a fairy den in here.' Above her, the trees arch together like the vaulted ceiling of a cathedral.

When she looks around, Lucasz is gone.

'Luc?' she calls, turning around in a circle. Aside from the wind rustling through the trees, there's no sound. 'Lucasz, where did you go?'

She spots her sandals, abandoned next to a patch of nettles. She bends to pick them up, one in each hand. They'll be late to the party now. 'Lucasz! We'll get in trouble and this time it'll be your fault!' she shouts into the wood. That would get him to come back if he could hear her. But still nothing, no sign of him. Where could he have gone?

Maybe he fell over, or down a sinkhole. Maybe there are old smugglers' tunnels or an abandoned mine. Maybe he's lying unconscious metres underground, unable to call for help. Or maybe he's hiding from her, sniggering at her worried face from behind a tree. The dick. That's more likely.

She leans against a nearby tree, propping one foot up behind her as if she doesn't have a care in the world. She must look pretty cool, leaning against a tree in this long dress in the middle of a forest. She hopes he comes back soon and sees her here, surrounded by spring greenery like a page from a clothes catalogue.

She starts to hum to herself and closes her eyes.

Lucasz's laughter explodes as he emerges from the thickest trees. 'Your dress is falling down again.'

She folds her arms. 'Shut up. Where did you disappear to?'

He points into the bushes where the ground slopes away downhill. 'Something's on fire.'

'What?' Now he says it, she can smell smoke in the air. Not a bonfire, but more synthetic, acrid.

Through a gap in the trees, a funnel of black smoke floats away on the breeze.

They push through the branches. Twigs catch on her hair and dress. She hopes her dress doesn't get torn; she doesn't need another reason to get into trouble.

Finally, she stumbles out of the trees and into a big open space where Lucasz is waiting. There, in a small clearing, is a house.

'It looks like it's mostly burned out. No flames anymore, just smoke. Round the back.'

The house is hunched over, like an ancient old lady with a twisted spine. The trees crowd it, getting in its space. The cracked walls are streaked with moisture, and one side is black and crumbled. A young tree grows through the empty space where the roof once was.

The ground floor windows are shuttered with metal, and an old car huddles outside, its tyres flat and cracked.

'I didn't know this house was here,' Cleo whispers. 'This is really cool.'

He grabs her hand and pulls her around the back of the house, pausing to step over the fallen fence, which lies flat on the long grass. They enter what was once the garden but has now become part of the forest.

The building is L-shaped, and the smaller wing of the

house is charred and black, its roof collapsed in at one end, like a stoved-in skull.

'The fire didn't spread.' She points at the untouched part, which looks almost normal. 'I wonder why.'

But the house isn't burning.

The smoke is coming from a tumbledown shed next to the building with planks of wood stacked against its walls like a bonfire. 'So the big house fire wasn't today. This is something different. Someone was here today, lighting things on fire.' She flicks a glance at Lucasz. 'They might still be here now.'

He covers his shiver with a grin. 'They probably did it hours ago; it's going out now. The best bit is there's a window that's broken. We can get inside!'

Sure enough, one of the windows has no glass in the panes, and the metal sheet lying on the ground is warped and broken.

'Let's go in,' Lucasz says.

She looks at him, surprised. Usually she's the one who pushes, dares, teases and pokes to get a reaction.

'I'm not wearing any shoes.' On the grass by her bare feet, little crystals of glass sparkle in the sunlight.

She's disappointed. She would love to go inside and explore the abandoned house. But they're already late for the reception and she doesn't want to cut her feet on broken glass and have to explain that on top of everything else.

He steps towards the window. 'I can't see a thing, it's too dark.'

She sticks her hand in his jacket pocket and he flinches. 'Keep still, I'm just getting your phone.' She turns on the phone's torch and shines it through the window. 'I left mine in Spider's car.'

She can see the outline of furniture, and other shapes too.

'Woah. It's full of stuff, like the owners just left for the day.' She turns to Lucasz. 'It's like a hoarder lived here.'

'Hang on, look – what's that?' Lucasz grabs her wrist and angles the phone down towards the ground just under the window. There's something there, something once white and now yellow. 'I think it's a newspaper.'

She leans into the window and a blast of mouldy air reaches her nostrils. She stands up on tiptoes and leans, but the threat of broken glass stops her bending inside all the way. Still, she can see the title. 'It's an *Abbeywick Gazette*. Can't see the date though. It looks old. It's all wrinkly from the rain getting in.'

She moves over and Lucasz leans in; he's taller so he can bend further. He straightens up, triumphant. '1986.'

'Wow, that's ages ago.'

'Do you think the house has been empty since then?'

'Or even before that – someone could have brought the paper here after.'

Lucasz wrinkles his nose and snaps up his head, scanning the trees. 'You think someone's here? Someone might live here now?'

'Who do you think lit that fire today?'

His eyes open wide, the whites visible around the entire iris. He peers into the woods.

She laughs at him. 'Don't freak out. It was probably something flammable kept in the shed that exploded. Like an old petrol can that got too hot.'

He looks up at the blue sky, peeking through the gaps in the trees above their heads. 'It's not that hot today.'

She walks around the other side of the house, towards the smouldering shed. As she moves closer, it shifts, sending ashes and embers into the sky with the smoke. She watches their orange glow as they float up into the sky and disappear.

She points at the desolate woodland around them. 'Everything around here is totally overgrown. There's no driveway, no way to reach the nearest road or town. There's not even a footpath. A thief couldn't drive that car out of here even if they wanted to steal it. No one's here. I bet no one's lived here for years and years. It looks like everyone's forgotten about it.'

Lucasz looks up at the scarred facade of the wrecked house. 'It looks like it was a nice house once. They had shutters.' He points up to the first floor where shutters, once sky blue, hang from their hinges at each window. And net curtains hover at each window behind the glass.

'This is our house now. We can make it nice again.'

He grabs her hand in his and holds it. She wants to let go of his clammy fingers and wipe her hand on her dress. But she doesn't want to hurt his feelings, so she stands there and counts to ten before she lets go and brushes her palm on her thigh.

'We'd better go to this stupid wedding party,' she says.

Chapter Three

Jamie

Jamie watches, transfixed, as Ant takes the largest, shiniest knife from their block and tests its blade against the soft pad of his thumb. She winces.

But Ant shakes his head. 'Not sharp enough,' he says with a smile. 'Honestly, I don't know how your mum survived without someone around to keep things in order.'

He crosses to the drawer and pulls out the sharpener. The knife glints in the kitchen's spotlights as he draws the blade against the sharpener in deft movements, over and over. After a minute or two, he stops, wipes the blade like a soldier after a battle.

Then he beckons her over to the cutting board. 'Watch this.' He holds a tomato with one hand and strokes the sharpened blade along its surface. With the smallest stroke, the tomato's skin ruptures and splays open, like he's undoing a zip. He looks at her, eyebrows raised.

'Wow,' she says, impressed. 'What are you making?'

'Ah.' He rubs his palms together. 'It's a surprise gourmet meal for your mum, inspired by an amazing meal we had together the night I proposed. I took her to Le Poulet Heureux over in Harrogate. Have you been? It has a Michelin star.'

'I don't think I've ever had a gourmet meal,' she says.

'Well, you're in for a treat. Your mum loved it. Anyway, in honour of that evening, tonight we're having pheasant surprise. As in, I know what it is, and you'll find out later.'

'Sounds great!'

'As you're my sous chef, I guess I'll have to let you in on some of the secrets.' He grins at her. 'OK, so while you chop, tell me about the documentary. If I'm your patron, I should understand what it's all about and how you're progressing. It's about arson if I'm right?'

'My patron?' She feels weird about that word.

'You know, like your sponsor. I believe in you, think you've got talent. I really liked that mini-doc you made about the park and ride planning permissions.'

Her cheeks flush. The way Ant says it makes the project sound infantile. At the time it seemed so important: her first undergraduate university project, shining a light on the Neolithic site being flattened into a car park for tourists. The documentary did draw attention from the council; they even talked about it at one of their meetings. But ultimately it didn't work: the Neolithic site was briefly excavated and then covered over with tarmac in the name of progress. And then everything went wrong and she dropped out of uni. A big, fat failure. She doesn't like thinking about it.

Still, for a brief moment she thought her documentary, her research and her storytelling might have an impact. Could preserve something priceless in the history of the area. And that felt amazing. She wants to claw back that feeling with this new project she's scoping out with Spider. Some hope and direction; a potential future career despite her failures. And helping people get answers to questions that have been asked for decades.

'So not many people know about it, but back in the Eighties, there were a bunch of unexplained fires in Abbeywick. At first, they thought it was accidental, but then someone died, and the police started to take it more seriously. But in the end, they couldn't find enough evidence or any suspects and eventually the case went cold. No one was ever caught.'

He frowns. 'Someone died, you say?'

'Yes, at least one death in a fire that we can find. So we thought we'd take a look into it, do our own investigation, basically.'

'You could see if you can get the police interested again.'

She nods. 'Definitely. It seems like for the investigators back then there was always something bigger or more serious, especially because so many of the fires didn't seem malicious: they were small or burned out quickly. Or were set in abandoned buildings, that kind of thing.'

'Fascinating.' Ant sets a big bag of potatoes on the counter next to Jamie and hands her the sharp knife. 'Can you slice these into thins?' He brings together his thumb and forefinger to indicate half a centimetre.

She nods and starts to chop. She's always enjoyed cooking, finds it soothing. A lot more than eating.

'I wonder what motivates people to set fires.'

'Arson motivations are interesting, I agree. But I really want to focus on the victims, you know? Too many documentaries are all about the criminals, and the victims get forgotten. That's not right.'

'So you'll interview people about this?' He opens the fridge and pulls out a massive Tesco carrier bag, dumping it on the worktop with a scatter of feathers as it hits the countertop.

'Yeah… definitely. I put a call out on social media for anyone affected by the fires. Already got some responses, mainly from weirdos though. One anonymous email address told me to scrap the documentary or they'd set me on fire.' Jamie gives a quick bark of laughter to show it didn't affect her. 'What's that?' She points at the Tesco bag, which is oozing blood and feathers.

'Oh, damn, I'm making such a mess.' He carries the bag to the sink and sets it inside. 'It's a brace of pheasants.' He pulls them out of the bag and holds them upside down by their feet. Their heads loll and sway.

Jamie swallows and wipes her hands on her jeans. They're beautiful birds, with green-black heads, white necks and brown bodies, feathers shining like oil rainbows on water. She's seen pheasants often in the surrounding countryside; clucking as they fly overhead, wandering the country lanes, and dead by the side of the road. But somehow she's never seen them this close before, never appreciated how beautiful they really are.

Ripping apart her admiration, Ant takes a big handful of feathers and yanks them from one of the pheasants. He throws the feathers in the sink and grabs another handful.

'Oh, don't. Please don't.' Jamie feels like she might cry.

Ant turns around, surprised. His eyebrows are high up his forehead, knotted together in concern. 'You're not vegetarian or anything, are you?'

'No, no, it's not that. I just…' She feels stupid. She eats meat all the time. 'It's just never this close up when you buy it in the shops.'

He rubs his cheek with the back of his hand, fingers still full of small feathers. 'What isn't?'

'The death.' She turns her back on Ant and tries to block out the crunch-thump sound as he rips the feathers from the skin of the pheasant.

'Who will you interview?'

She talks louder to drown out the sound. 'Spider is trying to get the headmistress of the local school. Their sports hall burned down.'

'Wasn't there a theatre fire too?' There's a pause in the feather-pulling.

She nods. 'That was the one where the woman died.'

The plucking resumes. 'And you're looking into that one? I could ask around, see if I know anyone connected. I've got great contacts in the area.'

She smiles at him, non-committal. She doesn't want Ant to think that just because he gave money, he can control the process. There's a neat stack of sliced potatoes next to Jamie now, and the chopping board is slick with white residue.

He's quiet for a moment before he finds a different way to interfere. 'Do you need any advice or tips for the interviews? I had a lot of on-camera training back at the start of my career and I'd be happy to help.'

Jamie's skin prickles with embarrassment for his unselfconscious pride. Just talking about his job makes Ant's voice shinier, louder somehow. He seems to think he's a lot more famous than the presenter of a morning breakfast show on satellite news. Once she saw him believe he'd been recognised in the street, when it was just someone nodding 'hello' like people do in a small seaside town in the off season.

He turns from the sink and leans against it, hands waving around like a politician delivering a speech. 'You see, to work with the public in such a demanding role, you have to be able to make quick decisions and respond to what's happening around you. What are you like under pressure? Can you be off the cuff, think on your feet?' He pauses, probably trying to find another cliché.

Jamie opens her mouth to reply.

'What I mean is,' he continues, pushing his sleeve up past his elbow, 'anyone whose main career is in broadcasting, particularly if they're on camera, needs to be able to put their own emotions aside in the name of journalism. If someone's telling you something absolutely horrifying – like their children drowned in a cruise ship disaster, etc.'—his eyes glint with glee at the scale of this drama, presumably excited by the number of viewers he'd get for this particular segment—'then you can't stand there and cry with them. It's just not professional. You can't say, "Oh, you poor thing, I'm so sorry."'

Jamie nods, swallowing the spit pooling in her mouth. She glances behind Ant to the pheasant carcasses in the sink. Now bald, their skin is a pale yellow; they look a bit like chickens, but more delicate.

'So interviewing victims of a crime is a tricky subject. You've set yourself up with a big challenge for your first feature-length doc, but I'm here to help.'

'Thank you. I'm looking forward to it.' She swallows and picks up the knife. 'Do you want me to cut anything else?'

He plonks a bag of carrots in front of her along with a peeler. 'So can you do it?'

'Peel carrots?'

He shakes his head and roars with laughter. 'Can you put your emotions away?' His expression becomes grave with the speed of a camera shutter. 'If there's this little old lady and her cat died in the fire and she's crying, saying it was the only love she had in her life or whatever… can you look her dead in the eye and keep asking her questions, probe her pain in the name of good TV?'

'I mean, these fires happened a long time ago. No one's going to be crying about their dead cat.' She picks up a carrot and runs the peeler along its length, letting the peel drop onto the chopping block. 'I think I can, but it would be hard. I'm pretty good at compartmentalising stuff, putting it away to deal with later.' *Control issues*, in the words of her old counsellor. 'Mum's the same. Contained, I guess.'

He gathers the pheasants by their scaly feet, drops them back on the counter and picks up a butcher's knife.

Jamie turns back to the carrots.

'Must have been a nice childhood, with your mum. She's a peaceful person.'

'Didn't rub off on Cleo, though.' Jamie laughs, but Ant gives only a tight smile. 'She's always been loud.'

'I wouldn't have got away with her kind of attitude where I lived.'

'In the foster home?'

'Yeah. Lots of shouting and tantrums and rage: kids from difficult circumstances. We were all angry about something. Anne and Fred were good at dealing with it though. Great people, those two.'

She nods. 'I liked them when we chatted at the wedding reception.' They seemed kind: two jolly, kind people who clearly love Ant. 'What about before that? Before foster care.' She wants to know more about this guy outside of the constant shiny public persona. He's constantly in 'make an effort' mode. She wishes he'd relax a bit, show his real self.

There's a pause so long that she turns to look at him. He chews his lip like he doesn't know what to say. Maybe this is him being real, now. He's rarely quiet, never short of something to talk about – must be the TV presenter in him, ready to improvise at any moment. She'll have to get better at talking to people, at asking questions and knowing what to say, if she's going to be successful at this like Ant.

Then the moment passes and his face clears. 'Before?' He smiles at her and shrugs, as if to say it's not a big deal. 'I don't actually remember much before Anne and Fred.'

Jamie's surprised. 'I chatted a bit with your foster sister the other day. Tamara? She said you were in a children's home.'

'That's right. For quite a few months before Anne and Fred found me.' He slams the butcher's knife down on the counter and it slices straight through the neck of one of the birds.

Jamie suppresses a shriek, more from surprise than fright.

'But I don't remember much about it. I remember rows of beds, and lots of secret bullying – from the staff as well as the other kids. It wasn't a very kind place. Some of the staff were wonderful, but they all went home at the end of the day and we had to stay there. I don't think about it much.'

'What about your birth family?'

He shakes his head. 'I don't know much about them. I don't want to. They gave me up and sent me to that home – and whatever the circumstances, they don't deserve my time or my thoughts.'

He slams the knife back down on the counter, slicing off the second pheasant's head in a clean cut. Jamie is ready for it this time.

'Anyway,' he says in a brighter voice. 'I'd better get this show on the road. Thanks for your help, kiddo. Now I ask you to leave me in my kitchen and I'll make the magic happen. It won't be a surprise if you know what exactly we're having.'

Kiddo. He's trying so hard, bless him. Jamie smiles and

leaves him to finish cooking his surprise dinner to impress Mum.

At the door, she turns to watch him for a moment, his knuckles white where he grips the knife. What does that do to a kid, knowing your family gave up on you?

Cleo

'Oh. My. God. Why are there feathers everywhere?' Cleo looks around the kitchen, shocked at the mess. 'It looks like a literal murder scene in there.'

Daisy sniffs the floor in huge gulps of air, inhaling the scent of death. Her tail wags like crazy.

Ant nudges her with his knee. 'Stop it, Daisy.'

The dog looks up at Cleo, a little white feather stuck to the tip of her black nose. Cleo cups her face, kisses the top of her head where the fur grows soft and fine. 'Poor Daisy. Was he mean to you?'

'No dogs in the kitchen. It's not sanitary,' Ant says.

'Don't make a fuss, Cleo. Just sit down for dinner, please.' Mum lays knives and forks on the dining table, ignoring the trickle of blood in the middle of the worktop as it oozes out of a Tesco bag and onto the granite surface.

Cleo leads Daisy out of the kitchen and closes the door. 'What are we having, roadkill?'

From her seat at the dinner table, Jamie rolls her eyes. Cleo grimaces at her and sticks out her tongue. She's such a suck-up.

There's a plume of steam as Ant opens and closes the oven door. 'Mind out of the way, please!' he announces grandly as he carries a huge casserole dish across the kitchen towards the dining table. It's Mum's best Le Creuset.

'I thought we weren't allowed to use that?' Cleo looks at Mum, waiting for her to challenge Ant. 'You said you wanted to keep it for best.'

Mum ignores her and scrabbles to arrange the heatproof mats on the table before he sets down the dish.

'Mum? Look, it's all black around the bottom.'

'Shut up, Cleo,' Jamie hisses.

'I just like to know if the rules have changed around here. You know, in *my home*.' She sends daggers at Ant through narrowed eyes. He clears his throat and lifts the lid from the dish with a 'tah-dah!'

It's just two dead birds. They look like little chickens, slightly charred in some kind of sauce.

'Oh, did I forget to mention? I'm vegetarian.'

Jamie groans. 'No, you're not.'

'Since when?' asks Ant, looking concerned. 'No one mention—'

'Ignore her,' smarmy Jamie simpers. 'She's just being difficult.'

'Seriously though, the meat industry is barbaric. In a few years we'll all look back at the abattoirs and intensive farming and we'll be shocked our so-called civilised society did things like that to animals in the name of food. We talked about this, Jamie – don't you remember? We watched that documentary and you said—'

'Stop it,' Jamie hisses at her. 'You ate a bacon sandwich yesterday morning. I watched you make it.'

'It's OK, Jamie,' Ant interrupts her. 'Cleo. Enough.'

Jamie closes her mouth, surprised.

Cleo's surprised too. She's not used to adult intervention:

38

Mum usually lets them bicker and doesn't say anything – it's over quicker that way. Also, it's totally none of his business whether they argue or not – he's not their dad and Cleo doesn't consider him her stepdad. He's only been living with them for a month.

'You'll be pleased to know that today's gourmet dinner doesn't contribute to what you refer to as the "barbaric meat industry". This is local pheasant, reared by the gamekeeper of an old schoolfriend of mine, actually – Lord Farrah – on the Langdale New Manor estate. It's organic, and these pheasants probably had a much happier life than the animals who produced the meat you can buy in the supermarket. No suffering either.' He mimes bringing a gun to his temple. 'Flying around happy one minute, dead as a dodo the next. It's a very humane death.'

Cleo snorts. 'Humane death? Humane. Death. That's a contradiction if I ever heard one.'

Mum gets up from the table and bustles around in the kitchen, clearing up some of the pots.

'And how did you even get the pheasants? Oh my God, you didn't pick them up from the side of the road, did you? They've not got tyre marks in them?' She stands up and peers into the casserole dish, but they look perfectly normal. They actually look tasty on second look, sitting in a thick reddish liquid full of root vegetables. It smells of wine, roasted meat and thyme.

'Lord Farrah had these two left over from the end of the season and had to make space in his freezer.'

'Does he make you call him "Lord" to his face?' She stifles a giggle. 'If so, he's not your real friend.'

Ant ignores her.

Mum returns to the dining table and strikes a match,

lighting the two red candles in the centre of the table. The flame reflects in her eyes as she concentrates on catching the wick with the flame. She looks sad, Cleo thinks. Maybe she should have married someone who makes her happy instead of this guy.

'There, doesn't that look nice?' Mum blows out the match and lays it on the candleholder, where a little thread of smoke rises into the air. 'This smells amazing, love.' She reaches out and places a hand on Ant's arm. He smiles at her.

'Thank you. So—' He sits up straight and rubs his hands together. 'Girls, this is braised pheasant with chanterelles and quail's eggs. Oh, and dauphinoise potatoes, thanks to Jamie here. A true winter warmer.'

Cleo doesn't mention it's actually spring, not winter.

Ant plates up the food and hands it out, passing a plate to Mum first. Cleo gets the next. 'Miss Cleo, here's a special plate for you.' He passes her one with breast meat and one chanterelle mushroom, which is clever of him. She can't fuss about bones. And with only one mushroom on her plate, she can't complain about not liking them and she also can't moan about not getting any. Check. Mate.

He winks at her as she takes the plate from him. She pretends not to see.

When everyone has a plate of food, Ant raises his glass to Mum. '*Bon appetit, mon cheri*,' he says, in imitation of a French accent. '*Merci beaucoup* for welcoming me into your beautiful family. I'm a lucky man.' They clink glasses and Jamie joins in because she's old enough to have wine.

Cleo stares at her plate, poking the pheasant and looking for feathers. She can't see any. It looks nice. She tastes it, and it's really, really good. The meat is tender but firm, with a rich taste that's stronger than chicken, but in a nice way. And the sauce is fruity but comforting somehow.

'Oh, Ant, this is amazing.' Mum looks at him gooey-eyed. 'Just like that meal we had—'

'The night we got engaged.' He beams at her. 'I'm so glad you remembered.'

They grin at each other, the candlelight making their eyes look teary.

'So delicious,' Mum adds.

Cleo wishes she'd stop inflating his ego even further.

Jamie nods and says 'mmhmm', her mouth full of potatoes. Cleo doesn't say anything, but does take another mouthful of pheasant.

There's a sudden, sharp pain in one of her teeth. It's crippling, and reverberates all along her jaw, clanging her skull. She shrieks and spits her half-chewed mouthful onto the table. It lands with a thick *splat*.

'Cleo, really.' Mum sounds disgusted.

Only Jamie stares at Cleo, a concerned look on her face.

Cleo examines her plate where the chewed-up lump of meat glistens in the candlelight. There's blood in it. Blood and metal. And that's what she tastes inside her mouth, too.

'What was that?' She pushes her fingers tentatively against her teeth.

Mum reaches out to Cleo, puts a hand on her arm.

Towards the back of her mouth, Cleo's fingertip finds a jagged edge. She's broken a tooth. She examines her fingertips, finding blood.

Ant is the only person not looking concerned. He laughs, throws his head back and claps his hands in glee.

Cleo drops her hands and stares at him.

He keeps clapping.

41

She can't think of anything to say. She's so shocked at his reaction to this.

'Congratulations, Cleo! You've won. You found the shot.'

'So you did this on purpose?' she mutters through saliva and blood.

'What? No, Cleo. You're misunderstanding.' Mum looks from Cleo to Ant. 'Ant, what do you mean? She won what?'

'I'm not misunderstanding. Mum, he gave me this plate. He planned this.' She points down at the 'special plate' he selected especially for her.

For a moment there's a flicker of doubt on Mum's face. Maybe she sees what Cleo sees, too.

'I'm so sorry, Cleo.' Ant hands her a napkin. 'I should have explained you might find a shot, the little pellets from shotgun cartridges. It's perfectly normal in game birds, and if I'd remembered to tell you, you might have chewed a little more carefully. I'm sorry I forgot to mention it.'

In the half-chewed mess she spat into the table, there's a tiny metal ball. In any other circumstances, she'd keep it in her little miscellaneous things collection, in an old biscuit tin in her underwear drawer. But she can't let him see her take it.

She crumples up her napkin, drops it on her uneaten plate of food. 'I've had enough.'

As she leaves the kitchen, she hears the conversation start back up again. Ant's voice sounds pseudo-wounded, the faker. 'I gave her all the nicest breast meat, poor Cleo. Had no idea there'd be a shot in there.'

Always the hero or the villain, that guy. The star of his own show.

Jamie

'I'm so sorry about that, love.' Mum pats Ant on the arm as Cleo storms out. 'It was a total accident, I know. Don't mind Cleo, she doesn't think before she speaks.'

Ant shakes his head. 'Please, don't worry about me. It's you I worry about.' He reaches out and brushes her cheek. She leans into his touch.

Jamie looks away, uncomfortable.

'This can't be good for your stress levels, especially when work's so busy,' Ant says.

Mum's a make-up artist on Ant's news show. That's how they met. But recently she's been contracted to a second show at the same channel so she's working longer hours.

'I suppose I am a bit stressed, what with the wedding prep and everything else.' Mum gives a half-smile, and Jamie's surprised: Dad was always drained by work, quick to snap. Mum's always been the calm one who doesn't react to anything. Mum's more measured, likes to think things through. Certainly not 'stressed'. What's changed?

Ant helps himself to another serving of potatoes and a pheasant leg. 'Has she always been this... undisciplined?'

Jamie frowns. There's something invasive about this question, as if Ant is criticising their family. Even so, maybe that's why Cleo's so wild now: she hasn't been disciplined since Dad left, really, and that must give her unspoken licence to do whatever she wants. In this case, it's being rude to Ant in his own home.

'She's probably just getting used to all the new stuff. It's easier for me, I was practically an adult when you split up. But for a fourteen-year-old... you guys used to hang out all the time.' She nods at Mum. 'Now you have a new husband, and there's a new girlfriend for Dad. Two homes, two Christmases,' Jamie says quickly, taking a slug of wine. 'She used to be fine, before the divorce.'

Mum flicks her head as if she hasn't heard Jamie, and glances at Ant. She doesn't seem to mind his questioning. 'I've always tried to encourage her to think before she speaks, that she doesn't have to express every emotion she feels. She's so angry recently.'

He holds her hand. 'That must be hard for you to see.'

She nods.

Jamie reaches for the wine bottle, her lips pursed. This doesn't feel fair. 'She's settling down. Getting used to everything again.' She tries to keep the uncertainty out of her voice.

'Maybe we should get her some help. It can't be good for her,' he agrees.

'I do wish she wasn't so volatile.'

Jamie's face feels hot, and she's not sure whether it's from the wine or something else. She lines up her knife and fork on her plate, staring hard at the table in front of her. She's never heard Mum talk about Cleo like this, and it feels like a betrayal. If there's a problem with Cleo, Mum should talk to Dad about it, not Ant.

'What kind of help?' Mum asks.

'Well, maybe we should do something about this anger management issue before she gets older. I'd hate to see it damage her schooling, or even her future career.'

Mum nods, her eyes sparkling in the light from the candle. 'We just want her to be happy, you're right.'

Jamie suddenly registers what she heard Ant say. 'Wait, what do you mean, "do something about it"?' There's a spike of annoyance; he shouldn't tell Mum how to parent Cleo, no matter how difficult she is. 'She's a teenager, she'll grow out of it.'

But Ant shakes his head. 'She sent you a warning, loud and clear, with that school incident last year. I've known kids like Cleo. They're in for a nasty trajectory: prison, drugs, or worse, unless they get a real short, sharp shock and it thrusts them out of it.'

'What do you mean?'

He takes a swig of wine and glances at Mum. 'I think we should think about getting her a counsellor. Just so she can work through some of these issues.'

Mum looks at him, her expression unreadable.

He tops up her wine glass and smiles at her. 'It'll give us some breathing room to settle in together, to our marriage.'

There it is, Jamie thinks. Cleo's in mourning for the familiar family unit they lost, and it's not convenient for the honeymooners. Counselling. Jamie raises her eyebrows and looks over at Mum, who has always resisted confrontation and talking things through.

Mum doesn't say anything, but Jamie thinks she sees her give a slight nod.

———

Cleo

Cleo shuffles through some of the clothes on her bedroom floor, kicking a pair of pyjama bottoms in the direction of her laundry basket. There's not much carpet visible, and it'll only be a day or two until Mum comes in with a bin bag and threatens to throw away everything that isn't in a proper place.

She shoves one of her drawers closed, trapping a bra half-in, half-out.

Her stomach grumbles. 'Screw you, Ant,' she mumbles. She grabs a little mirror from her bedside table and opens her mouth, but her tooth is too far back to get a proper look. It's stopped bleeding, which is good.

She lifts piles of discarded clothes, crumpled homework, and empty crisp packets. Finally, she finds what she's looking for: a half-eaten tube of salt and vinegar Pringles. Then she throws herself onto the bed. She chews tentatively, but all seems well.

Cleo: 'Emergency! Need to get away from Ant tomorrow. You free to hang out?'

He texts back straightaway.

Lucasz: 'Helping Dad on a job in the morning. Free after lunch x'

Good old Lucasz, she knew he'd say yes. His dad's an electrician and sometimes takes him along on jobs as a helper in the school holidays. Her phone buzzes again.

Lucasz: 'Wanna go back to the house in the woods?'
'Lets work out what happened to the people who used to live there??'

Cleo: 'Yesssss!!!'

She smiles at Lucasz the history geek, and flicks over to scroll through her Instagram feed. She's starving now. Her stomach feels like it's eating itself. She's just about to give up and creep downstairs when there's a knock on her door. 'Thank God,' she whispers. It must be Mum with some food; she'd never let Cleo go hungry. She's a good mum.

'Come in,' Cleo calls, and the door opens slowly, pushing against the pile of old magazines she's stacked behind it.

'What have you got behind here?'

Cleo suppresses a groan. It's Ant.

He shoves the door and the magazines crumple.

He walks in, and she glares at him. He keeps eye contact, challenging her to stop him. She *did* say to come in, after all.

'What?' she asks.

'Just came up to see if you're OK. I want to be friends, Cleo.'

'No, you don't.'

'Why would you say that? The shot was an honest accident. Your mum found one too, moments after you left the table. It's normal.'

'You don't want to "be friends".' She uses air quotes. 'You're just pretending for Mum. You wouldn't care if I died.' She's surprised herself with this, but she knows it's true: he'd be delighted if she wasn't around, if he got Mum all to himself.

'I would care very much. And I would hate to see how sad your mum would be too.' He sits down on the end of her bed and she pushes herself back against her headboard, as far away from him as she can get. He looks so out of place in her room, sat on her purple bedspread in his posh jeans. He's very tall and broad, and the room feels smaller with him in it. No matter how far away from him she tries to be, it feels like he's crowding her.

He leans towards her and she shrinks back even more. His thumb ring glints in the reflection from her overhead light.

'Your mum's worried about you, Cleo. She says you used to be a good girl. She's concerned about your recent behaviour.' His voice is quiet, almost a whisper. He doesn't want anyone else to hear. 'And that makes me worry about her. She's a very special lady—'

'I know that. I've known her all my life.'

He ignores her interruption. 'She's a very special lady, and my number one priority is to make sure she's OK, no matter what. And if something worries her and causes her stress, then my job as her husband is to get rid of that stress in whatever way I need to do that. To look after her. There's nothing I won't do to look after your mum.'

He stares at her, his eyes boring into her soul. He doesn't look away, and he's perfectly still, like a cat about to pounce on its prey.

A threat. Her skin prickles; the hairs on her arms stand on end, but she doesn't break his gaze. She might need to start checking for poison in her food. She wouldn't put it past him to try and get rid of her that way.

'Mum doesn't need looking after. Not by you.'

He shakes his head, like he feels sorry for Cleo. 'We all love her, Cleo. And we all want the best for her, don't we? We want her to be happy.'

She rolls her eyes. 'Of course I do. She was perfectly happy before you came along.'

His face clouds, and he frowns.

When he speaks next, it's an urgent hiss. 'Your mum and dad will never get back together. They're over. Let her have a new life.'

She stands up on the bed, her heart beating too fast. She can't believe he just said that. As if her dislike for Ant has anything to do with some childish Lindsay Lohan film idea that if only Ant was out of the way her *mummy and daddy would get back together.* 'That's unbelievably patronising,' she spits. 'All I want is for you to get out of our lives and get out of my house. Get out of my room.'

He gets off the bed and walks towards the door, a fake look of disappointment on his face. He keeps his voice low. 'You're making yourself look bad again. No one is listening to you. No one believes you.'

She groans with frustration. 'Cook in our kitchen all you like, but this will never be your house. You don't belong here.'

'I'm sorry you feel that way, Cleo. But I do have to warn you that your behaviour is causing your mum and I to consider drastic action.'

'What does that mean?' She picks up a hairbrush, pulls loose strands from its bristles. She tries to look like she doesn't care, whatever his answer.

'Like boarding school.' He pauses at the door, and whispers: 'You will leave before I do. And Jamie's old enough for her own place. Then it'll be just me and your mum.'

Chapter Four

Jamie

Documentary Proposal
HouseFire: 20 Years of Arson and No Arrests
A true crime documentary

Spider and Jamie, two investigative reporters, try to uncover the truth behind a series of cold case arson attacks across the Abbeywick area, dating back to the 1980s. But as our team gets closer to uncovering the mystery, an arsonist threatens their lives.

Filmed in interview style with occasional on-camera presenters for live-action and fly-on-the wall reporting in unfolding action sequences.

Film Synopsis
Spider Turnbull and Jamie Davidson are on the trail of a

notorious and ruthless arsonist whose fires have terrorised the county of North Yorkshire for over 20 years. Working in chronological order, they visit each arson location and interview the victims and their loved ones, gathering a portfolio of clues along the way. They connect with local law enforcement to learn the barriers to arrest that enabled this monster to walk free for so many years. They visit renowned experts in arson, including psychiatrists and criminal psychologists, gaining valuable insight into the inner mind of firesetters, and answer questions: why start fires? And why stop for so long? Is the arsonist still out there?

As our reporters begin to piece together the puzzle and get closer to identifying the arsonist, ready to present their findings to the police, they get the ultimate lead in the case, but will it make or break their investigation? Jamie and Spider fly too close to the sun, and the arsonist comes out of retirement to make contact with a sinister threat, warning them to stop their detective work or risk their lives by continuing. The investigators have a big decision to make: do they pursue justice but endanger their lives, or save themselves while risking future fires and further lives lost?

Arsonist Timeline*

- Approx. 1982/3(?): Small misdemeanours, mainly public or council property. Not confirmed as this individual but suspected due to higher than usual average annual reported arson rate and choice of accelerant: all fuelled by kerosene. Locations include bins, park benches and big bonfires in woodland, wooden shed at local cricket ground and beach hut.

- October 1984: Escalation begins – break-in and small amount of fire damage at Leisureland Amusement arcade, Moorburn Bay promenade. Empty kerosene container discovered at scene.
- April 1985: Signature kerosene lamp appears – Moorburn Bay bandstand burned to the ground; smashed kerosene lamp recovered from scene.
- November 1985: Abbeywick High School gym razed by fire. Kerosene lamp discovered smashed on vaulting horse.
- March 1986: Theatre Royal total burndown. One deceased. Fire source narrowed down to exterior of building. Damage too severe to identify accelerant, but curved shards of broken glass (lamp?) discovered in wreckage.

Note: as far as we can tell, the theatre was the final fire. Perhaps the arsonist felt remorse at taking a life? Jamie and Spider to investigate.

*Information taken from newspaper research and publicly available police records. Spider and Jamie expect to uncover further arson crimes attributed to the same perpetrator during filming.

Casting
Pamela Dunning, Manager, Theatre Royal Abbeywick
Headmistress, Abbeywick High School
Forensic psychologist – arson expert

Relative of Louise Alderton, who died in the Theatre
Royal Fire [Spider to sort this one]
Former arsonist?? [Can we get one? Jamie to look into
this]
Narrator: Ant Gardiner, news reporter [??? TBC –
Spider]

Contact Information
Spider Turnbull
Email: spideyt@hotmail.com

Jamie Davidson
Email: jamied1999@gmail.com

'What is this?' Jamie bursts through the doors of
Inktopia, pointing at her phone, Spider's email on the
screen.

Spider shakes his head, raising his eyebrows at the phone
sandwiched between his cheek and shoulder. 'Of course, we
have an opening next Wednesday at half two?'

Jamie paces the floor of the tattoo parlour, arms folded.
Before she met Spider, she assumed tattoo places were grubby
and seedy, but this one is clean and bright, more like a dentist,
doctor, or another medical practice. She's in the shop window
part of the store where clients come in to browse the tattoos
they can get. The walls are covered in options ranging from My
Little Pony to skulls and motorbikes.

There's a quiet buzzing from the back room where the
tattoos get done. It's Spider's colleague Tamara, drawing a
dolphin onto the ankle of a nervous girl who looks barely
eighteen.

'OK, all done.' He hangs up the phone and beckons Jamie

to take a seat on the other side of his table. He moves the plastic binders containing tattoo designs into a stack at the end of the table and opens a notebook. 'What's up?'

'What's this?' She holds her phone out to him.

'It's a pitch for funding. The Arts Council North opens for applications next week and we might have a chance.'

'It's full of lies. What's all this rubbish about us endangering our lives?'

'It's a narrative arc. We're investigating a cold case, so there needs to be some threat, something to make it exciting. Otherwise it's just old newspaper articles and grainy news footage.' There's a sparkle in his eye, and his dimples appear as his grin widens. 'And this is effective, right? You never know, we might be able to make the documentary look like we nearly got set on fire ourselves. You gave me the idea, actually.'

She folds her arms across her chest.

'The message you got. Telling you to scrap the documentary.'

'That was just a troll. The internet is full of them; it doesn't mean anything.' She picks up her phone and points at the screen where it says they find out the identity of the arsonist. 'We haven't even started filming yet. We haven't interviewed anyone!'

'I'm about to change that.' He's quiet for a moment, and Jamie hears the buzz of Tamara's needle in the back room, carving into that young girl's skin.

'Oh, are you?' Her cheeks flush with frustration. 'That's another thing. I'm the director. Why did you write this and why is your name listed first?'

'Woah, chill out. I'm not taking over. It's still your baby. You just needed a little push. I have a good feeling about this doc.

This is the one that'll get us noticed, J. Especially with Ant's help.'

'This is my project, Spider. My idea. We should have written this together.'

'Change what you like. I haven't submitted yet. And it's a fifty-fifty project. Equal work.'

'Why are we applying for this anyway? Ant's already given us what we need to make the film.'

'He has, but if we get a grant then we can take a few weeks off work, really give it the time it deserves. I didn't lie about everything.'

'Really? Because there's no arsonist anymore. He's probably dead. There haven't been any fires for thirty years.'

'Come on, Jamie. Of course there's an arsonist. Look at the Golden State Killer: hasn't killed anyone since 1986, but he was still alive and well.'

Jamie pauses, pulling one of the binders towards her and opening it on a page full of inked motorbike tattoo options, some with flames emanating from the wheels. 'I suppose.'

'For the purposes of our documentary storytelling, I choose to believe the arsonist is still alive, and we're going to find him.' He nods at the funding application on Jamie's phone, flat on the table before them. 'Before he finds us.'

She brings her hands to the sides of her head and grabs her hair. 'But documentaries are about telling the truth.'

'No, they're about creating entertainment. Invention, at least a little bit, is a well-known method in documentaries.'

Jamie raises her eyebrows at him, not believing a word of it.

'Really. The reason everyone thinks lemmings jump off cliffs is because they made it up for a Disney documentary; it's not true. And *Nanook of the North* from the 1920s – they faked a whole three-sided igloo just so they could film it from the inside. And Attenborough's sound effects are all pre-recorded. Most nature docs do their filming in zoos and then fake that they were in the wild. And those are for the BBC. This is just like that; the story we're telling is still true, we're just adding drama. Trust me. It'll make us famous.'

'What about integrity?'

'Fuck integrity. That's for successful people to worry about.'

The Arsonist

I watched from across the road, from the attic window of the old coffin factory. I crouched on the bare floorboards, the wood hard against my knees, my hands on the windowsill, the top of my head invisible from the street in case anyone looked up.

I smelled the smoke before I saw the flames; the wind was in the right direction. It started as a subtle, fragrant scent on the air: woodsmoke, like a bonfire. I breathed it in, filling my lungs and remembering happier times. Then, sooner than usual, the smoke became thicker, more acrid as the flames inside the building began to consume more than wood. Plastic began to melt, paint started to bubble, glass shattered, and plaster became ash. I pulled my clothes up over my face to protect my mouth and nose.

Then, the best part: the flames. By the time they're visible from the outside of a building, the inside is often destroyed, a shell. That's the part I waited for: the sight of the flames licking the sky, their luminous beauty, filled my soul with joy, made me want to sing and dance. But instead, I sat quietly and felt the tension leave my muscles as I relaxed for the first time in weeks.

My body waited for this release, patiently at first and then more urgently the longer it took. Where others needed a massage or a holiday, I needed a fire. It provided a balm to soothe my soul, and without it, I became a wreck of a person.

But then the fire department arrived. Doused the flames. And I watched them remove a body bag.

I'm not a murderer. I didn't want to hurt anyone. I didn't even want to destroy people's belongings – the places I selected were insured up to the eyeballs and I timed it to ensure no one remained inside the building.

That night I made a mistake. I couldn't have known the costume lady stayed late, catching up on some last-minute stitching before opening night. I didn't know. I didn't. If I had known… if her car had been in the car park. But she caught the bus that day. I would never have done it. I would have waited, at least.

I couldn't sleep for weeks, seeing her face staring out at me from the front pages of the local paper.

I've read a lot about what it's like to die in a fire since I killed that woman. It's the smoke and heat that kill, not the flames themselves. As the fire consumes the oxygen in the room, it releases carbon monoxide. As she inhaled carbon monoxide, it would have combined with haemoglobin in her blood where oxygen should be, suffocating her from the inside as she breathed.

Even worse, as her body detected higher levels of carbon monoxide and carbon dioxide, she probably breathed harder, deeper and quicker in a futile attempt to obtain more oxygen, inhaling more lethal gases. Next: incapacitation and then asphyxiation. If she was lucky, it was quick.

I haven't been able to access reports from the port-mortem, so I don't know if the flames touched her. What I do know is smoke is hot. And when it's inhaled, it sears the respiratory tract.

She burned from the inside out, because of me. Because of what I did.

I have to live with that. What surprises me most is that I can.

The House Fire

At first they thought it was an accident: she was smoking in the green room, and ash from her cigarette caught the costumes alight. But they started to investigate and for a short while I felt so guilty that I nearly turned myself in, stopped everything before it even began.

But I got lucky. It was a motiveless crime and they couldn't pin it on anyone. And soon the case went cold, and I moved on, too. It's a miracle what the human mind can rationalise and justify. I learned to live with what I had done, and the guilt began to fade. It'll never leave entirely, but I make up for it with other kind acts: charity donations, giving money to homeless people, little anonymous acts of kindness, helping others through life to make it easier for them. Anything to balance out my misdeeds.

And I managed to justify it in other ways, too. I dug into the life of that costume assistant and found she wasn't as angelic as the papers painted her. I'm not saying that justifies her horrible death in flames, of course. But when I learned that, I could live with myself a little easier.

Of course, I vowed after that night that I would never do it again. No more fires. But that was easier said than done, sadly. I lasted six months before my fingers itched and my lungs burned, and I couldn't sit still. I couldn't keep my temper, was unable to remain calm. I felt like I would tear off my own skin. I remember it like a nicotine craving, only multiplied by a thousand. I needed to watch something burn again.

So I carried on. I had no choice.

Jamie

'Episode one: the first death.' Spider's voice booms around the inside of the car, imitating the gruff anticipation of cinema trailer voice-overs.

Jamie turns to Spider and then abruptly turns away, covering her face. He's pointing a camera at her. Again. 'Don't, please. I just want to get ready for this, not mess around.'

The camera makes a small *ping* and a red light shines from the front, just below the lens. It's recording. Jamie holds out a hand, blocks the lens.

The camera is black, smooth, and shiny, its big lens wide and expectant, a microphone pointing forwards. Their equipment arrived in a big delivery to Spider's shop this morning. It's everything the internet said they would need, a beginner's documentary kit: camcorder, camera bag, rain cover, tripod, and a lapel mic like newsreaders wear on TV.

They're the only car parked outside the Theatre Royal on the town's clifftop. Through the windscreen, Jamie watches a seagull perch on top of an overflowing litter bin, its beak plucking at the Styrofoam of a discarded fish and chips box. Beyond that, it's just the sea stretching for miles.

'Jamie, you need to get used to being on camera.'

'This documentary isn't about us. It's about the arsonist and his victims.'

'Yes, but you're our investigator. Our presence on screen.' He reaches out and takes a section of her hair between his fingers. 'With that hair and those eyes, it'd be a waste not to get you in front of a camera. You'll bring the personality to our series, give viewers something extra to tune in for every episode.'

She mimes vomiting at his compliments. 'Oh, we're making a series now?'

'They're what's selling at the moment. But you're the boss.' He rubs at the corner of his mouth. 'This camera is awesome, by the way. Please thank Ant again for me. I'll buy him a case of beer.'

Jamie nods.

'And let him know if he ever wants a free tattoo, I'm his man.'

She laughs. She can't imagine anything less likely than Ant getting a tattoo. 'You could give him a massive cobweb across his back to match yours.'

Beyond the seagull and the bin, past the sheer drop of the cliffs, the sea churns grey as steel, with little white caps as the wind picks up the tips of the swell. She points at the little clock on the dashboard. 'OK, five more minutes before our appointment. Let's review what we know about our unsub.'

'Unsub.' He nods with approval. 'So it's all confined to a 20-mile radius of Abbeywick. And we think the crimes targeted buildings, not necessarily people, right?'

'Right. It didn't seem like he was trying to kill anyone.'

'So it was a compulsion?'

'I think so. From what I've read, it was probably something called "expressive arson".'

Spider turns to her, impressed. 'You've been doing your research.'

'Of course I have. This arsonist doesn't seem like he was—'

'Wait.' He holds out a hand and lifts the camera to his eye. 'Start again.' Seeing her discomfort, he lowers the camera and touches her arm. 'You don't have to talk directly to the camera. Look out to sea if it's easier.'

She watches the waves ebb and flow at the shoreline and takes a breath. She hears the short *beep* as he starts to record.

'We believe this arsonist was the expressive type, meaning he set things on fire as a way of...' She pauses, stumbling on her words.

Spider gives her a thumbs up. 'That's good, we'll keep rolling – just start from the top and we'll keep going until it flows right.'

She repeats herself and finds a better way to say it. '...as a way of expressing strong emotions. He wasn't trying to cover up a crime or hurt anyone, necessarily, but injuries, loss and death were the collateral damage of what he *needed to do* to survive.' She's enjoying herself, she realises: talking fluently to the camera, her brain working at full speed. She feels exhilarated. She stares into the lens, imagining making eye contact with an audience. 'It's a compulsion. So we're here to ask questions: who is he? Why does he do this? What made him who he is today? And why did he stop?'

Spider's mouth drops open and whoops with glee, his voice filling the car with sound. 'Jamie, you're a natural! That sounded amazing!' He high-fives her. 'We'll have to interview some experts, though. That kind of thing will look so much better coming from a psychologist or psychiatrist or something.'

Pamela Dunning is a big woman who perches on a red velvet stool at the hotel's bar. She fiddles with a Deuchars beer mat, spinning it on its point and snapping it between finger and thumb before she sets it spinning once more.

She's the theatre's manager and has worked here since

way before the fire. 'I started out as an usher and just never left.' Little lines pucker around her mouth, showing she's a smoker. Her magenta lipstick is applied thick specially for the camera.

Every now and again, her eyes flick to the camera and then back to Jamie.

'If you can just keep your eyes on Jamie, Mrs Dunning. Try to ignore the camera.'

She nods. 'Sorry.' She's got a broad Abbeywick accent, her vowels comfortable and round.

Even though it's a bright day outside, inside the theatre bar it could be day or night, rain or shine. There are no windows, and the light from the tobacco-yellow lamps bounces off the mirror behind the bar, giving the whole space a gaslit glow. It feels like this dark-wooded, red-velvet-shrouded bar hasn't been updated for decades, but Jamie knows they must have rebuilt it 20 years ago after the fire.

The whole theatre was gutted.

'Can you tell us a bit about the night it happened?' Jamie makes her voice as welcoming and calm as possible.

Pamela nods, and spins the beer mat again.

'Just look up at me for a sec – so Spider can get a focus on you.' She tries to make a subtle gesture, her hands saying, 'Stay still.' This lady is so uncomfortable on camera, Jamie has doubts they'll be able to use any of this footage at all.

Spider gives a nod.

'OK,' Jamie says, and puts a hand on Pamela's arm. 'We can do as many takes as you need, so don't worry if you stumble over a word. In fact, if you do stumble a bit, just start the sentence again and we'll keep going. No need to cut or anything – we can edit later.'

Pamela smiles gratefully. 'Sorry, love. Not been on camera

since it happened, you see. Haven't really talked about it since, either. Everyone sort of forgot about it.'

'I understand. I hope to change that.' She pauses to show there's no urgency here, even though her stomach is rumbling and she'd kill for a can of the Diet Coke she can see in the fridges behind the bar. 'So, the night it happened?'

'It was my fault. I practically killed her.'

At this, Jamie hears a slight shift behind her: Spider zooms in on Pamela's face, probably to get a close-up of her eyes glistening with as-yet-unshed tears.

'I didn't know she was there.'

'Louise Alderton?'

Pamela nods. 'I'd locked up for the night and gone home, the whole place was dark and empty. No cars in the car park.'

'So how did she get in?'

'There's a keypad on the stage door, at the back. I told the police at the time that no one had the code unless they worked here, and we changed it every six months or every time a member of staff left, whichever came first. It was pretty secure, I made sure of it.'

'And they had a theory?' she prompts, hoping Pamela will answer in complete sentences so they can cut Jamie's voice from the edit.

'In the end, their theory was that the fire was set from outside the building. So it wasn't necessarily set by someone who knew the code. And I'm proud that it wasn't some negligence on my part.' She falters here, and reaches a hand up to her cheek, but doesn't quite rest her fingers on her face – probably for fear of smudging the thick layer of foundation on her skin. 'But I do blame myself.'

Ant was right: it's tough. This feels exploitative. But she sticks to her script; she'll think about that later. Jamie swallows her disquiet. 'Can you tell me a bit more about that?'

'Louise was a stand-in for our costume designer, who went on early maternity leave.' Pamela picks up the beer mat again and turns it over in her pink-tipped fingers, her lips quivering.

Jamie doesn't say anything, and overrides her instinct to console, to reassure. It really wasn't this woman's fault. There's no way she could have known what would happen. But if Jamie interferes or talks, or touches Pamela, she knows it'll ruin Spider's shot; she needs to let Pamela 'ride her wave of emotion' for the camera, or something equally invasive.

Jamie shifts on her stool, rearranges her feet on the footrest.

After a moment, Pamela looks up once more. 'Louise worried she didn't have the skills, that she was too new to the job. I suggested she work as hard as she could, and quickly, so she had more time to fix anything that went wrong. You know, instead of it getting to opening night and everyone having a panic. She must have taken me literally because that very night she came back to the theatre to do an all-nighter, hemming the petticoats for the chorus dancers.'

At this, Pamela gives in to the tears and covers her face. Her shoulders shake. There's a whirring behind Jamie's shoulder as Spider zooms in even closer.

Jamie opens her mouth to suggest they take a break or stop altogether. But Pamela looks up, her foundation streaked with tears, mascara smudged under her eyes. She looks directly into the camera.

Spider clears his throat. 'Do you ever think "what if?" If you hadn't rushed her on the costumes, maybe she wouldn't have...'

Jamie stifles a grimace. There's something ghoulish about asking these questions, probing someone's emotional pain to get their reactions to make a documentary. She flicks a glance over her shoulder at Spider, half his face hidden behind the camera. A small smile pulls at the corner of his lip. He's pushing too hard, taking over. They're trying to identify an arsonist, not encourage this poor woman to take responsibility for a death.

Pamela shrugs, her face blank like she can't face Spider's question head-on. 'I think about Louise every day. Every morning when I come into this theatre, I walk into the old green room and I imagine what it must have been like for her, trapped in that windowless room with no way out, breathing in the smoke and knowing that was how she would die: surrounded by costumes at an amateur theatre in this crumbling seaside town. She was a mother, you know. She deserved better than that. I hope this documentary catches whoever did it, and I hope they rot in prison.'

'And what about people who worked here? Was there anyone you didn't trust or who seemed suspicious?' he asks.

Jamie interrupts. 'But the fire was set from the outside.'

He shrugs with one shoulder, keeping the camera steady with the other. 'Got to think about motive, too. Pamela? You said very few people had the door code.'

Pamela shakes her head. 'I'm sorry, it's such a long time ago now. But the police interviewed me back then and I gave them all this information. If you can get to it somehow. I don't have the best memory.'

A small beep as Spider switches off the camera.

'Pamela, thank you so much.' He steps forward, hand outstretched to shake. He looks delighted, puffed up and proud, as if he wrote the script for her or something. He didn't do anything except point a camera at her. 'You have been excellent, and you're right, that's exactly what we're here to do: shed new light on this case and finally bring the arsonist to justice.'

She smiles at him in that way a lot of women smile at Spider when they look past his tattoos and his big bushy beard and they see his dimples and his blue eyes. 'Thank you, Spider.' She takes his hand and shakes it. 'If there's anything else I can do, of course…'

Jamie holds her own hand out to shake, but Spider keeps talking. 'Actually, there is, if you have a few minutes?'

Pamela doesn't notice Jamie's outstretched hand.

'We'd love to get some footage inside the green room and the theatre itself? You know, so we can show what the theatre looks like now and what a good job you've done on the restoration.'

Jamie puts her hands in her pockets and follows as Pamela leads Spider backstage.

Chapter Five

Cleo

'Argh!' Cleo screws up her eyes against the blinding sunlight. It's so bright it hurts her head. She pushes her face into her pillow and groans. She needs more sleep. It can't possibly be morning already.

'Wakey-wakey, snoozer!' Mum sounds like she's in a good mood. She sounds like her old self. From before.

Cleo opens one eyelid and peers out through her eyelashes. Mum stands by the open curtains, hands on her hips, surveying the mess of Cleo's bedroom.

'It might be the Easter holidays, but that doesn't mean you get to sleep away every single day until you go back to school.'

'But I'm tired.'

'You'll feel more awake soon.' Mum climbs onto the bed next to Cleo and leans against the headboard. 'Come on, sit up.' She pokes at Cleo until she sits up, and they both huddle in the bed, the covers pulled up to their chests like Bert and Ernie.

Her eyes won't focus on anything yet, but her heart feels full with Mum next to her like this. She used to get into Cleo's bed every Sunday morning to drink her cup of tea before Ant started staying over. Now he brings Mum's tea in bed. No Cleos allowed.

'What time is it?' Cleo stares into space, still snoozy. She knows her hair must be sticking up everywhere and she's probably got creases on her face. She always looks wild when she wakes up in the morning.

Mum checks her Fitbit, Ant's not-very-subtle present to hint that Mum was growing thicker around the middle before the wedding. 'It's half past ten.'

'Mum! I could have slept way longer.'

Mum laughs. 'Such a teenager.' She claps her hands. 'Nope, no more sleeping for you today. I'm going to an antiques fair later, but before that we are going out for brunch. Just me and you. I think it's time we had a girly morning, don't you?'

Cleo suddenly feels more awake, and she's delighted. 'YES! That sounds great! Can we go somewhere that does pancakes? And bacon? And maple syrup on all of it?' She could cry, she's so happy. There's been no alone time with Mum since Ant arrived in their lives. He's always around, always at their house, always the topic of conversation even when he's not there.

'Maple syrup!' Mum laughs and mimes gagging. 'Sweet on savoury is disgusting. But if that's what the belated birthday girl wants, then go for it.' Then her face goes serious again. 'And I think we have some things to chat about, don't we? Ant told me you two had another run-in last night.'

Cleo slumps under the covers. Of course this isn't just a mum-and-daughter outing. *Of course* they have to talk about Ant. Even when he's not there, he controls everything.

'What if I don't want to talk about *Ant*?' She emphasises every letter of his short name, ensuring her tongue makes an unnecessarily loud *click* on the 'T' at the end.

Mum gets out of bed, no longer jovial or smiling. The moment is over; the window into their old life slams shut. She stands at the foot of the bed, arms folded. She's wearing a white knitted jumper with light blue jeans and the whole outfit complements her blonde bob. She looks stylish and expensive in a way she never looked before Ant came along. But he helps her buy clothes now. She thinks it's romantic. Cleo thinks it's twisted.

'Honestly, Cleo, it doesn't always matter what you *want* or *don't want*. You're not the centre of this household and we're not going to keep tiptoeing around you trying not to upset you. When, frankly, everything upsets you at the moment.'

Cleo opens her mouth and closes it again. This is unusual. Mum's usually so... meek. She doesn't stand up to anyone. 'Did he tell you to say that?'

Mum turns and starts to walk out of the room. 'Get dressed, please.' Then she stops again. 'And you'll tidy your room today, too. It's a disgrace in here.' She points at the clothes all over the floor and the drawers hanging open. The lipstick smear on the mirror.

Cleo waits until Mum's footsteps head down the stairs. 'I bet he told you to say that, too,' she mumbles.

Cleo orders the American breakfast: thick pancakes covered in syrup and the crispiest streaky bacon in the world, which shatters in her mouth when she takes a bite. Exactly as she likes it.

Mum's got a vegetarian egg white omelette and she looks like every mouthful is hard work.

'Bacon?' Cleo holds out her plate, but she's relieved when Mum shakes her head slowly. She looks tempted though.

'Why did you order that? You don't even like eggs.'

Mum shrugs. 'It looked nice in the picture.'

'You could have got cheese on it or something.'

'Cheese would defeat the purpose.'

Cleo waves her fork from side to side in the direction of Mum's omelette. '…Which is?'

She sticks out her top teeth and wrinkles her nose. 'Burning more calories than I consume.' She says it in a funny, nasal voice like a cartoon mad scientist.

'Why are you on a diet, though? You look fine.' Cleo means it too. Mum's lost about a stone in the last six months and doesn't need to lose more.

'Ant says we need to be as healthy as we can be at this age, so we don't stagnate and end up dying of a heart attack.'

'You're only forty-five. You're younger than Jennifer Aniston.'

Mum sputters on her green juice. 'I bet she eats this kind of crap too!'

Cleo shoves a huge forkful of pancake into her mouth and wipes a drip of syrup from her chin with a paper napkin. 'It's weird that Ant tells you what to eat and what to wear, Mum.'

'It's not like that.'

'Yes, it is.'

Mum's face shuts down again, like a shop's metal shutter at closing time. 'Give it a rest, Cleo. Ant wants us both – us *all* – to be happy and healthy. That's all this is. And because neither of us have our parents around anymore, we don't know what hereditary illnesses we might be susceptible to.'

'I wish I'd met your parents.' Mum's parents died before Cleo and Jamie were born, and Dad's dad too. 'I love Gran, but it'd be nice to have the full set, you know? Lucasz has all four of his back in Poland.'

Mum gives a small smile. 'Relatives are important. They would have loved you very much. Just like Gran does.'

'She says I should get the train to visit her.' Cleo shoves more pancakes into her mouth and talks with her mouth full. 'That's another thing. Why doesn't Ant have any blood relations?'

'He doesn't talk about it much. But you could ask him.'

Cleo pulls a face.

She shrugs. 'A few years ago, he went to the children's home and got his old records. He thinks his parents were unmarried, and in Yorkshire in the 1970s, that wasn't always accepted by people.'

Cleo tilts her head. 'But he wasn't a baby, right? I mean, giving up a newborn baby, sure, I kinda get it. Don't want the stigma of an illegitimate kid and so on. But he was almost a teenager when they gave him up for some reason.'

'We don't know the circumstances.'

'You've got to admit, that's strange. After raising them for years you love that kid, or you should.' She pauses and glances up. Mum's looking at Cleo, but her face is angled away as if she can't quite bear to look directly at her. 'Unless something goes wrong. Maybe he was a problem child, you know, like bed-wetting and killing animals and stuff.' Mum opens her mouth to interrupt but Cleo forges on. 'And the mum gave him up – the unmarried bit was just an excuse.'

'No one's a problem child here except you.' Mum winks to show she's joking and signals for the waitress. She asks for some grated cheese to add to her omelette.

Cleo grins, triumphant. 'I'll try not to let slip to Ant that you ate CHEESE.'

Mum sticks her tongue out, but then her expression gets serious again. 'There is something I wanted to talk to you about, though. As well as the fact that we haven't had any time together, just you and me, for far too long.'

Cleo nods, happy Mum's acknowledging how neglected she's been lately. It's been terrible. Anything could have happened to her and Mum wouldn't even have noticed. She could have been suspended AGAIN, got a boyfriend even though she's only thirt— fourteen now.

'Ant's worried about you.'

Cleo groans and lowers her forehead to the table. She shakes her head, feels grains of salt against her skin as she moves against the cold surface. 'No, he's really not, Mum,' she mumbles into the table.

Mum reaches across, strokes her hair like she used to when Cleo was little. Cleo closes her eyes, feels the familiar comfort of Mum's hand running through her hair. For so long she hasn't felt looked after or cared for. She's been so alone, untethered like a boat when the rope breaks the connection to the jetty. And suddenly, with one touch, she's certain that no matter what happens someone will be there to help when things go wrong. She almost cries with relief: this is what she needs. A mum, someone who's there all the time. Not this part-time thing they have right now, when Ant releases Mum from his clutches for a snatched minute. Relatives are important, just like Mum said. Mum is important.

'Ant's not worried about me one bit.' She raises her head from the table and looks at Mum, whose face is set in full 'flinch' mode. Her brow is furrowed and although she's looking at Cleo with her eyes, her head is still turned away. She doesn't want to hear what Cleo is about to say. Probably because, deep down, she knows it's true. 'The only thing that Ant is worried about is himself. And you. But believe me, if you were to get between him and what he wants, he wouldn't put you first either. He's selfish, Mum. He's mean. He's... he's a narcissist.'

Mum sits back in her seat, as if Cleo has hit her. 'Oh, come on, Cleo. Stop this. It's so dramatic. I understand that you've been learning about narcissists at school or on Twitter or something—'

'Please don't patronise me.'

'Well, where did you even learn about what a narcissist is? At fourteen years old?'

'Does it matter?'

'It matters if you're trying to diagnose everyone you meet with a different pathology just because you saw a new documentary on Netflix.'

Cleo tries to make her voice sound as calm as possible. 'All right, Mum. If that's what you want to believe. But I know deep down you see what I see, too. You see him turning every conversation to himself. You see him manipulating you and everyone who comes into contact with him just to get what he wants. You see him poisoning everyone against me so he can have you all to himself.'

'No, I don't see that. I see a man whom I love, who loves me back. Who deserves a happy family for the first time in his life. Stop this, please. This isn't fair. Everyone else likes him. He's a good man.'

Cleo folds her hands, interlacing her fingers. 'Is he really a good man if you have to say it out loud so much? All the good people I know don't need you to say it about them all the time.'

Mum pauses here. She stares at the table, hard. She's still and quiet for such a long time that Cleo begins to worry she's having a stroke or something. She's moments away from reaching out and poking her, just to see if she'll react.

Then she snaps out of it, a bright shiny look on her face like a robot. 'I'm sorry you're unhappy right now, love. I really hope things improve for you. You and Jamie will always be my priority, that goes without saying.' She smiles. 'But I also have Ant to think of now. And he has some concerns about you, as I mentioned. He thinks your recent... problems might be indicative of—'

'Recent problems? What recent problems is he on about? It was one thing, and it won't happen again. I've promised. I'm FINE.'

'You don't seem fine. You seem troubled.'

'I am troubled. By him.'

'Anyway, he wants us to consider sending you to a counsellor.'

'He's the one who needs counselling. He threatened me last night.' Her voice gets higher, which is so annoying. She so badly wants to hide that this bothers her.

'Threatened you?' She shakes her head, like she's getting rid of a mosquito. 'Please stop telling lies.'

'I'm not! He came into my room and he said he would send me to board—'

'Just listen, Cleo. I think a counsellor might do you some good, help you untangle some things in your head.'

'I don't have a tangled head!' Her fork clatters to the floor. Some people in the restaurant turn around and look at her. She ducks her head. 'Sorry,' she mumbles. She'd be a lot less likely to provide a replay of last year if people would listen to her for a change, instead of just telling her how broken she is all the time.

'We're thinking about it,' Mum whispers, smiling over her shoulder at the strangers who are more important than Cleo.

'I don't have to think about it, I know—'

Mum reaches out a hand and puts it on top of Cleo's, shaking her head. 'It's not you who has to think, Cleo. It's me and Ant. If you can be easy, in the house, kind to Ant, helpful and polite—'

Cleo sputters, indignant. '*He* should be the one—'

Mum continues as if Cleo hasn't made a sound. 'Then maybe a few counselling sessions and everything will be fine.'

'And if it's not?'

Mum doesn't say anything.

Cleo sits down. 'And if it's not fine, Mum? If he says it's not fine. What then? He sends me away to boarding school.'

She shakes her head. 'I don't know where you got that from. No one is sending you anywhere. I love having you around.'

Cleo's eyes fill with tears. 'If you love having me around, Mum, don't let him do this. He's tearing everything apart and he won't stop until he has what he wants: only you and nothing else. He hates me and Jamie because we take your attention away.'

'He doesn't hate you and Jamie.'

'It'll be the dog next. I bet you anything.'

'Thanks for brunch, Mum.' Cleo kisses Mum on the cheek and jumps out of the car. 'Enjoy the antique fair thing. Maybe you could actually buy something for once!'

Mum laughs. 'We have enough clutter. You know I just like to browse.'

She slams the door and runs up the gravel path to Lucasz's place. It's a huge house on the outskirts of town but instead of the creamy white paint of nearby houses, Lucasz's is slightly tired-looking. They've lived there for nearly a year – before that they were in a flat in the town centre, but when Jan became old enough to need his own room, they bought this massive six-bedroom tumbledown house and moved in, planning to renovate.

Lucasz says it's like a chef never cooks well for themselves: a house builder rarely has a nice house. Back in Poland, Lucasz's dad owned a successful company building mansions for rich people. In his thick accent, he's told Cleo many times that he employed a team of twenty men and was practically a millionaire before he sold it all to move to England.

She knocks on the door because the bell is broken, and Lucasz's mum answers with Jan balanced on her hip. He's sucking his thumb, the skin around his mouth covered in dried food.

'Hi Mrs Kowalski. Is Lucasz home? He said he's free this afternoon.'

She shakes her head, and Jan joins in, moving his whole arm so his thumb remains firmly in his mouth. Cleo pulls a funny face at him and he smiles, mouth gaping around his thumb.

'Jan just woke from his nap.' Like Lucasz's dad, her expression is always very serious. 'Lucasz is still out on a job. Be back soon though. Want tea?' She turns away from the door and walks into the house without waiting for Cleo's answer. Cleo pulls the door closed behind her, following Mrs Kowalski into the kitchen where she's setting the kettle onto the hob.

Her footsteps echo on the wooden floor of the corridor. One of Lucasz's chores for the Easter holidays – when he's not helping his dad at work – is to use a massive industrial sander to sand the floorboards. He'd rather be reading a boring book about a battle or a long-dead king, but the sanding looks like an exciting job to Cleo.

Cleo sits at their dining table and sips at her black tea. She'd prefer it with milk and sugar, but Mrs Kowalski is too scary for her to ask. Cleo quite likes her; there's something enticing about someone who seems so unimpressed by everything. It makes Cleo want to be the exception, the one who makes her smile or raise her eyebrows with surprise. But only Lucasz and Jan seem able to elicit any extremes of emotion from this stern woman.

'Luki is working hard for his dad lately,' his mum says. 'Weekends and holidays. But he got the day off for your mum's wedding. He said it was a good day?'

Cleo nods, too shy to tell the truth. 'Mum looked very pretty. And happy,' she mumbles.

The dining table is cluttered with straw placemats scattered at each seat, a couple of sticky plastic toy buses lined up along the edge, and a pair of sharp scissors with purple handles. Mrs Kowalski sees Cleo staring and stands to return the scissors to a kitchen drawer. Cleo's cheeks flush.

'Luki says you don't like your stepfather,' says Mrs Kowalski as she sits back down, scissors safely away.

Stepfather. Cleo suppresses a grimace.

'He's rich?' she asks, very direct. A British person would never ask, but Cleo likes it: there are no games, just clarity. It's comfortable, somehow, even when the questions and the subject aren't.

'Yes, I think he is.'

Lucasz's mum nods her approval.

'But he's not nice.'

'Oh?' She pushes a packet of Polish biscuits across the table to Cleo.

Cleo likes the way the letters look on the packaging: familiar but very different all at the same time. She takes a biscuit: they're chocolate-covered wafers with nuts. Super tasty.

'What has he done?'

'He's…' She can't find a description that this no-nonsense lady would nod and agree with. There's so little tangible evidence, but so many little things add up to a monstrous whole that can't be described over a cup of tea. 'He wants to send me away. To boarding school. He doesn't want me around.'

'He wants you to get the best education. And he has money, so he will pick a good school. This is a nice man.'

Cleo shakes her head. 'He wants Mum all to himself. He wants to get rid of me.'

She purses her lips. 'He has married your mum, a whole package with you and your sister too. He knows you are there, or he wouldn't have married her.'

She shrugs, not sure what to say. It's not possible to explain it.

'Even if you're right, your mum is your mum. You think she'd let anyone get between her and her children? No. She wouldn't marry a man like this. Trust me.' At this, Mrs Kowalski kisses Jan on the cheek and sets him on the floor, and he runs off into the living room to turn on CBeebies. 'Luki would miss you if you went to boarding school. I hope this doesn't happen.'

'Thank you.'

There's the sound of the old van pulling onto the drive, doors slamming. Cleo smiles as Lucasz storms into the house, singing at the top of his lungs. He stops as soon as he sees Cleo at the table and blushes. His mum smiles, the smile she keeps just for her sons. 'Cleo's here,' she says, her frown gone.

'Hey, Clee!' He ruffles his hair on his way past, grabs a banana from the fruit bowl and shoves half of it into his mouth. He's covered in dust, his hair sticking up everywhere. 'Mum, can Cleo borrow your bike? We want to go for a ride.'

Mrs Kowalski shrugs. 'Make sure the tyres are pumped.'

Chapter Six

Cleo

The abandoned house is unchanged from when they visited a few days ago. The car rusts in the overgrown driveway, the front door still has a panel missing where they can peer through into the entrance way, and the window at the back is still broken, open wide enough for them to squeeze through now that they're dressed ready to explore.

They shove their bikes into a huge rhododendron bush which was once a hedge and now dominates the remnants of a front garden.

'Why are we hiding these?' Lucasz brushes his hair out of his eyes. 'There's no risk of someone stealing them.'

Cleo folds her arms. 'One, your mum scares me and I don't want to lose her bike.'

Lucasz throws his head back and guffaws, as if the idea of being afraid of his mum is so impossible.

Cleo throws him a quizzical look, as if to say, *Have you* met *your mum?*

'And two?'

'Two, I don't know about you, but I don't want to leave visible evidence outside. Some dog walker could wander past and see our bikes, and then sneak inside to see what we're up to. And then I'd shit myself.'

He sniggers. 'I would too. Good point.' He stands back and examines the bush, then nods, satisfied the bikes are out of sight.

'Come on then, let's go find out what's left inside this place.'

She shivers. 'I'm excited.'

'Me too. And a bit scared.'

'Knew you would be.' She smiles at him and he grins back. His eyes are very blue, almost icy. She's never noticed that before; has he never looked her in the eye? 'I'll go first, shall I?'

'I'll give you a leg up.' He interlaces his fingers and boosts her through the window. She pulls her jumper sleeves over her hands to protect them from the broken glass, and slithers head first to the floor on the other side of the window, using her arms to break her fall.

'Very graceful.'

'Fuck off. Your turn.' She scrambles out of the way of the window and shrieks as something touches her back. It's an old sofa, pink and cream flowery print with frills around the bottom. Lucasz steps through the window frame, showing off his long legs and six-foot frame.

'It smells bad in here.' He pinches his nose.

She sniffs by reflex, and grimaces. The air is dusty and damp, like Gran's old shed in her allotment.

Little shafts of light streak through the gaps between the boarded windows. She drags her phone from her pocket and switches on the torch.

'What the frig?' Lucasz whispers, and she rolls her eyes. He tries not to swear since Jan started copying everything he says.

There's stuff everywhere; every space is covered in piles of junk. Magazines, newspapers, crumpled clothes. 'It looks like they got burgled?'

'Or like the opposite of burgled.' He starts to laugh. 'Like someone broke in and left loads of stuff instead of stealing it.'

Cleo giggles and mimes a phone call. 'Hello, 999? My emergency is someone gave me a bunch of old junk.'

'Or they got looted and messed up after they left? Who knows?'

'No one could live like this, surely?' She picks up a cassette tape from a pile of about sixty of them. 'Welsh men's choirs? Who listens to this?'

Lucasz pushes at a door, but it won't budge. 'Must be even more stuff behind here.'

'OK, be quiet, just in case.'

Lucasz's smile disappears. 'In case of what?'

'I don't know. But step carefully in case the floors are rotten. And remember the way we came in so we can get out quick if we need to.'

He pushes at the next door and this one opens about a foot. He squeezes into the gap. 'Ooh, it's a study,' he says, his voice low. 'Come see.'

She pushes through the door. There's stuff everywhere just like in the other room, but this one is more ordered. There's still a semblance of what the room used to be: bookshelves line the walls, with books stacked haphazardly, like broken teeth. A yellowing globe spins with a little push from Lucasz.

Lucasz forgets they're supposed to be quiet. 'Oh, I've seen these!'

She shushes him.

'Haven't these got—' He opens it up, lifting off the top half of the globe at a hinge. 'Yep. Amazing. Think it's still good to drink?'

There are six bottles there, their labels yellow and peeling. She picks one up and tries to unscrew the lid. It's stuck, welded together with decades-old sugar. Lucasz picks up another and manages to unscrew it. He sniffs it and mimes gagging. 'This one's not okay.' He shakes his head and puts it back to pick up another. 'This rum smells fine though.' He offers her the bottle and she shakes her head.

'Maybe next time. Or never.' In the corner there's a massive desk, carved out of black wood and with green leather on the top.

Lucasz picks up a pair of glasses, the lenses thick, with that little window of extra glass in the bottom half of the lens. The frames are thick, clear plastic, kind of old-fashioned while also being fashionable right now.

'Put them on!' calls Cleo, and Lucasz dutifully raises them to his face. Cleo bursts out laughing: his eyes are magnified almost two times their normal size. 'You look like a Disney character!' she snorts.

He turns to the speckled mirror over the mantlepiece and admires his reflection. Then he takes them off and folds them, placing them back exactly where he found them. 'I feel bad now. Like we're laughing at a dead person.'

'You're such a good boy, Luki.'

'Yep. Nothing wrong with that.' He throws her a sheepish grin.

He opens a desk drawer. Like everything else in this house, it's crammed full of stuff: an old pipe, cotton handkerchiefs, keys, a stapler, and a big envelope stuffed full of papers. There's a leather-bound Bible, an old brown glass pill bottle with the label faded beyond legibility, and a daily diary, dated 1987. She flicks through it, but there's no writing. All the pages are blank.

'A clue.' She holds up the diary. 'Whatever caused them to leave might have happened in 1986. They never wrote in this.' She pauses, puts on a whispery, creepy voice. 'They never lived to see 1987.'

Lucasz pushes back his hair. 'Or they just left and went somewhere else. Maybe they moved to an old people's home. I guess there was no one to clear out their house when they died.'

Cleo shakes her head. 'That's far too boring. Maybe they were murdered. Maybe their ghosts are here right now, begging us to find their killers.'

He shoves his hand into the drawer, trying to tamp down its contents so he can close it again.

Cleo shoots her hand out to stop him. 'Wait, those are letters.' She grabs the big envelope and motions for him to close the drawer. She's right: it's full of letters, tied together with ribbon. 'They might have a clue about what happened here. Why the house is empty. Or how that desk ended up here. We should take them.'

'No, we shouldn't.' Lucasz is uncharacteristically stern.

She looks up at him, shocked.

He looks back down at her, making eye contact again.

She looks away, fast. She's not sure how she feels about all this eye contact right now. 'We're conducting *historical research*, Luki. I thought you were all about that.'

'They're not ours. It's fine to poke around, to be nosy and look at this place. But as soon as we break anything or take something away, we're committing a crime. Seriously.'

She sighs and pulls the letters back out of her pocket. 'And how does that fit with drinking the rum, eh?'

She holds the stack up to the streak of light from the gap in the boarded window. The top one is a thin blue airmail envelope, addressed to 'The Old Manor', with a return address in Barbados. 'Barbados,' she whispers.

Lucasz shines his torch onto the letters. 'This is so cool. Look at all these old stamps.' He runs a finger over one of them. 'I need to find out what happened to the people who wrote these letters and lived in this house.'

'Yeah! And why half the house burned down.' She waves the letters at him. 'The answer could be in here. You can't make me leave these here.'

'Yes, I can. It's not right. Put them back, they're not yours.' He stands up straighter, broadens his shoulders and for a moment he looks like a man. Not the little kid she met on their first day at high school, whose blazer trailed over his hands and who got shoved from side to side along the corridor, bouncing off the walls. If he wanted to stop her, to overpower her, he could easily. But he won't; Lucasz doesn't fight, even when he needs to defend himself. Cleo fights for both of them.

She puts them back in the drawer reluctantly. 'But we can read them while we're here?'

'I suppose we can, yes.'

She slides the drawer closed, but not quite all the way. 'You're right. We should be honourable and good. Even while we're trespassing.'

He laughs. 'Even then. And being here isn't quite a crime, apparently. It's only a crime if we're carrying a weapon or if we break something, then it's aggravated trespass.'

'OK, Google.' She hangs back for a moment as he leaves the room.

They climb the stairs, shoulder to shoulder. With each creak of a step, they pause to listen to the house around them. Aside from their own movements the house is silent, but that doesn't stop Cleo's imagination going wild as she invents eyes which peer at them through the gaps in the cupboard doors, and movements in the shadows.

The first-floor landing is long, a threadbare rug running the length of the corridor. She can see six doors – three on each side – before the hallway turns out of sight into another wing, where the walls are black and everything looks unnaturally dark.

'That's the burned part,' she whispers to Lucasz. He acknowledges her with a nod but says nothing, his lips set in a thin line, his eyes huge as he scans for movement.

'We shouldn't go there. It might not be safe.'

'None of this is safe.' His skin is pale, his eyes dark. He looks terrified.

She punches his arm lightly. It's surprisingly muscular. 'Hey! This is an adventure. Nothing scary here.'

His smile doesn't reach his eyes.

'Where do you want to look first?'

He points to the nearest door, which stands open about six inches. 'Shall we check in here?' He glances back to the charred part of the house.

She raises her hand to push the door, but Lucasz's hand on her arm stops her. 'What?'

'Knock first,' he whispers.

'What?' Something about the way he says that makes her stomach flip with fear. She can feel the blood rushing around in her veins. 'Don't be stupid, there's no one here.'

'Just do it.'

She raps her knuckles twice on the wood, and the sound echoes through the empty hallway. Lucasz's face turns even paler. That was probably the loudest sound in this house for decades. She hopes it doesn't wake anything up. She catches herself, shakes the thought away. She doesn't even believe in ghosts, for goodness' sake. This is Lucasz's fault, making her knock on a door like a ghost hunter on TV.

She shoves the door open. There's a heart-wrenching shriek as the hinges give way after decades of quiet rusting, and Cleo hears a small squeak from Lucasz, which he tries to cover with a cough. She suppresses a smirk and decides not to tease him this time.

The room looks like it's been ransacked. Drawers gape open, splurging their contents all over the floor. The single bed sags in the middle; its dark wood frame probably once looked very grand, but now just looks creepy. 'I wonder if someone died in that bed,' she whispers to Lucasz to freak him out. He swallows.

It's a child's bedroom: there's a rocking horse and a little dressing table with trifold mirrors. Above the bed is a child's name laid out in carved wooden letters: *Tony*. 'It's cute,' she says, but Lucasz is pale, staring back the way they just came.

'Holy crap,' she shouts. There's graffiti all over the wall, huge black letters and shapes, illegible in places. It looks like black chalk or something. There's something so shocking about the juxtaposition: a child's toys next to destruction from intruders just like themselves. 'I guess we weren't the first people to find this place, then.' She shivers, creeped out at the idea that other people wandered in and out of these rooms, just like her.

'Is that written in charcoal? What does it say?' Lucasz squints, tilts his head. 'It looks like "say a word". What?'

She stares at the jumble of letters, looks to where Lucasz points. '"I won't say a word."' She shrugs. 'Weird. There's more over here.' She points at the wall beneath the 'Tony' sign, where something else is scrawled in black. '"Is dead." *Tony is dead.*'

Lucasz shudders. 'Told you someone probably died here.'

'Maybe he died in the fire.' She runs a finger over the coloured glass of the bedside lamp. It's so bright and cheery, in contrast to everything else in this house. 'I want one of these for my room.' She turns to Lucasz, who's shaking his head.

'Don't even think about it. This stuff isn't ours, and we're not thieves.'

Lucasz turns to the dressing-table mirror and reaches out to the frame. There's a photograph tucked into the corner. He holds it out to Cleo, and she crosses the room to join him. It's three people in glossy black and white, a mum, a dad and a little kid. The dad is wearing those thick glasses they found on the desk downstairs, his eyes massive behind their lenses. The mum has her hand up to her forehead, shielding her eyes from the sun and casting a shadow so you can't see her face. She's smiling. Something about the way she rests her open hands on her thighs makes Cleo sure that this lady is kind. The little kid has his hands in the pockets of his shorts, his face blurred because he moved while the picture was taken. He's got that bowl-cut hairstyle that all kids seem to have in TV shows from the Seventies and Eighties, like a blond helmet.

'I guess that's Tony.' Lucasz flips the photo: there's spidery handwriting on the back. 'Family day out, Moorburn Bay, 1985.'

'Moorburn Bay!' Cleo reaches out to point at the familiar

landmarks of the Spa, the Victorian bandstand and the arcade on the seafront behind the figures, but Lucasz moves it up high, out of her reach.

'Watch out for fingerprints.'

She pulls back. 'Still worried about being caught trespassing?'

'No, I meant your greasy paws might ruin the picture.' He replaces the photo, folds his arms and crosses to the doorway. 'Let's finish looking around and get out of here. It's too creepy, half of the house burned. Something awful happened here, and I don't like it.'

'What do you mean?'

'I mean, people don't just up and leave their houses like this. Even after a fire. Leaving their glasses behind, their rum, their toys.' He points at the rocking horse. 'It's weird and sad and scary and I don't like it.'

Cleo raises her shoulders up and tries to look nonchalant. 'I'm not sad. We didn't know these people. Maybe I'd be sad if *whatever-it-was* happened last week. But this is decades ago. Our parents were kids, it's that long ago.'

He nods. 'I guess it's history now.'

'Exactly. So it's interesting. A history mystery!'

Outside, they squint in the afternoon sunlight. Cleo peers through the wrecked car's window, cupping both hands to her face. An old Britain A-Z map pokes out from the back pocket of the passenger seat, its corners curling. Nothing else. The door handles won't budge, and the little nub is down to say the doors are locked.

Cleo turns from the car and looks up at the house, the dark burned side like a scar on someone's face. Her heart pumps hard, like she just rode a rollercoaster. She bounces on her toes. 'No one knows this is here, Lucasz. You know?

There's no road, no address, and no one owns it. This place is ours.'

'It's not, though.' He knits his eyebrows together. 'It does belong to someone, and it's not ours, legally.'

'True. But I don't think anyone wants it.'

'For the last time, Cleo, we can't take anything. It's stealing.'

'*For the last time, Cleo,*' she mimics. 'That wasn't where I was heading with this. I promise we won't take anything out of the house. Everything here will stay here, OK?'

'OK.' He trudges towards the bush where they hid the bikes, and she follows behind, almost skipping.

'What I mean is we can come here any time. We have the perfect hideout for the rest of the holidays. And then the whole summer.' She points at a bare patch of grass just outside the fallen garden fence before the woods begin. 'We can have campfires. It'll be like camping, but with a house. Maybe I could get one of those disposable barbeques. We could cook burgers.'

Lucasz is thawing, she can tell. There's the ghost of a smile on his lips.

She knows the next bit will persuade him, 'We can comb through the house, try to work out who they were and where they went. Solve the mystery.'

He's smiling now, and nodding.

She thinks for a moment whether this is a good time to do it. To test the little kernel of suspicion that's been burgeoning inside her mind for a few weeks, as Lucasz has stopped playfighting quite so much, choosing to avoid touching her instead. Except when he does touch her, very deliberately. Like when he grabbed her hand the other day. And he looks into her eyes a bit more... 'We could even sleep here. It looks pretty sturdy. Our parents wouldn't know. We could tell each of them we're staying at the other's house.' She reaches out and touches his arm.

His cheeks flush bright red but he doesn't pull away. 'That sounds fun. I guess it'll be great to have somewhere like this while the weather's nice. Somewhere to get away from the parents.'

'Bingo. Especially as…' She withdraws her hand from his arm. 'Well, you know. They don't think a boy and a girl can be friends, like we are.' She hooks a foot behind his leg and pushes his shoulders, hard.

The air leaves his lungs with an 'oof' as he falls to the grass, his long legs everywhere. 'Hey!' he shouts, but Cleo is at the bikes before he can scramble to his feet.

She jumps on his mum's bike and pedals through the trees, listening as he tries to catch up with her. She likes being chased.

Chapter Seven

Jamie

'Jamie?'

She groans, barely surfacing from sleep. The knocking at her door gets louder. 'Jamie,' the man's voice hisses once more.

'It's me, Ant.'

'What?' she mumbles, glancing at her alarm clock through blurred vision. It's not even 4 a.m. She sits up, her stomach clenched. Her deepest fears take advantage of her half-asleep state: Mum's hurt, Cleo's missing, Daisy's ill. 'What's wrong?'

The door opens a crack, and she screws up her eyelids against the hallway light filtering through the gap.

'What happened?' she shields her eyes with her hand, only able to see the dark silhouette in the doorway.

'Get dressed, we have to go out.'

'Why? What's happened?'

His voice is a whisper as he checks over his shoulder into

the corridor behind him. 'Put some warm clothes on. And bring your camera.'

He doesn't seem affected by the early hour at all, talking fast as they drive along the narrow hedge-lined lanes as they roar across the North Yorkshire Moors. The sun hasn't yet risen, and the gorse and heather are coated in a sheen of dew.

Although bundled up in her massive ski jacket, Jamie can't stop shivering. She's not sure whether it's the cold, the lack of sleep or nerves. Her fingers clutch at the camera balanced on her knee, holding it tight as Ant's Jeep swings around the sharp bends in the dawn light.

He tunes through local stations on the car radio, eventually turning it off with a nod of satisfaction. 'Nothing. It looks like we'll be the first on the scene.'

She rubs her eyes. 'So what's going on?'

'I got a call about half an hour ago telling me to get to Langdale Stables to cover a breaking news story. The whole thing is burning down, animals and all. Suspected arson.'

Her mouth falls open. She notices a slight haze on the horizon, the sky growing greyer as they climb the hill to the top of the moor.

'Thought it might be useful footage for your doc.'

'Wow, thank you.' Her first live fire.

'Do you want to pick up Spider on our way?'

She fumbles for her phone but pauses with her finger over the *call* button. After a moment she shakes her head. She doesn't need him. 'Just me is fine. I wouldn't want us to get in the way.'

'Good point. I shouldn't have told you – breaking news and

all. You'll have to stay out of sight or I'll get in a lot of trouble with the station.' He pulls to the side of the road, and they peer across the fields, towards the unmistakable inferno before them. Flames reach higher than the stable roof. The air smells of melting plastic, burning straw, and behind it all, a terrifying meaty smell, like barbecued beef.

Three fire engines are scattered in the field alongside the stable, their blue lights illuminating the dawn.

He slams the car door behind him, leaving Jamie to watch as flames consume the buildings, like a real-life horror film unfolding in front of her. This is someone's livelihood, someone's entire career, reduced to ashes in minutes while Jamie observes from the warmth of a car.

Somehow, fires from thirty years ago, before she was born, are a different thing to her: an entertainment, something to investigate and poke around at. But the destruction she's witnessing here in real time is visceral and raw, it's not something to capture in a documentary for entertainment.

She climbs out of the car, leaving her camera on the seat.

'Good morning.' Ant holds the microphone to his mouth, his nose red in the morning chill. He has removed his coat to reveal a suit and tie, with a scarf wrapped around his neck, its ends tucked into his blazer. 'As the local area waits to see what remains from the wreckage of last night's fire at Langdale Stables, you can see firefighters behind me struggle to control the blaze. It's not yet clear what, if anything, will be salvageable from the flames, and police are still trying to contact the owner of the stables to find out just how many animals may be missing, probably killed, in the blaze.'

Next to the cameraman, the producer gives him a thumbs up as he talks to the camera. She doesn't look much older than Jamie, who feels a pang of jealousy that she's working part-time in Abbeywick's only cinema while this girl runs local news.

'Great work, Ant. We've got a really good shot of the flames and the Fire Service efforts in the background while you do the intro.' She claps her hands. 'This is gold.'

The hungry glint in the producer's eye is eerily similar to Spider's expression while he zoomed into Pamela Dunning's tears in the theatre.

'Shall we see if we can get one of the Fire Service on camera? Ask them how it's going?' Ant pats his chest where his press card peeks out from under his scarf. He strides towards the fire, the producer and cameraman right behind him.

Jamie doesn't move, her boots sinking into the mud, holding her in place. Her toes begin to go numb, and for a moment she's tempted to walk closer to the fire just to feel the warmth. Bile rises in the back of her throat. She shakes her head to get rid of the thought: she can't warm herself on a burning stable full of dying horses. Jesus.

She watches as the crew approaches the emergency workers one by one, each one shaking their head or jogging away with hoses in their arms, too busy to stop and chat to a reporter, and for good reason. A thin layer of ice covers their jackets as the morning air freezes the water droplets splashing from the fire hoses.

After a few minutes, Ant strides alone back towards Jamie, his nose even redder from the cold. He shakes his head. 'They won't talk to the press. Keep saying their spokesperson is back at the station.' He folds his arms and turns back to watch the stables burn. 'It's not true; they can talk to us if they want to. They just don't trust the press.'

'Or maybe they've got more important things to do. Like put out the fire?' Jamie mumbles.

He turns to Jamie. His skin alternates between orange from the flames and blue from the fire engine lights, like a monstrous fairground ride gone wrong. 'Some crews are really helpful. It's in their interest to get this footage out there, engage audiences. Someone might watch our footage and realise they have key info, might give the police a call. We do good work. How else are we going to get little Doreen to realise her grandson came home last night smelling of kerosene?'

'Kerosene?' Jamie tenses. 'Was that the fuel used here? Was this arson?'

Ant shrugs. 'They're not giving anything away. But it does look like it.'

The producer and cameraman creep closer to the inferno, capturing as much footage as possible until finally one fireman loses his temper and sends them back to their cars with an angry point of his arm.

A rumbling fills the air. Engines.

Ant turns and peers down the hill, a hand over his eyes to shield against the rising sun. 'Here we go.'

'What?'

'The other networks are here.' He waves at the producer and cameraman, beckoning them over. 'Incoming!' he shouts.

They start to run.

'Other networks?' Jamie jogs to keep up with Ant as he runs back to the Jeep.

'Vans from other news stations. We've no longer got the exclusive on this story. So we're back to the studio to rush the story through.' He gestures for her to get in the car. 'Maybe you and Spider can come back later when the fire's out and everyone's gone, get more footage for your documentary.'

She shrugs, pulls the camera back onto her knee as she climbs into the passenger seat. 'I don't know. Our documentary's about the cold case, not about a stable fire.'

Ant turns his mouth down at the corners, disbelieving, as he pulls out into the lane and turns the Jeep in the direction of home. 'I'd say you've got an interesting story right here, right now, Jamie.'

'I cannot believe you were at the scene of an active fire and you gathered no footage. What the hell were you thinking, Jamie?'

She can smell the ash in the air when the wind picks up the soot and whips it around. Her jeans are light blue; they'll need a wash as soon as she gets home. 'Look, if you want to go off and make your own documentary, please go ahead. Stop trying to derail mine.' She looks across the fields, which all belong to Langdale Stables, or what's left of it. Now the sun is up, she realises she's been here before, years ago. 'Mum brought me here for riding lessons a few times. I hated it.'

Spider coughs and lowers the camera, frowning at her.

She hated riding around the paddock on a lunge rein, around and around and around. Hated heels-down-toes-up, hated that horsey smell of sweat and hay. Hated the burning in her thighs as she gripped the body of the horse. Hated riding the animals, as if she had the right to climb on the back of another living thing. She was relieved when she fell off and broke her arm and couldn't ride anymore. Mum didn't bring her back after that, saying the instructor was negligent.

But she did love horses themselves. Their shiny coats, kind bright eyes, unwavering stare. She could tell they are good-hearted creatures. She didn't have the right to ride them, that's how she felt.

The fields are empty now, the horses that used to canter about, eating the grass, dead in the fire.

'Don't ignore what I said, Jamie. You could have texted me, could have taken some footage. Even a few seconds would have been great.'

She ducks under the police tape, steps into the charred shell of the stable. There's a huge pile of ash in the middle, once a hay bale for the horses to eat. Poor things. They had no idea what was coming. They didn't deserve this.

'Our documentary isn't about some stable fire in the 2020s. We should stay focused on our subject. It's our second day of filming and we're already deviating from my plan.' She thinks again of that producer from this morning. Jamie wants to be like her, wants to clap her hands and have people leap into action. They need to stick to Jamie's vision, maintain the plan she made, as the director.

'An active crime scene is too good an opportunity to miss, you should know that. The footage would have been great b-roll.'

'Well, we're here now, aren't we? We can get loads of footage of this for your next project.' She gestures around them at the burned-out shell. Something clunks by her feet. She shuffles her toes, moving it around. It's metal. She bends, toes the ash. As she realises what she's looking at, her vision clouds with tears. It's a horseshoe, one nail still in it.

'What are you doing? This is private property,' a voice yells.

Jamie looks up: there's a woman in overalls striding towards them from her battered Defender parked on the lane. She looks a couple of years older than Spider, maybe late twenties, early thirties. She's beautiful and very intimidating: silver-white hair tied in a headscarf and earlobe stretchers. And a scowl on her face.

A sudden gust of wind, and there's an ominous creak as part of the wrecked building moves with the wind. Jamie ducks back under the police tape and away to safety.

There's a camera beep. Spider's recording, the camera held by his side, just out of the woman's eyeline.

'Seriously?' Jamie whispers to him. She blinks, holding her eyes closed for a beat longer than normal. Her eyes feel dry, her eyelids scrape. She rubs at them, pushing her fingers into the sockets. She opens her eyes again, and for a moment the world looks blue before her sight adjusts once more. She fixes a smile on her face and steps towards the woman.

'Are you Catherine?'

The woman tilts her head, the frown still there. 'Do you have a right to be here? Permission?' She looks them both up and down, her gaze resting briefly on the camera in Spider's hand, before she looks back up at both of their faces, new fury in her eyes.

Spider clears his throat. 'Yes, we're from the insurance firm.' He holds up the camera, as if that explains everything. 'For the assessment.'

The woman straightens up, takes a step towards Spider. Jamie eases back, but Spider doesn't move. 'Insurance.' It's not phrased like a question.

This close, Jamie can see the ash under her fingernails, ingrained into the creases in her palms, smudged on her face. She bends to pick something up from the ground, and when she stands, she's holding a five-pronged manure fork, its tines sharp and dangerous-looking.

Jamie takes another step back.

'Filming the damage, you know.' Spider tries again as he waves the camera. 'Taking pictures.'

'Bullshit,' she spits. 'The fire investigation hasn't even started yet. My insurance company hasn't touched this place. What are you doing, wandering around an active crime scene? Get the fuck out.'

'Woah, woah. Calm down.'

Jamie winces.

The woman takes another step forward, and in response, Spider raises the camera, pointing it at her.

'Stop,' she whispers to him. She touches Spider's shoulder, a silent plea for him not to act.

'I'm so sorry,' Jamie makes her voice as smooth as she can. 'We won't touch anything. We're not here to interfere with any investigation.'

The woman looks at Jamie hard. Jamie smiles, letting the woman stare. She seems to decide something, and her forehead relaxes slightly. 'What are you doing here? No lies. Filming without proper permission, that's clear.'

Jamie gives Spider a look, and he turns the camera off. 'Sorry,' he mumbles.

'We'll leave.' She hands the camera bag to Spider, indicating he should pack up.

Spider steps forward. 'But just so you know, we're investigating local arson attacks for a documentary. We want to find the person who did this to your livelihood. Make sure justice is done.'

Jamie glares at him. Liar.

The woman nods.

'But we're not here to upset you or ruin the investigation.

We want to give a voice to the victims, instead of a spotlight on the criminal. You should have a voice. On your terms.'

A genuine smile creeps to the corners of her mouth. 'I do like the sound of that.' She drops the sharp fork into the ash and sticks out a hand. 'Yes, I'm Catherine.'

———

'We'll have to do a bit of set up before we start. We need to find somewhere a little more sheltered from the wind, and I'd like to make sure we get the fire damage behind you, so it's in shot.'

Jamie hands her the lapel mic and Catherine fastens it to her overalls. Spider marches off towards the big oak tree and stands under it, looking up, listening. 'This is good. It's sheltered, but we'll have to pause if the wind picks up. Ready?'

'One moment.' Jamie closes her eyes and counts to five in her head, mentally cursing Spider for wasting their time with this tangent. 'Okay, let's go.'

Ping.

'Tell us a bit about how you got started?'

Catherine nods, her eyes scanning the horizon as if imagining her horses cantering across the fields in the distance. 'Horse riding was for the rich kids when I was young. Not for kids like me. But I loved horses so much, and I wanted to be near them, I didn't care how.'

Jamie nods, checks the mic is clipped properly to Catherine's lapel. 'So you worked at the stable?'

'Yes, from my early teens. It gave me an escape, you know. Got me away from the house when everyone else was drinking white lightning on the pier and playing the twopenny nudge machines in the arcades.'

'It's like you're describing my childhood.' Jamie thinks back to her own afternoons roaming the town at dusk, cold hands shoved into pockets. Huddling in doorways to hide from the sleet before they looked old enough to sneak into the pubs. Buffeted by the wind on the pier, making too much noise near the fishermen.

They smile at each other, and Jamie gets that feeling in her chest, the one that tells you that under different circumstances, you and this person would be friends.

Catherine's face relaxes and she gazes into the distance as she talks. 'Back then Sally Norton-Stanley ran it; this hugely posh woman who had a magnificent past in show jumping. The stable and tack room were covered in pictures of her at shows, but she hadn't climbed on a horse in years. She didn't have her own children, never married. She was very kind.' She pauses, gives a little twitch at the side of her mouth. 'But stern too. Better with horses than people.'

Jamie laughs, and signals to Catherine to continue.

'She taught me a lot, let me take on more and more responsibility. The other kids were quite jealous.'

Catherine's eyes glisten as she glances at the camera. She enjoys talking about the yard, her past. She slides her hands into her pockets. 'Stable yards attract kids. Loads of them: they spend their summers here, grooming their favourite pony, getting jealous if someone else takes "their horse" out on the moors. There's a lot of bitterness and resentment and jealousy around stable yards, for some reason. I guess when you get a group of teenagers, there's always rivalry, isn't there?'

'Is it possible a teenager was responsible for the fire? One of the stable kids?'

Her face clouds. 'I've thought about it. I can't think how it started, otherwise. We didn't have electricity in the stable buildings and the floor was rubber matting. Nothing to spark a fire. But a stray cigarette, an angry teenager. It's possible. It's likely. But why? None of them disliked me, not that I know of anyway. They wouldn't come here if they didn't like me. And I don't have any enemies. I don't think...'

'You don't think?'

'The hardest part about being one of those kids is money. They hang around here because they love the horses, but horses and riding are expensive. They'd come for an hour lesson but then stay here all day, or all weekend, helping out. They did help out when they weren't bickering or climbing on hay bales. And I was one of them, once. So I'd pay them when I could, but I couldn't guarantee it.'

'That's hard.'

'It's really hard. And I'm running a business here. I often have to sell a horse or a pony. And that's heartbreaking for these kids. It's like their household pet is sent away. They dream of buying *their pony* one day, and then some other little girl or boy, richer than them, privileged and happy, comes along and Mummy and Daddy buy the pony for them. And they take them home. It's devastating. So no, no enemies. But some hard feelings occasionally. Any work with animals is brutal at times. Owning a stable is no different.'

She looks down at her hands, picks some dirt from under a short fingernail. She smiles sadly. 'This was the muck heap, in Sally's time. Where we dumped out all the manure. It stank on summer days, but it was always hot underneath, like a furnace. We had to tidy it, making sure it was all contained, forking the dirt up the mound. I put a fork right through my boot once while I was tidying it. Sally laughed all the way to A&E.'

'What happened to Sally? Where is she now?'

She swallows. 'She died, about a year ago now.'

Jamie opens her mouth to console, but Catherine shuts her down with a look. 'Just old age.' She shifts in her seat, her tone more abrupt now, almost business-like. 'Anyway, she left me the stables in her will, wrote a letter to say I should look after the horses for her.' Her voice cracks at the end.

Spider shifts his weight and takes a breath. 'Do you feel in some ways like you failed her?'

'Woah,' Jamie whispers. She glares at Spider, but he refuses to meet her eye.

Catherine leans forward and puts her face in her hands, shoulders shaking.

Jamie signals to Spider: 'Stop filming.'

He shakes his head, and looks at Catherine over the camera, keeping the lens trained on her as she sobs. He has a small smile on his face. He's talked about this before: how the 'best' documentary makers capture unadulterated feeling on the faces of their interviewees, how the camera keeps rolling as they cry, zooms into their faces to display the emotions as they travel across the faces. Jamie gets it, she enjoys those documentaries too. But it feels very different when it happens right in front of her, when the questions she asks cause the pain, when her own boyfriend pushes and pushes, and she must watch the person in front of her go through so much pain.

She can't do it. This is exploitation. Their documentary isn't about this.

She walks towards Catherine, blocks the camera with her back.

Spider swears under his breath.

She holds there for a moment until she hears the soft 'beep' as he stops recording. Then she reaches out to Catherine. 'We can hold it there for today if that's best?'

'Thank you, but no.' She shakes her head, adamant. 'I have more to say.'

Spider flashes a triumphant grin at Jamie as he raises the camera back to his shoulder.

Jamie can't look away as tears course down Catherine's cheeks. The camera lens reflects in the dark brown of her eyes.

Jamie has never cried like this, with no shame. No one has ever watched as tears track down her cheeks. She has never let Spider see her cry. Come to think of it, Jamie can't think of the last time she cried at all. Years ago, probably. She thought that showed strength, used to boast to her new university friends that she'd trained herself not to show any strong emotion at all, especially not sadness. *I'm the ice queen.* But those quashed emotions found other outlets, more damaging ones in the end.

Yet Catherine has a quiet power to her tears. Her unwavering stare is glorious, dignified, and strong. Catherine isn't afraid of the camera showcasing her tears. She doesn't care that Spider and Jamie – total strangers – can see her cry. She sits up straight, the tears making tracks down her cheeks. She doesn't even wipe her nose where a clear line of snot trickles its way down to her top lip.

Jamie would love to offer her a tissue for that one.

'Ignore this.' Catherine gestures at her face. 'The tears happen when I'm angry.' She shrugs, accepting.

Jamie smiles weakly.

'I'm not sad, you see. I don't really cry when I'm sad, but hooo boy, when I'm angry you can't stop me. I'd rather they be laser beams instead of tears, but this is the way I'm wired, it seems. So I carry on.'

Jamie snaps back into interview mode. 'Have you cried a lot today?'

Catherine throws her head back and laughs joylessly. 'Non-stop. I brought the horses into the stables last night, so they didn't get cold. Closed them in and shuttered the doors. They couldn't escape when the heat and smoke began to rise.'

Jamie hugs herself and trains her eyes on the horizon, staring across the sheep-flecked valley towards the moors, a dark green line on the tops of the hills.

Catherine looks back at Jamie and her eyes are filled with fresh tears, about to spill over her eyelids once more. 'People teach little girls that anger is unnatural, unladylike.' Catherine finally reaches up to her nose and swipes at the moisture on her upper lip. 'As if their reaction is more important or more destructive than the thing that made them angry in the first place. Fuck that. So, yes, I'm angry because I lost my business, my horses, and my livelihood to an arson attack. I'm furious – because no human being died, the police won't consider it serious enough to continue their investigation, so they'll hand it back to the Fire Service. They've already said as much. Which will take twice as long. And the insurance won't pay out until the investigation is done. So yes, I'm crying because I'm angry.' She holds out her hands, palm up: a question. A request. 'But this interview should be about what happened here. The destruction it caused. It shouldn't be about me, or my reaction to that destruction, or the way the internet chooses to ridicule me.'

Jamie opens her mouth, ready to ask more, but Catherine continues: 'My reaction is FINE. It's healthy. It's normal to be angry or upset. What's not normal is that some fucking monster burned my stables down and now I'm going viral on

YouTube for being angry about it. What a fucking world we live in.'

'That was amazing. She's a natural. I think I'm in love.'

Spider barely reaches the car before he pulls out his phone and opens YouTube. 'She's already viral? The fire barely hit the news yet.'

'Just wait a second, please.' Jamie watches as Catherine wanders around the wreck, scuffing her toes in the ashes. 'Don't let her see you watching this.'

He ignores her. 'I hope she meant it, that she'd talk to us more as the investigation carries on. Can you imagine? We'll document the whole thing, from this fire to catching the guy.'

Jamie feels a frisson of panic. 'We can't just change our focus any time we come across something new.'

'You've got to admit, that interview was *fire.*'

Jamie winces, but can't suppress a smile.

Spider shrugs. 'It's our documentary; we can do whatever we want with it. And I say a contemporary arsonist is way more interesting than a long-dead one.'

'We don't know this was arson.'

'They found kerosene, apparently.'

'For setting the fire?'

He shrugs. 'Same accelerant as our unsub.'

She purses her lips. 'She said they didn't have electricity, so maybe it was there anyway, for lamps. And they need to investigate.'

'Exactly. Kerosene lamps. It's possible that this is our old arsonist, back for more.' He coughs. 'Even if it isn't, we can make it look that way.'

Jamie examines her hands, which are ingrained with soot even though she doesn't remember touching anything. She pinches the skin on her arm until it stings. 'We had a plan. And now we don't.'

Spider unlocks his phone, types into YouTube. 'We'll make a new plan. Go with the flow, J.'

'We did so much work on our original plan.' Jamie grits her teeth. She is not a *go with the flow* person. She's a *research, plan, execute* person. 'There'll be a big investigation here. For months.'

'And we'll be here for it, with Catherine talking us through it on camera. It's perfect!' He claps his hands. 'And you've got to admit, the footage we got today was amazing.'

Jamie purses her lips. She doesn't have to *admit* anything. They watch Catherine climb into her Land Rover and pull away.

'Here we go: YouTube. So there are two versions. The original, which has about 200 views, and the remix, which must be the one she's talking about going viral.'

'How many views does that one have?'

'Erm... twenty thousand.' He refreshes the page. 'Twenty-two. It's going up by the minute. This is crazy. I mean, this is a ready-made audience for our doc, too. They'll be gagging for more.'

'Shit. No wonder she didn't want us poking around. She must have thought we were here to make the next YouTube video.'

'Here's the original.' He holds his phone so they both can watch.

On the screen, Catherine stands in front of the burning barn in early morning light. This must have been taken by one of the news crews who arrived as Jamie and Ant left. Smoke still emanates from the wreckage behind her. Her face is streaked black with soot and tears.

Her voice fills the car, rendered shrill by the phone's small speakers. Just out of the shot, a red-topped microphone bobs into view, held by the disembodied hand of a news reporter.

She speaks clearly and slowly, staring straight into the camera. 'This farm was my life, you fucking imbecile, whoever you are. I had animals in this barn. Six beautiful horses with the kindest hearts. They didn't do anything to deserve this. You burned them alive.'

Jamie feels the prickling in her eyes and the sting in her throat that means she's about to cry. She shakes her head, hits the space bar. 'I don't know if I can watch this. It's too sad.'

Spider looks confused. 'They're just horses.'

'Don't say that. They were defenceless and they died.'

Spider hits the space bar and the woman addresses her interviewer. 'This place was mine.' She looks at the camera again. 'I have a message for whoever did this.' She pauses, and then she shouts, loud and clear: 'Do you hear me? The horses you killed were Flopsy, Mopsy, Cottontail, Peter, MacGregor, and Beatrix. You will remember their names.'

The video ends, and Spider clicks the second video, entitled 'Fire Feminist Flopsy REMIX', and hits play. It's still soot-blackened Catherine, but with a pumping bass track. Computer animated horses trot across the screen while she chants her horses' names over and over in a weird dance remix.

Spider's face is red. His hand covers his mouth as his shoulders shake trying not to laugh.

Jamie can't even look at him. 'What the fuck is wrong with you? Why are you laughing? This poor woman lost everything in this fire.'

'I'm sorry – I'm not laughing at this.'

'Could have fooled me.' She can't believe him. This whole project is harrowing no matter which direction they take: people's lives ruined and disrupted, and that girl in the theatre dying in that windowless green room. And Spider's laughing at this woman's pain.

'It's not that, honest,' he lies again.

Jamie stares at the paused screen. Tears sparkle in the eyes of the woman's soot-blackened face. 'I don't know if I can do this, Spider.'

He puts his hands on her shoulders and gives her tense muscles a squeeze. 'Like I said earlier, we're giving her a voice. She's getting drowned out with this remix. Not this time. Okay?'

Chapter Eight

Cleo

The letters are fascinating, the paper so thin that the slightest wrong move and she'll tear them. They're all addressed to The Old Manor, Langdale, North Yorkshire. Langdale: their village. The Old Manor must be the name of the house in the woods, the sign long gone.

She doesn't like lying to Lucasz, but she also doesn't agree that they shouldn't take anything from the house. It's practically theirs – no one has been there for years, clearly, and no one owns it anymore. It's like finding a treasure chest and refusing to claim the treasure in case the long-dead pirates want it back. Stupid.

The stamp Lucasz practically drooled over is silver-grey, with a white silhouette of the Queen in the corner. It cost 48 cents in Barbados back in 1965. The blue airmail envelopes are a clever design – the whole thing unfurls to reveal the writing on the inside of the envelope itself. The blue sticker says 'aerogramme/par avion'.

She checks the dates to make sure this is the first letter in the chronology and starts to read.

14 September 1965: Dear Vanessa, I know you told me not to write, that the separation would be too difficult if we stayed in touch. And I did try, I promise you.

'Wow, this guy's got it bad,' she whispers. It's unexpectedly romantic, this soppy professing of love. Especially in the Sixties; she didn't think people talked like that back then, so openly about their feelings. But then, thinking about it, people have been writing love letters and dirty poetry for centuries, so there's no reason why the Sixties should be any different.

She skips to the end, finds the writer's name: George, who's clearly pining for Vanessa. He writes vomit-worthy things like 'I remember the brief touch of your hand in mine before you had to leave me.'

He talks about transferring back to England from his temporary station in the Caribbean.

Did Vanessa feel the same about him? She saved the letters, so maybe they fell in love across the seas.

She finds the next letter, opens it carefully. She sniffs the envelope, trying to detect some remnant of the West Indies, but it just smells like musty paper.

He wrote it months later, sending thanks to Vanessa's mother for the Christmas card and cursing the slow delivery times. Vanessa hasn't replied to his original letter, yet he writes he's booked his passage back home, coming back to her. It's very romantic. Cleo can't wait to find out whether they get married. Maybe George died in a shipwreck and Vanessa always wondered what happened, why he didn't come back for her. It's like a soap opera only for Cleo. She feels a twinge of guilt that she's not sharing this with Lucasz, who loves anything about the olden days. But she shrugs it off: it's a love story and he's not interested in those. She promises herself she'll stop reading and wait for Lucasz if an actual shipwreck or pirates appear on the scrawled pages.

She skips through the letters; they're all from George. Did Vanessa like him back? Did she ever reply?

She's about to open the next one when someone knocks on her bedroom door. She shoves the letters under her pillow and then calls, 'Yes?'

Mum pokes her head around the door with a smile. 'Your dad just called – you're spending the night tomorrow, is that right?'

Cleo nods and sighs. A whole evening of him and Sahara. 'Can't I stay here? We could watch a film. There's a funny one just dropped on Netflix I thought we could watch?' Ant doesn't like comedies; he'd probably leave them alone.

Mum shakes her head. 'Sorry, love. I'm going out with Tina. Girls' night.'

Cleo purses her lips and moves them sideways. Going to Dad's is better than a whole evening with Ant hogging the TV and lecturing her about *behaviour*.

'Do you have to go out?'

Mum looks grumpy but keeps her voice bright. 'I'm taking Tina for dinner to thank her for our wedding present. I hope you're mature enough to accept I have my own plans?'

Cleo can't think of much to say to that, so she shrugs. She's glad Mum's getting away from Ant for a bit. 'Fine, I'll go to Dad's then.'

Mum smiles. 'Good girl. I'll text him to confirm.'

The next letter is mid-1966, and George is ecstatic because Vanessa replied. 'She does like him back!' Cleo whispers. 'It is romantic after all!' George even talks about marriage when he gets back to England. She remembers the picture of the couple Lucasz found tucked inside the mirror and wonders if that's them; if they married and had a child and went on day trips to Moorburn Bay in the Eighties.

Cleo is about to open the next letter when she hears raised voices from below. It's Mum and Ant, talking in the living room, their voices trickling up through the floorboards.

Cleo steps off the bed and opens her bedroom window. As she hoped, the living room window is open so she can hear every word.

'I just don't think she's in a good place right now,' Ant's saying, his tone urgent. Cleo's stomach flips. Is he talking about her?

'Exactly. She needs her friends.' Mum uses that voice she keeps for times when she's struggling to stay calm. Cleo holds her breath to hear better.

'I just care about you, babe.'

Cleo winces. Nicknames are gross. Babe is the second worst after baby.

Ant continues, his voice a nasal whine of affected concern. Cleo opens her window wider and leans over the windowsill, hooking her toes under her bed to make sure she doesn't topple out. Their shadows project on the grass as Mum and Ant pace back and forth. She feels a thrill of excitement: their first argument! Maybe they'll get divorced and she'll never have to see Ant again. That would be the best.

Ant says something else, but Cleo doesn't quite catch it. He must be pacing around the room. Then Mum's voice comes through clear and it's obvious what Ant said.

'Tina is not toxic. She's having a tough time, that's all.'

There's a pause, and then Ant talks again, his tone gentle but fake. 'I just thought, well, you said Cleo's going out tomorrow, and Jamie'll be round at her boyfriend's place.' He's almost crooning now. His manipulation tactics are disgusting. 'It's rare we get a night just the two of us.'

Cleo almost vomits from the window.

'It was meant to be a surprise, but I'd organised a night out for us. I guess I'll cancel it.'

'What was it?'

'No, no. I don't want to make you feel worse about going out with Tina, leaving me home alone.'

'Ant?'

'I just love you and want to spend time with you, that's all.'

'Tell me.'

'Oh, I had theatre tickets. And a table booked at that new restaurant near the pier.'

'As a surprise?' Mum sounds so happy. 'I love the theatre, but I haven't been in years. Ant, how kind of you—'

Cleo closes the window and throws herself face down onto the bed. Her face burns. Mum wouldn't stay home to watch a film with Cleo, but she'll cancel her plans to hang out with Ant, won't she? She'll really do that. Tears prick at Cleo's eyes.

Cleo and Jamie used to come first for Mum. And when Jamie grew up and went out more, it was just Mum and Cleo at home – two girls together, hanging out all the time, watching romcoms, cooking together every night. And Tina would come round and join in: Mum and Tina shared a bottle of red wine and Cleo drank hot chocolates as they chatted on the sofa together.

But that was all before Mum met Ant. Since then, it's like Mum's a different person: colder, distant. She has less time, and sometimes she looks at Cleo like she doesn't like her very much. It's clear Ant pours poison into Mum's ears. And now she sees Mum hesitate before she says, 'Yes, Cleo,' or falters a moment when Cleo asks for time together. She's heard him whisper, her ear pressed to the door: *Your relationship isn't healthy. You need to show her you're the boss, you can't let her take advantage of you like this. She shouldn't talk to you like that. Set some boundaries. She needs to respect that you're the authority, the adult here. You make the rules, she follows them. Cleo's selfish, Ella.* She can hear him say all of it.

She's losing her mum. Ant has ruined everything.

Cleo can't stand it anymore. She storms down the stairs and throws open the living room door, tears just a breath away. She swallows them down. 'You said you couldn't hang out with me! You told me you had to see Tina. But you'll stand her up for *him,* won't you?' She points at Ant, her finger sharp like a knife. Her voice cracks. 'Why? Why don't you want me?'

'Cleo, please—'

But Ant interrupts, his voice booming. 'Who taught you to talk to adults in this way? I've never heard any child so rude in my entire life. You need to respect the adults in your life, young lady—' In her bed in the corner of the room, Daisy flattens her ears to her head. She doesn't like shouting.

'I wasn't talking to you; I was talking to my mum.'

'Cleo. You stop this right now.' Mum never shouts, but she's almost there this time.

Cleo stops, her muscles locked. Mum won't hear her. She wraps her arms around her body, feeling her ribs hard under her fingers.

'Ant, can we have a minute please?' Mum says, in a more normal voice.

Ant stands up straight, his shoulders broad. 'Ella, I really think if I am to be part of this fam—'

Louder now: 'Can we have a minute, please, Ant?' Mum repeats, and Cleo holds her breath in hope.

As Mum looks away for a second, Cleo catches his eye and raises her eyebrows in victory.

His ears turn red, but he doesn't say a word, just turns and walks out of the room, pulling the door shut behind him.

Cleo and Mum sit in silence as Ant's footsteps echo up the stairs and creak overhead as he paces around their bedroom.

'I really don't know what to say, Cleo.' Mum's quiet now, talking very slowly. 'We don't shout in this family.'

'I didn't mean to shout, I just—'

Mum stops her with a quick shake of the head. 'We don't get angry. We talk things through rationally and clearly. We solve problems with logic and care.'

'Not now Ant's here. He's turned it all around, made everything feel wrong and bad. We were fine before, but now it's all broken.' Tears trickle down Cleo's cheeks, and Mum reaches out to wipe one away.

'You're all mixed up, my little girl, aren't you?'

Cleo nods, and sniffs up some snot. Mum hands her a tissue from the box on the coffee table. 'I just wanted to watch a film with you. I want my mum back.'

'And we can watch a film soon, I promise.' Mum puts her arm around Cleo's shoulder and pulls her close. 'I'm pulled in two directions here. Please try to understand. I have to make sure Ant feels welcome, too. This is his home now, too. And I'm his wife.'

'He's not welcome. Not by me. And it's my home too.'

'Cleo.' Mum's voice is harsh again, so different from the caring, quiet tone that Cleo's used to. Things never used to be like this. 'I won't ask you again. You do not get angry like this. You do not shout. If you still can't control yourself, we're going to have to get help.'

'Send me to boarding school, you mean?'

Mum looks at her hands, the fingers woven together, the knuckles white. A shiny flat scar snakes across the back of her hand, an old cooking burn. 'The world can't revolve around you. There are adults living in the house.'

Cleo paws away the remains of her tears and wipes her hands on her jeans. 'Sounds like he told you what to say again, did he?'

Mum's knuckles go even whiter. 'Go to your room.' She doesn't look up, but her voice is steady. 'I don't want to see you again tonight.'

Cleo wakes, her mouth dry. She reaches for the glass of water on her bedside table and drains it. Better.

She lays her head back on her pillow and closes her eyes, but can't fall asleep straightaway. Normally a heavy sleeper, it's unusual for Cleo to wake in the middle of the night like this, and even more unusual to be unable to fall back to sleep quickly.

She peers around her room; the streetlight outside her bedroom window sifts through a gap in her curtains.

Did something wake her? She clicks on her bedside lamp and sits up, her back resting against her headboard. Might as well go get more water from the kitchen.

Daisy barely looks up from where she's curled up at the foot of Cleo's bed.

She runs her hand along the wall as she walks along the

dark corridor, feeling her way down the stairs and into the kitchen. She loves to wander through the house at night, navigating only by the streetlights that filter through closed curtains, and the blue glow cast by the microwave's digital clock. It feels like she's discovered a secret world, one in which she's entered a dimension where the whole house belongs to her alone, and no one else exists.

She switches on the kitchen tap and fills her glass, dangling her finger over the side to feel when the water reaches the top. Tap off, she turns back to the kitchen and suddenly her skin prickles.

There's someone else in the kitchen with her. She can hear them breathing.

She freezes, her back to the sink, her eyes straining in the darkness to see who's there. Cleo's biggest fear has always been burglars. Hiding in the dark, watching her. A hand reaching out from under her bed to grab her ankle and yank her to the floor.

Water slops over the side of the glass and lands on the kitchen floor with a slap.

She steps towards the knife block full of freshly sharpened knives. She's not afraid to stab someone if she needs to. She's done it once before. It's self-defence this time.

She places her water on the countertop and turns her body towards the knives, keeping her gaze trained on the dark area of the kitchen where the streetlight doesn't reach. Where the quiet presence breathes in the darkness.

She grabs a knife, and at the same time flicks the switch for the fluorescent bulb under the kitchen cupboards. Light floods the room and she whips around, squinting through her eyelashes against the sudden onslaught of light.

There is someone in the kitchen, sitting at the table, their face covered with their hands.

'What are you doing?' she yells, holding out the knife.

As her eyes adjust to the light, the person at the table drops their hands from their face, squinting. It's Ant. He's wearing his big coat, which made him unrecognisable: he looked like a stranger, bulky and stout.

'Why are you here?' After she's spoken, Cleo realises she should have made her tone harsher. Sleep dulled her reactions. It's too late now, and she's too tired to fight.

Ant gestures to the mug in front of him on the table. 'Couldn't sleep, so I came down for some warm milk.'

'In the dark?' She slides the knife back into the block.

'My eyes are used to it. I didn't want to wake anyone.'

'In your coat?'

'Lots of questions, Cleo. I could ask you why you're awake, but I expect it's too much screen time.' He chuckles, but it sounds fake.

'Why are you wearing your coat? Have you been outside?' The kitchen smells fresh, like night air with a hint of bonfire.

He shakes his head. 'My dressing gown is in the wash. This was the closest warm thing I could find. There's even a single glove in the pocket in case one hand gets chilly.' He reaches into his pocket and waves it at her: it's black and knitted. He chuckles. 'No idea where its mate went. Want some milk? It's a great help for insomnia.' He slides the mug over to Cleo.

She shakes her head. She might exist in a different dimension in the middle of the night, but she's not insane.

He drains his mug and stands up to rinse it at the sink. 'Get yourself back up to bed. You'll sleep in no time.'

Chapter Nine

Cleo

Sahara has cooked, and, typical for her, it's a fruity and foreign dish to show off some exotic place she travelled before she met Dad. Today it's Morocco, and she's wearing a weird sequinned patterned top. Trust her to theme her outfit to go with dinner.

'I got this in a souk while I was backpacking around in my early twenties.'

'Not that long ago, then,' jokes Dad, winking at Sahara.

Jamie catches Cleo's eye and hides a laugh behind her hand, disguising it as a cough. Cleo glows with happiness. It's been a long time since she and Jamie had a laugh together. They were close once, or as close as two sisters can be when they have an eight-year age gap. Maybe this is a thaw, and they can get back to where they were.

'What's this?' Cleo lifts her fork; something brown and shiny with wrinkles squats on the end of the tines. She pulls her eyebrows into a deep frown and curls her lip. 'Did something fall into the pan?'

Jamie groans. 'Shut up, Cleo,' she hisses. Poof. The momentary unity is gone.

Sahara reaches over and takes Cleo's fork from her hand, pops the brown thing into her mouth with a smile. 'Ooh yum. You lucky girl, that was a date. They're delicious.'

Cleo's cheeks grow hot.

'If you're lucky you might find another in there.' Sahara hands back the fork with a wink.

Cleo pokes through the mounds of couscous and chicken and vegetables. 'I found one!' She waves it around on the end of her fork.

She pops it into her mouth and chews. She doesn't *hate* it. It's like a giant raisin, only grainier. 'Oh, wow!' she mumbles, her mouth full. 'That's amazing.' She hopes she sounds sincere.

Sahara looks delighted. She tucks her wild hair behind her ear and does a little dance with her shoulders.

Dad puts a hand on Sahara's shoulder, as if he's proud of her. Even Jamie looks pleased, flashing a grateful look at Cleo.

Cleo pulls her mouth into a half-smile, feeling a mixture of guilt and discomfort. If you're difficult and prickly, people value it more when you're kind or agreeable. Look at Jamie: always polite, always measured, and no one is grateful or happy for that. They expect it and take it for granted. Whereas difficult old Cleo: it's such a shock when she's easy that they all celebrate because she *ate a date* and didn't have a tantrum.

'How's the documentary going, Jamie?' Dad asks as he tops up Jamie and Sahara's wine glasses. His shirt strains at the buttons across his tummy, which is round and tight like a balloon. He's always been a big fat dad, good for cuddles and climbing on. Recently he's put on more weight, as evidenced by the buttons, but it suits him. His cheeks are ruddy and full behind his beard and he always wears half a smile on his twinkling face.

Jamie puts her fork down. 'Okay, thanks,' she says, without her usual chirpiness. Cleo looks up at her. She looks tired, a bit sad.

'Just okay?' asks Dad.

'We've interviewed a few people, but I don't know... it feels ghoulish, probing them to talk about their unhappiness and things they lost. It doesn't seem to bother Spider, but it does bother me.' Her gulp of wine leaves little maroon stains at the corners of her mouth. 'This one woman lost all her horses at her riding stable. Just a couple of days ago.'

Sahara lets out a small inhaled squeak through closed lips, her hands at either side of her face.

'That's awful. I hope she had insurance,' says Dad, always practical like the accountant he is.

Jamie shrugs. 'The whole project has changed, and I don't know if I want to carry on, honestly. It used to be about historic crimes, but Spider thinks we should cover recent fires too... maybe we just ditch the subject and find something else. Something less painful for people. We've still got all the equipment, so we haven't lost anything.'

Dad mumbles confirmation, chewing thoughtfully.

'How did you get set up?' asks Sahara. 'Must have been quite expensive to get everything you'd need, no? Cameras especially.'

'We were lucky. Ant helped us out.'

'With equipment from his work?' Sahara's wildly impressed that Ant's on television, even though he's not famous in the slightest. Literally no one knows who he is.

'No, he gave us some money.'

Cleo's fork clatters to her plate. 'He gave you money? How much?'

Jamie shakes her head. 'Not very much.'

Cleo's eyes burn. She reaches up and smears her fingertips across her eyelids, pushing away the sting. 'This is incredibly unfair. He's trying to buy you.'

'Cleo.' Dad gives her a stern look.

'No, I want to know. Me and Jamie should be treated equally. If one of us gets money from a parent – or a'—she swallows, because saying this out loud is grim—'or a *step-parent*, they should understand that the other sister also gets something. It's fairness. That's how things are. That's how things should be.' As soon as she says it, though, she knows she wouldn't accept a penny of Ant's money even if begged her.

But Jamie did.

'This was a loan,' Jamie says in a quiet voice. 'We're going to pay him back.'

'No wonder you pretend to like him.' She pierces Jamie with her eyes, looking right at her sister, the betrayer.

'Cleo, that's enough.' Dad's voice is loud and stern. 'You're not making a documentary, are you?'

She shakes her head no, then turns to Jamie, homes in on the real thing that's pissed her off. 'How could you take his money? And keep it secret?'

Jamie looks at her plate, pushes a chunk of chicken around with her fork. 'It's not like that. He helped us get started.'

'He bought you. He knew you'd be on his side if he gave you a bunch of money. He gives you thousands of pounds and—'

'Not thousands—'

'And I get cut off from everyone I ever knew, sent away to boarding school,' she mutters.

They're quiet now, looking at her. Their eyes are wide in shock as they stare at her, mouths half-open. This is Cleo's moment in the spotlight. She stands up. 'Yes, you heard me right. Ant wants to send me away, to boarding school. To get me out of the way. And Mum's going to let him.'

She throws her paper napkin to the table and turns away. Halfway to the door, she remembers. 'Thank you for dinner, Sahara. It was nice.'

Her room at Dad's feels weird. It's never really felt like home, even though some of her stuff is here. But it's like the reject stuff she won't miss from home: the T-shirts that shrank in the wash and pyjama trousers with loose elastic.

She's never had the heart to hang up posters or anything. Doesn't seem much point when she's only here for one or two days a week, max. More important to imprint her identity on her room at home, where she has covered her walls with posters and pictures cut from magazines.

She scrolls through TikTok to find something funny or shocking or interesting, but it's all annoying kids miming to rap songs.

There's a soft knock on her bedroom door and she slides her phone under her pillow. 'Come in?'

It's Sahara, holding out a bowl. 'I brought ice cream. Raspberry ripple okay?'

Cleo takes the bowl with a grateful nod and leans back against the bed's corduroy headboard, which is surprisingly comfortable.

'Mind if I join you for a minute?' Sahara doesn't wait for an answer, just sits on the end of the bed. It's not like when Ant shoved into her room to poke around for information to use against her. Sahara takes her time before she says anything. She shuffles her feet on the carpet and hums a little, as if she doesn't realise she's doing it. Then she uses two hands to lift her hair into a huge, messy plume on top of her head, and secures it with a bobble from her wrist.

Cleo takes a large spoonful of ice cream and slides it into her mouth and out again, shaping it smooth on the spoon. It's cold and creamy and very very good.

Sahara coughs. 'I went to boarding school, you know.'

Cleo bristles, ready to argue. 'Good for you.' All acceptance of Sahara is gone if she's going to jump on board with the 'Send Cleo Away' plan. 'And I suppose it was all jolly rousing games of hockey and midnight feasts in the dorm after lights out?'

Sahara blinks slowly, and then leans towards Cleo, grabbing the bowl of ice cream from her hands.

Cleo opens her mouth, astonished.

Sahara beckons for the spoon, and Cleo understands. Sahara wants to share. Cleo licks the last remnants from the spoon and hands it over. She's strangely pleased Sahara instigated this to show Cleo that they're family.

Through a mouthful of raspberry ripple, Sahara continues. 'We played hockey, sure. And had midnight feasts. But I wasn't invited. Or, worse, they invited me and then used me as the fall guy when they needed someone to get in trouble for them. I didn't have a great time. But this isn't about me, I came here to talk about you.'

Cleo reaches out for the ice cream.

'It was new information for your dad, what you said about

boarding school. Jamie, too. Are you sure your mum and Ant are talking about this as a genuine option?'

Cleo shrugs. 'He wants to get rid of me. He told me that.'

'Are you sure you're not just feeling left out now Mum's married?'

'No.' Cleo thrusts the bowl back towards Sahara. 'Is that what you're all saying behind my back? *Poor Cleo, jealous because she's not Mummy's number one anymore.* That's exactly what he wants everyone to think, by the way. And it's not true. If I had a problem with Mum having a relationship in general, I'd also have a problem with you and Dad too, wouldn't I?'

'Well...' Sahara's cheeks flush. 'You're hard to read sometimes.'

'I come and stay, don't I? I eat ice cream with you.'

Sahara looks unconvinced.

'Look, I don't hate you. I actually quite like you, especially in comparison to fucking Ant.'

Sahara laughs, then catches herself and covers her mouth, clearly wondering if she should disapprove of Cleo using the f-word. Then she gives a small shrug and drops her hand. 'Well, at least I don't have competition, I guess. For the best parental partner.'

Cleo laughs.

'There's no way you couldn't just be misunderstanding him? Maybe he's a nice guy who just doesn't know how to act around you. He didn't have an ordinary family life himself...'

Cleo shakes her head. 'It's not that. It's so many little things that if I try to describe them all I'll seem petty. They sound like nothing. Even saying that out loud makes me sound like a whiney little kid, I know.'

Sahara gives a wry smile but doesn't interrupt.

'But all those little things add together to make a really big thing – he's wrong for Mum, and he's wrong for our family. Since she met him, nothing has gone right. Everything nice about our lives is poisoned by him. Like, we can't just have a nice dinner, it has to be a giant palaver where he cooks something ridiculous and we have to tell him what a hero he is for cooking, and how he should open a restaurant or something.'

Sahara laughs and then stifles it quickly.

'It's not just dinner. It's the Ant Show. And he can't just get married – he has to scrunch up his vows and have this massive revelation in front of everyone. But he planned that. So then everyone gives him a standing ovation and he's the hero. Where's Mum in all this? She disappears behind him, in his shadow. He makes her invisible. And I hate that. She deserves to be her own person. Not to be eclipsed by him.' Cleo holds eye contact. 'Look, I want Mum to be happy.'

Sahara cocks her head to the side. Her messy bun slips slightly. 'And you don't think she is?'

'I think she *thinks* she is. But I think he's made her feel like that. He tells her she feels happy.'

'Well, that sounds kind of normal. Every—'

'No, I mean he manipulates her to believe she's happy when she's actually not. I've been reading a book; it's called *Happily Ever After and Other Fairytales*. Have you heard of it?'

Sahara shakes her head.

'Everyone at school has a copy. It teaches us what healthy relationships should look like and how to spot unhealthy ones. So we can break the cycle with our generation. You know, to stop us shacking up with pimps or whatever.'

Sahara splutters on her mouthful of ice cream, covering her mouth with the back of her hand. 'Pimps?'

Cleo grins. 'I can see Ant on every page of that book. All the unhealthy relationship parts. Like love bombing.'

'Love bombing?'

'They're kind and romantic and affectionate one minute, making the other person feel safe and loved. And then they take it all away so the person's confused and alone, and will do anything to get back the love they thought they had at the beginning.' Cleo brings her knees up to her chest and wraps her arms around them.

'Oh yes, I've heard of that. It's a manipulation tactic.' She stops, and looks hard at Cleo, her eyebrows pulled into a frown. She flicks her eyes from side to side: she's said more than she wants to. She tries to back out of it, holding out a hand to touch Cleo's arm. 'But your mum and Ant, it might not be that for them.'

'It is. Some days he brings home flowers and takes her out for dinner, the next day he says she's too fat for that dress and should go on a diet.'

Sahara's face drops. She quickly tries to rearrange her expression, but Cleo's seen it. Finally someone believes her.

'They had a fight the other day and I heard.'

'Cleo, I don't know if you should tell me—'

'Just listen, please. You're the first person who has listened and I really, really appreciate it. Please?'

Sahara gestures for her to continue.

'And Ant made her cancel dinner with Tina, said Tina is toxic. But Tina's, like, one of Mum's best friends. Then he suddenly had this massive surprise night out planned, tickets for the theatre and a dinner reservation so she couldn't say no, and she had to ditch her plans with Tina.'

'Why is Tina toxic?'

Cleo shrugs. 'He says she's a man hater. She whines about

her boyfriend sometimes, but normal stuff, like he forgets to put out the recycling when Tina's on the night shift or whatever.'

'Yup, sounds like pretty normal relationship stuff to me.'

'See, he says that's toxic. He's isolating Mum, making up reasons she needs to ditch Tina. And he wants Jamie to move out, he's sending me to boarding school, he's telling her what to wear.'

'But isolating someone is emotional abuse, it's probably not something Ant—'

'Yes! Emotional abuse.'

'This can't be right. He seems so nice. He clearly loves her very much; you could tell at the wedding. Why do you think your mum married him if he's so horrible?'

Cleo shrugs. 'Maybe she was lonely. Or desperate.'

'That's not a very nice thing to say about your mum.'

'I know. I don't really believe it. But I honestly don't know why otherwise. Like, she used to say she was happy on her own, didn't need a boyfriend, barely even missed Dad after they split up. She said we gave her everything she needed, me and Jamie. So it can't be that. She says she's happy, but if that's true, why does she always seem like she's trying not to cry?'

Sahara moves to sit cross-legged on the bed, like a yoga teacher. She takes a couple of deep breaths. 'I have friends who had bad experiences with men. One of them, a bit like this. And if you're right, this does need taking seriously.'

Cleo's heart soars. Finally someone has heard her. She would get up and dance, but it would look strange and undo all her hard work. 'When I say it all out loud it sounds like I'm making a fuss out of nothing, and maybe that's why no one believes me. But when you look at the whole thing it's massive. Your friend, what did she do?'

'People tried to talk to her and it didn't work. It just pushed her further away, closer to him. She had to realise on her own.'

'Like, she had to see evidence?'

Sahara shrugs. 'I guess, yeah. Because otherwise it's one friend's word against the partner, and they'll always believe the partner. She needed to see it for herself. But the most important part is that you're there for her, no matter what. If she needs your help, even if it's months or years from now, can you still be here?'

Cleo sits up straighter. 'Yes, absolutely.'

'Then just wait. And help when she asks.' Sahara stands and picks up the empty bowl and spoon. 'Thanks for sharing ice cream with me.'

'Thank you for talking to me. I'm glad you're with Dad.'

Sahara beams, and pulls the door closed behind her.

As soon as she hears Sahara's footsteps walking away, Cleo reaches under her pillow for her phone and opens a new message. 'She has to see evidence,' she mutters. 'I can get evidence.'

Chapter Ten

Jamie

J amie doesn't have her own room here, as the house is only a three bedroom. But she doesn't mind too much: Dad and Sahara's guest room is stylish, the walls covered with fabric hangings embroidered with little circles of mirror and patches of coloured fabric. An ornate copper lantern hangs from the ceiling, the light shining through holes which project speckles of light across the walls. Like sleeping in a Bedouin tent in the desert.

She loads today's memory card onto her computer and copies the contents carefully onto the cloud, watching the progress bar fill up as it duplicates everything. She surveys the files and clicks on one to open it and make sure it works. The video flicks up onto her screen and it's Catherine's face. She's turned away from the camera, looking towards the blackened wreck of the stable behind her, her mouth moving.

Jamie unmutes the speakers and Catherine's voice fills her bedroom, tinny through the laptop speakers. '…a glass clock on the wall in the tack room and it had shrivelled and melted, the heat must have been that intense. Every rug, blanket and brush burned beyond recognition, there's only a hoof pick left. We're far enough back from the road that no one reported it in time.'

Her own voice pipes through the speakers, louder than Catherine's: 'We've talked about the weekend kids, but what about other business owners? Do you have any competitors who might have wanted a boost?'

Catherine's eyes flick to the camera and away. She's a great interview subject but can't keep her eyes away from the camera. They'll have to use b-roll to patch over the moments where Catherine talks to the camera, shifts from foot to foot, or steps backwards and out of focus. Still, Spider was right: they got a lot of good interview material today, and some great b-roll of the charred buildings before Catherine arrived.

On the screen, Catherine talks: 'No rivalry really. We're all pretty friendly around here.' She pauses for a moment, and Jamie makes a mental note to cut the long pause as the mic fills with the crumpled sound of wind hitting electronics. 'They were standing on hay, my horses. In their stables. And that's probably what went up first. They would have been surrounded by flames when they died. They wouldn't understand what was happening. How could someone look into my horses' faces then set their home on fire? Then they walked away, left them to burn. My poor, poor animals.'

Jamie's chest tightens. Injustice or cruelty to animals makes her rage. There's so much innocence and trust smashed when animals are mistreated. Those horses thought they were safe. A person who burns horses needs to be brought to justice by the police. Interfering with an official investigation is no place for an amateur documentarian.

There's a knock at the door, and Jamie pauses the video. Sahara pops her head around. 'Sorry to disturb you; your dad forgot to mention'—she rolls her eyes with a smile—'a parcel came for you today.'

Jamie frowns. 'Here?'

Sahara opens the door wider and holds it out. 'Not expecting anything?'

'Nope. Barely anyone I know has this address.' She hasn't ordered anything from Amazon lately and wouldn't get it sent here even if she did. She takes it and thanks Sahara.

A large brown padded envelope. She turns it over. Her name and address are written on the envelope, handwritten in block capitals but no stamp or sticker or payment. Weird.

On the back there's a hot pink Post-it in Dad's handwriting, which is scratchy and spiky, like a bird walked over the page: 'Jamie – this came for you today.'

She tears open the envelope and slides the contents onto the bed next to her. There's a sheet of paper wrapped around something bulky. 'What the...'

She shifts in her seat. But then she catches her breath. What is that? She can smell a charred charcoal-like scent: something burned and cooled, like the old embers after a barbeque.

She leans forward to the blackened thing which pokes from within the paper.

She recoils with a scream. She's going to be sick. She runs across the room to the bed and curls up against the wall, as far away from her desk as she can get, tears of horror filling her eyes.

Her heart pumps in her chest, breath fast like she's been running,

How did it get here? It's a taunt. A message: *I know where you live. I know where you film. I can get at you whenever I want.*

She can still see it from across the room. It's a horse's hoof, blackened and shrivelled.

Her hands shake as she reaches into her pocket for her phone and dials Spider. Her voice quakes as she describes what it is. But Spider sounds calm, his tone steady.

'Spider, they know where I live. They followed us today.'

'Woah, woah. What's happened? Who followed us?'

He's silent on the other end of the line as she tries to get her words out between sobs. Across the room, the hoof glitters in the light from Sahara's ridiculous Bedouin lamp.

'What's on the paper?' he whispers.

She swallows acid in her throat and her hands shake as she peels back the filthy paper wrapped around the charred hoof. She takes a deep breath, and her eyes focus again. There's writing scrawled all over in black permanent marker, all capitals: YOU WILL FIND NOTHING. STOP FILMING OR BURN.

He's quiet for a moment. 'That's pretty messed up. Are you okay?'

'How did they know we were there?' She tries, but she can't get enough air into her lungs. 'Spider, we need to stop filming. This isn't safe.'

He takes a breath before he speaks. 'No. Jamie, don't you get it? This is exactly what we needed. It's the hook and the drama.'

'Spider, we need to go to the police.'

'No way.'

'Are you kidding?'

'No police. If we're right, they'll stop our documentary

right at the point where it's getting interesting. The police don't appreciate civilian investigators.'

'Yes, exactly. They will catch whoever did this, and then we can start work. Not now.' Her eyes blur as they skim over the scrawled black text.

'We're making a documentary, not solving a crime. We're no threat to the police. Jamie, we're documentarians. This is perfect. Can you open the package again tomorrow and we'll get you on camera? Remember how you felt so you can replicate it for the shot.'

She pulls the phone away from her face, looks at her screensaver: a picture of her and Spider, his lips pressed against her cheek. It used to be her favourite picture, set to pop up every time they spoke on the phone.

'We should definitely change direction – ditch the old stuff and focus on recent fires in the area. When you look at statistics in other local towns, Abbeywick has way more criminal property fires. Especially over the past couple of months. It's exploded. Pardon the pun.' He chuckles at his own joke. 'Our documentary should work out what's going on, why there are so many. It's perfect, J, don't you see?'

'Who are you right now? Are you not listening to a word I'm saying?'

'OK, take a deep breath. This probably isn't as serious or scary as it seems right now. Do you want me to come over there? I mean, clearly this guy is a total sicko.' He's silent for a moment. 'We must be onto something. We must have him rattled, like when Zodiac contacted the cops. You know, this is actually a good sign, J.'

She shakes her head even though he can't see her. 'How do they know where Dad lives, Spider? And how did they know where we were filming today? That fire had barely even

finished burning. Did you tell anyone where we were going?'
Her mind whirrs, and for a moment her vision clouds. She's
thinking so hard that she's forgotten to breathe.

'It's viral, J. A million people know there was a fire at
Langdale Stables. It's probably just some internet creep. Look,
I'll tweak our Arts Council proposal. Have a read and tell me
what you think.'

The funding pitch. Spider wrote about a threat in the pitch.
He wanted this to happen. Did he plan this? Maybe one of his
friends was there, crouched behind Catherine's Land Rover,
waiting to enter the wreckage and grab a horrifying keepsake.
Did Spider do this?

She can't stop staring at the charred hoof.

She takes a sharp breath, and her world refocuses. If he is
ruthless enough to threaten his girlfriend's life for the sake of a
documentary, what else might he do?

He's pushing so hard to refocus the documentary on what's
happening now. Would he set a fire to capture the footage? Or
worse?

She needs to think.

She holds the phone away from her face again, takes one
last look at the screen, at the two of them together, a happy
smile on her face as he kissed her with what she thought was
love and what might be something more calculated and not
caring at all. 'I can't do this right now, Spider. I need to think.'

'About what?'

'About what we do next, what our documentary looks like.'

'But—'

'It's my decision.'

She hits the red button, turns off her phone and throws it
onto the bed next to her. She curls up with her back to the
desk, pulling her laptop with her. Her dinner feels heavy in her

stomach, and she wishes she hadn't eaten so much. She wishes her stomach was empty, hollow. Light.

As she opens the application, the next of today's videos starts to play automatically. This one's some b-roll. A steady pan: Spider filming on a tripod. The wind buffets the camera's in-built mic, and when it occasionally drops, she hears Spider breathing.

The stables look even worse than she remembers; Spider must have found a good angle to shoot them. Everything in the shot is charred. If not for the green leaves on the trees in the background, this footage could be mistaken for a black and white film. Catherine's stable is a pile of ashy planks in a heap, an old bonfire. Some vertical posts remain where the walls stood, but everything else has collapsed into old kindling, with the occasional metal object that survived: a mop handle, a spade, the tines of a pitchfork.

The panning slows, and she hears Spider's intake of breath, then the camera zooms in. In the ashes, something metal shines. The camera shakes as he moves towards it, then steadies as he focuses. What is it? Jamie can't tell. It's small, about the same width as Spider's shoe, which is also in shot.

Then Spider starts talking.

'And here we have something of utmost interest to the ghoulish out there at home.' He nudges the metal with a foot.

It glints in the sunshine as Spider focuses the camera on it from different angles, clearly looking for the best way to show it on screen. She understands that he would want to show parts of the stable that got destroyed, really highlight the elements of loss Catherine must feel every time she returns and finds a new piece of her lost livelihood and animals.

At first, she doesn't understand what she sees next.

The camera swings around to a close-up of Spider's face, a

weird smile at the corner of his lips as he addresses the camera. This close, his features are distorted: his nose huge, his eyes small. He looks shifty, untrustworthy, and gleeful.

He holds up the piece of metal next to his face. It glints in the sunshine as he moves it back and forth.

'Before the devastating fire consumed Langdale Stables, this was inside the mouth of one of the victims.'

It's a horse's bit, normally attached to the reins. He moves it into his mouth and bites down on it; its shape distorts his mouth into a grotesque slash. Then he gives a little whinny, like a horse, and laughs.

Chapter Eleven

Cleo

Cleo sighs with relief as Daisy dozes on her knee and the film's opening credits showcase the bubble gum fluff of music, colours, and teenage hopes about to rinse her mind clean. She wishes she went to high school in America. It looks idyllic in the movies: everyone has a perfect clique where they belong. Not like Cleo's ragtag band of friends from different places who don't really like each other, like Lucasz and Cleo with Peach, Leonie and Tara. But those three aren't her friends anymore, not since that art lesson last term. She could have claimed it was an accident if the teacher hadn't turned around at the wrong moment. And if Peach hadn't shrieked so much and bled everywhere. Drama queen.

The first scene's starting as the door bursts open and floods the room with light. Ant strides in and grabs the remote control. The screen goes black.

'I was watching that,' she scrambles up from the sofa, her feet tangled in the blanket. Daisy leaps to her feet. 'What are you doing?' Cleo grabs for the remote but he holds it out of her reach, a cruel smile on his face.

'I'm trying to concentrate, and that racket is too loud.' Daisy jumps at him thinking he's playing with a ball. 'Get down, bloody dog.' He shoves her away and she slinks to her bed in the corner, tail between her legs.

'Leave her alone.' Cleo tries to grab the remote again, but he lifts it above his head, goading her. 'So what? Just ask me to turn it down, don't come in here and switch it off.'

He pockets the remote and folds his arms. 'I can do what I want, it's my house too.'

'No, it's not.' Cleo sits back down on the sofa, pulls the blanket over her legs, and opens her phone, flicking to Instagram. It's important he doesn't see she's bothered by his actions, that he's disrupted her. She flicks through the feed, doesn't look at him. 'It's Mum's house. It's in her name. She bought Dad's half.'

'Not anymore.' He turns to leave, his hand on the doorknob.

'What?' She gets up again, follows him into the kitchen. He sits at the head of the table, surrounded by piles of paperwork.

'"Not anymore", I said. If you didn't have your face buried in your phone all the time maybe you'd understand. The house is mine too. Your mother signed it over to me.' The chandelier over the dining table illuminates him from above, its yellow light casting shadows that turn his eyes to dark holes in his face.

'She wouldn't.'

He smirks. 'Why wouldn't she? We're married, she trusts me.'

Cleo's mind whirrs. She can barely swallow the spit pooling in her mouth. Why would Mum do that?

'She's terrible with paperwork and money, you know it and so does she. It stresses her out. So now we own the house jointly and all the bank accounts are in both of our names. She doesn't have to worry about a thing. She doesn't even have to work if she doesn't want to. She could hand in her notice tomorrow.'

'The bank accounts too?' Cleo's skin prickles. She shouldn't rise to his bait; he knows this bothers her. He'll provoke her and she'll react, get angry and then look bad. It's what he wants. 'She's given you all her bank accounts?' This feels so wrong.

'She just wants someone to take care of her, Cleo. Like your dad couldn't. He focused too much on his business, his clients, you two girls. Your mum craved someone like me to look after her, to shoulder the burden she carried by herself for so long. She loves how I care for her.' He sits up straighter, almost preening.

'Dad looked after all of us just fine. And he never tried to steal her money.'

Ant laughs, a spiteful little sputter. 'This really isn't any of your business. This is an adult discussion. I have no need to steal from your mother. You think I don't have enough of my own money?' His voice is soft, mocking her. 'I'm a successful television presenter, Cleo. Your mum doesn't even need to work if she doesn't want to. She can just relax, browse antiques fairs all day if that's what she wants. My wage will look after us both. And pay your school fees, boarding and all. I'll make sure all of you are looked after in the right ways. With enough left at the end to donate to charities. I'm very generous, you know.'

She shakes her head, wants to leave and get as far away from his soft voice as she can. It's not that he wants Mum's money, it's that he wants her to have to ask him for things, unable to make her own decisions, to rely on him for everything. Eventually she'll be unable to leave. She's read about this.

'Give me back the remote.'

He takes the remote from his back pocket and places it on the table on top of a folder labelled 'Ant: birth cert etc'. Then he raises his gaze to look at her, inviting her to come and get it. He could have just held it out towards her, but this is a power play. She has to walk to him and get the remote that he took in the first place.

'For fuck's sake.' She strides around the table to Ant's side and reaches out for the remote, but Ant grabs her wrist, squeezing her bones. 'Ow, get off me.'

He pulls her towards him and stares into her eyes. It's a threat. 'You don't use language like that towards me. Your behaviour is a problem; one I'm determined to solve. And believe me, Cleo, I always get what I want.'

He tugs her again, and as he does, he reaches into her jeans pocket and pulls out her phone. 'I'll keep this until you give me a proper apology.'

She swings to get her phone back, but he holds it out of her reach, just like he did with the remote. Then he slides it into his own pocket.

'That's stealing. Mum won't let you do that. You give that back. That's my phone, it belongs to me.'

He shakes his head, as if regretful of the information he's imparting. 'Cleo, you're a child. Nothing belongs to you. Everything in this house belongs to your mum and me, including your phone.' He waves his hand over the piles of paper all over the dining table. 'I presume one of these bills is your phone bill, and you don't pay it yourself, out of your own money? That you earned yourself?'

Cleo says nothing.

'I thought so.' He releases her wrist, and she rubs it like a prisoner released from handcuffs. He raises an eyebrow at her, daring her to refer to him grabbing her. 'I'll talk with your mum when she's home and we'll discuss what's next. Whether you get your phone back and when. And next steps to ensure that this behaviour of yours, and your blatant disrespect, does not continue.'

She hums to herself as she picks up the remote and walks away from him, determined to prove she doesn't need her phone, that his threats don't affect her. But back in the living room, Cleo can't concentrate on her show. She needs her phone back.

She stares at the action on the screen, eyes unfocused, until she hears the click of the front door and the cheery greeting of Mum returning home. Then the rumble of Ant's voice as he greets her.

'Muuum.' She tries to sound even more upset than she is. She needs Mum's attention and she needs it fast, before Ant can tell her his side of the story. Before they look at her phone. The rumbling, mumbling voices continue. It's not working. 'Mum, help!' she shrieks, and slithers off the sofa onto the floor, trying to look like she's hurt. 'Owww,' she shouts. Still nothing; the conversation continues. She listens for a moment, her face pressed against the itch of the carpet. She wraps her right hand around her left wrist and squeezes hard, twisting until a red ring of sore flesh encircles her wrist where Ant grabbed her.

Whatever Ant said to Mum as soon as she walked through the door, it worked. It got her attention, and nothing can pull her away. Not even a daughter in distress. Well played, Ant. But Cleo can do better, surely.

Daisy trots over and sniffs, the dog's nose wet against her cheek.

She gets to her feet and pushes open the kitchen door, her hand wrapped around her wrist. 'Mum, my wrist. He really hurt—'

She stops. Ant and Mum are at the table, huddled over something. As she enters the room, they both look up at Cleo, their eyes cold, even Mum. Her mouth is set in a hard line, her eyebrows pulled down as if guarding her from Cleo.

Cleo holds out her wrists, still red from Ant's grasp. 'Mum, he hurt me—'

'Just stop right there. Don't say another word.' Mum's voice is clear and sharp.

Cleo freezes in shock. She's never spoken to Cleo like this before.

'But Mum—'

'Shut up,' she snaps, and looks back down at what Ant holds in his hands.

Cleo rushes forward, her arms outstretched, the sting of her wrists forgotten. Mum and Ant were going through her phone.

Mum puts out an arm, catches Cleo by the shoulder. 'No. Not one step further. You have done enough.'

Cleo stops. She knows what they found.

'You need some serious discipline,' Ant snarls, and Cleo opens her mouth, eyes wide.

'Mum, you can't let him talk—'

Mum shakes her head with such force that Cleo stops.

She tries again. 'What am I supposed to have done? He stole my phone. It's my private proper—'

'Stop, Cleo.' Mum reaches up and smooths the sides of her

150

hair, tucking loose tendrils behind her ears. 'I want you to go to your room. Ant and I will discuss what happens next. But you have crossed a line and things have to change around here.'

Cleo folds her arms and leaves the room. She knows exactly what they found on her phone, and it's bad. *The evidence.*

There's no coming back from this.

———————

Out of her bedroom window, the late afternoon sun shines over her swing where it hangs from the apple tree, swaying in the breeze. In the flower beds around the garden's edges, the daffodils are starting to droop, their short-lived spring visit coming to an end as they make way for summer flowers.

A magpie hops around the lawn, pecking the soil. One for sorrow. Cleo looks around, hopes for a second or a third: no single magpies today, please. No more sorrow.

In the distance she can see the moors, the hills rolling, the occasional tree squatted against the harsh winds of the open moorland. And then, even further away, a little glimmer of the sea peeks at her between the hills. She loves this place, this house – the only house she's ever known.

They can't send her away from here. She couldn't bear it.

There's a knock at her bedroom door. 'Come in,' she shouts, but doesn't turn around. She wants a second magpie.

'Hey.' Cleo hears the springs creak as Mum sits on the bed. 'We need to talk, Cleo.'

She keeps looking out at the garden, hoping for a second magpie. Its mate. Two for joy.

'You're sending me away.' She doesn't want to move out, to spend every term living in a boarding house full of other girls. She's never found it easy to make friends. She knows she's overbearing, a bit bossy sometimes. She can tell when they have enough of her, start to pull away, find new friends.

Only Lucasz stays, always available to hang out on adventures and explore the countryside. He's kind and good, and resilient. He knows when to leave her alone, let her rant and rave without a word from him. He doesn't take it personally, just waits for her to finish, and then he's there just the same as if nothing happened. Calm, strong and steadfast Lucasz.

She should tell him how much she appreciates him. But she doesn't want him to get the wrong idea, so she fights for him instead. Peach knows to leave Lucasz alone now, not to tease him about his complicated name and his parents' thick accents. And eventually Peach's hand will go back to normal. It's not like it was her right hand or anything. And the boys stab each other with compasses all the time. Apparently, scissors cross the line. Who knew?

'Cleo, come and sit down, please.'

So boarding school means leaving these hills, the moors, the sea, this garden. Leaving it all behind to Ant, who would immediately cut her swing from the tree and turn her bedroom into a home gym so he could pump his biceps all day. It means leaving Mum alone with him and relinquishing the house to him. Like he's won.

'Cleo.'

Cleo wrenches her eyes away from the garden and turns. Mum looks tired, sad. Her hand is flat on the bed next to her, patting the duvet cover to invite Cleo to sit. She holds Cleo's phone in her other hand, pink-tipped nails across the cracked screen.

Cleo's stomach drops.

She sinks to the carpet, her back against the radiator. If

she's going to sit, it'll be on her own terms, not next to Mum where Mum could put her arm around her any minute. If anyone touches her she'll cry and she can't cry, not now.

Mum unlocks the phone screen with a swipe of her finger, and Cleo curses herself for not setting up a passcode. If she'd done that, none of this would have happened.

'When we confiscated your phone—'

'When Ant *stole* my phone, you mean.'

Mum pretends there was no interruption and carries on. 'You had a new message, from a name familiar to Ant. So he opened it, as he couldn't understand why you would be messaging that person.'

Cleo sinks her head into her hands.

'For the record, Cleo, the message said she had no idea who you were, and she had never been married to a man named Ant.'

Cleo looks up, bewildered. 'But I saw her tagged in his old profile pictures.'

Mum shrugs. 'Anyway, what worries me more is what you said in your message to her. We're lucky she didn't go to the police.' She swipes up on the phone and opens the message and reads it out loud: 'My new stepdad is a monster and is abusing my mum. Did he abuse you too? Please tell me so I can save my mum from him; no one believes me.' She shakes her head, swallows.

Cleo hugs her knees to her chest, grips her right wrist with her left hand so tight that her hand goes white. 'It's true, Mum. On a checklist of controlling behaviours, he ticks all the—'

She shakes her head, her perfect bob swinging. 'Stop this. I don't want to hear it. You're wrong, Cleo.'

Cleo punches her knee with her fist. 'I'm not. Why can't anyone see it? I'm not wrong.'

'You've crossed the line with this message. You contacted people outside of our family and exposed your identity to strangers on the internet. You told people that Ant is abusive. He is my husband, Cleo. It's too much. You don't know what abuse looks like. You haven't seen it, and you don't understand.'

'But—'

'No, Cleo. Abuse is a terrible, life-changing thing. It's violence.' Her voice cracks and she coughs. 'It's shouting, threats and fear.'

'It's other things, too. It's—'

'It's so many things that are nowhere near this house. This house where I'm happy.' Her face is pale, her cheeks sunken where they used to be plump.

'You keep saying that, but I can't see it. You don't seem happy. We were happy before him, don't you remember? I just want my mum back.'

Mum closes her eyes, holding up Cleo's phone. 'This is a serious accusation and a serious situation you created. And we can't just let this go. You stabbed a girl at school—'

'It wasn't like that, I—'

Mum ignores her. 'You ran away from our wedding, ruined your dress, tantrums in public, arguments at the dinner table, and now throwing around this accusation to a stranger. Ant is trying to be your stepdad. He's trying to create a relationship with you, but you won't let him. He's a kind man, Cleo. A good man.'

She splutters at this; she can't believe Mum is saying these things. She's so wrong.

Mum stands up, throws the phone onto the bed. 'When you marry into a family with kids, parenting is hard. Ant is your stepdad, and we are taking your actions seriously. So you know you can never do this again. You can have your phone back, but we will monitor it. You must show us your phone whenever we ask to see it, so we can check you aren't contacting strangers and sharing personal information. You are grounded for the rest of the Easter holidays, no going out. And we will submit your application to boarding school this week, so you are in a new school for the summer term in a couple of weeks. It's a good school with great facilities, and perhaps some space might do you good, help you see things more clearly.'

In a couple of weeks. Cleo rests her forehead on her knees and moves her head from side to side, her eyelids scrunched against tears. She doesn't want Mum to see her cry, to tell Ant she's upset. Mum's footsteps move towards her, a shuffle on the carpet. Mum rests her hand on the back of Cleo's head, smoothing her hair. A tear escapes from Cleo's eyes and plops onto her trousers, leaving a small wet circle of dark fabric.

'I love you, Cleo. And I want you to be OK. But I have to protect our whole family.'

Mum's footsteps fade as she leaves the room and walks away down the corridor. 'Then you should divorce that monster,' Cleo mumbles into her knees.

This is bad. She's losing this battle and it's all her own fault. They'll wrench her away from her family and Lucasz and send her away, and she has only a few days left to gain an advantage.

She hasn't processed any of this yet; she has a couple of hours before it all really hits her. Right now is the time to act before she starts to feel wretched, before her brain soaks in that Mum doesn't want her around anymore. *Mum doesn't want me anymore.* The words flicker around her brain, like breaking news tickertape along the bottom of a TV screen.

Mum doesn't want me anymore.

She shakes her head, hard.

She'll use this time for action. She gets up, opens the drawer under her bed and pulls out her giant camping backpack. She throws clothes into it, chucking in the first things she comes across.

They can't send her to boarding school if she's not here.

Chapter Twelve

Cleo

Her reflection in the speckled mirror shows her propped up against the headboard, the book on her knees, unread. From the cocoon of her sleeping bag, she can see the little photograph shoved into the edge of the wooden frame where Lucasz carefully replaced it a few days before.

Through the doorway the dark corridor looms at her like the open mouth of a monster. She closed it when she first arrived, but the looping graffiti bristled and moved in the half-light. *I won't say a word. Tony is dead.* A dressing gown hanging on the back of the door looked like a man staring at her, so she propped the door open. Better to hear intruders that way.

'What's your plan, dickhead?' she asks herself. Her voice pierces the quiet of the house, but the sound is sucked away almost immediately, absorbed into the darkness like the walls are hungry for company. When she left home earlier, this seemed like the best plan in the world: get to the derelict house, light a fire to warm it up, live here for the next few days while she makes a plan. Possibly move in with Lucasz and his family for a while until Mum finally realises the truth about Ant and divorces him, and then begs Cleo to come home. And, as a last resort, she could escape on the train and go hundreds of miles south to Gran's house. Maybe Jamie would give her some of Ant's bribery money for the train ticket.

This plan isn't working. She shivers in her sleeping bag, huddled up in her fleecy tracksuit trousers, hood over her head and the drawstrings pulled tight to keep the warmth in. She found the sleeping bag in their garage: Dad bought it for a camping trip up in Scotland years ago, so it's good quality and warm, despite its musty smell.

She's trying to make this fun. Her torch stands on its end, shining its beam at the ceiling in Dead Tony's bedroom. She stole a bag of food from the kitchen at home: crisps, apples, nuts, and a bottle of water. She even brought a pack of cards in case she wanted to play patience.

She tried to light a fire in the living room grate, but the flame wouldn't pick up. The chimney must be blocked. Plus it's probably dangerous to light a fire. Someone already burned down half the house and the shed was on fire just a couple of weeks ago. Maybe they're coming back. No smoke should escape this chimney to alert anyone that she's here.

She considered exploring the burned wing before the sun started to set, but couldn't gather the courage to poke around on her own. It's too dark, the walls a level of blackness that creates a deep fear in her chest.

She's scared, she's lonely. She wishes Lucasz would come. She's so much braver when he's around. His cautious nature allows her to be the brave and daring one. He'll say no and hold them back. She can't be brave and foolhardy alone. Without him, she's a wimp.

The wind picks up outside, and a draught chills her face. There's so much noise: a drip from the leaking ceiling; the windows rattling in their frames; the bowels of the house groaning as it shifts, unused to weight on its floors and warmth in its bed. And then, somewhere downstairs, a sound like footsteps. And a cough.

Every muscle in her body is tense, ready to run. Ready to fight.

She climbs out of the sleeping bag. She's careful where she places her feet, ensuring her weight is on only one floorboard at a time: less likelihood of creaking and alerting the intruder. She switches off the torch.

While her eyes adjust to the darkness, she listens. Another creak from downstairs. Her stomach roils, empty and fighting against the fear. Her bowels squeeze. She can't decide if she needs to vomit or shit. She has no idea what the bathroom is like here. And she didn't bring toilet paper. 'You idiot, Cleo,' she whispers to herself.

It could be nothing.

It could be something. Someone.

The person who lit the shed on fire the day Mum married Ant.

The ghost of Dead Tony.

She shuffles to the wardrobe and climbs inside, pulling the door closed behind her. She huddles on a pile of shoes; it smells leathery and damp. Something cold and flesh-like brushes her face and she startles, shoving it away with a squeak. A wax jacket, not the skin of a dead body. She grabs her phone and unlocks it, clicking on Lucasz's name.

But she can't do it. She can't admit to him that she's afraid. She turns off her phone to conserve battery and shoves at the shoes until she finds a comfortable position, cushioned by a coat and with another on top of her.

She lies in the wardrobe for hours, listening to the house. The footsteps don't come back. Was it her imagination? Eyes open, she peers into the darkness, trying to stay awake. As her eyelids float closed, she pretends she's at home, curled up in her own bed, warm and comfortable.

When she wakes, she has no idea where she is. It's black as night, her neck is sore, and her legs cramped.

Half awake, she reaches out and smacks her hand against the wardrobe wall with a huge *whack*. The door flies open and she crunches her eyes against the light. Her heart pounds, and she rolls out of the wardrobe onto the floor.

She scrambles to her feet, ready to defend herself against an intruder, but there's no one there. The house is quiet.

Low sunlight filters through the torn net curtain that hangs over the sash window. Unlike the ground floor, the upstairs windows aren't boarded up. She peers through the grimy glass into the woods, admiring the golden morning light and the dew-covered trees. It must be early.

She drinks long and deep from her water bottle and crunches on an apple, trying to work out what to do. Now it's daylight, the house doesn't seem scary at all. It's shabby and grubby but homely. Her feeling from yesterday returns, from before the darkness descended: she can stay here for a while. Until she works out what to do next, so she doesn't get sent to boarding school.

What she needs to do first, she decides, is explore every inch of this place, so she knows it inside out and when night falls again she understands that nothing hides in the darkness, ready to pounce. First she'll use the toilet, and then she'll tackle the door which won't open, then make her way through the house systematically until she knows every inch of the place and it's hers. The only place she won't go is the burned wing, that's dangerous and black. Nothing can hide there, it's just a shell.

The bathroom is bile green: the sink, bath, and toilet all a shade that no sane person would ever choose. How does this even get designed and manufactured, never mind bought and installed? There's matching green carpet on the floor and creeping up the sides of the bath. Carpet. In a bathroom.

She's glad she's got her shoes on. Generations of urine must have splashed onto the carpet around the toilet.

The toilet seat is dark wood, and the bowl is dry. She sits down anyway and empties her bladder with relief. The flush does nothing. It doesn't matter, it's not like she'll get in trouble. She does miss washing her hands.

She rubs her palms on the seat of her jeans as she trudges down the stairs and faces the locked door with dread. The paint is cracked and scratched. She wraps her fingers around the handle and tugs. No movement. She pulls with all her strength, leaning back with her body weight until the handle groans under the strain, but still the door won't move.

She gives it a kick.

She could leave it locked. An unanswered question.

But last night was terrifying and Cleo knows herself: she can't spend one more night in this house without knowing every inch of it. There could be a dead body behind this door.

Or worse, someone still alive. Someone who's been listening to her as she wanders through the house. Someone waiting to emerge and attack her while she sleeps. She shivers. Nothing behind this door can be as bad as what her imagination creates.

She presses her eye to the crack between the frame and the door itself. A lock shaft glints in the early morning light. She needs a key.

She stands and runs to the study, pulling open the desk drawers she pawed through with Lucasz on their first visit inside the house. She tosses aside a stack of folded handkerchiefs and there it is: a bunch of keys.

The fourth key she tries fits the keyhole. The lock's mechanism is seized, but with a struggle she manages to turn it with the scrape of rusted metal.

The door creaks and struggles against its hinges, darkness oozing through the gap. She pushes, shining her torch down the steps. A basement.

She reaches out and breaks a couple of cobweb strands which have spanned across the door frame and starts to descend. The stairs are unvarnished wood, their treads open at the back. Someone could reach through and grab her ankles from underneath, drag her down into the darkness.

The walls are bare brick and the floor is concrete. Heavy-duty metal shelves line the walls, each shelf full of storage boxes. There's a workbench, a lathe and a lawnmower shoved into a corner. Abandoned in another corner is a lop-sided tricycle and a deflated football.

She shines her torch across all the shelves, looking for something useful or interesting. But it's all DIY tools and horse-riding stuff, including a dusty riding helmet and a leather crop. Then, as she turns back to climb the steps, her torch catches on something metal glinting under the stairs. It's dark down there; no daylight reaches that part of the room from the small windows. She takes a step forward and stops.

Something feels wrong. What is that?

She takes another step forward, points her torch and squints her eyes.

As soon as the torchlight steadies, she shrieks and drops the torch.

She scrambles up the basement stairs, her feet pounding on the wood, almost slipping as she runs. Without pausing on the ground floor, she runs to the bedroom and starts shoving the sleeping bag into its sack, punching her fist into it over and over again to get it into the bag, her breath ragged and sharp.

She needs to get out. She can't stay in this house anymore. Her plan doesn't matter.

She shoulders her backpack and steps towards the door, and that's when she hears it: footsteps.

She freezes. It's not like last night, when the footsteps were just out of range, her brain playing tricks. Now it's the unmistakable rhythm of a person striding through the house, opening doors, their shoes on the lino of the kitchen and the bare floorboards of the hallway.

She drops the sleeping bag and clamps her hands over her mouth, suppressing a scream. She kicks it under the bed and follows it with her backpack. Then, just like last night, she climbs into the wardrobe and pulls the door shut behind her, curling into a ball with her hands over her ears.

She takes one brief moment to open her eyes, typing frantically into her phone: 'HELP AM AT THE HOUSE. SOMEONE IS HERE. HELP.'

Jamie

'Why are you here?' she asks. It's so early. She folds her arms over her chest to cover that she's not wearing a bra under her pyjamas.

Spider points to the boxes beside him on the doorstep. It's all their kit: the camera, the lights, the mics, the covers.

'Sorry to come over like this, but I wanted to return things before I open the shop.' He looks tired, like he's just woken up, his eyes crinkled and his nose squashier than usual. He runs a hand through his hair, and it sticks up, adding to his dishevelled, cuddly look.

Jamie suppresses an urge to step into his arms and press her face into his hoodie. She shakes her head. She's still angry. She still doesn't trust him. 'You didn't have to do that. I would have come to collect it sometime.'

He bends to pick up a box. 'I didn't want you to think I stole it. You know, it's more yours than mine. Ant paid for it really.'

She moves to the side to let him into the house, and then picks up the second box and follows him to her room. They stack the boxes on her desk, and she perches on the side of her bed, looking at him.

'Jamie, I really like you.' His voice is steady and calm. He's clearly thought through what he wants to say. He pulls out the desk chair and sits, then he looks at her, eyes open wide, bewildered. 'I want us to keep filming.'

'You wanted this whole mess to happen. A threat because we were getting too close. You wrote that in the funding application! You said it would be good TV.'

'I wish I hadn't. But that's all I did, J. I just wrote it in the proposal, nothing else.'

'What a coincidence, then.'

'That's exactly what it was.' He stands up, crosses the floor towards her. She holds still, doesn't move, keeps her eyes fixed on a spot on the carpet. 'I wanted to pretend this happened. I didn't want you actually threatened. That's crazy. I really care about you.'

She shakes her head. 'They know where my dad lives, Spider. They have my email address. You know who else has that information about me?'

'What?' His face pales behind his beard as he realises what she means. 'NO, honestly. Please believe—'

'You sent me a threat. You threatened my life for documentary fodder.' She shakes her head. 'How can you ask me to believe you, when you've shown me over and over that you'll go to any lengths, tell any lies necessary to make a good documentary, on your terms? "Fuck integrity", isn't that what you said?' She looks into his eyes, which once made her stomach flip but now has very little effect. 'Who was there at the stable? Who did you rope into your sick little plan, to go into that burned-out shell and steal part of a dead horse? I can't bel—'

'I didn't. Jamie, please. I didn't do th—' He grabs his hair again, almost yanking out a tuft. 'I promise I didn't. I wouldn't do that. It's disgusting. This project means a lot to me, I think it could be great.'

'Yeah, you showed me how important it was when you disregarded all my concerns. Practically told me to suck it up and get on with it.'

'We were getting some amazing footage and I got carried away. The documentary is important to me. We could work out a way forward.'

'I don't know if there is one.'

He swallows. 'You can't give up. Where does that leave me? It's all your equipment. You pull the plug and we're left with nothing.'

She purses her lips, glances out of the window. 'You're right. I mean, top marks for perceptiveness. But you can't guilt-trip me into this when I'm so uncomfortable. I owe you nothing. I'm not continuing with this documentary right now.'

'What about me? I could keep filming while you…'

'I really don't know how this threat could have been anyone else, considering only you and I knew where we were going that day. Whether it was you or not, I need to think: both about this documentary and our relationship. I need a break.'

'Wait. A break from what? Me, or from the documentary?'

'Both.'

'I don't want a break.' His shoulders slump, and he looks at the ground. Are those tears in his eyes? 'It wasn't me, J.' He stands, wipes his palms on his trousers, then leans down and kisses the top of her head. 'I'll text in a day or two, maybe we can talk again.'

'Please don't.' A pressure builds in her chest. She's going to cry. She needs him to leave.

He pauses. 'I'll text.'

She shakes her head, walks to the bedroom door, and holds it open. She closes it behind him and presses her forehead against the cold wood. As she listens to the trudge of his footsteps descending the stairs, she hears him sniff.

She curls in a ball on her bed, scrolling through Instagram. Her heart beats so fast it feels like it's trying to escape from her chest. Did she really do that? It's possible this is the end of her relationship with Spider. How does she feel? She's never been able to process big things straightaway; always feels numb first. It could be days before she really knows how to react.

Would she be different if she had ever allowed herself to have tantrums and cry, if she was more like Cleo? Maybe now as an adult she would feel something – anything – in response to the end of her first serious relationship.

Since she first met Spider he felt right, like coming home. She thought that meant everything, but now she doesn't know. Maybe that's how relationships always feel, even if they're not right. What if that just means she has bad judgement? That she can't see what's good for her and what's bad? That's scarier than anything.

He seemed so broken, so genuine when he said it wasn't him. But the coincidence of the threat and the funding pitch is too much. It's unbelievable that the threat could have appeared from another source.

Her skin is clammy. It feels like she's about to have a panic attack. She can't drag a deep breath into her lungs, and every time she sucks in air, her lungs contract and force it out again. There's only one thing she's ever found that helps when she feels like this. But she can't go back. She can't undo the progress she's made.

Her hands shake as she opens her desk drawer, the bottom one. It's full of chocolate bars: Wispa, Twirl, Mars, Snickers. They look the same coming back up as they do going down. Less disgusting, somehow.

She stares at their colourful wrappers, her vision blurring them into a stained-glass window. She's about to reach for a Mars bar when there's a knock on her bedroom door. Mum strides in, looking around. Jamie slams the drawer shut, closing her eyes in silent thanks that Mum didn't come in just thirty seconds later.

'Cleo's not in here?' Mum's eyebrows are pulled down into a frown and there's an air of agitation around her which is unusual. Mum's usually very calm, quiet. Today she bustles to the window, looks out over the garden, eyes scanning the fields around their house.

'Isn't she asleep?'

Mum shakes her head.

'Haven't seen her. Why?'

'She's gone. Packed a bag.'

Jamie sits up. 'What? Why?'

Mum shakes her head, takes a shaky breath. 'She got in trouble again, and we grounded her.'

'Shit,' mumbles Jamie. 'Where has she gone?'

Mum's already tapping on her phone. 'I'll call your dad. Can you have a look around her room, see if there's anything that might give us an idea of where she's gone?'

'Let me know if Dad has heard from her.' Jamie stands up.

It's not like Cleo to disappear. She might be badly behaved and cheeky and rude, but she's never run away before. 'I'll text Lucasz, too. I think I have his number.'

Cleo's room is disgusting. There are dirty clothes all over the floor, an apple core browning on the nightstand, cobwebs in the corners of the ceiling and a weird smell, a bit like a hamster cage. Jamie doesn't know what she's looking for, so she gathers clothes from the floor and throws them all into one corner. Occasionally she comes across an item that belongs to her, something lost months ago: a make-up brush, a halter top, a spiral hair tie. She throws these out of Cleo's bedroom door and into the corridor.

When she can move around in the room without stepping on something, she opens the desk drawers one by one, excavating old mobile phone chargers, HDMI cables, a calculator with no batteries, a 2017 diary and loads of biros. Nothing interesting.

Finally, she finds a battered old biscuit tin under some bras in Cleo's underwear drawer. Inside are lots of little trinkets: pebbles, shells, some old costume jewellery, and a large battered envelope containing a stack of letters, their papers old and yellowing. She kneels on the floor and slides them out carefully.

They're far too old to belong to Cleo. But where did she get them? They look like they came from the Caribbean in the Sixties, sent to an address in their village. Somewhere called The Old Manor.

'Mum?' she calls. 'Where's The Old Manor?'

No answer. Mum must have gone downstairs.

Jamie pulls her phone from her pocket and opens Google Maps.

Google Maps can't find 'The Old Manor, Langdale'.

Make sure your search is spelled correctly. Try adding a city, state, or zip code.

Jamie clicks Google Search and tilts her head as search results come up. At first, it all seems so familiar, like her research for the documentary: articles in the *Abbeywick Gazette* and *Moorburn Bay Evening News* archives, all from 1986. *Arson attack? Witness appeal… Devastating fire on Langdale Lane…*

Why does Cleo have letters from an old house that burned down? And why are they hidden in her drawer? And fire, again. Creeping into every part of Jamie's life. She tries to connect these dots together, to understand what's happening.

She pulls up Google Maps again and zooms into Langdale Lane, shifts to satellite view. And there, in the woods off the lane she sees a small clearing, and a little dark square which must be the shell of a derelict house.

Chapter Thirteen

Jamie

The house is a burned-out shell. It's partially collapsed, with a sagging roof and a whole wall gone, the charred insides exposed to wind and rain. There's no way Cleo found those letters in here. Nothing survived this fire intact.

She circles around to the other side to find the other wing of the house. The walls are crumbling, ivy slowly pulling apart the bricks, but there's no fire damage on this side, only the damage of time.

She's spent so much of these last few weeks absorbed with burned buildings that it feels normal to find a blackened shell in the woods. But this is different; she checked before she left the house, and despite all her research into local unsolved fires, The Old Manor wasn't on their list. Her research was thorough, and it's the right era: right in the middle of the 1980s. It should have come up in her initial searches: she wouldn't have missed it. Unless Spider removed it from their list, which doesn't make sense.

She finds a broken window and climbs inside, careful not to catch herself on the shards of broken glass. It's creepy inside, smelly and damp. Something tells her Cleo's been here, even though this place is fit for nothing but demolition.

She checks the ground floor, opens cupboards and peeks behind doors. She's reluctant to touch anything and dirty her clothes. Off the living room, one door won't open and another leads to a study with an ancient carved desk. There's so much stuff here, she notes with surprise. The whole house is crammed. As if no one returned after the firefighters doused the blaze decades ago.

She's about to force the stuck door when she hears a creak from above. Her heart starts to pound, and her skin goes clammy. 'Hello?' she calls, but there's no reply. If Cleo's here, surely she would respond? 'Cleo?' Nothing.

She looks for a weapon, something she can hold.

She picks up a kerosene lamp, heavy and cold in her hands. A potential bludgeon. She doesn't want to use it, but she feels better carrying its chilly weight.

She steps lightly on the treads of the stairs. In comparison to the burned-out wing, this part of the house is remarkably intact. There are signs of leaks, some mould and peeling wallpaper, but other than that, it's like a messy family went out for the day. Like she could turn a corner at any moment and find someone sitting in an armchair, watching her. Behind every door and inside every cupboard is the possibility of someone hiding, or something hidden. She can't imagine why Cleo might come here.

At the far end of the landing, the walls creep black with soot. She imagines one of the family standing in that corridor, back to the raging fire, staring at her, begging her to help as the flames consume that part of the house.

She turns away with a shudder. A door stands ajar, a beam of morning light projected across the thin rug that runs along the corridor.

The room is empty, and she releases a huge breath. It's a child's bedroom, with a rocking horse, a little dressing table with trifold mirrors, and on the bed there's a toy clown, its face burned off.

Jamie walks to the bed and stares at the clown. There's something so unsettling about the destruction of a toy.

The single bed is covered in a hand-knitted patchwork quilt, squares about the size of a man's open hand, sewn together with thick yellow wool. It's stylish and would be fashionable now, although she can tell in this case it was made with wool remnants to be thrifty. There's a threadbare rag rug on the floor, and an old shipping trunk at the foot of the bed.

The door slams closed behind her, trapping her in the room. With a shriek, she throws the clown on the bed and turns to face the exit. Her heart stops. It must be the wind. It must be the wind.

This wall is covered in graffiti. Big, bulbous letters shaded and wrought in what looks like charcoal. *Tony… is dead.* As untouched as this house appears, others found it first. She shivers. Others wandered in and out of these rooms after the fire, just like her.

She grips the oil lamp harder and pauses to listen to the sounds of the house shifting around her.

What happened to Tony, whose bedroom this once was? Why did he leave all this stuff behind? They probably couldn't sell such a fire-wrecked house, but there must have been insurance money. Perhaps he found it easier to just leave it all behind, start a new life.

Jamie pauses, staring closer at the graffitied walls. *I won't say a word*, reads the scrawled charcoal writing. This whole house gives her the creeps. She doesn't want to be here any longer.

As she shifts, she hears a noise in the room with her, a thump of flesh against wood. This is a distinctly human sound, a body moving, skin against wood. It's distinct from the noises of a shifting house, or wind in the trees outside. Jamie grimaces in fear.

Her sweaty palm slides on the oil lamp. There's someone in the wardrobe.

She steps forward, the lamp raised above her head. And then she flings open the door, ready to fight. But there, curled up in the bottom of the wardrobe, her eyes screwed shut and her hands clamped over her ears, is Cleo. She's crying and shivering.

'Cleo! It's me, it's Jamie.' She places a hand on Cleo's shoulder.

Cleo flinches away, as if it takes a moment for her to reassure herself it's really Jamie. Curled up like this, her cheeks wet with tears, Cleo looks like the little sister who begged Jamie to act out scenes from their favourite Disney movies long after Jamie felt too grown-up.

Jamie feels a surge of love for her little sister, so spiky and sarcastic now she's a teenager. She used to be so sweet, so loving. Cleo is the baby of the family, the one who would suck her thumb and cry at the end of *Dumbo* just like everyone else. And then suspension from school, the poor girl who needs minor surgery to repair the tendons in her hand.

The whole family brushed off her recent change in character with a shrug, and a muttered *'teenagers'*, *'hormones'*, or a whispered *'divorce'*. There's always been a spiky side to Cleo, a tendency to tell tall tales. But this isn't just hormones, or the occasional white lie. This is something bigger, something darker. She needs more attention than a shrug. Cleo needs help.

'Poor Cleo,' whispers Jamie, and holds out her arms for her little sister.

Cleo looks at her from the wardrobe, and Jamie's ready for a big reunion hug, but it doesn't come. Instead, Cleo regards her with a blank stare for a moment. 'Well, get out of the way then. I can't get out of this bloody wardrobe if you block the door.'

Deflated, Jamie's shoulders sag and she drops her arms to her sides. She steps back and Cleo tumbles out, all legs and arms and a couple of shoes that fall out with her.

'I need to text Mum, let her know you're safe.' Jamie gets her phone out of her pocket, but Cleo places a hand on her arm, shakes her head.

'Not yet.'

'What are you doing here?' Jamie asks, putting her phone back in her pocket. She'll text in a minute. Cleo needs her attention.

'I could ask you the same question.' Cleo sniffs. 'You know why I'm here. I needed to get away from Mum and Ant.'

Jamie resists rolling her eyes. 'And your plan was what? To hang out here, foraging from the forest until you're too old for boarding school?'

'Just make them worry enough that they realise what a bad idea it is.' She pauses, her body still. 'I just want Mum to care about me, like she used to. To tell me I can stay.'

Jamie swallows the lump which gathers in her throat. 'Do you even want to stay, though? Doesn't seem like you're very happy.'

'Of course I'm not *happy*. But you'll probably move out

soon, and I don't want to leave Mum on her own with *him*.' She practically spits as she says that final word.

Jamie shrugs. 'Fair enough.'

'How did you find me, anyway?'

Jamie reaches into her coat pocket and pulls out the envelope, the letters tucked back into its folds.

Cleo's eyes light up. 'You found them! Aren't they amazing? So romantic.'

Cleo takes the stack of letters from Jamie and unties the ribbon, letting it fall from her fingers as she fumbles with the letters, their paper so thin. The big envelope slips from Cleo's knee and onto the floor.

'Be careful.' Jamie stoops to pick up the large envelope, the one that housed all the other letters for so many years. She opens it to check inside. 'Oh, wait – there's more writing.' There's spidery handwriting scrawled all over the insides.

Jamie holds the envelope wide so Cleo can see.

'I can't read what it says.' Cleo grabs it, hooking her index finger under the bottom flap and the desiccated glue crunches as she wrenches it apart.

Jamie winces. 'Wait, slow down. You don't know what's in there, what you might destroy.'

Cleo rolls her eyes but changes her movements, unpicking the envelope's seams, meticulous in her efforts not to tear the paper. She unfolds the yellowed envelope and flattens it out onto the patchwork blanket, then looks up at Jamie, confused.

'They've written on the inside of the envelope!'

'It's another letter.'

To my baby,

If I knew then what I know now, I would have burned these letters without ever opening them.

This cloying control is not love. He maybe thought it was at first, as I did. But the sweetness quickly curdled into resentment, force and isolation, a punch and a shove when I was not the meek pet he thought he was promised.

It looks like romance. But it is not.

Of one thing I am certain: he will never touch you. I would kill him first.

Ness

'Oh my God.' Jamie's skin is cold, the damp of the house soaking into her clothes.

'Oh shiiit,' Cleo mumbles, her mouth open.

Jamie frowns, looks over at her. 'What?'

Cleo stands and walks to the mirror, picks up the photograph and holds it out to Jamie. 'This is them. The family who lived here.' She points at the picture, her finger hovering over the woman's face. She's shielding her eyes from the sun, a shadow cast over her eyes. But her mouth is smiling. 'She wrote this. She's Vanessa.'

Her eyes flick to the man, leaning against the railing of the bandstand. He looks so charming, his arm around his wife, a smile on his face. It's all a lie, a pretence at being a normal human. He goes to work, shakes people's hands, talks about his family as if everything is normal and good. And yet years of charm and calculation. Then violence and fear.

'Hello?'

A man's voice from below, and a clunk reverberates up the stairs as boots clamber in through the window.

Jamie grabs Cleo, a small shriek escaping from her lips. 'We should hide.' The footsteps start to climb the stairs and Jamie leaps to her feet, wrenches open the wardrobe doors. 'We shouldn't be here. Quick, get inside.'

But Cleo stays on the bed, a big grin on her face.

'For God's sake, Cleo.' Jamie reaches out and grabs her arm, trying to pull her to her feet.

The footsteps grow louder by the moment.

'Hi, Lucasz!' Cleo shouts.

Jamie bends double in relief, her hands on her knees, gathering her breath once more. 'You could have said.'

Cleo grins and shrugs at her. 'We're in the bedroom,' she calls out.

Lucasz bustles in, so tall he has to stoop so as not to bump his head on the doorframe. He gives Jamie a small smile; always shy, but such a sweet boy. He brings with him the clean smell of spring from the woods, a bright contrast with the musty odour inside the house. 'Anyone lose this?' He holds up a black woolly glove. 'I found it outside, near the broken window.'

They shake their heads.

He frowns. 'Someone's been here. It's new since our last visit.'

They're all quiet for a moment, listening. The house is silent except for their breathing.

'We found a new letter.' Cleo thrusts the unfolded envelope at Lucasz. 'The dad was a wife-beater.'

'What?' Lucasz takes the letter and skims it before handing it back to Cleo.

'Isolation, it says.' Cleo points. 'Like Ant not letting Mum see Tina. And sending me away. Isolating her.' She shakes her head, her fists balled at her sides. 'It explains what I found in the basement.'

'There's a basement?' Jamie and Lucasz ask at the same time.

Jamie doesn't want to be here anymore, in this charred house of pain and fear. But Cleo pulls a key from her pocket and unlocks the door, then runs down the steps to show them what she's found. Cleo is different now she's got company, a wild contrast to the huddled, tear-stained child hiding in the wardrobe. It must be the presence of others; her superior knowledge of the house, as if it's hers, has given her a javelin-throw of bravery.

Cleo stands in the centre of the dank basement, gesturing towards the corner of the room, under the stairs.

It looks like a dog bed, nestled into the corner. A big pile of blankets, about five of them all stacked on top of each other to create a pseudo-mattress a few inches deep. There's a pit worn into the middle, where the dog slept.

But why would your dog sleep in the basement? Why not in the kitchen, or even in a kennel in the back garden? Daisy sleeps on Cleo's bed.

Jamie steps forward again, and this time raises her hand to cover her mouth. She swallows, keenly aware of the disgust roiling in her stomach.

Deep in the corner, almost invisible even in the beam of her phone torch, is a pair of handcuffs attached to a metal chain embedded in the wall. Handcuffs.

Still, though, her brain doesn't quite make the connection. Until… you can't handcuff a dog.

Someone imprisoned a human down here.

Lucasz folds his arms, his shoulders hunched as if trying to make himself smaller. 'I dunno, maybe it's not as bad as we think?'

Both girls turn to him. Jamie hopes he can offer an

explanation which stops her skin crawling and her hair standing on end. Cleo looks defiant, her head tilted and chin jutting, challenging him to come up with an alternative narrative.

'Maybe they had a dog? Like, this was its bedroom?'

Jamie shivers and looks away. 'More likely the woman who wrote that letter.' She mutters. 'Her punishment for not being… what did she write? His "meek pet".' It's a pitiful little prison. Horrifying; grey and bleak, so cruel. She can't believe a human being could treat someone like that, could tie them up and treat them worse than she could imagine even treating an animal. And with a child in the house, too. What kind of impact would an upbringing somewhere like this have on a small child?

She climbs the steps up to the ground floor. 'I can't stay down here any longer. Come on, guys, we need to leave. It's not safe in here.'

Cleo runs up the stairs to grab her stuff, and Jamie listens to the ceiling's creaks as she moves around on the top floor.

Lucasz gives Jamie a small smile, making brief eye contact.

'Let's wait outside. She'll know where we've gone.' She doesn't wait for his answer, climbing through the window and out into the woods with a huge feeling of relief. She hadn't realised how much tension she was holding throughout her body, screwing her shoulder muscles tighter and tighter the longer they stayed inside. She strides away from the house, into a patch of sunshine and lets the light warm her, seeping into her bones. She takes a breath of the fresh air and clears the dust from her lungs with a hearty cough.

Moments later, Cleo tumbles from the window, all legs and arms, and crosses the grass to join them. She throws herself to the ground and stretches her legs out in front of her, tipping her toes back and forth. She points to the shed, set back a little way from the house. 'That's how we found the place: it was on fire and Lucasz saw the smoke.'

Jamie looks up at the charred wing of the manor, her gaze settling on the green weeds poking through the cracked brickwork. The main house hasn't been alight for decades.

'The shed was burning. The day of the wedding. It went out pretty quickly.'

Jamie tries to process what Cleo just said, peering at the scorch marks around the base. A fresh fire just a couple of weeks ago, at a house which burned down in the Eighties.

Cleo inhales. 'It's nice to be in the fresh air. The smell in there was almost as bad as our house when Ant's home.'

Jamie shakes her head, filing everything away to think about later. 'It's been pretty tense lately.'

Cleo stands and shoulders her backpack. The letters are poking out of Cleo's coat pocket, Jamie notices. 'You know he's taken over all the bank accounts? Says he wants Mum to be able to give up work. And she's signed the house over to him.' She picks up a big stick and whips at the bushes as they enter the woods, walking away from the house.

Jamie's footsteps slow. 'Why would she do that?' she asks.

Lucasz clears his throat. 'He's just winding you up, Clee. What if he knows you're reading that stupid book about unhealthy relationships and he's giving you clues to make you paranoid.'

Cleo stops and turns to face him, the stick held in both hands now like a baseball bat. The air changes, becomes still. The wind dies for a moment. 'It's not a stupid book.'

Lucasz and Jamie stop walking.

There's a flicker of wariness on Lucasz's face as he looks at

Cleo, but he quashes it and smiles. 'He's a dick, but I don't think he's evil.'

Cleo's shoulders loosen and she swipes at a bush again.

As they walk on, Jamie flicks a glance to Lucasz, whose face has its normal, relaxed, faraway gaze again. 'Why would he take all the money?' Jamie asks.

Cleo links arms with Jamie. 'He wants control, I've been trying to tell you. He wants me gone, her to give up her job, no more friends, the house is his, the money is his. He wants you to move out. He's taking away everything she ever had.' She punctuates her speech, whacking at the bushes as she walks past. 'I can't get sent away; I can't leave her alone with him. We're not far from Mum being chained up in the basement.'

Jamie has seen them laughing and happy, holding hands. Ant brings Mum flowers, takes her out for dinner, makes her smile. But Cleo's right when she says it always seems a little too saccharine and sickly. Like something forced. He moved in, told her he loved her, proposed, and they got married; all so fast. As badly as Cleo has handled everything, Jamie can see something in what she says. *The sweetness quickly curdled*, the letter said. Something about that line really resonates.

'I just need some evidence she can't deny. You know?' Cleo throws her stick into the trees with a clatter. 'Something to prove to Mum how awful he is. I wish she could hear some of the things he says to me when she can't hear.'

Jamie feels a surge of frustration and impulsiveness. She's fed up with Cleo's desperate entreaties for attention as she repeats the same arguments. It's time for this to be over, one way or another. 'Okay. You win. Let's find out how dangerous he really is.'

Cleo stops walking and drops Jamie's arm. 'What do you mean?'

'I have all this recording equipment just sitting around, not doing anything. Spider brought it back yesterday. And we have a little budget left over.'

Cleo looks confused. 'What about it?'

'You said you want evidence, right? That he's not a good man.'

Cleo's eyes are wide, her mouth open with shock. She looks close to tears. 'I don't... Jamie, what?'

Lucasz stares at Jamie as if she's gone insane. He has grasped what Cleo hasn't yet. 'You're going to bug your house?' he asks, incredulous.

'We're going to bug the house.'

Chapter Fourteen

Cleo

L ow voices filter through the kitchen door. Cleo steps loudly so they know she's coming; she wants them to think she's more mature than to eavesdrop. She can listen to them whenever she likes now, even if she won't bother most of the time. They're probably talking about when to take the bins out and what to have for dinner.

As she opens the door the voices stop, Mum and Ant look up at her from the dining table, empty cereal bowls and a half-drunk cafetière of coffee between them. Mum smiles at her, but Ant places his spoon in his bowl and glowers.

Cleo smiles at them both. 'Good morning. Mind if I join you?' She can't help but check the dresser, a flick of her eyes to the side. She can't see the small camera hiding behind the decorative plate. There's another in the living room, both with microphones. Jamie had some money left from the documentary fund, so she bought three little ones, like baby monitors but for house security.

'Very formal.' Mum laughs. 'Of course you can join us. It's your house too.'

Not if Ant gets his way, Cleo would have said before, but now she bites her tongue and pulls out a chair, her back to the camera. 'I wanted to apologise.'

Ant barely suppresses a snort, but Mum doesn't notice. Cleo glances at him to show she heard him but wills herself not to narrow her eyes at him in a glare.

'Cleo, it's not as easy—'

She holds out a hand to stop Mum. 'Can I talk for a minute?'

Mum blinks a yes and lifts her coffee cup to her lips.

Cleo musters up every dredge of acting skill and humility and sits up straight in her chair. 'I agree with you both that my behaviour hasn't been great over the past few months, and I'm really sorry for that. I have found it difficult to have a new adult in the house, and I've been acting badly because of that.' She swallows. She can't give Ant everything he wants.

She flicks him a glance, and then looks back to Mum, who has a wary expression on her face. 'It's not because I want you and Dad to get back together, even though I understand why you might think that. I want you and Dad to be happy, and I understand that couldn't happen when you were married.' She likes that line; Jamie helped her hone that one in whispers while they set up the equipment late last night after Mum and Ant went to bed.

Mum's eyebrows lift high on her forehead, her lips pressed together. She looks like she's waiting for an unexpected blow, and Cleo's pleased she's not going to deliver one.

'I want to be better. I know it doesn't undo anything, but hopefully I can show you I've grown up a bit.' She smiles at

Mum and flicks her eyes to Ant, pretending the smile is for him too.

He shakes his head, a movement so small that it looks almost like a tremor, but Cleo sees. A player can spot a player. Game recognises game.

But Mum beams, her eyes shining. 'I'm really proud of you, baby.' She grabs Ant's hand and looks to him for agreement. Mum's smile wavers as she realises he's not quite won over.

Ant shifts in his chair, moves away from Mum. Withdrawing from her, just like *Happily Ever After* says abusers do when they don't get their way.

Mum shifts closer to him, narrowing the gap he's created. 'Ant?'

'A few empty words over breakfast won't change anything overnight,' he mutters.

Mum frowns and puts her hand on his arm as if to stop him. He shakes her off and stands, picking up the bowls and carrying them to the sink.

Cleo bristles, but keeps a neutral expression. She won't let him provoke her. Jamie warned her: if Ant's as calculating as they think he is, he wants her to react. Everything he does is designed to provoke Cleo, to make her look bad while he appears to be the victim of her wrath.

Part of Cleo's plan includes strenuous efforts not to play into his hands. She sits up straighter. Cleo can play a game too. She pulls a bowl towards her and pours cereal. 'Of course. I know nothing can change overnight. But I'd like to try.'

She watches as Ant places their bowls on the counter and moves away without loading them inside the dishwasher. Mum's always annoyed that everyone expects the 'dishwasher fairies' to load it up for them. Cleo waits a moment until Ant's hand touches the doorknob.

'Don't worry about the dishes, guys. I'll load the dishwasher before I go out later.'

Mum coos with happiness, but Ant stops in his tracks, his back to them, shoulders high and tense. He turns back to face the table, tall and glowering as they look up at him from the breakfast table. Cleo sets her face into the most innocent expression she can muster: clear forehead, eyes wide.

'Go out later?'

She keeps her face blank. It's very difficult not to smile.

Mum coughs. 'Where are you going, love?'

Ant grasps the back of a dining chair, his knuckles white. 'You're grounded. That hasn't changed.'

Cleo looks at Mum and measures her tone. Soft, entreating. Almost asking for permission, but not quite. 'Lucasz and I are researching for a history project at the library.' Not a lie.

Ant's knuckles go whiter. Then Mum and Ant speak at the same time:

'Be back by three,' says Mum.

'Grounded is grounded,' says Ant.

They look at each other, the air crackling with tension. This is interesting, a nice little bonus of the plan. It seems when not united against Cleo, they are pitted against each other.

Cleo will remember this.

Jamie

Jamie wakes late, and lies in bed staring at the ceiling, listening to the rumble of voices in the kitchen below. She's surprised but impressed that Cleo's up so early, starting the plan she has named Operation: Dirtbag. Cleo's first self-appointed mission is to persuade Mum that she's turned a new leaf, while letting Ant relax and think he's won. To let down his guard, then Cleo will catch it all on tape.

If she's right.

Jamie has always been the type of person who can see both perspectives, examining a situation from all sides: what if Cleo is correct, and Ant is waging a cold war of attrition aimed at the isolation and control of their mum? If that's right, they need to act, and fast. Like it says in Cleo's book: women try to leave an abusive relationship seven times before they are successful and leaving is the most dangerous time for them. Jamie and Cleo need to protect Mum even if she doesn't realise she needs protecting.

And the other perspective: what if Ant is just a kind, misjudged man who loves Mum and wants her to be happy? Meanwhile his new stepdaughters wage a campaign to discredit him, spy on him in his own home and ruin his new marriage.

Then there's Cleo. It's probably just normal teenage hormones in combination with a new family situation, but she has been acting differently since the school suspended her. Much more erratic, heedless of the consequences of her actions. Almost self-destructive. It's worrying, and Jamie does understand why Ant and Mum would consider a change for her, something to give her more discipline and direction, for her own good as well as the peace of the house.

But no matter what, Jamie just wants her sister to be okay, and right now it doesn't seem like she is. So the current plan is win-win for everyone: while Cleo's on her best behaviour, there's peace in the house, which makes everyone happy, especially Mum. Jamie hears it in her voice reverberating up from the kitchen, a chirpy, sing-song sound she hasn't heard in months. She pulls her quilt up to her shoulders and snuggles into her pillow.

And Cleo feels supported, with an ally in Jamie. Jamie will listen to the plotting and contribute ideas of how to be nice to Ant to put him at his ease.

Her eyes wander to her laptop on her desk, where she can view the camera feeds any time day or night. She must make sure the cameras remain hidden. That part of the plan is a little uncomfortable, but it's not like they're in the bedroom or the bathrooms. That would be too far, even for Cleo.

Jamie's phone buzzes, and she picks it up from her bedside table. Ten missed calls. She groans. Spider.

She's got voicemails and texts too. She drops her arm to the bed, letting the phone fall from her hand.

A huge wave of doubt lurks in her chest. She doesn't know if she did the right thing. She misses him so much that her collarbones ache. She feels stripped back, like a layer of her skin has been peeled off, leaving her open and vulnerable to the world. But it was the right decision, it had to be. Who knows how far Spider would go to get this documentary footage?

She misses him presenting her with a cup of tea in the morning when she stays over at his house, eager for her approval and affection in return. And he got it; she still cares for him, but she couldn't ignore the prickles of doubt she felt in response to his ruthless drive to make the documentary, exposing people's grief and pain like that, with no sympathy.

But does she miss Spider, or the *idea* of him? At first she loved his drive and focus, thought it sexy that he had such ambition and motivation. She wanted to be more like him, to impress him, and to succeed alongside him. So she dove into preparing for the documentary, thinking about story boards, research, arcs, and interview technique. She loved it, felt like they could make a difference to the case – uncover the truth of who set those fires, their gathered footage revealing clues that lead to an arrest. They would be heroes.

But then filming began, the stables caught fire, and suddenly for Spider it's not about investigating cold cases anymore. They're attending live fires, still burning. Her plan and their research mean nothing, and the project isn't hers anymore. He's taken it and shaped it into something different.

She doesn't want to exploit people's pain, probe their unhealed wounds, and force them to pick their scabs in front of her and bleed for the camera. And when she looks over at Spider to check how he feels, she sees no remorse or hesitation. In his eyes she sees the glow of excitement, almost lust.

She doesn't want that. She feels her ambition crumbling and there's nothing else to cling to. And most of all she doesn't want to hand over control and direction to someone else: this is Jamie's documentary, her future career. Who would she be without this project? A university drop-out with a part-time job in the cinema of a crumbling old seaside town, still living at home in her twenties.

Her phone buzzes again. She switches it to silent and pulls the quilt over her head.

Cleo

At first, she doesn't recognise him. In her mind Lucasz is still the kid she met on their first day of secondary school, a thick bowl cut sliced across his forehead, teeth too large for his face, sleeves too long for his arms.

But today an almost-grown man stands outside the library, leaning against the bike racks. The kind of guy she'd glance at from the corner of her eye as she walked past, too shy to look directly at him. He's grown into his sleeves now, with arms almost too long for the rest of his body. His sandy hair is tousled and wavy. He taps his foot, moves his shoulders a little bit to the music that pipes from his headphones as he stares into space, waiting for Cleo.

As she moves closer, he turns and sees her approach, and his face breaks into a wide smile, teeth still too large for his face. There's the Lucasz she knows. Her body relaxes. He's still her geeky little friend, nothing more.

'Hey!' He pulls his earbuds from his ears and rolls them up into his pocket. He pushes off from the bike racks and strides towards the wheelchair ramp at the main entrance.

She has to take two steps to every one of his long strides.

'Ready to work out what happened to the people who lived in that house?'

'We don't normally let people use the microfilm unless they know exactly what they're looking for.' The librarian is obviously not used to teenagers coming in to do anything other than look up porn on the ancient library PCs. 'Do you have a particular edition of the *Gazette* you'd like to review? An issue number?'

Cleo glances at Lucasz, who wears the smarmy smile that he reserves for grown-ups. She resists the temptation to poke him in the ribs and ruin his 'perfect kid' act.

To her surprise, he pulls a notebook from his back pocket and flips it open. 'We'd like to review issues of the local papers from a range of dates, as we're not sure what date this might have been reported on. So the *Moorburn Bay Evening News*, the *Yorkshire Post* and the *Abbeywick Gazette*... from,' he flips a page, 'from...' His voice fades.

The librarian unfolds her arms, her unimpressed expression melting as she watches Lucasz consulting his notebook. She's clearly got a soft spot for studious boys. 'The microfilm comes in rolls covering a couple of months for the daily publications. Do you have any idea of what you're looking for here? It might take you some time, with that number of papers and no clear date range.'

Lucasz pockets his notebook again and puts on his best smile. 'There was a fire in July 1986, and we're interested in the investigation over the following months. Anything from July 1986 to the end of the year. Is that possible, please?'

Cleo darts him a smile, impressed. He used to mumble and falter in the face of adults, but now he talks to them like they're equals.

The librarian shuffles off and comes back with a selection of reels which look like the old film you used to put in cameras. She shows Lucasz how to load one into the machine, pointedly ignoring Cleo.

'You'll have to scroll through everything, I'm afraid. Nothing is indexed. Hope you find what you're looking for. Whatever that is.' She shrugs and makes as if to walk away, but then turns back at the last minute, staring hard at Cleo. 'Don't touch the lens.'

Cleo raises her eyebrows at Lucasz.

The library is so quiet that she can hear the blood rushing around inside her ears. It's too hot, and her body itches to move.

'It's like we're in a film,' she whispers to him, giggling.

'An old film. This is a cool machine.' He pats the side of the microfilm reader as it whirs to life, surprisingly noisy in the silent library. He turns the wheel to run through a projection on the old, boxy blurred contraption. Cleo swings on her chair, staring at the other library users. An overweight guy with a stain on his T-shirt sits at the next bank of desks, checking over his shoulder to make sure no one can see his screen. As he catches her gaze, Cleo points at her own eyes and then to him: *I'm watching you.* He packs up and leaves pretty fast. She stifles a giggle.

Next to her, Lucasz is quiet, the only sound the whirr of the machine. The muscle running along his forearm flexes as his fingers turn the reels. Finally, his body stills, and his breath speeds up. He's found something.

'Woah, Cleo. Check this out.' He steps to the side, letting Cleo see the article.

The image accompanying the article is fuzzy and black and white, but shows a family of three: Dad wearing thick-lensed glasses which magnify his eyes, Mum half-smiling and their child between them, face blurred for anonymity. But Cleo knows it's the same kid from the picture in the house.

'It's their trip to Moorburn Bay.' Cleo hops up and down in her seat. She feels like a detective.

Lucasz frowns. 'Read the rest of it. It's not pretty.'

Tragedy at The Old Manor: Vanessa and George Kerr perish in fire
19 August 1986

Image copyright NORTH YORKSHIRE POLICE
Image caption: The family in Moorburn Bay, 1985. George

Kerr and his wife Vanessa died in a house fire in July 1986. Their child survived with only smoke inhalation.

NO ARRESTS have been made over a house fire which killed a mother and father in Langdale last month, leaving behind their orphaned pre-teen.

George and Vanessa Kerr died at their home in Langdale Manor, Langdale on 10 July 1986, police said.

The child, who cannot be named for legal reasons, was in the house at the time of the fire, but managed to escape through a first floor window. The child will make a full recovery and is assisting police with their enquiries.

North Yorkshire Police officers made no arrests relating to the deaths of Mrs Kerr, 55, and her husband George, 60.

The cause of the fire is inconclusive, although investigations are continuing. North Yorkshire Police are looking for anyone who saw anything suspicious in the area on or before that date and would particularly like to speak to a man wearing dark clothing seen walking along Langdale Lane in the Abbeywick direction at around 9.30pm that evening.

She finishes reading, and looks at Lucasz, eyes wide. 'Their kid survived.'

Lucasz nods. 'The house belongs to someone.'

'Dead Tony.' Cleo swallows, remembering what she thought were footsteps that night she slept there. The fire in the shed, the timber stacked against it like a bonfire. 'Do you think he goes back there? To visit the place his parents died?' She shudders, hugging herself.

Behind them, someone clears their throat.

They turn, startled, to find the librarian standing there, arms folded. 'Are you finished with the microfilm?'

Lucasz nods. 'I think so. Thank you. It's been really helpful.'

'If you want a photocopy of any articles it's 10p per sheet.'

'No thanks,' Cleo says, holding her phone up to the display and snapping a shot of the article. 'We've got everything we need.'

The librarian's cheeks flush and she narrows her eyes, but clearly decides against arguing.

'Want to come for dinner at mine?' asks Cleo on the way out of the library. 'We can tell Jamie we've got more stuff for her documentary.'

Chapter Fifteen

Jamie

As soon as she opens the front door, something seems different about the house. It feels warmer, somehow, the atmosphere lifted from the chilly tension of recent months.

She steps into the hallway and listens for a moment as she removes her shoes, sticky with spilled fizzy drinks and encrusted with popcorn dust from all day behind the cinema counter. She hangs up her jacket on a hook by the door. There's a rumble of contented voices from the kitchen. Ordinarily she'd go straight upstairs and wash the sweaty cinema out of her hair, but today she wants to join in the family time, hoping this signals the dawn of a new era in their house. It would be so nice.

Cleo is sitting at the dining table with Lucasz opposite, playing some elaborate and fast card game that involves slapping their hands on the table as hard as possible when they run out of cards. They're chattering away to each other, having a great time.

Mum and Ant are cooking together in the kitchen area. There's a song on the radio and they're both moving with the music, humming.

Jamie stops in the doorway and watches for a moment. Ant places a hand on Mum's hip as he shimmies past her on his way to turn on a hob ring. Mum catches his eye and smiles up at him. They look happy.

'What's the song?' She hasn't heard it before, but she quite likes it.

'"Ace of Base".' Mum's shoulders bop in time to the beat. 'This was a hit when I was a teenager. They played it all the time at the amusement arcade on the seafront. And I remember sneaking into the pub before I was old enough to drink and putting it on the jukebox.'

Ant laughs. 'I must have been about the same age, but I didn't sneak into pubs. It was more likely to be on the radio while I poked around with motorbike engines in Fred's garage.'

'Ooh, you had a motorbike? I would have been so impressed,' says Mum, her tone lighter than Jamie's heard for a while.

'Wow, motorbikes and underage drinking. Now it's all organic farm shops and antiques fairs.' Jamie laughs. 'Never get old, Cleo.'

Cleo sniggers. '*Browsing* at antiques fairs, which is even worse! You never even buy anything.' She grins at Mum.

'Us oldies have got to get our kicks somewhere.' She reduces the radio volume and turns to Cleo. 'Packed your bag for Dad's? It's two nights this time, remember?'

'Yep!' Cleo and Lucasz exchange an incomprehensible look.

Mum holds out a bottle of wine to offer Jamie a glass. She nods yes.

'How's your day been?' asks Ant, as he chops onions into small cubes. 'Been out filming with Spider?'

She takes her wine to the table and sits next to Lucasz, who smells faintly of aftershave. Jamie resists the urge to tease him. 'Not today. I've just been at work.'

Ant slides the onion into the frying pan with a loud sizzle. 'Haven't seen Spider around here for a while.'

Jamie takes a slurp of wine and doesn't answer.

'Jamie?' Mum says. 'Ant's talking to you.'

'He didn't ask anything,' Cleo mumbles, too quietly for Mum and Ant to hear over the frying onions. Lucasz frowns at her, shakes his head to remind her she's supposed to be nice to Ant. She gives him a nod.

'I haven't seen Spider for a while either,' she says reluctantly. 'We're taking a break.'

'Oh, Jamie. Why didn't you tell me?' Mum drops her tea towel on the counter and crosses to Jamie's side, putting a hand on her shoulder. 'Are you OK? What happened? You made such a lovely couple.'

Cleo laughs. 'Yeah, his tattoos really matched your eyes.'

Lucasz hides his giggles behind a fake cough.

Jamie glares at her across the table. She hesitates, feeling everyone's eyes on her, watching her. Her cheeks grow hot. 'I don't feel like talking about it right now, okay?'

Mum squeezes her shoulder and returns to cooking. Jamie leans back in her chair, resting her feet on the strip of wood that runs along the centre of the dining table base.

'What about your documentary?' Ant asks, clearly ignoring her request not to talk about it. 'You'll still be working on it, right? That fire up at Langdale Stables is calling your name. It's like the arsonist wants to be caught.'

Mum frowns at him and shakes her head slightly, but he's

not looking, his gaze focused on the chicken breasts he's slicing into strips.

She shrugs, pinching the skin on her arm between her fingers until it turns white. 'I think they call it creative differences.'

'Woah, don't be hasty.' He crosses to the sink, runs his hands under the hot tap. 'What about the theatre, that poor girl who died? She deserves some justice, don't you think? You said it yourself when we first talked: you want to showcase the victims, not the perpetrator. Your idea has the potential; you shouldn't give up so easily.'

Jamie puts her head in her hands and rubs the heels of her palms into her eyes. 'I don't know right now. He wanted to ditch the old stuff and focus on recent fires like the stables.'

He looks up, stares at her across the kitchen. 'What a shame, Jamie. This project could be your future. A direction to head in, at least.' He doesn't even notice Jamie's distress, just carries on. 'I just want you to be successful. I thought this was your dream. I dreamed of working in television and I got there, and if I'd let anyone else's plans get in my way or derail me, I wouldn't be where I am today. Your relationship with Spider shouldn't dictate your success like this.'

Jamie groans. There's a tightness in her chest and she tries to breathe through it, ignore the quiet roar blooming inside her with Ant's every word.

She had a direction and now she's lost it. She doesn't need Ant to 'helpfully' point that out. She slaps a palm on the table, signalling for him to stop.

Cleo and Lucasz stop their game, reacting to the new tension in the room. 'What's going on?' Cleo asks.

Ant walks to the sink and rinses the knife under the tap, his movements slow and careful. There's a cold knot of dread in Jamie's stomach.

'You have an investor you need to keep happy. You made a commitment.' He tries to make it sound like he's joking but he's clearly not.

'I'm thinking about what to do next.'

'You and Spider need to work through your little tiff. It's not a good look, giving up at the first hurdle like this. And not for the first time.'

She looks up, her eyebrows pulled down in a frown. Why won't he just drop it? 'No offence, Ant, but what does it matter to you whether I make the documentary or not? I'm grateful you got us started, but I can use the equipment for another documentary any time; it doesn't have to be this one.'

'You've invested your time and resources in this one. You've conducted interviews, done research. It sounded promising.'

She stares at him. 'I'm not giving up. I just need a break.' She stops. She doesn't owe an explanation of her relationship to Ant.

He shrugs. 'You sound like a quitter, Jamie. When you're so close to a breakthrough.'

Mum says his name, but he shakes his head, ignores her.

'Don't call me a quitter. We've got a lot of good footage already. I'm going to edit, see what I can make of it. And I own all the equipment so I could even start making something new on my own.'

Ant's shaking his head and makes a *hmmm* sound before he starts talking. 'It's not a good idea to have your career dreams rely on a relationship, especially if it's early days.' He points a knife at her as he talks, waving it around like a conductor at an orchestra.

She grits her teeth against this onslaught of unsolicited advice. He's totally tone-deaf, this guy.

'Relying on others for your own success is the route to failure, in my opinion. You need to be independent, rely only on yourself. What are you going to do if Spider refuses to let you be involved in the next phase because you had a bad breakup? If he locks you out of your shared files because he's angry? Or because he wants to take control of the project? Your project.' He shakes his head. 'This isn't good planning, Jamie.'

She can't focus on the conversation anymore. She's too distracted by what Ant just said. *If he locks you out of your shared files.* 'I don't need your advice on this, thanks.'

Mum draws in a breath through her teeth, throws Jamie a warning glance. 'It's dangerous, though. Perhaps Jamie's being sensible, protecting herself from this criminal. You never know what she might uncover.'

'Don't let one pathetic threat with a hoof stop you. It means you're on the right track. You've got 'em scared.'

His brow furrows as he talks, a little speckle of spit on his chin. How does he know about the hoof? Mum's biting her lip. Ah.

'You should go to Spider and work out a way forward. Be professional. Don't let your relationship get in the way. You shouldn't give up on anything once it gets tough. Like your degree. Sounds like you need some staying power.'

'I didn't *want* to quit my degree. You don't know what you're talking about.' She's had enough. She just wants him to shut up.

She puts her head in her hands and mumbles through her fingers: 'Mum, I don't know what you've told him about university and why I dropped out, but it's no one's business but mine and I want you to stop talking about me behind my back.' She stands, the legs of her chair scraping on the floor. At the stables, Catherine was proud of her anger and didn't care if people called her crazy. She just wanted justice for her horses. And all Jamie wants right now is Ant to leave her alone, stop badgering her in front of everyone. 'I can't stand this anymore. Mind your own business, Ant. Shut up.'

Mum inhales through clenched teeth with a *hiss*. 'We don't talk like that in this family, Jamie. We keep our tempers.'

Jamie rolls her eyes at the same line she's heard repeated since before she can remember.

Lucasz's cheeks flush crimson.

'What I do is none of your business, so get off my back, Ant. I can tell you've never had kids because you have no idea how to talk to them.'

Ant looks crestfallen, but it's all an act. He needled and poked at her until she reacted, and now he's won: he can behave like he's hurt by her reaction in front of witnesses. It's just like Cleo said.

Cleo and Lucasz remain frozen over their card game. Cleo's hand hovers over the table, about to place a card on top of a stack. She stares at the table, her eyes wide and eyebrows raised. She looks like she's trying not to burst out laughing.

'Jamie,' Mum growls. 'You apologise to Ant. He cares about you and he is asking out of concern.'

Ant picks up a tea towel and dries his hands. 'No, Ella. Please don't worry. Clearly Jamie has a lot on her mind. We can talk another time if she doesn't want my advice today.' He throws the tea towel onto the counter, and Mum scurries to pick it up and fold it. 'I was just trying to help, but it's clear she isn't ready to hear it.'

'If I want your advice, I will ask for it.'

'Jamie!' Mum slaps the folded tea towel onto the counter. 'He's trying to help.'

'He's not helping. I just broke up with my boyfriend, I don't need a lecture on professionalism. I'm just trying to work out how to be okay right now.' Her voice cracks on the last few words, and her eyes start to prickle with unshed tears. She's mortified that she's about to cry in front of everyone, but again she remembers Catherine, how she owned her emotions and knew she had a right to them. She didn't squash things down like Jamie has tried to her whole life; Catherine feels things and communicates those feelings, owns the mess and the tears and is better for that. Maybe if Jamie had been more like her from the beginning, she'd be graduating from university with a degree right about now.

'Don't get upset.' Mum's trying to soothe now, her voice soft.

Ant scowls at Mum, a warning not to take Jamie's side. Mum flinches.

Jamie stands up. 'For the record, Mum, I can get upset if I want to. Breaking up with Spider is upsetting.'

Mum opens her mouth and closes it again without saying anything.

'Don't tell me what I should and shouldn't feel. I'm so fed up with being told to not get angry, to not react, to not cry, not shout, not feel anything. *Keep your temper, blah blah blah.* It's unhealthy. Repressing everything made me ill.'

'Jamie, no one's telling you what to—'

'Yes, you are. Always. And I need you to stop.' She glances at Cleo, who is watching her with a half-smile of approval. Cleo who has always bucked against Mum's directives of unemotional stiff-upper-lip squashing of feelings. Jamie realises with a sudden rush of emotion that she admires Cleo for her rebellion. She looks back at Mum. 'I've tried so hard to be like you, but I just can't. Uni didn't work, I dropped out, and now I'm trying to fix it, to feel like less of a failure.' She points at Ant. 'He isn't helping.'

At the kitchen door, she turns back to the room, everyone watching her leave. Mum flicks a glance to Ant and then back to Jamie. 'I'm going to be sad for a while. And you're going to let me. And Ant – either I'll keep making a documentary or I'll pay you back the money, but stop asking me about it for one minute so I can get my head straight on my own.'

She closes the door behind her and climbs the stairs to her bedroom, and as she walks upstairs, she hears Cleo giggle. 'Usually it's me making the big scene!'

———

Jamie ignores her stomach rumbling. She's not going back downstairs tonight, not while Mum and Ant are in the kitchen. But she can see on the cameras when they leave the room. She grabs a chocolate bar from her desk drawer and opens her laptop, clicking into the documentary file she shares with Spider. *If he locks you out of your shared files.*

She frowns. Her mouse hovers over a video file she doesn't recognise. The file name reads 'Expert' and it's dated just yesterday.

Her fingers tighten on the mouse. He's filming without her.

She clicks on the file and presses play.

Text flashes up on screen:

Interview with an Arson Expert
Professor Maria Cuevas, Forensic Psychologist, University of Durham

It's a one-on-one interview with a lady in her mid-thirties, long black hair shining under the lights of her office. She sits at a desk with a wall of books behind her, looking slightly off camera at Spider.

In lightly accented English, the professor starts talking. Her expertise is clear in her precise word choices, even though she's speaking in a second language: 'First, we have to think about the victims. Whether or not an arsonist means to hurt other human beings, that often does happen. People die, lose loved ones and their homes. Even while we talk about the arsonists themselves, we should never forget the victims of their crimes.'

Jamie nods along with Maria's words, imagining the b-roll they could play over the top of this: archive footage of people surveying the wreckage of their homes, a clip of Catherine wiping tears from her cheeks with sooty hands... she gets goosebumps just thinking about how good this would be after post-production.

Voice muffled as he's not wearing a mic, Spider interrupts: 'But we also have to ask ourselves why. Why start fires? Why these locations?'

She nods and tucks her shiny hair behind her ear. 'In my opinion there are two types of adult arsonists: those who burn to destroy something, to hide something. To cover up a crime or attempt to get an insurance payout. And then there are the people who set things on fire because they can't help themselves; it's like a compulsion, and I definitely view it as a mental illness, a pathology. These are the types of fires we're looking at here in North Yorkshire, the ones your documentary is investigating.'

'And how do people like that choose their locations? The victims?'

'There's often no discernible target victim unless it's accidental, like in the Theatre Royal. When they're small fires which burn out quickly, it's like the firesetter is trying to get something out of their system and then can move on. We call this type of fire-setting *expressive arson*. I've reviewed your cases and that's what I believe we're looking at here.'

Jamie nods: this is what she read about right when they first started the project. It's exactly what she said to Spider, in the car on their first day of filming. When he said she was excellent and that her words would be much more impactful coming from an expert. And now he's found one. He's pushing Jamie out.

She hears a quiet 'mmhmm' as Spider encourages the psychologist to say more.

'Expressive arsonists, in my opinion, are angry. They use fire as a way of getting that anger out, processing it. They can't help it, it's a compulsion. They can't process extremes of emotion, and eventually it all bursts out and they need to set something alight to cope. That's what I'm seeing here.'

'Do you think our arsonist is a pyromaniac?'

She shakes her head. 'Providing a potential diagnosis is not recommended without meeting the patient. But you're not necessarily dealing with a pyromaniac here.'

'No?' Spider sounds surprised.

'Your arsonist is careful, selective. It's an impulse issue, sure. But it's within their control to an extent. The fires suggest a capacity to make choices.'

'Do you think the locations are important? Or random?'

Jamie sits up on the bed, her face close to the screen.

Maria pauses, looks off away from the camera for a moment while she thinks. 'It's hard to say. In pyromania the act of fire-setting is like a compulsion. For them the location is anywhere they are in the moment. For yours, I feel that part of their compulsion is choosing to burn something significant, an important location to them.'

'And the timings? We're looking at two time periods: a spate of fires in the 1980s, and then some which started up more recently, like the stables. It was in the file I sent over...'

Maria nods. 'Now this is where it gets interesting. If there wasn't such a large gap in time between the two sets of fires, I'd swear they were set by the same person. Matching accelerants in most... and the fires are similar in style, size, and method. In both cases, the buildings are often empty for the day or derelict.'

'Yes!' Spider's hand edges into the frame as he gesticulates. 'It's not like it's a skip fire one day and a hotel the next.'

Maria nods. 'And the arsonist is clever: the fires don't seem like they're targeted at ending lives, so the police don't treat them as urgent cases.'

'So the arsonist was free to start again. A pattern across decades.'

She hesitates for a moment. 'But it's very unusual for an arsonist to stop setting fires and then begin again.'

'Even expressive arsonists?'

'We may have an exception here. If they have a very specific trigger that creates their need to set fires, and then that trigger goes away, it's possible—'

'Possible they'd stop?' She hears the eagerness in Spider's voice.

'And then if the trigger comes back...'

'They start setting fires again.'

'Exactly.'

The screen goes black.

Jamie releases a breath. Spider's good at this. He doesn't

need Jamie. She swallows. He has done a great job without her. 'I would watch this documentary,' she mutters.

Eyes barely focused, she reviews their footage and to-do lists: their interviews from the stable she went to for riding lessons and the theatre where she performed in school plays. Next on the list was the principal of her secondary school, but she shut down production before they could schedule the interview. All familiar places which played a big part in her childhood. Burned by the same arsonist who set Catherine's stables alight just this week.

She wants to know more, to understand why this arsonist makes the choices he does. What's the trigger? And why the long break?

But the hoof, the note. *Stop or you will burn.* A very clear threat, with Spider's name all over it, manipulating reality to create good documentary footage. And Spider has an accomplice: whoever sent the package. He's proved that this documentary means more to him than integrity, than his relationship. She's surprised he didn't make sure he was with Jamie when she received the parcel, so he could film as she opened it.

She needs to change that password. It's even more important now they've stopped filming: she can keep Spider out of the recordings while she works out what to do next. Keep the project hers for the next phase where she links together the old cases and the new.

She clicks to the *Settings* and changes the password to their shared drive.

It's Jamie's documentary now, Spider is out of her life, and she'll solve the arson mystery on her own.

Chapter Sixteen

Cleo

The kitchen is Cleo's favourite part of the derelict house. *Her* derelict house. Of all the rooms, it's the one where the abandonment is both stark and almost non-existent at the same time. There are dishes stacked on the draining board next to the sink, as if someone just finished washing them and carefully laid the cloth over the long neck of the tap to wait for everything to dry. But when she touches the cloth, it's stiff and solid, frozen in time.

Turning on the tap elicits a dusty gasp from the pipes, but no water.

The cupboards are still full of tins and jars: a rusting tin of Lyle's golden syrup, a jar of marmalade with a gollywog on the label, its rotten contents unrecognisable: a terrarium of sludge. On the dining table, cut glass salt and pepper shakers sit on their own little silver tray, ready to be shaken over dinners that never arrive. The bumps of the cut glass feel nice under her fingertips.

When Lucasz is here with her it's cosy and fun; not scary at all. It's an adventure. They've both brought candles from home and scattered them around the living room. Their orangey light dances up the walls as the draughts nudge the flames.

It's warmer than the night Cleo stayed here alone. Spring is advancing, the sun drying out the bones of the building.

They've pulled the cushions off the saggy old sofa and laid them out on the floor, where they sit in front of the laptop where Lucasz has queued up a pirated horror film his dad brought back from his last visit back to Poland. It's in English with Polish subtitles. Cleo likes to see the foreign words and sometimes practises saying them out loud, much to Lucasz's mortification.

'What? It's a cool language.'

'True. No matter what Peach says. Before… you know.' He mimes stabbing himself on the hand.

She giggles. 'Well, I showed her. You should be proud. Poland is BADASS. She's just boring English.'

Lucasz laughs. 'Does that make me a badass, then?'

She shoves him. 'You're not Polish, dickhead. You were born in Moorburn Bay Hospital.'

'More Polish than you.'

'True.'

'I read something about the Winged Hussars the other day, did I tell you? They were so cool.'

Cleo rolls her eyes. 'Geek.'

'They had twenty-foot lances and would remove the heads of their opponents. Just pop them off like bottle tops.' He mimes jabs with a lance. 'And they had massive metal wings on the back of their armour, just to scare their enemies with the terrifying sound they made when they banged together as they rode into battle. Just a big battle flex.'

'Totally badass,' she agrees.

She reaches out to a candle, waves her fingers through the flame 'You even did the lance actions. Very sexy.'

His cheeks flush, two dark spots at the top of his cheekbones, stark against his pale skin in the candlelight.

She loves to push him, make his cheeks pink.

He mumbles something but she can't catch it. She rolls to face him and cups her jaw in the palm of her hand, trying to look as cute as possible.

'What did you say?'

'You're good at a lot of things, too.'

She grins. 'You think?'

'You know it, Cleo. You don't need me to tell you that you're great.'

She reaches out and pokes him. 'On the contrary, dear friend. On the contrary.'

He pokes out his tongue. Then he resets his face to a serious expression. 'And what do you think of me? Really?' His tone is grave, his body still.

She pauses. They've been best friends since their first day of secondary school. He's her only friend, now. But lately it's harder to be just friends, getting teased that they fancy each other. Friendships at school have gone from innocence, with no consideration of gender, to a minefield of analysis, rules, and assumptions. Lucasz barely notices, and Cleo enjoys the attention and the questions. The endless questions.

But it also complicates their friendship in a new way. She doesn't want to spend time wondering what his actions *mean*. She just wants to know, to have things stated out loud so she knows where they stand. But then she's also started to notice his wide shoulders, the little muscle in his jaw that pulses when he's uncomfortable. The blond moustache which fuzzes his upper lip. It's confusing and she doesn't like it.

She's not ready for it, that's the thing. She's angry that a whole new phase of life is being forced on them and it's moulding their friendship into something new, something unfamiliar. What *does* she think of him?

She rolls onto her back, stares at the ceiling: whitewash threaded with black beams. 'I think you…' She feels a buzz in her pocket. 'Sorry, I got a message.'

Perfect timing. She pulls out her phone. It's from an anonymous account, one with no headshot and just a string of numbers where there should be a name.

'This is weird,' she says, trying to distract Lucasz from his question. She sits up cross-legged, the phone in her lap.

He leans over to see. 'Who's that from? I didn't even know you were allowed a Facebook account without a proper name.' The faceless avatar stares back at them, offering no clue about the sender.

Cleo shrugs. 'No idea.'

She clicks on the link to open a long message, a wall of text peppered with grammatical errors. 'Woah,' she says to Lucasz. 'Check this out.'

I heard your looking for info about Tony Gardiner well he was my mum's second husband. I bet you didnt know he was married before did you? He probably lied about it. He probably lied about a lot of things – thats what happened to us. At first he was like the perfect guy he bought Mum flowers all the time, took her for fancy dinners, showed up in his flashy car to take her out and parade her around. She thought she'd won the lottery. He was nice to me, too – i was little and didn't know my dad so i was just super happy to have a guy around making mum happy and chucking me around the garden in playfights.

He moved in fast and they got married, then everything changed. No more fancy dinners or flowers, and mum didn't go out with her friends anymore. Next he told her she was fat and her skirts were too short for someone her age. She stopped laughing so much and she barely went out except to the supermarket. She was scared of him.

Finally, he told her her relationship with me was unhealthy that we were too close and she needed to set boundaries and discipline me better. We stopped talking like we used to. He took her away from everyone who loved her and everyone who might help her get away.

He never hit her, he's too clever for that. It was always there, though, in his movements and his eyes one time he called her a cunt and then when she cried he said she heard him wrong. And he'd stand really close to her while he shouted at her for not putting something away right or not loving him enough.

She never escaped – he left her for someone new so I don't know what advice can help you get your mum away from him. He sucked all the goodness and life from her and then he left her. He told her she was crazy and broken and no one would ever want her again and she believed him because no one came to help. He'd chased them all away.

'Holy shit.' Cleo hands the phone back to Lucasz, who's still reading. He reads slower than her and she feels like she's won a race. She waits quietly, staring around the cluttered living room while he gets to the end.

Lucasz's eyes flick back and forth over the last few lines, and then they come to a stop as he finishes reading. But he doesn't move.

She fizzes with excitement, desperate for him to say something. She wants to get up and shout, shake him, jump around, anything. Finally she's got proof. Another person has seen what she sees. She can show people it's not all in her head.

He's very still, staring at the phone, his eyes unfocused. She wants him to read faster.

She waits another ten seconds.

He takes a breath and clicks into the profile that sent the message.

She can't stand it anymore. She retrieves the phone from his hand, her fingers brushing his. 'Well? What do you think?'

He looks at her, finally. He's not smiling.

Her new-found joy begins to sink. 'What? This is amazing.'

He nods. 'I mean, that's a bit weird. To say it's amazing, I mean. If this is real, your mum's married to an evil guy.'

'Why wouldn't it be real?' She holds her phone out to him, as if the message is total confirmation.

He shrugs.

She wants it to be real so much. 'But yeah, I know. That bit about Mum being married to someone evil is not amazing. What I mean is I can show it to Mum and she'll believe me, and she'll leave him and we'll be back to how we were before, just the three of us: me, Mum, and Jamie. No Ant. She'll tell him to get out and never come back.'

'You think?' Lucasz's eyebrows lift in the middle, creating a little crinkle on his forehead. 'Your mum's really nice. I hope he doesn't make her into a husk, like that other woman.'

Cleo brings her knees to her chest, wrapping her arms around them while she scrolls through the message over and over, committing it to memory.

'Be careful, Cleo. Don't do anything too quickly with this. Make a plan.'

'Yeah, I know. You're right.' This is the evidence she needed. It was always part of her plan.

She's about to press play on their film when shattering glass pierces the heavy quiet of the empty house. They look at each other, eyes wide in the half-light of the candles. Lucasz's face goes pale. Her stomach flips.

'Did you hear that?' she asks. The smash came from upstairs, and it sounded faint.

He nods. They both sit still, listening. No other sound.

He stands to blow out the candles and they're plunged into darkness.

She gets to her feet, grabs her black duffle coat, and pulls the hood over her head. Without waiting for Lucasz to follow, she climbs the stairs, careful where she puts her feet to make the smallest possible sound.

She glances behind her out of the corner of her eye. He's right behind her. They climb slowly, stopping to listen every few steps.

At the top of the stairs, she pauses and scans the corridor for movement. Nothing.

'Can you smell smoke?'

An otherworldly roar sounds from the dark gaping hole at the end of the corridor. The black, charred and burned part of the house. A flutter of movement. Smoke curls up the walls and along the ceiling.

'RUN!'

The house is on fire.

217

The Arsonist

No one knew the house was here, no one lived there. The back wing was already a shell from the first fire. So I returned whenever I needed to, to burn a section at a time. It was a victimless crime. After all, it belonged to me. You can do what you want with your own belongings.

Most people don't realise how hard it actually is to set fire to a house and succeed. It's difficult; they're cleverly built, and fire-retardant materials are everywhere. As my addiction has grown so has my expertise.

I know how to burn a property to the ground, but I also know how to set fire to a small portion, how to get those flames to six feet and have it burn itself out in under an hour.

I make sure I can escape once I set the fire. I leave a door open so I can get out quickly. It would be damning to be the charred body left behind in the ashes of the house when I just wanted to watch it burn from afar.

Crouched amongst the trees, hunched against the world for generations, this house became my punching bag. It is an outlet. My voodoo doll. Every time I poke it with another burst of flame, I get my revenge. In the fire I see my mother's face as she cries, begging him to stop. The roar of the blaze is his roar of fury as he launches himself at her, at me.

And in the quickening of the embers, I see a child exacting revenge, unaware of the horrifying consequences and unintended destruction.

Fire comes from nothing, leaves as nothing, and leaves nothing behind.

Setting a fire is an escape. Since before I can remember, when the shouts turned to punches and kicks, the only thing that helped was watching flames. Observing the inferno that I caused as the heat ravaged the area around it, leaving nothing behind.

As I gaze at the burning, I feel something inside me uncurl, like a rattlesnake moving from crunched defence to sibilant movement, the pain slithering away.

It's always been a reaction for me. A compulsion. I feel my insides seethe and writhe with pain, like that feeling you get when you've eaten something bad and its remains gnaw at your stomach; your stomach pulses and squeezes, desperate to get out before it destroys you from the inside. It's an instinct: your body tries to rid itself of a poison. And then, after the purge, relief and relaxation as you know you have saved yourself from what your body couldn't process, couldn't handle. For me that is lighting a fire and watching it burn.

So, like a murderer might join the army to find a government-sanctioned way to kill, so a troubled soul finds an empty house to slowly ravage when the need arises. Better that than another theatre, a sports hall, a barn full of horses.

I regret those. I regret all the death.

But in those moments, I had no choice. I am an addict pursuing their next fix, an alcoholic alone at the bar sinking spirits long after his wife begs him to return home. It is a sickness, but not one I want to recover from.

I think often about dying in flames. I take a step forward, feel my skin blister in the heat. But something always stops me. There are always more fires. And more life to live in between.

Chapter Seventeen

Jamie

Her phone won't stop buzzing. When he's not calling or leaving voicemails, he texts.

There it goes again. She turns her phone to silent and leans back on her pillows, grabs her Kindle. But the blue light on the top of her display flashes with every message, and then keeps flashing its little reminder. Every time her phone catches her eye, a sinking feeling of dread fills her stomach. *Please, not again. Leave me alone.*

Her friends told her to just block his number. That you can't be friends with an ex. That he's a creep at best, a psycho at worst. She would give the same advice if one of her friends was in the same situation. 'He thinks he can just click his fingers and you'll hand over the documentary as if it was his idea all along,' Sarah messaged, with a smattering of mind-blown emojis. 'But he has to learn he can't just take what he wants, like he was trying to take your project and make it all his.'

All the girls in the WhatsApp group chat agreed with this. Fenella sent a clinking-glasses emoji and added: 'This is your future career, for him it's just a hobby.'

Now, watching her phone flash, Jamie still knows it was the right advice. But she reads his stream of messages and, although persistent, there's a new level of desperation that wasn't there before. *Please answer, J. I need to tell you something.*

He's just saying that to get her attention. To get the password. So he can steal the documentary back.

What will he do if she blocks him? He could turn up at the cinema while she's at work, or at her house. He knows her routine. At least while he's still able to call her, she knows where he is and what he's doing. She can still receive a text message which says *I'm here, please come outside.*

She doesn't *want* that text message. But she does want to know if he sends it. So she can prepare, mentally, to see him, instead of him just springing up out of nowhere.

She reaches for her phone again just as Spider's name flashes up on her display. She's long since deleted the coupley picture which used to appear when he called. It is too sad to see him kissing her cheek.

Her finger hovers over the 'block' button. It's a shame you can't just mute someone for a while, like on Twitter.

Her right eyebrow starts to pulse. She reaches up and presses her fingertips to her browbone. Fine. She hits 'block' and chucks her phone across the bed.

Straightaway her chest feels lighter, her shoulders looser. That was a good move, for now.

Voices wake Jamie from downstairs in the kitchen. Mum. Ant. Cleo. Something about their pitch makes her heart beat faster, her skin flush with anxiety. Their tone is curt and urgent. Something's happened.

The clock says 1.55 a.m. A full moon shines a faint blue-white light through the gaps in her curtains, and she can see the outlines of everything in her room. She doesn't need the light.

She pulls on her dressing gown and runs downstairs. She almost trips on an upturned piece of carpet as she runs down the stairs and stands at the kitchen door, waiting.

Cleo's crying and talking really fast. She sounds like a little girl again: 'We weren't doing anything, and there was this horrible smashing noise. And then fire was everywhere. Like a massive ball of it and we ran and ran, and it was so scary and dark. We ran all the way home—'

Jamie pushes the door open. Everyone stops talking and turns to her, surprised. Daisy glances up from her bed and slumps down again, eyes closed. She looks annoyed that everyone's awake when it's sleeping time.

'What's happened?' Jamie asks. She shields her eyes from the bright overhead light with one hand and smooths her hair with the other.

Cleo and Lucasz sit at the dining table, wearing their coats. Their faces are pale beneath a layer of dirt. Their cheeks are sunken, eyes ringed with dark circles. They look haunted. Mum doesn't look much better; she's in her pyjamas, wrapped up in a dressing gown. There's a big frown on her face: Jamie can't tell if she's angry or worried. Ant looks like he's still half-asleep; his hair sticks up on one side and his eyes are puffy and baggy. Then, conscious of Ant and Lucasz and their eyes on her, she pulls her dressing gown around herself and ties the cord tight.

'Everything OK? Why's everyone up?'

Ant switches on the kettle and chucks a handful of teabags into the pot. 'We're just trying to get to the bottom of that ourselves.'

Cleo stares at Jamie, either willing her to help or begging her not to ask questions. Jamie can't tell.

Lucasz just looks dazed.

'Why are you both so dirty?' she asks. And then she smells it: burning. It's not the smell of something on fire right now, but the smell of old charring, like the wind caught the ashes of an old bonfire. Like the scorched hoof.

Mum clears her throat, her voice shaking even though she tries to sound calm. 'These two went on a little adventure, didn't you?'

Lucasz stares at the table. Cleo folds her arms and shakes her head.

'Just tell me what the punishment is. We don't need to go through all these stupid theatrics for Ant's benefit.'

Mum ignores her, and flexes her hands, opening her fingers out, watching the sinew on the backs of her hands stretch as they move. 'They played that clever old trick: Cleo told me she was staying at Dad's house, told her dad she was at Lucasz's, and Lucasz told his parents he was staying here.'

'Bloody stupid, that is. Dangerous.' Ant mumbles as he pours water into the teapot and slams the kettle back down onto its stand. 'There are people who care about both of you, who need to know you're safe. This is just selfish and thoughtless and bloody stupid. We're going to be having a word with your parents, young man. This won't do.'

'Oh, be quiet,' mumbles Cleo.

'That's enough,' Mum says, her voice firm. 'Ant's right. What you did tonight was reckless, and you could have been hurt. Those old factories aren't safe, especially now we know that local… yobs hang out there.'

Jamie's stomach clenches. 'Wait, what happened? What old factories? I thought it was the Old—'

Cleo shakes her head. Her eyes beg Jamie not to say anything about the house. More lies from Cleo. Same as always, ever since she was a toddler pretending she didn't eat Jamie's birthday cake, shouting indignant denials through a mouth stained by blue icing.

'Will someone tell me what happened?' Jamie asks.

Mum holds her hand out to Cleo, as if inviting her up on stage. 'Go on, tell your sister.'

'We were camping in the old factory by the river,' she looks at Jamie, eyes shifty. She's lying. Again. 'And something happened,' she mumbles.

'What?'

Ant brings the teapot and mugs, slopping tea onto the table as he sets a mug in front of everyone. 'Someone set a fire while they were in the factory, apparently. There's a bloody arsonist on the loose and you're off gallivanting around when no one knows where you are in the middle of the night.'

Jamie sits down, throws a look at Cleo, who shakes her head. 'Don't,' Cleo mouths.

'I should teach you both a lesson. Some parents would whip you both with the buckle of their belt.'

Mum puts a warning hand on Ant's.

'That's illegal now.' Cleo stares at him coldly as she says it.

Mum looks shocked. 'I'm sure Ant didn't mean that. No one will be hitting anyone.' She shakes her head, as if to cast away what Ant just said. 'But what you two did tonight can't go unpunished. We'll tell Lucasz's parents and they'll make their own decisions about him.'

Lucasz doesn't move, his hands folded in his lap.

'And we will deal with you, Cleo,' Mum says. 'Somehow.' She pushes a cup of tea towards her.

Cleo shakes her head violently. 'We barely even did anything. Jeez. You guys are just looking for an excuse to be angry with me. Because of *him*.' She points at Ant, her finger quivering with rage. 'It's normal to go camping, it's the Easter holidays. If we'd asked, you'd have said no, for no good reason. Just to say no.'

'You're grounded,' Ant adds. 'That's reason enough.'

She groans.

Lucasz shifts, uncomfortable.

Mum rubs her finger and thumb together in circles, like she's trying to remove the residue of something from her fingertips. Her skin makes a quiet hisssss of friction. 'Where have you gone, Cleo? Where has my sweet little girl gone?'

Cleo looks like she's about to cry. But she clearly can't bear the idea of showing emotion in front of Ant, or Lucasz for that matter. She scrapes a hand across her eyes and mumbles. 'Oh, get lost, all of you. I hate you all.'

Jamie's heart squeezes for Cleo. She doesn't hate anyone; she's hurt and tired, rejected by their mother and lashing out.

There's a silence for a moment before Ant sucks in air through his teeth. 'You see, Jamie,' he announces, sitting up straighter 'Another fire. Cleo and Lucasz could have been seriously hurt.'

Jamie frowns at him. Lucasz hunches over, wanting to disappear.

'Your documentary is more important than ever.'

She glares at him. She needs to get Cleo on her own, find

out what happened. Was the arsonist creeping around, lighting fires while Cleo and Lucasz slept? Would he do something to get at Jamie through Cleo? To hurt Cleo and Lucasz as a warning to Jamie? The note, the hoof, and now this. She shudders. The whole thing is too close.

Just then, the doorbell rings. Daisy gives a half-hearted bark, and Ant hisses at her to 'shut up' as he walks to open the door. There are voices, and loud footsteps boom down the hallway and into the kitchen. It's Lucasz's dad.

'What have you been doing?' He grabs Lucasz by the arm and almost lifts him from his chair. Lucasz gets to his feet, standing one head taller than his dad, who glowers up at his gangly son. For a moment, it looks like Lucasz's dad will hit him, but then his forehead clears and he grabs his son into his beefy arms and holds him tight.

The whole room takes a collective sigh of relief, and Cleo grins at Lucasz over his dad's shoulder. Lucasz blushes. It looks funny, this muscular Polish man in his pyjamas in their kitchen in the middle of the night, hugging his son.

'You be more careful,' his dad says in his thick accent. 'Come home to me and your mother.' He leads Lucasz to the door, thanking Mum and Ant as if they personally rescued Lucasz from the jaws of death.

As soon as the door closes behind them, Cleo pounces again. 'See, he was pleased to see Lucasz. Lucasz isn't even in trouble.' She stands up, chair legs scraping on the kitchen tiles. 'Mum. Can you come upstairs? I want to talk to you alone.'

Mum stares at her. She doesn't move.

'Mum?'

Cleo

Ant shakes his head at Mum, willing her not to let Cleo win. But Mum can't say no, not when they've just seen how a parent *should* behave in a moment like this: just glad she's okay, like Lucasz's dad.

Cleo grabs Mum by the hand and pulls her away from Ant. She pulls Mum out of the room and up the stairs into Mum and Ant's bedroom. Mum sits on the bed, her hands resting on the quilt on either side of her. She looks up at Cleo, eyebrows raised. Her expression says, '*This better be good.*'

Cleo looks around Mum and Ant's bedroom. Mum's room used to be chaos, before Ant moved in. Not as bad as Cleo's, sure, but not great. Then Ant started coming round, looking at everything down his nose like there was a bad smell. And he chided Mum: *Ella, you should show some self-respect in the way you keep your house.* As if she was a little kid. Now, everything is put away neatly and even their shoes are lined up on a shoe rack against the wall. Her make-up table with its lightbulb-surrounded mirror is so neat and clean, just like a Hollywood make-up artist. The only messy thing is Mum's running shoes, caked in mud. They look strange next to all of Ant's posh shiny brogues.

This has to stop. Mum has to be allowed to be her happy, messy self again.

Cleo opens her phone to the new Facebook message and hands it over. 'Read this,' she says.

Mum holds the phone far away from her face, squinting. Cleo watches as her eyes skim the text. The two little lines between her eyebrows deepen as she reads, and the corner of her mouth twitches. It bothers her.

Finally, she places the phone on the bed next to her. 'Where did you get this? Who sent it?'

Cleo shrugs. 'I don't know. It's anonymous.'

She rubs her face with both hands, like she's washing it. 'I have so many questions, Cleo. Why did this person know you? And why do they say they heard you were looking for information?'

'I don't know.'

'What's going on with you? You've been messing around in derelict buildings—'

'That's got nothing to do with this!'

'What it has "to do with" is that I don't know what you've been doing or why. I don't know who you are at the moment and that scares me.'

'But the message, Mum…' She's so tired, her skin is gritty, and she smells of smoke. She's still shivering with terror from the shattering of glass, the heat of the fire, but she was excited to show Mum this message. She thought Mum would read it and look at her, amazed. That she would realise everything Cleo's been telling her for so long is true. It must be, mustn't it, if someone else experienced it too? It's not just Cleo anymore, not just her word against everyone's. This is *evidence*, just like Sahara said. 'And you told me to show you my phone when you asked, and I'm doing that.' She points at the screen. 'I haven't replied or anything.'

Mum doesn't move.

'He's done this before, don't you see? He breaks up families. Hurts people. It's evidence.' Her voice gets higher and louder. 'Why don't you believe me? What do I have to do to get you to listen?'

Mum is still as a statue. It's like she can't hear Cleo at all.

'If I'd died in that fire, you'd all be sorry. I'm telling the—'

'Stop, Cleo. I know you don't mean that.'

'I do. You'd have to listen then. You'd all be so sorry you didn't listen to me if I was dead.'

Mum stands up, wraps her arms around herself. 'That's enough. I won't listen to this in the middle of the night.'

Cleo can't hold it in anymore, and she throws herself to the bed, covering her head with her arms, sobbing into the pillows. The pillowcase smells of Mum's perfume. They're real tears. But she does make them a bit louder to make sure Mum hears.

The door creaks open and closed, and she hears Mum in the corridor. 'Oh, there you are.'

Cleo stops her sobs, listens hard. Ant's voice rumbles in the corridor outside the room.

He was listening.

The Arsonist

I've always been drawn to fire, hypnotised by the birthday candles as they dance. I never wanted to blow them out. I didn't care about the cake. I'd watch, mesmerised as the flickering tongues licked the air, breathed and flexed and grew like they were alive.

I hid my need to watch flames, sneaking off into the woods with a packet of matches while my parents fought. The only thing that released the tension in my chest was the spark and the burst of flame. I told no one about my need to light fires, yet it was so deeply a part of me that I didn't understand it wasn't normal.

It got worse, the shouting, the violence. I would lock myself in the bathroom, where the tiles, the sink and the bath weren't flammable. I'd hold a match to my mother's can of hairspray and push down the nozzle. Fireball. So big, so noisy that it drowned out the yells, the begging, the sobs. My fear.

As the urges grew, I wondered sometimes if there was a way to stop them. My targets got bigger, the fires I needed to see to quell the roiling in my guts got larger, more dangerous. I took risks, hurt myself. I'd hold the spark to the vellus hair on my arms, watch it sizzle and curl away. I'd set fire to my sleeve, test how flammable my clothes were.

But I couldn't stop. I didn't want to. And I knew I needed more.

Then came the day I found myself standing in front of the house, listening to the shouting, the pleading. It was the worst one yet. My mother kissed me goodbye as he bundled her into the car bound for the hospital, a tea towel pressed to her split brow. She said she'd probably have to stay overnight, to check for concussion.

I could stop this.

After he returned home hours later, the car's engine still ticking as it cooled in the drive, I lit an old kerosene lamp and climbed into the plum tree.

The bedroom window was open. I've always had good aim. SMASH.

Before I knew it, the fire surged up the walls. They licked the wallpaper, tickled the curtains. It was the biggest fire I had ever seen, and the biggest I had ever set.

As I watched from the tree, I could feel the heat on my face.

As the fire spread into the roof, I shuddered with joy. All these years of pain and fear, up in smoke. Mum would come home to heal her wounds in a peaceful house. No more shouting, no more punches, no more terrifying silence, creeping around the house afraid to speak. I listened to the crackle of the flames I had made, but then, when a gust of wind caught the smoke, I saw through their bedroom window: she was there with him.

She didn't stay overnight at the hospital.

He'd brought her home, wouldn't allow her to stay away from him where nosy nurses could ask too many questions. The kerosene lamp had smashed on their bed, covered them both with fuel now alight.

There they both were, visible through the window, wrestling with the smouldering blankets as the smoke filled the room and the flames consumed their skin.

I scrambled to descend the tree. I needed to save Mum, to get her out. I never meant for this. But something went wrong; my foot slipped off the branch and I fell headfirst to the ground. The fall knocked me unconscious, the first and last time in my life.

When I revived, the inferno had taken hold of the entire upper floor. I couldn't get inside.

Both of my parents were dead.

I never said a word.

Chapter Eighteen

Cleo

It's the first summery day of the year, even though it's still technically spring. The air smells like cut grass and on the other side of the fence the next-door neighbour sings to himself as he shuffles about in his shed.

Cleo has dragged the rusty old hammock frame out of the shed and strung up the hammock under the plum tree. Her head and shoulders are in the shade so she can read her book, and her legs warm in the sun. Daisy snoozes on the grass next to her, occasionally lifting her head to snap her jaws at a fly.

The house is quiet, with Mum and Jamie both out at work.

Ant's shuffling around somewhere. He leaves her alone when it's just the two of them in the house; he doesn't talk to her unless there are witnesses to see what a *hero* he is for putting up with his evil stepdaughter, when there's someone to witness the strain she puts him under, so he can roll his eyes at them in solidarity. Dickhead. He's getting ready for an evening shift covering the dinnertime news while the normal presenter is on holiday. You'd think he was co-starring next to Beyoncé the way he's swaggering around the house like a peacock.

She feels calm for the first time in a long while. The sunshine warms her skin and the sky is blue. Her shoulders relax.

'Cleo?' It's Ant. His shouts are aimed at the inside of the house; he hasn't seen her in the garden.

She puts her headphones in her ears.

'Cleo.'

She doesn't play music, but she just wants him to know she won't come when she's called. Not called by him anyway.

She shifts in her hammock, sits up a little higher to see him through the kitchen window. His mouth moves as he mutters to himself. Probably slagging her off. He tidies the kitchen, moving dishes into the dishwasher and wiping down the surfaces. He likes a tidy house and he wants everyone else to fall in line with his cleanliness demands too. Some mornings he stands at the bottom of the stairs and bangs a pan with a wooden spoon, shouting that it's time for Cleo to get out of bed, to help with the cleaning up. Even at 9 a.m. on a Sunday. He just wants people to do what he says, it's not about tidying.

She watches him lumbering about the kitchen, brushing his hair out of his eyes as he scrubs something at the sink. He's wearing Mum's yellow Marigolds, probably to protect his precious manicure so his nails look immaculate under the studio lights while he reads the news.

'CLEO!' he snarls. He points at her with a yellow rubber finger through the kitchen window; she can't pretend she can't hear him anymore. 'Come here.'

She makes a show of pulling out an earbud and shakes her head, miming that she didn't hear him through the window.

His face turns purple with rage and she covers her laughter

as she swings her legs out of the hammock and wanders across the lawn, stopping to pick a buttercup on the way. Daisy trots along behind her. 'Yes, Ant?'

He rips off the rubber gloves and turns away from the sink. He has his back to the window and his face is in shadow. He looks angry. His eyes are black with barely any irises: all pupil, like a wild animal. Almost scary.

He stares at her unblinking, like a predator watching its prey.

He takes a step towards her, and she's struck by how tall he is, how broad. No one else is here, it's just her and Ant in the house. He could murder her if he wanted to. This might be the day he finally snaps. She glances up at the dresser: behind the decorative plate, the little black eye of the camera lens blinks at her. At least it'd be caught on film if he did.

'I've been calling you for ten minutes and you're lazing around in the garden in a hammock.'

She affects a light-hearted giggle. Don't ever let him know you're afraid. 'My bad. Didn't hear you.'

'Bollocks.' He slaps the gloves onto the kitchen counter. 'While your mum's out we're going to clean up a bit, make the house nice for when she gets home from work.'

'Mum doesn't care if the house is tidy or not.'

'Yes, she does.' He holds out the tea towel, raises his eyebrows at her. 'And if you want to be in the good books, you'll help.' He tries to be jovial in his tone, but she can tell he's seething. There's a quiet rage underneath his skin; he's like a lion pacing its cage desperate for the zookeeper to open the door and let it bite.

She looks at the tea towel. He shakes it at her. When she meets his eyes, the pupils are a normal size again.

'Come on, we've got to be a team here.'

She takes the tea towel and swings it by her side as she crosses to the sink to dry the pots.

'Bros?' he asks.

'What?'

'Duran Duran?'

She shakes her head, trying to look exhausted. 'I don't know what you're talking about, mate.'

He waves his phone at her and then paws at the screen until music plays from their Bluetooth speakers on the dresser. The kitchen fills with the awful electric drums of Eighties music. She groans and turns back to the dishes.

'See?' He moves his shoulders with the beat. 'Doing dishes can be fun. You should try it some time.'

'Stop dancing.' She shudders. It's so uncharacteristic that it feels intrusive, like seeing your worst teacher in the supermarket buying toilet paper.

She dries a few plates and glasses, enough to clear a space on the draining board, and then grabs a pan from the cupboard and lights a gas ring on the stove with a tick tick tick.

'What are you doing?' asks Ant without turning around from the sink.

'Making popcorn.'

'Not until you've finished the dishes.'

'I'll finish them later. I'm going to watch a film now.'

'You'll do them now.'

'You're not my dad and this isn't your house.' She turns away from him and opens the cupboard, grabbing a bag of popcorn kernels and tipping them into the pan with some butter. She likes the clink-clink the kernels make as they hit the metal. Kah-ching! Like she just won on a one-armed bandit in a casino.

236

She hears him cross the kitchen towards her and tries not to flinch.

Without warning, the popcorn pan is wrenched from her hand. An arc of kernels skitters across the kitchen floor.

'Hey! Don't touch me.'

Daisy rushes over to sniff the spilled popcorn, giving an experimental lick.

Ant kicks out at the dog. 'I'll do what I like, and it is my house.' He grabs Cleo's arm and stares right at her, his whole body moving with every breath.

'This is assault.'

'You have no idea what "assault" actually means.' He snarls, and then something flickers across his face. She tries to pull her arm away from his grip. Ant pulls back, until suddenly there's a searing pain in her hand as it meets the blue gas flame of the stove.

'Oh SHIT. OH MY GOD,' she screams. The palm of her hand sizzles.

He pulls his hands away from her, releases his grip. 'What are you doing, you stupid girl?' he shouts, and drags her towards the sink by her elbow. His face is pale, a sweat breaking out on his upper lip. He slams on the cold water tap and pulls her hand under the running water.

'I can't believe you did that. You burned me.' Tears spring to her eyes and she wipes her face with the forearm of her free hand. The skin on her palm sears with pain.

He shakes his head. 'For God's sake, Cleo. You burned yourself.' He releases her and gestures to her to keep her arm under the running water. Then he crosses to the pan and moves it off the stove, turning off the gas ring. 'Stay there.' He sweeps up the spilled kernels, batting at Daisy with the brush to keep her away.

Cleo watches the water cascade over her burned skin, triumphant as her fingers turn numb in the cold water. It's like a gift. As much as it hurts, she's delighted to have something even Mum can't dismiss or ignore. This is the proof she needed to get Ant gone for good. *Evidence.* And she's got it on film.

With her other hand she pulls her phone from her pocket and opens Google.

'What are you doing?' he asks.

She switches the phone to speakerphone and presses 'call'. 'I'm calling Childline.'

'What the fuck?' The broom clatters to the floor as he wrenches the phone from her grasp and hangs up, pocketing it.

She barely suppresses a giggle. He's too easy to wind up.

'I'm trying to call for help.' She raises her voice over the sound of water cascading over her injured hand and down the plughole. 'Help!' she calls.

As if by magic, the front door opens. 'Hello?'

Ant's mouth drops open.

She almost laughs out loud. It's Jamie.

'Cleo? You OK?'

He runs his fingers through his hair, and when he takes his hands away his hair sticks out in all directions. He looks insane. He whispers at her as Jamie's footsteps get louder: 'You've got a serious problem. You're mentally ill. Ella says you're just going through a phase, that you'll grow out of it. But it's more than that. You're deranged. Not even boarding school will fix you. You need to be institutionalised.'

She holds out her hand which glistens with water, the skin red. 'I'm not deranged. I'm not the one who burned a little girl. You're an abuser.'

He hisses. 'Ah yes, sent yourself any more fake little

Facebook messages lately?' He gets his own phone. 'I'm calling your mother.'

Mum won't answer her phone while she's at work, they both know that.

The kitchen door opens and Jamie enters, her cheeks flushed pink with her walk from the bus stop. 'Everything all right?' She looks from Cleo to Ant, brow furrowed with confusion at what she's seeing: Cleo by the sink, hand under the water, Ant pacing around the kitchen, phone to his ear, as far away from Cleo as he can get while still in the same room. Popcorn kernels all over the floor.

'Fine, thank you Jamie. Your sister has had an accident with the stove.'

Jamie rushes to Cleo and examines her hand under the tap. 'You poor thing.' She puts her arm around Cleo. 'Does it hurt?'

Cleo nods and glances at Ant, who's still pacing.

'I know you don't like me, Cleo. I'm fine with that.'

Cleo stares at him over her shoulder, her hand still under the water.

Jamie looks confused. 'What's going on?'

Ant ignores her. 'You're making your mother incredibly unhappy. Do you realise that?'

'I'm not doing that to her.'

'You are. All you need to do is grow up a little bit and stop making our lives a nightmare. Stop being so selfish.'

Jamie pats Cleo on the shoulder and leans against the counter, her arms folded. 'Hang on, Ant. I don't understand what's happened, but let's just make sure Cleo's all right before we talk about anything else.'

Cleo smirks at him.

He growls.

Jamie turns Cleo's hand over and stares at it.

'It looks bad,' Cleo says. 'I might need an ambulance.'

The skin is red raw, and blisters are forming all over her palm. Jamie winces. 'Right, I'll find some burn cream from the first-aid kit. And I'll call the doctor too. This does look pretty serious.'

'There's no need to call—'

Cleo interrupts him. 'Please do, Jamie. If we go to hospital, I can tell someone what happened.'

Jamie brushes past him on her way out of the kitchen, not pausing to look at him.

'They'll get social services involved,' Cleo adds in a low voice only Ant hears.

'There's no need to call anyone,' he shouts. He glances at Cleo once more and then stalks out after Jamie. 'Jamie, wait.'

She hears them talking, a few sentences she can't make out. Ant's voice gets louder.

That's when Cleo hears Jamie's ear-splitting scream, followed by a huge crash.

And then silence.

The scene in the hallway is horrifying. On TV shows when they say, 'It all happened so fast,' it always sounds like a silly cliché, but that's how it feels to Cleo right now.

She hears Jamie scream, and runs to the sound, the tap still gushing into the sink. She forgets about the pain in her burned hand. All that matters is Jamie.

Jamie's body crumpled at the bottom of the stairs, her head at a funny angle. Ant stands over her. Her attacker.

'You've killed her.'

Cleo tries to be brave and tough, but in this moment, she is neither. She bursts into tears and slumps to the floor. Jamie is dead. Murdered by Mum's husband.

'You're a murderer.' As annoying as Jamie is as an older sister, Cleo loves her and definitely doesn't want her to die. If only someone had listened. For a brief, inhuman moment Cleo feels a little twinkle of something resembling hope, though: if Ant *has* murdered Jamie, Ant will go to prison, and he'll finally be gone from their lives.

But then, through her tears, she hears a groan from Jamie. She's still alive.

'Get off her,' she shouts at Ant through her tears.

He shakes his head, holding his phone to his ear to call for an ambulance.

'We need the police, too,' she shouts at Ant's phone, hoping the dispatcher hears her. 'This is an attempted murder. He tried to kill my sister.'

Ant puts a finger in his ear so he can hear the person on the other end of the phone over Cleo's shouting.

He mumbles about Jamie falling down the stairs, says the word 'accident' over and over again as if that makes it true.

But Cleo knows the truth.

Chapter Nineteen

Jamie

Someone has their hand down her throat. They reach inside and yank her insides out through her mouth. Her body raises off the bed, following the movement as she coughs and splutters.

'It's okay, Jamie. You're in hospital. Settle down, everything's all right.' A hand on her shoulder pushes her back down onto the bed. The pulling finishes, a tube removed from her throat. 'You've been in an accident but you're going to be OK. You've been in surgery. You go back to sleep and when you wake up, you'll be with your family. They're all here waiting for you.'

Her eyes drift closed.

When she wakes up again, she doesn't know if it's day or night. There are no windows, but there's so much noise: voices, beeping and bustling.

A blue curtain encircles her bed, and an empty chair to her left. On her right-hand side is a table with a plastic cup and a little jug of water. Her tongue is parched and the roof of her mouth feels scaly. That jug is so small, it probably doesn't have enough water in it to quench this thirst.

She tries to reach towards the water, but her arm won't lift. Her muscles feel disconnected from her brain. Her body and mind feel smooth and relaxed, like she's floating in a boat on the sea. She doesn't remember an accident, but she's clearly in the right place.

'Hello?' she says, but it sounds more like a groan. She can't open her mouth. No one comes. Footsteps move back and forth outside the curtains, but no one stops. She tries again. This time, someone pulls back the curtain.

It's a girl about her own age, wearing light blue scrubs. Her hair is tied up in a high ponytail, and her eyes are coated in thick black eyeliner. 'Hello, Jamie!'

She's very chirpy. It makes Jamie's head hurt.

Jamie smiles weakly.

'How are you feeling? A bit groggy, I expect.'

She lifts a finger to point at the water.

'Thirsty? I bet you are. Suspect you're hungry too. It's nearly dinnertime, so there'll be some special food for you coming round soon. And a nice cup of tea too.' The nurse holds out the cup with a straw and passes it towards Jamie's face. She lifts her head and drinks deeply until the nurse takes the cup away. 'That's all you can have for now; we'll take it slow. Let's check your bag.'

Bag? The nurse leans down the side of the bed to look at something. 'All looks good, Jamie. A normal colour.'

Jamie realises with a start that the nurse must be referring to a bag of pee. There must be a tube going into her bladder. Her cheeks burn with shame. What's wrong with her? What happened?

She remembers being at work at the cinema, cleaning out the fizzy drink machine and tearing tickets for the matinee. Sneaking kernels of popcorn into her mouth when no one was looking to quieten her rumbling stomach. She remembers returning to the house, Ant and Cleo arguing in the kitchen. Then nothing else.

'Where are my family?' She tries to say, but again the words don't come. She shifts her legs under the tangled blankets. It's too hot in here.

'Your mum is in the waiting room. Do you want to see her?'

She nods.

Moments later, Mum peeks her head around the curtain, her face drawn with worry. Her usually flawless make-up is smudged, eyeliner shadowed under her eyes and lipstick faded to leave only lip liner at the edges. 'My baby. How are you feeling?'

'Tired,' she tries. It's all she can feel right now, except for a dull ache in her face and ribs.

'You fell down the stairs.' Mum takes her hand. 'It's so lucky Ant was there. He put you in the recovery position and called the ambulance. He saved your life.'

Mum strokes her head, laying a cool hand on Jamie's forehead. Mum nods. 'It's not...' She swallows. 'It's not happening again, Jamie?'

She frowns, confused.

Mum whispers it, as if someone might hear. 'You've been eating properly?'

She tries again to talk, but nothing comes out.

Mum shakes her head. 'Don't try to talk. You broke your jaw.'

Her stomach plummets. Can she talk? Will she look different? She looks around, searching for her handbag. There's a mirror in there, she could see her face… but it's not there. There's no stuff. Her eyes blur with tears.

Mum leans forward and places a hand on Jamie's cheek. 'They've wired your jaw to help it heal. You won't be able to eat or talk for a couple of weeks.'

The nurse mentioned special food. Nutrition shakes, probably. She hates those.

'Cleo wanted me to tell you she loves you. And that she's going to come and see you every day. She's already looked up the bus routes, apparently. Doesn't want me or Ant giving her a lift and cramping her style.'

Jamie smiles, or tries to. Her face feels numb on one side. She's not in pain, but her body feels battered and bruised in a strange disconnected way: she knows the pain is there but the pain relief blocks it from reaching her brain. Her heart beats over 90 beats per minute; the little clip on her finger betrays her. Her body knows something is wrong, and it's sending those messages to her brain. Be scared. You're in danger. Something terrible has happened. Run. But her brain can't catch up.

'Jamie, if you're not eating properly, we need to get you seen by a specialist, okay? We can't have this happen again.'

Jamie shakes her head, but her neck muscles twinge. *I'm fine*, she wants to say. *That's not what's happening. I didn't pass out, not this time*. Did she?

Mum hands her a notepad and pen. 'This is to write down anything you need. I brought some odds and ends for you, but if there's anything else you need next time I come in, write it down in a list.' She opens the locker next to the bed and shoves a Tesco bag into it, patting it to show Jamie where it is.

Jamie nods and picks up the pen, but her hand shakes and

she can't grip it properly. She's too tired. She hands it back to Mum, closes her eyes.

Mum strokes her forehead. 'Yes, you sleep. You're going to be OK, Jamie. The surgeon says you'll make a full recovery. It's so lucky Ant was there.'

She remembers Ant now, crouched over her, looking worried. And Cleo crying, watching from the doorway.

She remembers shouting. And fear.

Cleo

Cleo stands at the curtain and watches Jamie sleep. She looks terrible. The right-hand side of her face is swollen and starting to bruise. She doesn't look like Jamie at all, but like a cartoon version of her, a caricature. Her face all puffed up and swollen.

Cleo's stomach clutches with guilt, as if it should have been Cleo who fell, or as if somehow she caused this to happen. That's not possible: she wasn't even nearby when it happened, but Cleo's looked at it from every angle and there's a lot of 'what ifs'. What if Ant and Cleo hadn't been fighting when Jamie came home? What if Cleo didn't get so angry, didn't wind Ant up on purpose? What if Jamie hadn't been rushing upstairs to get the first-aid kit to help with Cleo's burn? A lot would be different right now, and Jamie wouldn't be lying in a hospital bed with a broken jaw and fractured ribs after being attacked on the stairs.

Jamie wakes with a sharp intake of breath and opens her eyes. She smiles at Cleo with one side of her face, and it's shocking: she's missing one of her teeth. Gauze covers a wound near her neck and cheek in front of her ear. That must be where they cut her face open for jaw surgery. Cleo tries not to wince.

'Hey,' she whispers, and walks towards the bed. She hates visiting people in hospitals. Especially Jamie. There's something so awkward and strange about it, like visiting an elderly relative she barely knows; not that she has many of those. In hospitals she always wants to leave as soon as she arrives. Her body goes into flight mode, and she has to force herself to sit down on that plastic-coated chair and reach out to touch Jamie's hand. Everything feels terrible. But this isn't about Cleo, it's about Jamie and about helping her get better. And finding out the truth.

Jamie looks tiny in the hospital bed, her legs spindly under the sheet. She's kicked the blue blanket off and it's crumpled at the end in a heap. Her face is a weird orange near the surgical site with some kind of goop they must have put on before they operated. Hospitals are supposed to be clean but everything seems dirty and disgusting. Cleo doesn't want to touch anything. She folds her arms.

'You don't remember what happened?' Cleo asks. She knows she should ask if Jamie is okay, how she's feeling, etc. She'll ask later when she's found out.

Jamie shakes her head. *No.* But then she tilts it.

'Anything?'

Jamie nods and reaches for the notepad and pen. *'Not much,'* she writes.

Interesting. 'Do you remember anything up to when you fell?'

She nods again.

'Did he make you fall? Did he attack you? We were arguing; he was angry. He's dangerous. It's possible, right?' She squeezes Jamie's hand. Cleo's own hand is bandaged too, the two of them both victims in different ways. 'Jamie. Did he push you?'

She looks at Cleo, makes eye contact for a moment. Then looks away. Does Jamie look afraid? Cleo can't tell.

'Jamie, this is important. If he attacked you, if it's his fault you're here, he needs to be in prison. He's alone with Mum in the house right now.'

She shrugs and looks away. On the paper, she scrawls: '*I don't remember.*'

'OK. Well, I'm going to write down everything I remember, and then when your memory comes back, we'll call the police, okay?'

Jamie closes her eyes.

Cleo gets home an hour later after a long bus journey and tries to open the door without them hearing. She sneaks along the hall and manages to pass the living room door. As her foot touches the first step, the TV in the living room pauses.

'Cleo?' Mum calls.

She climbs the stairs faster, trying not to make noise.

The living room door opens just as she gets to the top of the stairs and out of sight. Safe. She opens her bedroom door and freezes.

There's a suitcase open on her bed, some of her clothes neatly folded inside. 'What the fuck?' she whispers.

'Cleo.'

She spins around.

Mum's in the doorway, looking sad and tired. Her mascara has run, smudged beneath her eyes. Has she been crying? Her cheeks look hollow. She's lost more weight.

Cleo's skin prickles in fear. 'What happened? Are we leaving? Did he hurt you?'

Mum grabs Cleo's arms on either side, a firm hold. It's not a hug, it's more forceful than that. She pushes Cleo to sit on the bed and sits down next to her.

'We're not leaving, Cleo. I'm married to Ant and I love him.'

Cleo scoffs.

Mum ignores her. 'We've decided it's best for you to go and stay with your dad for a couple of weeks, until you start the new school. Maybe this house is just too small for all the big personalities right now. All on top of each other because it's the Easter holidays.'

'You're getting rid of me. This is exactly what he wants, you know. He's winning, and you're letting him.'

'No one's winning anything. In this situation everyone loses. Maybe a break from each other would help.'

'I can't believe you're letting him do this. He's got rid of Jamie and now he's sending me away.' Mum flinches, but Cleo carries on. 'He's got you all to himself, just like he wanted. He's isolating you. He made you fall out with Tina, too. I heard you.'

Mum's cheeks flush under her foundation. 'You've got this wrong. He's a good man.'

'He's a monster.' Cleo pushes the suitcase off her bed and it turns over, spilling her clothes all over the floor. Something unfamiliar slips out from among the clothes; and as soon as she sees what it is, she starts to cry deep, wracking sobs: it's a box of Cadbury's Milk Tray. Her favourite.

'You bought me chocolates,' she manages through her tears. That little gesture from Mum is too much to bear. She's being discarded and rejected by the one person in the world who should love her unconditionally, who should believe her and protect her but who sends her away at the bidding of an awful man. Why can't she see he's evil? Why doesn't she listen? But at the same time, Mum is still Mum: she still loves Cleo, still remembers her favourite chocolate and hides them in her suitcase. It's all so fucked up.

Mum stares at the clothes on the floor, her mouth a thin line.

'That was Ant, actually. Something of a peace offering.'

Cleo kicks the chocolate box across the room and it slams against the wall.

Chapter Twenty

Jamie

B*eep.*
    Jamie frowns, becoming aware of the bright lights and the bustle around her once more. She's used to the constant alarms and machine noises, but that *beep* was a new one. New, yet familiar.

She opens her eyes slowly, adjusting to the hospital lights. She's alone.

But is she?

The curtain moves, a flutter where the two halves meet at the entrance to her cubicle. She blinks, trying to clear her vision. All the medication makes her groggy, slow to wake, easy to drop off to sleep. Everything's blurry as she blinks and blinks.

Something in the gap between the curtains. A black shape, a winking red light, pointing at her.

A camera lens.

Someone is filming her.

She squeals, sitting up in bed. She pulls the blanket up to cover her head, protect herself from the camera, sending a stab of pain through her ribs. She looks around for the alarm to call a nurse, to get help. Since the accident she feels so exposed, more vulnerable. Before this she felt immune to pain and danger; that kind of thing happened to other people. Since waking from her surgery, she feels the opposite: like her life is the most fragile thing in the world and the slightest misstep or moment of bad luck can crush her. Everything looks dangerous, everyone frightens her, anything might cause her pain.

She finds the 'help' button and presses it to set off a shrill, constant alarm and a flashing red light above her bed.

'Woah, woah, woah.' The curtains part and in steps Spider, the camera by his side. 'I'm sorry, I didn't mean to scare you. It's just me.'

She lowers the blanket to her chin and glares at him. He thinks this is a joke, that it's funny to film her in her hospital bed, her face broken, unable to speak. Her eyes fill with tears of rage and she curses herself for crying. She's furious that he's here, seeing her like this.

She wants to shout, to scream with rage, but she can't open her mouth. Her jaw aches with the need to open it and screech loud enough to wipe the stupid grin off Spider's face. It makes it even worse that she was pleased to see him for a split second before he opened his mouth. Her heart lifted for a moment. Before she remembered.

'Hey, what's wrong?' He sees her tears and his tone is soft, caring. He crosses to the chair next to her bed and sits down, laying a hand on her arm.

She whips her arm away, turns her face from him so he can't see her tears. She scrapes them away with her fist.

What would she say to him, if she could? So much about not respecting her, not thinking about her, being selfish and insensitive and stupid.

Why is he here? Why did he keep calling? She asked for space. She made her boundaries perfectly clear and he trampled all over them again and again, as if his needs were more important than hers. She wants to scream again.

She picks up the pen and paper and starts to write.

The curtains open with a whoosh. Martha, her favourite nurse, stands in the gap, staring at them with a frown. She's a big woman, wide and strong. 'Everything okay? Your alarm is going off.' She glances from Spider to Jamie and back again.

Jamie isn't sure how to answer. A nod gives the wrong impression to Spider, that he's welcome here and that she's happy about how he entered her cubicle. But if she shakes her head to say, 'No, everything's not okay', it feels like an overreaction. Like she's asking the nurse to force him to leave. That would be dramatic and awful, and she doesn't want that. She settles with a closed-mouth smile and raises her eyebrows to give a signal of… something in between.

Martha narrows her eyes at Jamie and then glances again at Spider.

'I'm Jamie's'—he pauses—'boyfriend.'

She doesn't react.

'Just dropped by to see if she needs anything.'

Martha gives him a long, cold look and then crosses to the alarm and silences it with a sharp poke of her index finger. 'Visiting hours finish in ten minutes,' she says, and pulls the curtains closed with a swoop.

'Short visiting hours today?' Spider asks, and Jamie suppresses a smile, thankful for Martha's perceptiveness.

If Spider notices anything, he doesn't show it. He carries on talking as if Jamie doesn't exist, as if their conversations are always one-sided rambles with occasional murmurs of assent from Jamie. Does he even need her input? Maybe this is what their conversations were always like, even when her jaw wasn't wired shut.

Finally, he looks up at her while he talks about some botched tattoo he'd been asked to fix and catches her staring at the ceiling. 'I'm talking too much.' His cheeks flush red. 'I didn't come here to blabber at you. I came here because I miss you. And I've been so worried. I hope you've missed me too.'

He pauses as if she could answer. She doesn't move.

'I've been working on the documentary. That's what I really wanted to tell you. I spent a bit more time with Catherine up at her stables, and Lucasz helped with some fact finding. That kid is a brilliant researcher.'

Jamie's gaze snaps back to Spider. How has he continued without access to the drive?

She grabs the pen and paper and writes her first message to Spider: *'I miss our documentary.'* As she writes, she realises it's true. It was her outlet for creativity, that little spark of hope that her future could be exciting and creative and fun. Taking a break extinguished that little candle of hope, and every day turned into a drudge. She needs a route into the future, a goal. The documentary was it. She still wants to tell stories, to ask questions, to investigate and research. But she doesn't want to share or relinquish control in the process.

He beams as he reads her note, his teeth white against the dark of his beard. But then he looks serious. 'Actually, that's one of the reasons I came to see you. And why I kept calling.'

She closes her eyes for a moment. Of course.

His cheeks flush. 'I mean, first I came to tell you I'm so sorry this accident happened to you. When Lucasz told me, I wanted to visit straightaway, but I knew it was best to give you some space, some time to recuperate. I want you to know I respect you and your decisions, I'm not here to try to persuade you out of what you want.'

She nods to show she understands, despite the little voice in her head that reminds her of the glint of the camera lens at the curtain, the ten missed calls on her phone.

How unexpected that Lucasz and Spider have become friends of a sort. She wonders what they talk about. Jamie and Cleo are very different characters, and so are their boyfriends. Unlikely friends.

'You know your sister and Lucasz were hanging out at that derelict house? The one that partially burned down?'

He waits as if she can reply and then carries on when he remembers she can't.

'I know you were looking into it; turns out so was Lucasz. Back when the first fires happened in the Eighties, the police and Fire Service investigated it and dismissed it. It was inconclusive whether it was arson or not, so they never charged anyone. In the end it was officially declared an accident.'

She nods. She knows all this. It's a race between her and Spider, and she'll win because he thinks they're still working together.

'But I've been looking at all the unsolved fires in the area. I think it's possible that our arsonist was involved in The Old Manor one too. The timeline fits, and so does the choice of kerosene lamp fuel as accelerant. And I've also been filming more with Maria and she says—'

Jamie reaches out and places a hand on his arm. *'Maria?'* she writes. She doesn't want him to know she's seen his interview file on their shared drive.

'Oh, you know? The psychologist? She's a professor who specialises in studying arsonists. She's incredible; she has so much to say about all this stuff.'

She watches his eyes sparkle as he talks about Maria's interview, about the 1980s arsonist taking a break until now.

'…And she thinks they're all connected: the theatre, the school, The Old Manor and even the stables. I've learned so much about why arsonists do what they do. I can't wait to tell you.'

She nods. Hearing him lay it all out just cements her feeling that this has the makings of an amazing documentary. One she nearly gave up on. Her stomach clenches.

'Oh, and there was a problem with the shared drive. But don't worry, I've reset the password. We'll work it out when you're feeling better.'

He's taken it back. He's got the files. Her mouth goes dry.

She wants him to leave. She picks up the pen to write that she's tired. But she's not tired. Why should she pretend? *'I'm ready for you to—'* then she spots something on his checked shirt. Something that glints between the buttons down the front. What is that? It looks like a black button, but his shirt buttons are white.

Spider continues talking, unaware Jamie has noticed anything. 'Anyway, she said a lot of arsonists come from homes where abuse happened. It's a cycle. So I talked to Lucasz about those letters you found, and we have this wild theory…'

Jamie can't take it anymore. She throws the notebook against the curtain, the pen clattering to the floor.

He trails off, distracted from his speech.

She reaches out and grabs his shirt, pulling him towards her until her other hand reaches the little black button. She rips it away from him, tugging the wire towards her. She growls in anger. She was right.

'Now, Jamie, please don't break that. Look, I just thought it would make good documentary footage, me telling you this theory.'

She pulls the wire free of his clothes and holds the camera in her hands. It's no bigger than a button, the lens the size of a thread hole.

'You in hospital, it's like the arsonist tried to stop you making the film. You got too close to the flame and got burned, you know? It's great material.' He rubs the back of his head. 'I didn't realise you wouldn't want to be filmed.'

She throws the spy camera at him and presses the alarm button again. The ear-splitting alarm rings through the air.

'As soon as you asked me to stop filming with the other camera, I did.' He grabs at the camera before it falls and shoves it into his pocket, looking like he's about to cry. She doesn't care. Let him feel sorry for himself, let him be hurt and rejected. He cares so little about her that he would film her at her lowest place. This arrogant disregard for her feelings. And it's all the worse for her because she had no chance to say yes or no, and she can't even speak to yell about how fucking unreasonable it all is. She's so frustrated she can barely see.

Martha returns with a whoosh of the curtains just as Spider is gathering his backpack.

'Is everything all r—' She stops, and bends to pick up the notebook at her feet. 'This yours, hun?' She hands it to Jamie.

Jamie immediately scrawls: '*GET HIM OUT*'. And Martha

practically lifts Spider off his feet with the force of her push out of the curtain.

'It's not a big deal, Jamie,' he calls as Martha closes the curtain on him.

Jamie shuffles down in bed and pulls the covers over her head to hide her tears. For a moment she was pleased to see him. That's why she's sad: she's a tragic idiot for believing something might have changed.

Chapter Twenty-One

Cleo

She's having the best time. They're in Dad's garage, where Dad set up a bar and an old pool table he got off Facebook Marketplace as soon as he moved in. Sahara perches on a bar stool, with a fixed smile on her face. As soon as they get more serious, Sahara will empty this room out and turn it into a gym or something. This 'bachelor pad' Dad created when he and Mum split up won't last too much longer.

For now, though, it's great; they're playing old music on the paint-spattered boom box as Dad beats her at pool. She's making him play left-handed, which should even them up a bit, but he's still winning by a lot.

'Cleo, come and get your drink.' Sahara points at a tall glass on the bar, a little umbrella sticking out of the top with a maraschino cherry speared on the stick.

'One sec.' She bends, closes one eye, and almost manages to pot one of her balls into the far pocket. Her hand's still sore from the burn, but it has healed enough that she can hold a pool cue without trouble. She's developed a style she secretly refers to as 'pool roulette', where she has so many balls left on the table that if she hits the white ball hard enough, it'll bounce around enough times that statistically she will pot something eventually. So far it's not working and Dad only has one ball left on the table.

She leans her cue against the wall and crosses to the bar. 'Cheers,' she says, holding out her glass to Sahara and clinking it against her martini, then takes a sip. It's deliciously sweet: grenadine and lemonade. A Shirley Temple. She's been alternating between those and a summer sunrise – a tequila sunrise without the tequila. Her body buzzes with the sugar and she almost feels like she could be drunk. Like the grown-ups. Dad and Sahara have had at least two cocktails each: Sahara is on dirty martinis, which sound very sophisticated but taste like poison. They're starting to get giggly and out of the corner of her eye she's seen Dad snuggling up to Sahara while Cleo's been lining up her shots. It's fine, it doesn't bother her nearly as much as if Mum acted like that with Ant. There's something innocent and real about Dad's relationship with Sahara; whereas Mum and Ant seem like they're performing all the time, Ant checking around to make sure people have noticed him. *Look how happy we are. Look what a great husband I am.* Everything for show.

Dad pretends to miss his shot and takes a slug from the strong IPA he buys in barrels from his favourite brewery.

'I've put our plan into action, by the way,' she says to Sahara as she sinks the white ball again and heads back to the bar. Dad lines up his second shot, his tongue sticking out of one side of his mouth.

Sahara's hair is falling out of its stylish pile on top of her head. 'Mmm? We have a plan?' She looks a little baffled and lets out a little hiccup.

'You know, the plan to get evidence on Ant. Something to prove what's happening.'

Sahara looks blank.

Dad finishes his shot and comes to the bar, propping himself up on his cue like it's a walking stick. 'Your turn, kid.'

'You know, with Mum. You said your friend…'

'Oh!' She lifts a hand to her ear and fiddles with her feather earring, running her fingers over the feather again and again.

Dad downs his pint and starts to fill his glass from the barrel. 'What's this about? You're trying to dig up dirt on Ant?'

Cleo runs her teeth over her bottom lip, scraping against her skin. 'Yes, Sahara said Mum needs my help to get away from Ant.'

Sahara nearly chokes on her martini. 'No, Cleo, that's not what I said.'

'You did.' Cleo tilts her head at Sahara. 'What did you say then, Sahara?'

There's a quick silence.

'You said if I wanted to prove to Mum that he's evil and abusive, I should collect evidence and present it to her so she would realise. It's what I've been—'

'I'm sorry if you misinterpreted me.' She turns to Dad, her cheeks flushed. 'Cleo and I were talking about abusive relationships, in the abstract. I shared a story about one of my friends and how she needed help, and – I'm sorry if this is my fault, Cleo – and Cleo must have assumed that meant I agreed that the same thing was happening to Ella.'

Cleo groans in frustration.

Dad takes a slug of his new pint. 'I don't know what was said, but Sahara shouldn't be giving you advice on dealing with your mum's husband.' He puts a hand on Sahara's shoulder and squeezes lightly. 'Cleo, if you have a problem with Ant, you should talk to your mum, or Ant. Not Sahara.'

'I've tried, but they won't listen.'

Sahara leans into him. 'Look, I'm sorry about that. I shouldn't have talked like that with Cleo. It's a misunderstanding, but it's really not my place.'

Cleo's mouth falls open. 'What? No, it was good. It was helpful. I'm—'

'Forget everything I said, Cleo. I wasn't giving the right advice. I forgot how young you are for a minute. You're getting so grown up.' Sahara reaches out as if to ruffle Cleo's hair.

Cleo steps back. She can't react, can't speak.

Dad kisses Sahara on the cheek. 'We know it's difficult for you at the moment, Ant being new to the family and everything. You can talk to us both about anything, you know.'

'That's not true. You just said I shouldn't talk to Sahara.' Cleo returns her Shirley Temple to the bar, slopping pink liquid over the side of her glass. 'What wasn't "right" about the advice you gave?' she asks Sahara.

'It's just… I'm not used to…' She stops, looks to Dad.

Dad rubs his hand on Sahara's shoulder.

'You believed me.' Cleo's chest feels hollow, like everything's been scooped out of her insides, nothing left behind. 'You were the first person to believe what's happening is real. Except Jamie and look what happened to her. She started to hear me, and she nearly died. And now… what? You think I'm lying?' Her voice cracks.

Sahara reaches out to put a hand on Cleo's shoulder, but Cleo pulls away.

'I'm going to bed,' she lies, escaping through the back door and into the night.

They won't even notice she's gone.

She feels less alone wandering through the quiet fields than she did in the house, surrounded by even more people who won't listen.

It's colder than she expected; she's glad she stole Dad's fleece from its hook behind the door. In the pocket she found a packet of giant chocolate buttons, so she's been sucking on them as she trudges across the fields.

Her feet ache a bit; Dad's house is nearly two miles from Mum's and she had to walk over the fields so she didn't get clipped by a car speeding down the winding lanes. In the dark, the sound of sheep chewing grass is really loud, their teeth grinding together. Their eyes glint as she shines her phone torch around her to avoid breaking her ankle in a rabbit burrow.

As she climbs over the fence and onto the lane, she spots a dark shape lurking by the postbox at the end of the street. A man, just outside the circle of light cast by the streetlight.

She slows her pace, takes care not to make any noise on the deserted road. Why did she do this? It was stupid to storm out of Dad's house late at night, but she needed to get away from them.

She pauses, watching the man. He looks up and down the road, his head moving from side to side as if he's waiting for someone. Other than him, there's no movement, no sound. This village is dead.

Then, he unlocks his phone and his face is lit blue by the screen. Cleo gasps.

'Lucasz!' she hisses. He looks up with a grin as she runs towards him. 'I didn't think you'd come.'

'I got your text,' he says, putting his arm around her. 'Let me warm you up, it's freezing out here.'

Her body relaxes into him and her insides feel warm. This is what she needed. She hadn't expected him to see a text which arrived after midnight – he usually turns off his phone when he goes to sleep. She's lucky that tonight was an exception and he read her message: *'Everything is terrible. Walking to Mum's on a top-secret adventure mission to liberate some stolen goods. You in?'*

It seems he is 'in'. She pulls away from under his arm and explains as they walk the final half-mile along the lane to the house.

'Jamie's cameras must have caught something. If not him pushing her down the stairs, definitely when he forced my hand onto the gas ring.' She shows him her bandaged palm, the once-white gauze now grey.

Lucasz frowns. 'It's crazy he did that.'

'Absolutely. We need to do something, and soon. Before I get sent away. So that's what we're here for.'

———

There's always an unlocked door at Cleo's house. People in their village lock their front doors, but there's often a side or back entrance which they don't bother to lock.

To avoid disturbing the rusty hinges on the gate, Lucasz gives her a boost over the back fence. He scrambles after her without much effort. Safely inside the back garden, Cleo glances around. No lights flick on in the windows like they do in the films.

She tries the back door, but it's locked. Ant must have been on patrol. She creeps across the lawn, watching out for squeaky dog toys. Nothing. The garden looks neat, grass recently cut.

At the patio door to the living room Lucasz stays close behind her, his breath tickling and hot on her neck.

She pulls the sliding door, as slowly as she can. There's a low scraping noise as the glass door moves along its runners. It's nowhere near as loud as it used to be, back when Dad lived here. Ant must have oiled it to sneak around. He must need it to be quiet, need the dog not to bark as he creeps in and out.

The door opens about a foot, and then she pauses, listens. Daisy must be going deaf. A few months ago, she'd be standing right there, tail wagging to greet them. She must be fast asleep on Cleo's bed. Missing her. No way would Ant let her sleep on his bed, that's for sure.

She shrugs at Lucasz and steps inside.

In and out as fast as possible, that's the plan. In the kitchen she points up at the camera Jamie secreted behind the plate on the dresser. 'Can you get that?' she whispers, and Lucasz darts forward. 'Careful,' she hisses, her hands already shooting towards her ears in that reflex your body does when it doesn't want to hear a loud sound about to happen. 'Don't knock the plate.'

'Duh,' he whispers, as he steadies the plate in one hand while he removes the camera. It's small, about the size of a plum. Lucasz slides it into his hoodie pocket and they head towards the living room.

This one's on top of the curtain, taped behind the ball on the end of the curtain rail. She stands on a footstool to grab that one and shoves it deep into Lucasz's pocket with a quick poke to his belly. He stifles a giggle.

'Are there any more?'

She shrugs. 'One more, I think, but I don't know where Jamie hid it. I'll check with her next time I visit. If we miss any it'll be fine, as long as Ant doesn't find them.' She beckons him up the stairs towards Jamie's room. They're safe now; if they're caught, she'll just say she felt homesick or something.

It's unsettling inside Jamie's room. Everything looks exactly as it was the day of the accident, Jamie's bedclothes thrown back from when she got up to go to work that morning; a neat stack of orange peel drying next to the open laptop, its light still blinking in sleep mode.

She picks up the laptop and its charging cable and cradles them in her arms. Then she turns to Lucasz, who hovers in the open doorway as if waiting to be invited in. She rolls her eyes at him. He's so awkward.

'Let's go.' She steps towards him, but he doesn't move.

'Where's the dog?' He frowns. Lucasz and Daisy have been best buddies for years, to the point where Mum used to joke that Lucasz was friends with Cleo just for the dog.

Cleo stops, raises her shoulders in a shrug. It is strange that Daisy hasn't greeted them. Even if she doesn't bark, she knows when people move around the house.

Just then, there's a muffled noise from downstairs. The sliding door.

They stare at each other, eyes wide. Did they close it? Did they leave it open? Who could that be? It can only be Ant. She remembers him weeks ago offering to take Daisy for her night-time walk, as if he was a massive hero for doing it. Maybe that's where he's been.

Cleo grabs Lucasz's shoulder and pulls him into Jamie's room, closing them inside. She presses her ear to the bedroom door and listens as someone creeps up the stairs. Socked feet pause on every step, measuring their heft before they commit to their weight on the tread. Whoever it is, they're trying really hard to be quiet.

The footsteps pass Jamie's room without stopping, and then the quiet *click* as Mum and Ant's bedroom door closes behind them. Ant, with Daisy. It must be.

Cleo's clammy all over, even the back of her neck. Her armpits feel sticky even though it's not a warm night. She swallows and gives Lucasz a nod.

He doesn't respond, staring at her with the most bewildered look on his face. 'What if he thinks we're burglars? What if he attacks us? Or pushes us down the stairs like Jamie?'

She shakes her head, but he's got a point. Ant could be dangerous. 'Then we'd better not get caught.' She opens the bedroom door and does a quick left-right check. No light shines under the door to Mum and Ant's room.

They sneak out of the house, silent, the laptop under Cleo's arm and the cameras in Lucasz's pocket. Much better than Ant at creeping around. Out on the street, Lucasz looks shaken. Now it's Cleo's turn to put an arm around him, snaking around his waist and pulling him close until a smile plays on the corners of his mouth.

'Come on, let's go review this footage.'

The fire didn't cause as much damage as they thought. It smells a bit smoky in the living room, but everything is more or less the same in the derelict manor except for a smashed window on the first floor. The fire must have gone out before it properly took hold.

Even in the dark, this house feels way less scary than their first visit, or the first night Cleo spent here on her own, curled up in the bottom of the wardrobe. When she thinks back to that night, it's a younger, more naive Cleo that she pictures, not someone as mature as she is now. Even though it's only been a few weeks.

She feels like she's been hardened by what's happened in her family. Mum's gone, as if Ant sucked out her soul like a dementor and made her into a zombie-like creature. She misses her real mum, the one from before. The mum who used to lean her head against Cleo's shoulder to snooze while they watched a film on the sofa. The one who used to dance around the kitchen while they cooked dinner together. The one who used to laugh at Cleo's silly jokes and make even sillier jokes back. But that mum is gone.

And Dad, too. He joined forces with Sahara, took away Cleo's hope that she might have found an ally, someone to confide in. He destroyed the little rivulet of hope that someone believed her. She's alone.

'How's things at home?' Lucasz asks, as if he can read her mind.

She looks at him, surprised. They're sitting on the living room floor, backs against the chintzy sofa, Jamie's laptop open on Lucasz's knee. Lucasz always believes her. He's so constant and steady that sometimes she forgets he's there, like a photograph she once loved that she no longer notices now it's on the wall every day.

She pulls her knees up to her chest. 'Grim. I'm banished to Dad's and Jamie's still in hospital. We're running out of time.'

He shakes his head and puts an arm behind her, draping it along the sofa. He sits in silence, the side of her body warm where they almost touch.

'Jamie and Spider broke up,' she says.

'Oh yeah, I saw Spider the other day. He's on some mad research bender and wanted my help.'

'Oh? He's still doing that fire documentary?'

'Think so. He asked me to bring him here, poke around. He thinks this place was a purposeful arson attack before it was abandoned.'

She shivers. 'What, and then they came back a couple of weeks ago to have another go at the shed? Twenty years later or whatever?'

He shrugs. 'Ask Spider, I guess. He's the one with the theory.'

Cleo leans towards Lucasz and slides the laptop from his knees and onto her own.

'You going to review the footage from inside your house?' he asks through a yawn.

She nods. 'I'm going to see if I can get anything on him. There must be something. I want to take it to the police station tomorrow.'

'The police. That's serious,' he mumbles, and shifts to curl up on his side, facing her. It's late, the sun almost rising through the curtainless windows. He pulls his hood over his head and wraps his arms around his body. His eyes close, his eyelashes resting on his pale cheeks.

She turns to the screen, squints as she runs through the motion-activated clips of people wandering around the house.

She scrolls back to a few days ago, the night Jamie argued with Ant about her documentary. She watches Jamie storm out of the room at quadruple speed, Lucasz waving as he headed home, Dad collecting Cleo. Mum and Ant sit at the table for a while.

Next to her, Lucasz's breath deepens as he falls asleep. She plugs headphones into Jamie's laptop, slows down the footage to real-time play. This feels creepy.

On the screen, Mum's talking. 'We've seen the improvement in her. She's friendlier, she's chatty. I'm really impressed.'

Ant pours them both a top up of wine and sits down. 'Of course you are, Ella. And that's why she's doing it. She's a clever girl, I'll give her that.'

He lifts his glass to 'cheers' her but she doesn't raise hers.

'What does that mean?'

'She's smart. Like her mother.'

'Ant, just say what you mean. I don't like this dancing-around-the-subject thing you enjoy so much. Please don't play games.'

'What I mean is that Cleo has lived with you her entire life. She knows how to wrap you around her little finger, how to get you to believe her lies. Nothing has changed except she's conning you and Jamie into thinking she's sweet and innocent. The moment you sign her up for another year at that local high school, she'll be right back exactly the way she was before: rude and belligerent and making our lives hell.'

Cleo tightens her lips and nods. She knew Ant said shit like this about her. It's exactly as she expected.

Mum stares at the table, her face blank, her hands cupped around her wine glass. 'This is my daughter you're talking about. Please don't forget that.'

'I haven't forgotten that, but I do wonder if you have, Ella. She is your child and should treat you with respect. Instead, she's either fawning all over you begging for your attention and pretending to be your best friend, or she's shunning you, slamming doors, screaming and swearing. She's a monster.'

'I used to have a lot more time for her. It's bound to take some getting used to…'

'Your relationship with her isn't healthy. She needs boundaries.'

Cleo rolls her eyes when she hears this. Again.

'With all respect, Ant, you haven't had children. I appreciate your advice and input on the marriage and the house, and even how we help Cleo as she grows up. But I raise my children as I think is best for them. I know them.'

'She's playing a game.'

'Well, you'd know about game playing, wouldn't you.' Her whisper is so quiet Cleo has to turn the volume right up so she can hear.

The camera quality is good, the image sharp. Even from six feet away, where the camera half-hides behind the old plate propped on the dresser, the feed captures Ant's face. It's like a cloud has passed over the sun. His eyes darken. His knuckles whiten as he grips the edge of the table, his arms shaking.

Cleo's heart beats faster. She wants to help Mum, to stop the conversation. But she can't. Whatever she's about to see on this recording has already happened.

'What?' Ant stands up so fast that the legs of his chair scrape on the tiles, just as Jamie's did when she stormed out. He balls his manicured hands into fists. Daisy leaps from her bed and skitters from the room.

Mum shrinks away as he towers over her. Why is she flinching like that? Mum raises her arms up to cover her head. She expects him to hit her. Has he hit her before?

Cleo's stomach drops. She covers her mouth with her hands.

Ant stands over Mum, raises his hand.

Unexpectedly, Ant places a gentle hand on Mum's

shoulder. Her shoulders relax, she drops her arms, and looks up at him, grateful. For a moment she looks like a dog rescued from a shelter, gazing at its rescuers with wary gratitude. Cleo has never seen this expression on Mum's face. Mum's usually strong, self-contained. Not open, grateful, enslaved.

The hair on Cleo's arms stands on end. Has he hit her before?

With his hand still on Mum's shoulder, Ant slides a piece of paper in front of Mum, and hands her a pen.

'We need this. It's for us as much as her, love.'

The boarding school application. Cleo's lungs contract, her fingertips sweaty on the mousepad.

Without hesitating, Mum signs it. Cleo suppresses a howl. Beside her, Lucasz sleeps, unaware of what happened. What already happened, days ago.

On the screen, Ant stands up and grabs his coat. 'I'll take Daisy for a last walk.'

As if she understands, Daisy leaps from her bed, tail wagging wildly.

Mum glances to the clock on the wall above the oven. 'It's late. Stay here.'

He shakes his head. 'She's too excited now. Plus, you need more help with the house. Let me take this task. Let me help.' He grabs Daisy's lead and hooks it onto her collar. 'I could do with a walk before bed. You'll be asleep when I get back. Night night.'

He kisses her on the head and walks out of the door.

Cleo feels shell-shocked, like she just witnessed a crime. Mum so skittish and afraid, and then Ant put that form in front of her, stood over her while she signed. She signed it.

Cleo's going to boarding school. Soon.

Chapter Twenty-Two

Jamie

Another mealtime, another nutrition shake. 'Chocolate milkshake today, Jamie!' the nurses sing-song at her, big smiles on their faces as they hand it to her. But they're not actual chocolate milkshakes, they're mealy and gritty with vitamins, minerals and protein added so you don't starve to death while you can't eat. All washed down with sugary tea and orange squash.

It's a horrible flashback to before, forcing down meal supplements three times a day, nurses checking she consumed every calorie, the sinking feeling of failure and desperation while her friends passed exams, celebrated the end of term, and moved on with their lives.

She forces it down, trying to quash the urge to throw the whole thing against the curtain with a splat.

Just as she finishes her 'milkshake' and sets her cup on the table by her bed, the curtain sweeps aside and Cleo stands there, a massive grin on her face. She looks like a magician who's just performed her best trick.

'Jamie!' she shouts.

Jamie giggles and raises a finger to her lips, indicating that there are other patients on the ward too.

The doctors say she'll be able to open her mouth soon, once they loosen the wires fixing her broken mandible in place. She can talk through gritted teeth, but people don't understand her, so she's given up.

'How are you feeling?' Cleo asks, and Jamie realises it's rare that Cleo asks her a question about her feelings, her welfare. Usually it's all Cleo drama.

Jamie nods. She's recovered enough for them to reduce her morphine dose, so she feels the ache in her ribs when she breathes. Her restlessness and frustration tell her she's on the mend, but they won't discharge her until they're certain her swelling has reduced. They're worried the floor of her mouth might swell and cut off her airway. Which is terrifying.

Cleo steps into the cubicle and throws herself into the plastic chair. She's about to talk when the curtain opens again and it's Lucasz, dragging another chair behind him. He sweeps his hair behind his ear with an apologetic motion; he doesn't want to be here. Unlike Cleo, he knows hospital visits are for family, not your little sister's best friend. Poor Lucasz. 'Hi, Jamie,' he mumbles, blushing.

She waves at him.

'Oh, Jamie.' Cleo practically bounces in her seat. 'I got your laptop last night. I sorted through all the surveillance camera footage and took it to the police station.'

Jamie frowns. 'My laptop?' She shakes her head. She needs that for the documentary. Her body starts to sweat. All she's been able to think about while she's been trapped in this bed is that the first thing she'll do when she gets home is change the password to the shared drive once more. Take the files back from Spider. Again. She needs her laptop.

'Cleo, I nee—'

'I said I had evidence of domestic abuse on it. Hopefully it caught the moment Ant pushed you down the stairs or burned my hand.' She holds up her palm, which is shiny and red but almost healed from the burn.

Jamie's eyes widen. She takes a deep breath, but that doesn't help. So she clicks the little morphine button and feels the wave of cool silver creep into her veins. That helps.

'Don't stress, Jamie. They took copies and gave it back straightaway. Your laptop is safe and sound in Dad's car. I hid it under the passenger seat so no one will find it.' Cleo turns away, a proud smile on her face. She thinks she's thought of everything.

'Did you get the bus?' Jamie asks through her wired teeth, and to her delight they understand her the first time.

'Oh, Spider brought us,' Cleo says brightly.

Jamie throws her head back onto her pillows. This guy will just not leave her alone.

'We were in town and saw him in the tattoo place. Said I was heading over here and he offered me a lift. He's just parking his van.'

Jamie tries to think of the clearest way to explain to Cleo that she doesn't want Spider here. That it's not some incredibly romantic gesture to trample all over your ex-girlfriend's boundaries again and again.

But before she works out how to say it, and be understood through her wired jaw, the curtain scrapes back and Spider's here, holding a box of chocolates and a bunch of pink carnations.

'For fuck's sake,' she hisses, but no one understands.

'Hey, Jamie. I hope you don't mind me coming—'

'I do.' She stares through the gap in the curtain into a waiting room, where a big man has squeezed himself into a metal chair, the arms cutting into his thighs. Above his head, posters paper the walls: moderate your alcohol consumption, quit smoking, get your flu jab.

He carries on, 'But I wanted to tell you about a bit of a breakthrough with the documentary. I didn't get a chance to tell you last time I was here.'

She shakes her head, incredulous. Her fingers itch to press the alarm button.

Cleo's eyes flick between Jamie and Spider, like she's watching a tennis match. Lucasz just looks like he wants to sink into his own hoodie.

Spider perches on the bed and talks faster. 'We wanted to know what happened to the child whose parents died. We wanted to know if he was still alive. Best case scenario, we'll find him to ask him how the fire started, what he remembers.'

Despite herself, Jamie's intrigued. This doesn't feel quite as ghoulish as zooming in to people's tears. This is interesting research, what she envisioned back when they first started the project. Detective work.

'First we tried to find out whose name is registered as the legal owner of the property. That was surprisingly difficult. We don't know the official address for the house, or the postcode.'

'It's not even on a proper road!' Cleo adds, clearly proud that it's her discovery fuelling this investigation.

'From the newspapers we knew the surname of the owners when the house burned down, and the age of the child when the fire happened, so we trawled birth records.'

'Come on, Spider. Get on with it or visiting hours will be over before you tell her everything.' Cleo grins at him.

Jamie nods, and reaches for her water glass, pressing the straw between her clenched lips. Despite herself she's interested. She wants to know what they've found out, and Spider is telling this story in as long-drawn-out a way as possible. 'We found county birth records for a few people that matched: born in 1974 with the last name Kerr, like the parents.'

'How many?'

Spider pulls a list from his pocket. 'Fifteen. But one is particularly interesting. His name is Tony Kerr.'

Tony. Jamie shifts around in her bed, propping pillows behind her back.

'Like the sign on the bedroom wall,' adds Lucasz.

Cleo places her hands on the armrests of her chair and lifts herself up, crossing her legs underneath her. 'Yeah. Tony. Like Anthony. Or Ant.'

'What?'

'And Ant was born in 1974 as well.'

It can't be him. It's too much of a coincidence. Spider must see the shock on Jamie's face and looks triumphant for a moment. He knows he's got her attention now. Then he replaces the triumph with a look of hesitation. 'I mean, we don't know anything for certain—'

'But it all fits!' Cleo stands up. 'Don't you see? Ant doesn't have any parents, won't tell anyone where they are – says he doesn't remember his life before the children's home.'

'That is strange,' Spider adds, trying to sound impartial. 'Most people have some memories of their childhood, even if they had some trauma.'

'You think he's lying about his memories?' asks Lucasz.

'Definitely!' Cleo answers, even though Lucasz asked Spider. 'He says he lived in a children's home, right? Of course he did, his parents died in a fire. Then Anne and Fred fostered him a few months later. It all makes sense.'

'I mean, it's a coincidence at least,' Spider says.

'And he's a sociopath. So are pyromaniacs.'

'Woah, woah, woah.' Spider holds out a hand to Cleo, stopping her. 'We're talking about whether his house burned down when he was a child. Whether he was orphaned. Not whether he set his own house on fire and burned his parents to death. And not whether he's an arsonist.'

But Cleo bounces in her seat. 'And another coincidence: the first fires stopped when Ant moved fifty miles away to live with Anne and Fred. Then when he married Mum and moved back here, they suddenly start again. It's a pattern.'

Lucasz clears his throat.

Everyone turns to him, interested to hear what he's about to say. But he's staring at the gap in the curtains, which move slightly as if caught by a breeze.

Someone was listening.

Cleo

Cleo leaps from her chair. A nurse walks away down the corridor, her crocs squeaking on the floor. 'What a creep,' she whispers, and Lucasz shushes her.

She carries on, in a quieter voice. 'We were at the house last night in the middle of the night—'

Jamie holds out a hand to interrupt. 'Why?' she says in her weird gritted-teeth voice. 'Aren't you staying with Dad?'

'Mmhmm,' Cleo says, and grabs the box of chocolates Spider brought for Jamie. She holds them up to ask permission but doesn't wait for his answer before tearing into the plastic wrapper.

Spider looks annoyed.

Cleo raises her eyebrows at him as if to say, *'What are you doing to do?'* After all, Jamie can't eat them. She pops one into her mouth and shoves the box at Lucasz, who sits with it on his knee like a grandma.

Then, mouth full of truffle, she explains about their middle-of-the-night adventure to get Jamie's laptop. 'We were in your room, and we heard someone creep into the house and up the stairs. It was obviously Ant, out for one of his insomnia walks. It's his evening routine. First he sets something on fire, then he drinks a mug of warm milk and falls asleep like a giant baby.'

Cleo and Lucasz burst into uncontrollable giggles.

'We don't know anything about this.' Spider shakes his head at Cleo.

She rolls her eyes at him.

'All we know is the child who lived in that house had the same first name and year of birth as your stepdad.'

'He's probably been spying on us. And if we're right and that kid is him, he'd be so pissed off if he saw me and Lucasz poking around in his childhood home.' She looks around at them all, triumphant. 'He probably set it on fire while we were in there to punish us.'

'Hold on. None of this implies anything about him being the one who set it on fire or set any of the other fires in the area—'

'But it's possible!' interrupts Cleo.

'It also suggests why he might want Cleo to go to boarding school next year.' Lucasz speaks up, and everyone pays attention. When quiet people choose to contribute, people always listen, and Lucasz often has good things to say. She's envious, especially as most frequently people seem to want Cleo herself to stop talking, not say more. Lucasz continues: 'We're having sleepovers where his parents died. That's kind of weird. Maybe it's easier for him if Cleo's not around for a bit.'

Jamie nods, agreeing with Lucasz.

Cleo opens her mouth to tell them what she saw on the recordings, but then she closes it again. She's not ready to tell them yet. There's still time to fix it if she can get something on Ant. 'Or he's a pyromaniac and we're getting closer to discovering his secret fetish for setting things on fire,' Cleo repeats. It's almost too good to be true that there might be something this big to pin on him. He'd go to jail, no question.

They're all quiet for a minute, thinking everything through. Jamie keeps looking at Spider, her face very serious. It looks like she wants to talk to him alone. Proud of her perceptiveness, Cleo nudges Lucasz. 'Let's go get some doughnuts from the Krispy Kreme near Reception.'

He nods and stands up.

'Spider, we'll see you at the exit.' She gives Jamie a kiss on the cheek, even though Jamie smells like hospital chemicals and her cheek is a yucky green colour at the edges of her bruise. But a kiss on the cheek is what a good sister would do.

Out in the corridor, she looks around. There's no eavesdropper, just nurses in their blue scrubs bustling around. They follow the signs through the windowless corridors to the exit.

Lucasz pulls her back, out of earshot. 'Do you want to go back to our house tonight? We could look through the paperwork in that office, try to find something else.'

She shakes her head. Everything bubbles up inside her, becoming hotter and more fiery by the moment. Mum signed the papers. 'I don't care about the history research project with Spider. I just need something that shows Ant is an arsonist, okay?' They round the corner into the open foyer, flooded with daylight from the glass roof. 'Lucasz, they'll send me away if I don't find something. Do you want that?'

Lucasz folds his arms, and his eyes become expressionless. Blue screen of death.

She checks her phone. Nothing.

'It's so annoying, you'd think they'd have gone through the footage by now and called me.' She shoves her phone into her pocket. 'There's bound to be something on it that incriminates him.'

Lucasz shrugs and walks faster as they reach the doughnut shop. It's unnaturally bright; fluorescent strip lights bounce off white surfaces, and there are no windows to allow daylight inside. Lucasz's skin looks yellow as he peers through the glass at the rows of doughnuts.

She turns to lean against the glass counter. She notices the shape of his shoulders: tense. And the balled fist he holds by his side. 'Just a little bit more evidence and we'll have him. In prison for arson, miles away from us.'

He pulls his phone from his pocket, doesn't look at her. 'My mum said she'd come pick me up about now.'

Lucasz is normally oblivious to time, and usually looks disappointed when he has to go home. But today's different, and Cleo doesn't understand why.

She frowns and turns back to the doughnuts. Some of them are Easter-themed: bunnies and chicks, pinks and yellows. 'Mr Cheerful not out to play today?' she says in a baby voice. It's what his mum used to call him when he was really little, apparently because he was such a smiley baby.

He turns to her. A frown mars his usually smooth forehead. 'Give it a rest, Cleo.'

'Seriously, though, what's up with you?'

'I dunno.'

'Yeah, you do.'

He glances out of the shop doorway at the people bustling through the hospital, looking for his escape. 'You could, like, care a bit that I've been looking into that house and its history. Me and Spider worked hard on it, we were in the library until it closed the other night, looking up stuff. I thought it was really cool.'

'Geek,' she teases, but gently. Even Cleo knows it's not the right time for that.

'I believe you, Cleo.' He pulls his hoodie sleeves over his fists and sits at one of the tables. 'When everyone else thinks you're a liar, I always believe you. When you said Ant was an abuser, I believed you. When everyone else said you were wrong, or paranoid, or jealous, or telling lies, again.'

She sits across from him, shaking her head. 'You're supposed to. People are supposed to believe women. Not take the abuser's side. I can't believe—'

'Stop it. I don't want your rambly rant right now. This isn't about whatever is going on in your family.'

She closes her mouth and pulls her hood up. She can tell by the tone of his voice that this will get heavy. 'What is it about, then?'

'You're my best friend.'

'You're mine too. I—'

He holds out a hand. 'Let me finish. Just stop talking for like one minute. Not everything has to be the Cleo Show.'

'Ouch.'

'I just wish you'd see me more.' He stops, glances out into the hospital again.

She tries not to talk, but… 'I don't… what do you mean? I see you all the time. Practically every day in the holidays—'

'That's not what I'm talking about. I wish you'd give me some credit, you know? For listening to you. For sticking by your side all the time.'

She bristles. She's read about this kind of shit in *Happily Ever After*. 'What, so your friendship has some kind of cost now? I have to pay you back for your good friendyness? You sound like an internet *nice guy*.'

He groans and covers his face with his fists. 'Stop twisting everything.' He checks his phone. 'My mum's here. I'm going.'

She scrambles to her feet but he's too fast, and he's out the door before she can catch him, ask him what that was really about.

She checks her pockets, but she has no money for doughnuts anyway; she had hoped Lucasz would pay. She sighs, and heads back in the direction of Jamie's room to ask Spider for a lift home.

She can hear a man's voice as she nears Jamie's cubicle. It's not Spider. She pulls back the curtains, the rings squealing on the rail. It's Mum and Ant, both with wide, fake smiles on their faces. They're wearing his 'n hers outfits: navy blue jumper with white shirt underneath and artfully distressed jeans. Gross.

Mum gives Cleo a tight smile. 'We're here to take Jamie home. She's being discharged.'

Ant barely acknowledges her. He's probably decided that the best way forward is to pretend she doesn't exist, which must be easy now he's managed to ship her off to Dad's. Cleo wishes she could do the same thing and pretend Ant doesn't exist, but it's difficult when they're cosplaying Barbie and Ken, and Mum's voice has turned just as cold as Ant's.

She watches his shoulders and twitching knees as he sits beside Jamie's bed. She examines his hands, looking for evidence of something. A burn, ash, anything. There's nothing; his hands are as perfectly manicured as ever.

She lingers outside the curtain, pretending to read noticeboards or look at signs. But Mum notices, beckons her inside. 'Cleo, love. And Jamie. We have something to tell you.'

She tries not to roll her eyes. There's always something to tell her, something serious that they can be dramatic about. Ant probably planted something in her room. Or he's decided military school is better than boarding school and there's an armoured van on its way to bundle Cleo off in handcuffs.

'Someone broke into our house a couple of nights ago.'

Cleo freezes. That is a surprise.

Jamie's pulse-o-meter thing beeps quicker. She flicks her eyes to Cleo and away.

Ant turns his head towards Mum, but his eyes don't leave Cleo.

Cleo swallows. Her surprise must show on her face. They didn't leave any evidence. She didn't break anything, and she took only Jamie's computer. Unless… She straightens her spine.

Unless Ant knew they were there. Unless he saw or heard them on his night-time roamings. Maybe he watched from the lane as Lucasz boosted her over the fence. And then decided to get the police involved, force their silence with the threat of discovery.

'We've spoken to the police, but there's not much they can do after the fact.' Mum shakes her head. 'Just a couple of things taken. But that's not the worst part.' She pauses, clearly struggling to say it.

Cleo frowns. She has no idea what she's about to say.

Mum reaches out and places a hand on Jamie's arm. 'Girls, I'm afraid we have more bad news. We can't find Daisy. She must have got out when the burglary happened, and she hasn't come back.'

Cleo gasps, brings her hands to her face. She doesn't have to look surprised at this, she's shocked. She can't talk. She can't think. It can't have been her fault.

Chapter Twenty-Three

Jamie

The drive home is uncomfortable in more ways than one. Each lurch of the car jolts Jamie's fractured ribs, and Mum and Ant chatter away. It sounds almost desperate.

Mum talks about her morning doing make-up for a bridal party, and how pretty they all were as she waved them off to the church. 'It's like coming full circle.' She squeezes Ant's hand as they reminisce about meeting on set and then their own recent wedding.

They talk about the shrivelling daffodils in the back garden as spring continues, and the wild garlic flowering in the woods behind the house. Anything except Cleo's banishment to Dad's or Jamie's accident. They clearly want to keep a cheerful mood; Mum compensating for her guilt at not being there when Jamie fell.

Cleo's silence is heavy. Her pale face stares out the window, and she occasionally checks her phone for messages. Dad and

Sahara will meet them at the house, so everyone can look for Daisy around the village.

'And you still can't remember?' Mum asks after a long-winded monologue about the neighbours who asked after Jamie. She must have run out of subjects and circled back to the reason they're driving Jamie home from the hospital in the first place.

As Mum turns around in her seat to glance at Jamie, Ant's eyes flick up to the rear-view mirror and meet hers. Then he looks back at the road. Her skin prickles.

She shakes her head. She can talk better today, especially now they've loosened the wires. But it's still painful and the doctor told her to take it easy, not talk too much for too long. It's easier not talking anyway.

They pull into the driveway, tyres crunching on the gravel. Mum slaps her hands lightly on her thighs and sing-songs: 'Here we are, home again!'

Jamie tries not to groan. She doesn't have the energy for this forced chirpiness. It's not even Mum's true personality. Mum's quiet and calm, not Little Miss Sunshine.

Cleo is out of the car almost before they pull to a stop on the driveway. She runs through the side gate, slamming it behind her as she enters the back garden.

Mum opens the car door for Jamie and helps her out; walking is still painful but it's OK if she takes her time. Ant grabs her bag from the boot and Jamie nods to thank him.

She pauses in the hallway. She thought she'd remember something about the accident when she came home. She looks around, her eyes roaming over the art deco side table with the antique miner's lamp, the varnished floorboards. A flash of memory: shouting in the kitchen. Ant following her out. His rapid footsteps, his panicked breaths. Then nothing until her face was pressed against the wooden floor. Did he push her, like Cleo says?

She glances at him. He looks pale and uncomfortable. The muscle in his jaw flexes as he clenches his teeth. He's watching her. He's acting strange, but is it guilt because it happened while he was there, or because he did something to make it happen?

She gives him a weak smile.

He looks away, drops his car keys in the bowl next to the lamp, and heads into the living room. She catches a glimpse of Daisy's empty bed next to the fireplace before the door swings half-closed behind him. Poor Daisy-dog, all she wanted was to sleep next to her humans and get taken for walkies. She would never run away.

She frowns. 'What got taken? What did they do?'

Everything looks normal, nothing smashed or broken. The front door intact. She's heard stories about thieves smearing their own shit all over the walls, smashing things for the sake of smashing. None of that happened here. The only difference is the house feels empty and sad without Daisy running to greet her.

'They must have got spooked, left early. The only thing missing is your laptop.'

Jamie gasps and opens her mouth, ready to explain. But Mum rushes towards her, arms outstretched for a hug.

Jamie shakes her head, not understanding. 'I mean, how did you even notice someone had been in if only my laptop was stolen?' She can't tell them. Cleo was so proud of their midnight raid.

'It was poor Daisy. She could never have got out by herself.' Mum straightens herself, trying not to get too sad. She rubs her hands together.

No way would Cleo have let Daisy out. 'Have you looked for her?'

'Ant walked around the village all day, calling for her.' She gathers Jamie into her arms. 'I'm so sorry, Jamie love. Someone must have left a door unlocked. All your documentary footage. I know it's a big loss, it must be.' Mum squeezes her a bit too hard and Jamie groans.

'I backed everything up. It's OK. Daisy is the most important. I can't believe she's gone. You called the police?'

'Oh, Ant did everything: called the police, talked to them, gave them a statement. He went through every cupboard to make sure nothing else was missing. He's been great. So strong. Such a rock to me.'

Jamie's stomach churns.

'Want to get settled back in? I can make a cup of tea.'

Jamie shakes her head. She's had enough NHS tea to last a lifetime. 'I'll just go to my room,' she mumbles. She pulls herself up with a hand on the bannister and winces.

'I'll bring you some water. Jamie, love, it's such a relief you didn't lose all your footage, that it was all backed up. Ant will be so pleased; I know how important it is to him to see you succeed.'

She turns to climb the stairs and catches sight of a movement on the other side of the half-open living room door. Ant, hovering. Listening.

Cleo

'Such a shame about Daisy,' Sahara says to Mum and Ant. Dad and Sahara are on the sofa Daisy used to sit on because it's nearer the fire. There's still fur all over the blanket that Sahara sat on in her immaculate white jeans, Cleo notes with a smirk. 'I know how much you loved that dog.'

Mum and Ant are squeezed together on the big sofa, closer than necessary.

'Love. Present tense,' Cleo shouts. 'She's not dead.' Her eyes fill with tears, thinking about poor Daisy, lost and alone, looking for her family. She says in a low voice: 'She'll wonder what she did wrong, why we've left her.' She can't bear it. She clenches her fists so hard that her fingernails mark her palms, creating little crescent moons of pain.

She sends herself back through that night, mentally replaying everything, from Lucasz boosting her over the fence to their silent creep up the stairs.

She texts Lucasz, her thumbs flickering over her screen.

Do u remember if we closed the patio door at Mum's when we were here????? Daisy's missing.

The ticks turn blue; he reads it but doesn't reply.

She doesn't remember. Lucasz was behind her, though. Kind, reliable Lucasz.

'Look at these posters.' Mum holds them out to Cleo, a huge thick stack.

Cleo takes the posters into her hands, still warm from the printer. She wants to press them against her face. Little Daisy peers out at her from the poster, her eyes even more sparkly than usual.

'Ant designed them,' Mum says proudly, smiling up at him.

Cleo hands the posters to Sahara, not wanting them anywhere near her anymore. 'Did you Photoshop her too?' she says to Ant. 'Use a bit of Facetune to make her eyes extra sparkly?'

Ant pulls a fake confused face.

She types again.

When we went inside. Did you close it behind us? LUCASZ PLEASE ANSWER

He would have closed the door behind them, surely. She doesn't remember the shuuuurrrrp noise though. Did he leave it open? If they left the patio door open, Daisy would have got out into the garden. She has never run away, not even when she chases squirrels in the park. Not even if there was a hole in the fence. She wouldn't leave the garden, and her comfy bed, and her humans.

Mum clears her throat and picks up her teacup with a warning glance at Cleo. She puts a hand on Ant's knee. 'Great posters, love.'

And we closed the gate too? Lucasz, please answer.

No ticks arrive. He must have turned off his phone. She sniffs.

Cleo shakes her head. 'I don't know why we're acting like he's some kind of hero for printing out a couple of posters. I could have done that in Microsoft Word.'

'Awww.' Sahara sticks out her lip at the picture. 'She's such a lovely dog. I'm so sorry, guys. I really hope we find her safe and well soon.'

Dad nods. 'Daisy's so big, so noisy. It's hard to imagine her getting lost. Someone's bound to have picked her up.'

'Everyone loves Daisy,' Sahara says.

'Ant doesn't,' Cleo mumbles into the knees she's hugging to her chest.

Sahara looks at her, eyes wide. Dad is about to chip in when the living room door opens.

'Hey, guys.'

Everyone turns to Jamie and coos a greeting, talking in that weird simpery tone people use when someone's been ill. *'How are you?' 'You poor thing.'* Blah, blah.

'Hey, Jamie,' Cleo says loudly, to show them how normal people should speak to other normal people.

Jamie looks better: less sleepy and out of it than under the glare of the hospital lights. The angry bruises around her jaw have softened to a sickly greeny-yellow, and her face swelling is starting to reduce. She still looks like a Moomin with her lower face puffed up from the surgery. Cleo watches her, seeing how she acts around Ant, whether she's had any memories of the accident, if Ant really pushed her.

But Jamie's not looking at Ant, she's staring at Cleo with an urgent frown.

'Cleo, can I borrow you for a sec?' she asks in her new gritted-teeth voice.

Cleo can't tell if Jamie's angry or if that's just how she talks now she's got a broken jaw. She gets up from the hearthrug and follows Jamie out into the hall. 'You OK?' She tries to sound nonchalant.

'What the fuck, Cleo? They called the police. Why didn't you tell them you took the laptop?' Jamie sits on the stairs, wincing as she lowers herself down. 'And wouldn't the police know if you supposedly took the laptop to the station today so they could copy our files?'

Cleo opens her mouth to reply, but Jamie interrupts. 'More

lies, Cleo? And what happened to Daisy? Where is she? Don't tell me you did—'

Cleo shakes her head violently and grabs Jamie's arms. Jamie flinches and Cleo lets go quickly. 'Sorry.'

Jamie rubs her arm where Cleo gripped her.

Cleo looks over her shoulder to the living room, but the grown-ups have started talking again, their voices a low rumble through the closed door.

'I didn't do anything to Daisy,' she hisses. 'How could you even think…'

'So what happened then? All I know is the night you broke into the house, our dog disappeared.'

'Ant did it. I know he did.'

Jamie takes a step back, folds her arms. 'Oh, come on. Stop it with that shit. You and Lucasz were here in the middle of the night and Daisy got out. Just admit it.'

Cleo shakes her head, starts to explain, but Jamie continues: 'And where is my laptop? I need it, Cleo. You can't just take things that don't belong to do you, and… and, what? Drop them off at the police station as if it's some kind of active investigation? Are you a fantasist? How long will they keep it for, anyway? Did you even ask?'

Cleo's cheeks burn and her body tenses as Jamie's volume increases. She doesn't want the grown-ups to hear. 'I'll get it, okay?'

'You'd better. I want it back. All my documentary stuff is on there and I need to…' She trails off.

There's a tentative knock at the front door. Cleo crosses the hall and finds Lucasz on the doorstep, his arms folded. 'I got your texts about Daisy. I wanted to come help look for her.' He speaks to Jamie, looking past Cleo as if she isn't there.

'I don't get it, guys. Why not just tell them you took the laptop? That you borrowed it, that I said it was OK?'

'You really don't get it, you're right.'

'Go on then. Help me understand why you're telling lies and letting Mum and Ant believe they've been burgled.'

'Ant knows it wasn't burglars. He knows I was here.'

Lucasz shrugs at Jamie. 'I don't know why we can't just tell them.'

Cleo feels a prickle of irritation, watching Lucasz team up with Jamie like this. Lucasz should be on Cleo's side, always. He's her sidekick no matter what. And here he is making her look like a liar when she's not. Well, two can play the blame game.

'Lucasz didn't shut the patio door behind us when we came in.' She throws him a look, as if to say, *I'm not finished with you.*

'Stop lying. What's the point?' Lucasz leans against the bannister, his jaw set. 'The truth is fine. We were here, she's not lying about that. And maybe we left the patio door open. But Daisy wasn't here when we arrived. Whatever happened to Daisy had already happened.'

Cleo nods, her cheeks hot. Lucasz is right. 'You know what Daisy's like, she would have been right there as soon as me and Lucasz got into the garden, sniffing around ready to play, rushing over to lick us and swipe things off the coffee table with her tail. But she wasn't here. Not a sign. I even whistled for her and she didn't come.'

Lucasz groans. 'No, you didn't whistle.' He turns to Jamie. 'We didn't make a sound.'

'Okay,' Jamie looks from Cleo to Lucasz, confused.

'Ant was wandering around the house in the middle of the night. We heard him.'

Jamie looks at Lucasz for verification of this, and Lucasz

gives a small nod. 'We heard someone, she's right. They came in after us. It was just footsteps. We didn't see anyone for sure. It could have been a burglar.'

'A burglar who took nothing? There was no burglar, Lucasz.' Cleo tries to catch his eye, but he won't look at her. She shrugs; clearly he's still angry with her about something. 'So Daisy was already gone when we got here. Ant must have gone out with Daisy before we even arrived and dumped her somewhere. Then when he came back, we left the patio door open, so he knew we were in the house.' She flicks a dirty look at Lucasz. 'And Jamie's laptop was gone when they checked the next day. Which means Ant knew we were in the house that night. So he reported a break-in to the police, which gave him the perfect cover for ditching Daisy. He's set me up.'

This whole thing is a warning to Cleo, straight from Ant. He's telling her he knows her game, and he's not afraid to play.

'Why get rid of Daisy now? Why not months ago, if your theory is right?' Jamie asks.

'Good question,' mumbles Lucasz.

Cleo thinks for a moment. 'You.' She nods at Jamie. 'He knew you were getting discharged the next day; he needed to get rid of her while he had an empty house. Mum'll sleep through anything, and he knows I can't blab because I'd have to admit to creeping around here at night when I should have been at Dad's house. More reasons to ship me off to boarding school.'

The voices in the living room stop, and Cleo, Jamie and Lucasz look at each other, eyes wide. Did someone hear?

Footsteps move towards the door, and Mum comes out. Cleo catches a glimpse of Ant and Sahara laughing together as

Mum closes the door behind her. She looks from one to another, a half-smile on her face.

'Everything all right?' She lets out a little breathy giggle, her hand still on the doorknob of the living room. 'You lot look like you're plotting something.'

An awkward silence. Cleo wants to tell Mum, to talk to her like she used to, just open her mouth and let everything spill out exactly as it is in her head. No lies, no manipulation, just the truth and have someone listen to her and take her at her word. But that doesn't happen anymore; everything she says is questioned, interrogated, and doubted. For a long time, she's had to calculate what she says to even have a shot at being heard. It's exhausting.

Is it too much to ask to have Mum take her at her word?

She stares at Mum, at her tidy blonde bob, her engagement and wedding rings glinting on her manicured hand. She looks prettier and more expensive than Cleo ever remembers seeing her look. Her nails are perfect, her jeans look like they were made to measure. She's lost weight again, the product of Ant's rigid diet and the Peloton bike he bought her for Christmas. She looks good. But around the eyes, she looks haunted.

'Just talking about looking for Daisy. Lucasz came to help.'

'That's lovely, Lucasz. Thank you.' Mum walks away, heading towards the kitchen.

'I see it, Mum,' Cleo says quietly. She follows Mum, leaving Jamie and Lucasz on the stairs. She's tried the truth, she's tried lies. None of them work.

Mum frowns, shakes her head.

'I see you're not happy. Not really. It's in your eyes.'

'Stop, Cleo. I'm very happy. Jamie's home and my whole family's here, all together.'

'Except Daisy.'

Mum nods, her face sagging. 'Except Daisy.'

'Ant's not a dog person, is he?'

Mum's eyebrows raise in confusion.

Cleo has to talk fast if she wants to be heard. 'He's never liked Daisy. He doesn't want her on the sofa, doesn't feed her or give her cuddles. I've seen him kick at her if she's in his way.'

'This isn't true.'

Cleo shakes her head. 'You must have seen him. He shoves Daisy's head off his knee and then washes his hands, as if she's disease-ridden. And he hates her shedding on his posh clothes, drooling on the sofa. He spends most of his time trying to pretend she isn't here. And now she's not, so he's got his way. Again.'

'He takes her for a walk before bed each night. Can't have disliked her that much.'

'He didn't want her,' Cleo calls as Mum turns away. 'He said she was getting old.'

She just shakes her head.

This is Cleo's only chance. 'I was here last night. And Daisy wasn't.'

Mum freezes, her hand hovers in mid-air, reaching for mugs in the cupboard. 'What? You were at Dad's.'

'When Daisy went missing.' In a rush, Cleo tells Mum about creeping into the house, the footsteps, no dog to greet them.

Forgetting the tea, Mum turns around and stares at Cleo through narrowed eyes. She looks like she's thinking.

Cleo needs to fill the silence. 'He's dangerous, Mum. We've found something out, something about his past. And the fires, the arson ones Jamie's been looking into—'

'Get out.' Mum's voice is quiet, but her clarity pierces the air, like a sharp knife through the skin of a tomato. 'I need you to get out.'

Cleo's stomach burns. 'What?'

'Go and do something useful. Take the posters and get out of this house.' She thrusts a stack of posters at Cleo, and a few slide onto the kitchen floor. 'I can't look at you right now and I don't want you here.'

Cleo's eyes fill with tears as she scrabbles to pick up the fallen papers. 'I just want you to—'

'I don't CARE, Cleo,' Mum roars, her voice so loud that the light fitting above their head seems to hum. 'I've had enough.'

Cleo opens her mouth, shocked. She's never heard her Mum shout like that.

'I can't look at you right now and I can't trust myself not to…' Mum trails off, turns away to fill the kettle. 'Go and put up posters with Lucasz. Be back at seven to leave with your dad.'

'Everything all right?' Ant pokes his head through the door.

'Here he comes,' Cleo mumbles.

As suddenly as she shouted, Mum plasters a fake smile on her face. 'Yes, thank you love. Cleo's just going out to put up your lovely posters.'

She glares at Cleo and shakes her head slightly, the smile fixed to her face, but her eyes twinkle with unshed tears.

Mum has always been good at pretending.

Chapter Twenty-Four

Jamie

The house is finally quiet, everyone gone out to distribute posters, knock on doors and ask neighbours if they've seen Daisy. Jamie agreed to stay home in case Daisy returns, and she's grateful to get some peace and quiet, the first alone time in days with no noise, no alarms, no bustling.

Jamie seethes with frustration at Cleo; she can never tell what's true, what's a skewed version of reality and what's just an outright lie. Did Cleo take Jamie's laptop to the police station, or did she just say that as part of some unfathomable game? It was the same even when Cleo was a little girl: 'But Daddy said I could' and 'It was like that when I found it.' She has never understood her younger sister, why everything has to be complicated and twisted and turned into drama and lies. Surely life is simpler if you just tell the truth and let things go as they must?

As soon as the door closes behind everyone, she heads to Ant's study. The desk is piled high with paperwork: bills, folders and forms from the wedding stacked up to create a little barrier around the desk. Next to the desk, the wall is damaged: a fist-shaped hole.

She moves a manila folder off the chair and sits down, waggling the mouse to wake up the computer.

Her heartbeat slows as the desktop icons appear. She opens a browser and enters the URL for her cloud service, sighing with relief as she clicks 'Forgotten password?' and enters a new one.

The documentary is hers again, even though her laptop remains AWOL with Cleo.

Job done, she settles on the couch with Netflix, browsing for something mindless and easy to watch. She's about to choose an old romcom with Matthew McConaughey when the doorbell rings.

She groans. Probably Cleo and Lucasz, pretending they've put up all their posters so they can raid the snack cupboard while everyone's out. She pulls herself up and hobbles to the door, the pain in her ribs accentuated by movement.

She frowns at the outline of a person through the frosted panes on the front door. It's not Cleo: too tall. Not Lucasz either: too broad.

Her stomach flips. The arsonist sent that parcel. Knows where she lives.

She brushes the fear away. It's just her body's reaction to the accident: telling her to be more careful, to not get injured again. She's afraid of everything now; something horrendous could happen to her at any moment.

She opens the door a crack and peeks out. As soon as she sees who it is, she almost slams the door again. Does he already know what she's done?

'What do you want, Spider?' she asks. 'You said you would

stop doing this.' There's that fear again, the palm of her hand sticky against the door frame. Out of his sightline, behind the half-open door, she draws her phone from her pocket and unlocks the display. She might be paranoid, but at least she can call for help if anything happens, if his persistence is a sign of something more sinister, more dangerous.

'I'm really sorry, Jamie. Lucasz texted me and told me about Daisy.' His eyes look glassy.

She nods and opens the door a little more. He really loves Daisy. And Daisy loves Spider too; they play together for hours in the garden. Like Lucasz, as soon as Spider arrived at the house, Daisy would run off to find her ball or her tug toy, trotting around after him until he followed her into the garden. Then, when they'd finished playing, she'd climb onto his lap and become a massive, furry obstruction to any conversation.

'I came round to see if there's anything I can do. I could set up a Facebook page or something. Make some posters.'

'Ant's already made some. They're out putting them up right now.' She wants to thank him, but she also doesn't want to give him the impression he's welcome here, or that they need his help.

His face breaks into a smile, the laughter lines creasing up his cheeks and making her stomach flip.

He's so handsome.

No, Jamie. She shakes the thought away. *You can't trust him.*

'I missed your voice.' His eyes rake over her face, settling on the bruises and then back to her eyes. She feels her resolve weaken as she retains eye contact, taking in the icy blue of his eyes, the love she sees reflected in the soft way he looks at her. *Can* she trust him?

'You look much better.' He lifts a hand towards her and then changes his mind, moving to scratch his nose. He's trying.

She thanks him and shifts from foot to foot. Her body aches from standing at the door, her feet cold on the wooden floor. There's a twinge of guilt about what she's just done, but she shakes it off: it's her project, and she needed to regain control.

'Sorry, Jamie. I'm sorry for everything. There's a lot I'd like to talk to you about—'

She shakes her head, and he stops talking immediately, his expression open, ready. He wants to hear what she has to say, she can tell. 'I've felt so… trampled by you. Every time I said I felt uncomfortable about the way we were making the documentary, or I wanted some space, you acted like you knew better, like your feelings were more important.'

He's still listening. 'We made a plan for the documentary, and I needed us to stick to it. You were rewriting it while we were filming, without us even talking it through, and it was freaking me out.'

He nods, slides his hands into his pockets. He looks down at his shoes, and back at her. 'I'm sorry,' he whispers.

'I know I'm a bit of a control freak. I need to get better at that. But I've asked myself over and over why you wouldn't listen. It wasn't like you. You became someone else, someone pushy and thoughtless.' Now she says it out loud, she wonders if she is the person who has changed. If he has always been this way but she hadn't noticed until now.

'I should have told you from the beginning,' he almost whispers.

She opened her mouth to carry on, certain he would let her talk. But his whisper stops her. 'Told me what?'

'I haven't been entirely honest with you about everything.'

She knew there must be something she didn't understand. That it couldn't be just that he didn't care about her and her feelings.

Without warning, the world tilts. She's been standing too long, and the pain in her body gets too much. She's dizzy, her skin covered in a light sheen of sweat, like she has a fever. She reaches up and props herself up on the doorframe with one hand, clinging to the door handle with the other.

Spider takes a step forward. 'Woah, Jamie.' He wraps her arm around his shoulders, propping her up. He's gentle but firm. 'You've gone really pale,' he says as he manoeuvres her into the house.

She catches sight of herself in the mirror by the door and he's right: her eyes are dark holes in her grey face. The only colour is the angry purples and greens and the huge slice of red which is her surgery scar. It's the first time she's seen herself since the bandages came off. She looks frightful.

He moves her swiftly past the mirror and sits her on the sofa. 'I'll go make some tea.'

She hears him humming to himself as he fills the kettle, pulls the mugs from the cupboard. He returns quickly, a steaming mug in each hand.

'There's two sugars in yours. I think you need it.' He smiles at her tentatively as he puts the cups on the coffee table.

How can he look at her with such love when her face is so monstrous? Can he really see past all the swelling and bruises?

He sits next to her, jostling her slightly as his weight lands on the sofa. 'Sorry,' he mumbles, and puts a hand on her arm.

'What do you need to tell me?' she asks quietly.

He leans forward to pick up his mug and holds it to his lips, blowing on it. Without taking a sip he puts it back on the table. He's stalling.

She puts her phone on the table next to the mugs.

'First, I'm sorry I didn't listen when you weren't happy with the documentary. I kept pushing, I know that. I know you, and I know you need to feel in control. That it bothers you when you don't. And I'm sorry if that freaked you out when I came to the hospital. When I heard about your accident, all I wanted was to be near you, to make sure you were OK. I didn't think it would seem strange or horrible to you that your ex-boyfriend turned up when you couldn't talk or tell me to go away. I didn't think about anything except needing to see you. I'm such a selfish shit sometimes and I really want to be better. You make me a better person and I want to improve.'

She nods slowly. He's considered things from her side and he understands. There's no anger or blame from him, just a sincere desire to understand her perspective and share his own. She feels her uneasiness dissipate like fog on a spring morning. She's not there yet, not ready to start again, but she's willing to listen some more.

'So you needed to tell me why you were so fixated on this documentary?'

'Yeah. The whole reason I'd even heard about the fires in the first place. It's not like they're common knowledge around here.' He leans forward, his forearms resting on his knees. 'The woman who died in the theatre fire. She was my mum's best friend. They were practically sisters, grew up together.'

Jamie's mouth falls open. She leans towards him, her shoulder touching his. 'I'm so sorry.'

'I thought we could get some answers, you know? Especially when it seemed like the arsonist might still be around.' He leans against her too, and she feels the warmth of his body along the length of her, the hairs on his arm tickling the skin of her own.

She shivers, and goosepimples rise on her skin. Her cheeks flush. 'I had no idea. That theatre interview must have been weird for you.'

He shakes his head. 'I didn't know Mum's friend or anything. But it devastated my mum. My dad said she was never quite as fun after that, like it took something away from her.'

'I wish you'd said something. I wouldn't have been so quick to shut it all down.'

He shrugs. 'You were right, though, Jamie. I pushed too hard. I was so desperate to make people feel something about these fires, because the police treated it like a victimless crime. But there are victims and lives ruined by these fires. You were right to feel uncomfortable. I prodded people too deep, made them relive their pain for the camera over and over. I thought I needed to connect the arson to emotion and make people care, but I didn't need to be so pushy about it.'

Jamie turns to look at his profile. His nose is so exactly right for his face. His dark beard contrasts with the smoothness of the skin on his cheeks. 'And then I broke up with you.'

'I wanted the documentary to be brilliant, to be a well-rounded thing that didn't all hinge on this one death. I wanted it to be ground-breaking. But I had some kind of misguided notion that I could solve the arson attacks and get justice for Mum, her friend and her family, give Mum something to be proud of me for.'

'She's not proud?'

He shrugs. 'A tattoo artist faffing around with a camera in his free time doesn't really cut it for her.'

She leans into him, and he curls his arm around her. He smells like washing powder and shower gel, and a faint undertone of his skin which makes her want to bury her nose in his neck and inhale deeply. 'You've got a lot to make her proud.'

He stiffens, leans away from her. 'Jamie. I want to respect

what you asked for.' He stands up, straightens his hoodie with both hands. 'I will leave you alone. I'm so pleased you're OK. And I'm sorry to come over again. This'll be the last time, I promise. But I'll keep an eye out for any news about Daisy. She's an amazing dog.' He starts to stand up.

Jamie's stomach plummets. 'Wait. Please finish your tea.' She indicates the half-drunk cup which still steams in front of the seat he just vacated. 'I'd like to hear some more about what you said in the hospital. About the person who owns the house in the woods. The orphan.'

———————

Cleo

After an hour of trudging around the village, Cleo and Lucasz buy Cornettos at the village shop and rest on a bench, quietly licking their cones.

She nudges him with her shoulder. 'Can we be friends again now? I don't like it when you're cross.'

He shrugs. His cheeks turn pink as he pays extra attention to his ice cream to avoid looking at her.

She grins. 'What if I tell you you're a total badass?'

A twitch plays at the corner of his mouth. She's getting there.

'A Winged Hussar!'

He laughs. 'I'll think about it. Where shall we put up posters next?' he asks, his frown disappearing as he starts to thaw. All he needs is attention and he can't help but like her again.

'Who cares? We won't find Daisy anyway.'

'What do you mean?'

She folds her arms. 'Exactly that. Ant took her and dumped her somewhere. Or chased her off. Either way, he won't shit on his own doorstep. She's probably miles away. Posters around the village won't help. We're wasting our time.'

Lucasz pauses mid-lick, frowning.

She shrugs. 'I'll make a Facebook page instead. It'll reach more people.'

A car slows and stops by the side of the road, its engine idling. Cleo looks up from her ice cream and sees Dad staring at her through the window.

He lowers the window. 'Working hard, I see,' he calls.

She grins and waves, crossing the road to lean against the bonnet of the car. 'You going home?'

Dad nods. 'We've done all the little lanes, stuck posters up on the lampposts. Getting home now as we've both got work in the morning. You coming?'

Cleo pauses. Mum might hate her, but there might be another chance to get her to listen. 'Do you mind if I stay here? I'd like to keep helping to find Daisy.'

Dad nods and shifts into gear.

'Wait!' she shouts, opening the back door to pull the laptop bag out from behind the passenger seat.

'What's that?'

'Secret!'

Dad just shrugs. The least curious man alive.

As they pull away, Sahara leans over in her seat and gives a small smile through the open window. 'Hope you find Daisy, Cleo. Keep an eye out.'

'Will do,' Cleo mumbles, her voice lost under the grumble of the car engine.

Back home, Ant's car is still gone, but there's a beat-up Corsa van at a jaunty angle on the drive.

Lucasz's face lights up when he sees it. 'Spider's here,' he says brightly.

Cleo pushes the front door open and leaves it swinging; it's not like Daisy is here to get out. She hears Lucasz following behind her but doesn't wait for him.

'Caught you!' She bursts into the living room, expecting to find Spider and Jamie in some sort of reunion embrace, but instead they're hunched over the coffee table, surrounded by pieces of paper.

They both look up, startled. Spider had started to gather up all the papers, but as soon as he sees it's Cleo he relaxes. 'Thought it might be your mum or Ant.' He lays the papers back on the table with a smile.

'What are you doing?' She nonchalantly wanders to the table, trying to hide her curiosity. It's a bunch of printouts, photocopies, and scans: old newspaper articles, photographs, and official-looking documents. She recognises some of them: there's the picture of the family she found on the mirror in the old derelict house, and another one from the same day, with their hands and faces in slightly different positions.

'Spider's showing me some information he's got about the theatre fire, from his mum.'

'And we got the title deed information back,' Spider adds.

'Stuff about the burned house being Ant's house?' Cleo asks.

'Shhhhh,' Jamie hisses. 'Be quiet, OK?'

'Is that my laptop?' Jamie spies the bag slung over Cleo's shoulder. She grins and hands it over. Job done. 'Told you I'd get it back.'

'Better late than never, I suppose.' Jamie rolls her eyes.

Cleo sticks out her tongue in reply.

Spider hands her a piece of paper. 'These are The Old Manor's deeds; they came through this morning. I submitted a request on the government portal a few weeks ago to see who owns the house. The system was down, so it took ages before they got back with a scan.'

Cleo takes the paper and nods, trying to look impressed, but really just looking for something that says 'Ant' or 'Tony'. It's a very old document copied on grey recycled paper. It's pages and pages long, most of them handwritten in that illegible old handwriting people used to learn in school before typewriters were invented. She flips through it and hands the papers back to Spider. 'Fascinating.'

He laughs. 'These are too early.' He takes back the stack of paper, pulls one sheet from the stack and hands it to her. 'This is the one you want to see.'

This one is newer; it's typewritten with some signatures.

Spider points at part of the paper where a name is written. 'It matches what we found in the birth records. The house belongs to a Tony Kerr.'

'Ant!' she squeals.

'What are you doing?' It's a snarl. It's him.

Cleo covers her mouth with her hands, as if she could claw back the sound of his name as it still reverberates through the air. None of them heard the door open.

Jamie looks up, the colour draining from her smashed-up face.

Spider draws his finger back from the paper as if he's been burned. He picks up the deed and slides it into a bigger pile of newspaper clippings. Then he grabs Jamie's phone where it's been lying on the table and quietly presses RECORD. He props it against a mug on the table, aimed at Ant, who doesn't notice: he is so focused on the papers scattered across the table.

Cleo draws a breath, but resolves to stand firm, to not let him scare her. She stares at him, dares him to make a move.

Ant stands in the doorway, his eyes tracking over the papers spread around. He strides to the coffee table and picks up the deed, the page with *Tony Kerr* all over it.

For a moment he looks confused, and then Cleo is positive she sees a flicker of fear cross his face as he stares at it, the paper shaking in his hand. He's silent. He must be afraid they know about his past. His psychopath pyromaniac past. She suppresses a grin. *Gotcha.*

Behind Ant, the front door closes, snapping him out of it. He drops the deed back to the table and looks around at all three of them, his cheeks a blotchy mix of red and pale white skin. His eyes are wide, his face haunted.

'I don't know where you got any of this.' He gestures at the table, his movements jerky. 'But you need to get rid of it. NOW.' His final word is a bark.

Jamie tries: 'Ant, it's for the documentary. I thought—'

'Drop it immediately. That paper… if I'd known what you were… what this…' His voice fades as he hears Mum's footsteps, but the tension remains in every tendon of his body. 'Clear this up before your mother sees,' he snaps, as he crosses to the living room door and pokes his head outside. He murmurs to Mum, 'Go put the kettle on, love,' in a fake calm voice.

'Why, though? Have you got something to hide?' Cleo asks. She picks up a newspaper clipping which shows a blurry black and white image of the house in the woods, its damaged wing burned out and gaping at the camera. The headline reads:

Devastating fire kills two, leaves orphaned child. 'What's this house got to do with you, *Tony*?'

He turns back into the room. 'That's not my name. Get this stuff out of the house. Burn it for all I care,' he hisses. 'Do not let your mum see it.'

Cleo stands up. 'You have no right to tell them to do that. This is their research. You wanted Jamie to make this documentary, right?'

His face is chalk-white, a thin sheen of sweat on his top lip. His expression changes then, his forehead smooths out and his eyes turn black as the pupils dilate. He looks like a snake about to strike.

Jamie clears her throat. 'It's for the documentary, Ant.' She's trying her nice voice; the reasonable one she uses when Cleo's about to have a tantrum. It doesn't work on Ant.

'What's wrong, Tony? Did we find out something we shouldn't have?'

'My name is Ant.'

Cleo watches his manicured hands. And then she sees it and takes a breath: his knuckles.

She remembers his silent fury on that video, the night he loomed over Mum and forced her to sign the papers. Mum's flinch away from him, scared of his physical power.

'Stop this immediately.' His knuckles are red raw. The remnants of a punch. 'Believe me. It's not worth it.'

Cleo's skin prickles all over.

'Get out, all of you.' He points at the table and whispers, 'And take this with you, or you'll wish you never saw that stupid fucking house.'

Chapter Twenty-Five

Jamie

As he sweeps from the room, something in Ant's tone makes them all pause, silent. They listen to his footsteps on the floorboards in the hallway as he stalks away.

Spider catches Jamie's eye, gives her a look as if to say, *Woah, what was that?*

She shakes her head, a request that he stay quiet and not comment. This is her family, no matter how awkward the situation. Her cheeks burn with shame. So much drama in their once-peaceful home.

Cleo is the first to break the silence. 'Whew, he was ANGRY. Guess we discovered his secrets,' she whispers. 'What did he mean, "you'll wish you never saw that stupid fucking house"?'

'Don't.' Jamie shakes her head. It's too much to think about. 'That's a threat.'

Lucasz stands up. 'I'm going to go, guys.' He looks shaken and small, like a kid again.

Cleo moves to stop him, but Lucasz shakes his head. 'I think it's best that it's just your family around here right now.'

Jamie gives him a smile.

Lucasz glances at Spider from under his hair. Spider gets the message and stands up, too. 'Yeah, family drama and everything. The fewer witnesses, the better, I say.' Spider tries to laugh to make it a joke, but no one joins in. He gathers the papers from the table, tucks the stack under his arm.

Cleo stamps her foot. 'Shit, guys. If you're both going, I'll come too. Don't leave me in this madhouse.' She pats Jamie on the head. 'Sorry, sis. Broken ribs'll just slow us down.'

Jamie remains on the sofa as the others leave, her senses attuned to the tension in the house. She opens her laptop and checks it's working properly after its little adventure with Cleo. It seems fine, and she logs into ComCo Home Surveillance to see what Cleo messed with. She stops, her mouse hovering over their feeds. She thought Cleo removed all the cameras, but she must have missed one. There's a live feed of Mum and Ant in the kitchen, talking. Before she can debate if it's a good idea or not, she unmutes the feed and their voices pipe out from her laptop speakers.

'We need to talk, Ella,' Ant says.

Jamie's stomach plunges. She pulls her headphones from her pocket and plugs them in, stuffing them into her ears as fast as she can.

Mum mumbles something, but the microphone doesn't catch it. Jamie sees her body language, though: she's hunched, like she's broken. Ant paces around the kitchen like a caged tiger, looking like he wants to hit something. Or someone.

Jamie leans forward; her nose almost touches her laptop screen as she watches the feed, a copy of what's happening in the kitchen just on the other side of the wall. The way that photograph trembled in his fingers… she grabs her phone from her pocket, ready to call someone if Ant hurts Mum. If Cleo's right.

'I don't know what Cleo and Jamie are up to but it's serious. They're about to cause a big problem for us. For you. Cleo is a liability. Either she's making up crazy stories, sending messages to strangers, or she's running away, or burning something to the ground.'

Mum looks up then. 'What? Cleo burned something?'

'Jamie's documentary is giving her ideas. Cleo sees the attention it gets. That fire in the middle of the night. Coming home covered in ash. She'll get herself killed. Or worse.'

'She's not setting anything on fire, Ant. Please don't accuse her of that.'

He stops pacing and runs the hot tap. It's loud and Jamie pulls the earbuds from her ears. When she puts them back in with the volume lowered, he's still ranting: 'She's wound everyone around her little finger, and they all believe her lies.'

'Stop, Ant. Please. This is my daughter you're talking about. You can't say these things. I know it takes time, but you need to give them a chance. Cleo and Jamie are your stepdaughters.' She rubs her eyes, smudging mascara underneath until she looks exhausted. 'All I want is a peaceful life where my family cares about each other and no one hurts each other.'

'I want that too, I—'

'Then drop it with Cleo. Stop picking at her, stop demanding we send her away. *My daughter*, Ant. You want to send my daughter away. I wasn't ready to sign that boarding school form.'

Jamie gasps, and opens her phone to write a new text to Cleo:

Mum just admitted he forced her to sign your boarding school papers.

'This isn't working out, is it?' Mum's voice is calm, but a tremor betrays her feelings.

Ant opens and closes his mouth, speechless.

Mum carries on: 'Maybe it's because you don't have your own kids, or maybe it's because you didn't grow up in a family home and you just don't get it. But whatever it is, you know what?' Mum stops for a moment as if waiting for an answer.

'You know what?' On the screen, Mum's whole face is red and swollen, tears coursing down her cheeks. 'She wins.'

Jamie's phone buzzes with a text from Cleo, and her skin prickles as she reads:

And I think he hits her. I have to get rid of him.

'I don't understand what you mean.'

'If you constantly ask me to choose between you, I choose Cleo. I have to.'

'I'm not asking you to—'

'I choose Cleo.' Mum slaps a hand on the table.

'Right.' With his back to her, he speaks quietly, his voice eerily calm: 'I thought I could wait it out, you know? Wait until she went to boarding school and everything would calm down. All I wanted was to take care of you and make you happy.' He turns around, and there's a knife in his hand.

Jamie gasps, raises her hands to cover her mouth.

'Ella, I need your help and I need you to tell me the truth.' His movements are wild, as if now he's lost Ella, he's got nothing left to lose, no reason to hold back anymore. 'I pushed Jamie to make this documentary because I thought maybe it would bring me some answers, for the children who lost parents like I did. But when I saw all that paperwork they had in there... everything changed.'

He waves the knife around as he outlines the deeds, the photographs, and the newspaper clippings he saw spread all over the coffee table. The blade glints in the reflection of the kitchen spotlights.

He paces around the central island: round and round and round. His voice cracks. 'Spider has a photograph of the family whose house burned down, two parents who died in the fire, and a child who survived. They are somehow convinced I am that child. That I own that house in the woods. That I set it on fire, killed my own parents.'

He points the knife at Mum, inches from her face. Jamie braces, ready to run to help.

But then Ant turns back to the sink. He picks up a sponge and wipes the blade, throws it down onto the draining board with a clatter.

He stops washing up, stands with his hands on either side of the sink, his shoulders shaking. He raises a hand to his cheek, and Jamie realises with shock: he's crying.

Mum sees at the same time and crosses to his side, places a hand on his back.

He tenses under her touch and steps away from her. He swipes at his cheek with a balled fist.

She shakes her head. 'Ant, I don't know what you're—'

'Yes, you do know.' He gestures at the living room. 'I know the child in the picture. And so do you.'

Mum gasps and pushes him away. 'You're wrong.'

He shakes his head, his shoulders slumped in defeat. 'The name on the deed of that burned house is Tony Kerr.'

There's a silence so deep that for a moment Jamie thinks the feed has frozen. She reaches to press crtl–alt–delete, but then Mum's breath comes out in a rush of static through Jamie's headphones. She throws her hands in the air and steps back from him, knocking over one of the stools from the breakfast bar with a clatter.

Ant grabs her arm, steadying her, but he doesn't let go. 'Ella, you know who it is. And if I'm right, you know what it means for me.'

Tension crackles in the air as she watches Mum storm away from Ant on the fuzzy camera feed of her laptop. Jamie hears her stomp up the stairs, sobbing. It's a strange sound, not one Jamie has heard before, Mum crying. She never cries. This must be bad. She hears their bedroom door slam.

How does Ant know the kid in the picture? And what does he think that has to do with Mum?

On the screen, Ant sits at the breakfast bar, his head in his hands, his shoulders shaking. She watches the camera feed for a few more minutes as Ant stands up and clears away pots in the kitchen, his movements sharp and angry. Then he leaves the room.

She removes her headphones and listens, trying to discern where they both are in the house. She listens to Mum's footsteps stomping around, hears doors slam and then silence. Over the whirring of her laptop fan, there's the sound of voices in the garden outside: Cleo, Lucasz and Spider.

She closes the laptop and climbs the stairs to her room, hand on the bannister, her feet still unsteady. She pulls her headphones back on and clicks to Spotify, laying back on her bed. She needs a break from this mad family and her own crazy head, so she cranks the music right up and closes her eyes.

The Arsonist

It's an addiction and I can't control it. I've always been this way, ever since I knew what fire was, what it could do.

My fires were not about revenge. Nor about hurting people. In fact, I barely thought about the property owners at all. It was about convenience, ease of access, what would create the largest inferno and provide the simplest escape route. Leave the least evidence behind.

It was always like this: an incident triggered me, and something had to burn. What started as bonfires, benches and haybales led to the total destruction of a theatre and watching my own mother burn alive.

So I tried to stop. Succeeded for years. Taught myself to hold it in, squash it down.

And then out of nowhere, nearly a lifetime later, my fingers itched once more with the need to strike a match. I missed the ROAR. I knew if I didn't see flames, feel their heat, listen to their crackle, and observe their destruction – if that didn't happen soon, I would die. It's an animal urge, as much a part of me as thirst or hunger.

And I began once more, cautious and careful with my addiction. A derelict shed on a warm day, where an old petrol cannister could ignite after years of neglect. A stable full of dodgy electrical circuits, machinery, heating devices and a huge amount of fuel for flames. And if a hay bale is too moist, it can spontaneously combust. BOOM. Barn to ashes. Horses dead.

I thought I knew it all.

But I didn't know horses can scream.

As I lie awake each night, I listen to the sounds of the house as it settles and I imagine burning it to the ground.

I've seethed and raged and swallowed all my frustrations. I can't do it anymore. Can't see all my secrets laid out like a patient splayed open on the operating table.

I'll burn the past, burn the present, and start again.

I open the window a small crack. A fire needs oxygen to breathe, to thrive.

It's inevitable: fire investigators will find your start point, so choose something that looks like an accident. An almost-empty aerosol can heating up next to a hot chimney pipe, ready to explode at any moment. Like a Rube Goldberg machine of fire: the can explodes, the carpet catches and then WHOOSH. House in flames.

Flick-fizz. I watch the flame dance on the end of the match, creeping up the wood towards my fingertips. These fingertips shiny and white with the scars of previous match burns. Just before the flame touches my skin, I drop it into the bathroom bin, and the contents catch light quickly. The fire's tongues creep and crawl over the waste, creating a neat little campfire in the cupboard. It gets warmer; it'll be only moments before the discarded hairspray can ignites and then BOOM. House gone.

Fires tend to spread vertically unless they meet an obstacle. Or they're helped.

A few scattered polyester blouses around the bedroom floor and the fire has a little path it can follow to the curtains.

I have a few moments before the BOOM, so I cross to the window. Cleo's still there, on the phone now as the boys watch, helpless.

And then the wind changes, and I hear what she says: 'Help, please. Please send the police. It's my stepfather. Anthony Gardiner. He's out of control.'

I crouch to push my ear to the gap in the window so I can hear her.

'He's always been abusive, but this is the first time it's gone this far.' She lets out a sob, but I see her smiling at the two boys.

Her voice gets higher, more panicked. 'We need your help now.

He's right here. Smashing things up, I'm so scared.' *The distress in her voice is countered by the pride and glee on her face. How easily she lies.* 'He's going to hurt someone.'

She crosses to the little plum tree at the edge of the lawn, places her hand on the head-height knot on the trunk, cupping it in her palm as she talks.

'He's coming. Please. This is an emergency,' *she shrieks. And then she really does wink; just before she drives her own eye right into the knotted wood. The knotted wood which is the exact size and shape of a fist.*

She planned this just as I plan my fires.

The crackling behind me is louder now, the air stifling. I turn towards the room, and am greeted by a wall of flame, an old friend. It's as tall as me, and broader. A human-sized fire which licks outwards, desperate to spread its wings. It's beautiful. I made this.

I'm sweating, and it's harder to breathe. With regret, it's time to go.

I turn to the window one last time, just in time to see Cleo punch herself in the face and shriek. 'Please, come quickly! He's hitting me!' *she screeches down the phone to the poor, unsuspecting operator.*

'Cleo!' *Lucasz shouts, his face wracked with distress. He looks broken. I pause for a second to stare at him. He had no idea until this moment. I see his world crumble as he realises who she really is. He runs to her, tries to wrap his arms around her, to stop her somehow. But she uses this. She wrestles him and shouts,* 'He's on top of me.'

Lucasz lets her go, his hands held out to show he means no harm.

Spider sinks to the ground, his head in his hands. 'What are you doing?' *He shakes his head.*

Then Lucasz straightens up, looks around. Sniffs the air. 'Is that smoke?'

My shirt sticks to my back, the heat intense. 'Oh, shit.' *Lucasz points a trembling finger at the roof.* 'The house is on fire,' *he shouts.*

I duck below the windowsill, eyes just high enough to see them.

'Jamie's in there. Your Mum. And Ant.'

Cleo stands on the lawn, the phone still pressed to her ear. A trickle of blood runs down her face from her split eyebrow. 'He's set the house on fire,' she says into the phone, her voice calm. 'He wants the insurance money.'

Ignoring Cleo, both boys sprint towards the house. Doomed heroes.

Jamie

Jamie pauses, sniffs the air. It's so faint she could be imagining it, like all the other paranoid times recently when she's imagined the arsonist has acted on his threat to punish her for making the documentary. She shakes her head. It's not real.

It's not until a gap between the songs that she hears something. A bang.

Her eyelids fly open. There's a haze in the room; gossamer threads of smoke float on the air currents, like the aromatic curls of smouldering incense sticks. But she hasn't burned incense for years. She sits up, sniffs again, and her stomach roils. It's not her imagination. Something is on fire. A sharp clatter against the glass. She shrieks in surprise and rushes over to the window. Outside, Spider stands on the lawn with one bare foot, a discarded shoe lying next to him. That must have been what hit the glass.

She fumbles to open the window, but Spider screams 'NO!' He drops his folders, and papers fly across the grass. All his research scatters across the lawn.

'Don't open the window,' he shouts. 'Try and get out. Stay low. Hold your breath.'

She gives a quick nod and turns back to the room, which has filled with smoke in the moments since she looked out of the window. It seeps in through the gaps around the door. The room is unnaturally dark, like a solar eclipse on a sunny day.

She thinks back to the costume designer, caught in that windowless green room in the bowels of the theatre. Not knowing where the fire started, where it has spread, which way to run. Even though Jamie knows her house's familiar corridors and the route to the front door, how can she be sure that's the right way to escape? It could be the path towards more danger. Towards getting trapped.

She gives a little cough. Sweat breaks out on her forehead and upper lip. The longer she hesitates, the thicker the smoke becomes.

She fumbles for a scarf and wraps it around her face, and then lays a hand flat on the door. The door's surface is warm against her hand.

Scrunching up her stinging eyes, she opens the door a crack.

There's a *whoosh* as the fire sucks the air from the room.

Somewhere out in the corridor, the inferno roars like a wild animal. It's pitch-dark and the smoke is thick. She peers down the hallway towards Mum and Ant's room, where the smoke grows thicker. She lets out a little whimper.

Somewhere to her left, there's the sound of breaking glass.

'Jamie!' Ant crawls up the stairs, holding his phone as a torch. The beam of white light pierces the smoke like a needle but doesn't clear a path. She can barely see him. As he moves closer, she can just make out his eyes, which glitter with tears from the smoke. There's a dripping tea towel wrapped around his face. 'The fire's in our bedroom.' He points down the hall, where the smoke is thickest.

How does he know? It's too dark to see from here.

Her toes catch on the carpet, and she stumbles. Her ribs pulse in pain as she tenses her body and finds her feet.

'Just do what I say. Don't make me lose you and your mum too.' He takes a breath. 'Get outside and call 999.' He doesn't wait for an answer – he crawls along the landing, his whole body low to the ground like a snake.

She crouches down like Ant, pushes her face into the carpet and takes in a breath, as deep as she can through her sore ribs. It's slightly cooler on the ground, but it's growing hotter by the second.

Lungs full of air, she pulls herself to her feet and peers through the smoke. She taps the ground ahead of her with her toes as she moves forward, trying to find where the stairs descend. It's so disorientating; if she's not careful she'll lose her way in the darkness.

She flattens one hand to the wall, feels the way. Her lungs are bursting. She must have moved six feet, no more. The lack of air makes her feel faint, and she crouches low to take another drag of air. Her whole body shakes; her legs barely hold her up.

Behind her, the roaring sound mingles with shouts and the crackling of smouldering wood. She sobs.

Finally, the carpet drops away beneath her feet. She grabs the bannister and runs down the stairs. She bursts through the front door and out into the fresh air, coughing and coughing.

She gasps, dragging the fresh air deep into her lungs. She's doubled over, her hands on her knees. She is safe. She could have died. She'll never know how close she was.

Spider is immediately by her side, a bottle of water held to her lips, an arm around her heaving shoulders. She shrugs him off, nodding to indicate she's OK.

Cleo and Lucasz stand together. They watch her with concerned looks on their faces.

'Where are the sirens?' Lucasz peers down the road. He hops from foot to foot, pacing, his arms folded. 'We called ages ago.'

'Where's Ant? And your mum?' Spider squints up at the house. He fiddles around with his phone, pointing it up at the house.

He's *filming*.

Jamie sinks to the grass, too exhausted and breathless to even protest. 'They're still inside.'

There's surprisingly little smoke in the air compared to inside the house. It must be building up as the fire takes hold. She's seen it in films, when the heat gets so intense that the windows shatter and all the smoke pours out.

Spider takes a step towards the front door, his phone out of sight. 'They should be out by now. What's going on?'

She stares up at the house through stinging eyes. She can barely breathe, but it's fear, not smoke holding her back.

'Maybe Ant's dead,' Cleo pipes up.

Jamie swears at her. 'If Ant's dead, Mum's dead, you stupid shit. Shut up if you can't say anything helpful.' Jamie's anger descends into coughing.

'I've got to do something.' Spider paces around, running his hands through his hair. 'Do you have a fire extinguisher in the house?'

'Don't. It's safer to stay out here.'

Spider takes another step towards the house, shouting over his shoulder. 'Jamie? Fire extinguisher?'

She can't stop him. 'Under the kitchen sink, I think.'

He shoves open the front door, holding his phone ahead, camera first. He steps back, and smoke pours out, filling the air and obscuring Spider from view.

In the distance, the faint sound of sirens starts to move closer. 'Thank God,' Jamie mumbles.

As the first plume of black smoke clears, she sees Spider hasn't entered. He's helping Ant, who emerges with Mum thrown over his shoulder. Ant staggers under her weight, his clothes and skin black with soot.

He loses his footing as he reaches the driveway, and Spider helps him lower Mum to the ground.

Ant sinks to his knees on the gravel drive, his lungs wracked with coughs. He shakes his head slowly, heaving for breath. Then he looks up at the house. Plumes of smoke pour from the broken windows and the open front door, drifting up into the slate-grey sky overhead.

Mum is covered in soot, her clothes charred and torn. She breathes faintly, her eyes closed.

Between coughs, Ant says, 'She fought me.' He shakes his head, bewildered, lost, his arms wrapped around his knees. His eyes are icy blue, the whites riddled with red veins. Tears course down his dirty cheeks, and Jamie doesn't know if he's crying or if it's the effects of the smoke. 'She didn't want to come.'

'She must have been confused.' Jamie turns Mum on her side, the recovery position. As she does, something falls to the drive. She gasps.

Cleo steps forward. 'What's that?'

Jamie snatches it up, shoves it in her pocket and glances at Ant. 'Nothing,' she says to Cleo. 'Just a lip balm. I'll look after it for Mum.'

Ant meets her gaze, his eyes wide. He freezes, and then

something in him releases. He says nothing, just shakes his head and stares at the gravel of the driveway, his eyes flicking around as he thinks.

Jamie watches his face as Ant processes what this means. She knows too. The box in her pocket digs into her thigh like an accusation.

The sirens grow louder; Jamie covers her ears to block out the deafening shrieks. The fire engine noses its way through the gate, and firemen pile out of the truck, barely paying them any attention as they unload the hoses and the ladders.

A man runs to Jamie, barks something at her and she points in the direction of Mum and Ant's bedroom and mutters, 'Upstairs.'

Another fireman checks Mum's airways and examines her all over. Cleo, Jamie, Spider and Lucasz watch in silence until he nods and puts an oxygen mask over Mum's face, and hands one to Jamie and one to Ant, who pulls the elastic around the back of his head.

As soon as the fireman leaves, Ant pulls the mask away from his face to speak. Low, so only Jamie hears, he says: 'Ella told me in there.' He coughs again, covering his mouth and hacking deeply until he reapplies the mask. The clear plastic fogs with his breath.

Jamie opens her mouth, closes it again behind her own mask. She can't speak.

'It was the only way to get people to listen,' he croaks.

Cleo

Ant sits there on the drive, his head in his hands. His thumb ring glints in the afternoon sunlight. His hair doesn't look so luxurious anymore, with little pieces of it shrivelled from the heat of the flames.

He plays a good part, sitting there looking like the rescuing hero and the victim all at once. She has to hand it to him, he's a good actor. Good at swooping in at the last moment and claiming the credit for everything, like the lazy kid on the school football team who hangs around by the goal waiting to kick the ball in while the rest of the team do the hard work.

When the true hero, the one who got the ball all the way to the end of the pitch, is Cleo. She called the emergency services even before the fire took hold, and made sure Spider alerted Jamie so she could get out in time. No need for posturing or getting burned for attention. Ant is such a dick.

And the fire. If he even dares to try and claim it was an accident... she shudders in anger and frustration. He's an arsonist; he planned this all along. Maybe he wanted the whole family dead in the fire: Jamie and Cleo out of the picture. And with their deaths, he also perpetuates the cover-up of evidence of his own past crimes, recently discovered and about to blow up in his face. Very convenient.

The firemen emerge from the building, their uniforms dripping with water. The smoke is worse now, but the leader nods, tells them the fire is out. That they've localised the source to Mum and Ant's bedroom (what a surprise) and Ant is a hero. Cleo rolls her eyes so hard that she almost sprains something.

More sirens and lights trundle around the corner. A police car.

Two police emerge from the car, a man and a woman. They both have very serious expressions on their faces. Cleo suppresses a smile and points at Ant.

They glance at her and then speak to Jamie and Spider. 'We're had a report of domestic violence at this property.' The woman police officer glances over the scene: the smouldering building, the firemen clearing away their hoses.

Jamie opens her mouth to speak, but dissolves into coughing.

Spider steps forward. 'I don't think—'

'He's there, officers.' She finally follows Cleo's pointing finger to Ant, who has put his oxygen mask back on and is wrapped in a foil blanket like he's just run a marathon.

'Sir? Anthony Gardiner?'

He looks at her over his mask and nods.

'Does he need medical attention?' She turns to one of the firemen.

'Needs a once-over for smoke inhalation.'

The policeman nods. 'You're going to have to come with us, and we'll get you checked over at the station. We've had a call about domestic abuse.'

Ant shakes his head, the oxygen tube flapping around so much it nearly knocks over the silver cannister of gas next to him.

Jamie steps forward and pulls her own mask aside. 'No, this can't be right. It must be a mistake. He just saved us all from a fire.'

Lucasz nods in agreement. 'The call wasn't tru—'

Cleo shoves him out of the way. 'Mind your own business,' she hisses at him.

The woman shrugs. 'We take reports of this nature very seriously. We need to speak to Anthony at the station.'

She glances at Cleo, nodding at the cut above her eye. In all the fire excitement, Cleo nearly forgot about that, about ramming her head against the tree and calling the police, crying that Ant was hitting her. How clever she is.

'He do that?' the officer asks.

She tries to look cowed, scared as she glances at Ant, whose eyes are wide in confusion and rage.

'He did,' she whispers. 'Right before he set the house on fire.'

The policewoman starts to recite the TV thing about *anything you do say may be used against you* and Cleo straightens her spine, holds eye contact with Ant.

In a quiet voice, he talks over the policewoman, his eyes not leaving Cleo: 'I want you all to know I didn't do anything she accuses me of. I never touched Ella, nor Cleo.'

'You took over her bank accounts—' Cleo shouts.

'To pay off her debt with my savings.'

'You wanted her to quit her job.'

'Because she was stressed.' His voice is strained, like a teacher trying to control an unruly class, desperate not to show they're bothered.

She shakes her head. 'Liar.'

'That's enough.' The policewoman moves him into the patrol car.

As the taillights of the police car turn the corner, a fireman approaches, removing his helmet. His face is red and sweaty, his skin covered in a sheen of soot. He's so tall that Cleo has to tilt her head to look him in the eye.

'From what we can tell it's mainly smoke damage, which is good news.' He gives a small smile. 'The structure of the house is safe, except for the master bedroom.'

'That's fantastic news,' Jamie agrees, and Spider takes her hand. Cleo sees her flinch a little at his touch.

'You can go back into the house to gather some belongings, but often people prefer not to re-enter the property. The smoke can irritate your lungs.' He hands Jamie a piece of paper. 'Call this number to request temporary accommodation if you need it. And get checked out at the hospital as soon as you can; you weren't exposed to the smoke for long, but they'll want to monitor your CO_2 levels.'

Jamie nods. 'Thank you. Thanks for everything. We'll sort something out.'

'Don't sleep here,' he adds.

Very quickly, the firemen are gone, Mum with them for her own check at the hospital.

A flock of crows bursts from the branches of their plum tree. Cleo looks from Jamie to Lucasz to Spider, all very still and quiet as they stand on the driveway, staring up at the house. None of them will look at Cleo or each other.

'He's finally gone, guys. Can you believe it? We're free.'

Jamie stands up, steps over Spider's scattered research paperwork all over the driveway, some of it torn and stained, and walks away towards the house without looking back.

Lucasz just shakes his head at Cleo, his eyes cold. 'I don't know who you are. You're not my friend.' He doesn't look back as he walks away.

Jamie

It's a sunny afternoon outside, but inside the house it is as dark as night-time. There's a steady *drip, drip* as water from the firemen's hoses settles in the furnishings on the upper floors. In the study, she grabs the manila folder from Ant's desk and carries it outside, back into the fresh air as quickly as possible. The writing on the front confirms what she remembers from seeing it on the desk chair when she used the PC earlier. This is where the answers are.

'What's that?' Spider sits on the drive, his face smudged with ash.

She joins him on the ground, showing him the folder. His eyes widen as he reads the label: 'Ant: birth cert etc'.

Her lungs ache from the smoke. There's ash up her nose, coating the insides of her nostrils. She opens the folder, Spider leaning against her. She shifts away. She doesn't want him to touch her.

The top of the stack is an official-looking document on yellowed paper with red ink. The letterhead says Abbeywick Children's Home. 'He must have got his old records somehow.'

'He's Anthony Gardiner, fostered aged 12. Birth father unknown.' Spider traces the words with his fingers. 'His name was never Tony Kerr, like the kid from the derelict house. And his birth mother was... holy shit.'

'What? What's holy shit?' Jamie leans over him to see the paper.

'Ant was orphaned by a fire, but he's not the owner of the house.' Spider shakes his head. 'Louise Alderton, deceased. Occupation: Costume Assistant, Abbeywick Theatre Royal.'

'Your mum's friend...?' Jamie's head hurts.

Spider nods. 'Her best friend.'

'So Ant's mum died in the theatre fire.'

'And that's why he was fostered.' He runs his hand over his face. 'I mean, Mum mentioned she had a son. But I assumed he lived with his dad after Louise died or something. I never looked into what happened to him.'

Dad arrives as the sun starts to lower in the sky, the corners of his mouth tight with worry. He gathers Cleo in his arms, checking her for injuries, making sure she's OK. He smooths Cleo's hair, kisses her forehead.

Jamie looks away, but he calls her over, pulls her to his chest.

'Jamie,' Dad mutters into her hair. 'We've found Daisy.'

Jamie lifts her face, wary. Too much has happened today. *Please let this be good news.*

He whistles, and Daisy trots around the corner, tail wagging so wildly that her whole body wiggles with joy. Cleo squeals with joy. Jamie can't help but smile, reach down and cup each side of her lovely furry face.

'I bumped into your neighbour on the drive, bringing her over. She got through a hole in their fence and trapped herself in their shed. Poor little thing. At least she wasn't in here for the fire.'

Cleo smooths Daisy's ears and mumbles, 'Dogs don't lock themselves in sheds. People lock them in sheds.' She flashes Jamie a dark look, and mouths *Ant.*

While Cleo and Jamie fuss over the dog, Dad sets about doing the dad stuff: finding the insurance details, locking up the garage and the back door, ready for them to leave the house. He tells Spider to head off home, and he retreats, grateful to put distance between himself and everything that happened today.

The carpet squelches under her feet as she climbs the stairs to her room. The walls have a dark, greasy sheen and the wallpaper feels gritty to the touch.

She's distracted by the darkness, the stink of smoke, the

Fire Service-branded sheet of paper in her hand entitled '*The fire is out, what do I do now?*' She raises her foot to the next step, but something goes wrong. Her toe catches, slips on the lump in the carpet and she's plummeting once more, down and down the stairs, the carpet burning her skin as she falls.

'*Jamie, careful!*' *Ant shouts.*

And then the wooden floor of the hallway against her cheek.

She catches her breath, opens her eyes. Ant isn't here. He's gone, with the police. She's not on the floor, she didn't fall. Her ribs ache, but it's not the searing agony of before. She's still standing on the stairs. She caught the bannister, stopped herself from tumbling down.

And she remembers.

Ant didn't push her. She tripped.

———

'Jamie.' Mum is wearing the same clothes she wore earlier, but now they're charred and blackened. One of her arms is bandaged, and a white hospital bracelet encircles her wrist. A transparent tube bisects her face, piping oxygen into each nostril. Her skin is grey, and Jamie isn't sure whether that's stained from the smoke or her pallid skin.

'They checked me over. I'm fine to leave once my oxygen levels rise.' Mum pats the hospital bed, inviting Jamie to sit.

Jamie wants to be as far away as possible; she doesn't want to be in this hospital cubicle surrounded by blue curtains. She backs away, leans against the windowsill, her arms folded. 'I should call the police myself.'

Mum shakes her head, feigning confusion.

'Why did you have these?' She pulls the box from her

pocket, drops it to the bed where Mum's hand lay a moment ago. She feels the tears coming and lets them fall.

Mum glances at the box as if she's never seen it before.

'It fell from your pocket.' Jamie picks it up once more, slides the box open. It's half-full, with a rolled-up piece of paper slotted in alongside the remaining matches. She pulls out the paper and unrolls it. It's a sales receipt: kerosene lamp oil, 1 litre.

There's no denying this, no matter how practised a liar Mum might be. 'They use kerosene in antique lamps, don't they?' Like the one Jamie held as a weapon that first time she visited The Old Manor to look for Cleo.

Mum nods. 'I see them a lot at antiques fairs.' Her voice is scratchy.

Jamie's jaw aches with tension. 'The arsonist used kerosene at the stable fire last week. And before, in the fires we looked at for the documentary. The amusement arcade, the bandstand, the high school. Smashed kerosene lamps, thrown like grenades.'

A small frown crinkles Mum's brow and she waves a hand like she's batting away a fly.

'You set our house on fire.' Her hands shake, the matches rattle in their box.

Mum looks down at her hands, flexing open and closed in her lap, a burn scar shining across the back of her hand.

Jamie wants to reach out and grab her by her charred clothes, to shake the truth out of her. 'And The Old Manor.'

At this, Mum freezes. Her eyes slowly raise from her clenched hands, up to meet Jamie's gaze. Jamie's stomach clenches. She doesn't want this to be true. She wants Mum to have some kind of plausible explanation, anything that makes

Jamie wrong about this. 'You've been to the house in the woods.'

Mum gives a tiny nod.

'You set it on fire when Cleo and Lucasz were there?'

Mum doesn't move.

Jamie picks up the box of matches and slides them back in her pocket. 'I don't have to stay here, Mum.' The word 'mum' feels wrong in her mouth. The woman sitting in front of Jamie is her mother, but she's not the person Jamie has called 'Mum' for her whole life. The person Jamie thought she knew no longer exists. 'I can leave right now; go straight to the police and I'll never understand who you are. This is the time you get to tell the truth. After this, there's no chance to help me understand what this has all been about, convince me why I should ever speak to you again.'

Jamie pulls her jacket over her shoulders, ready to leave.

'Stop, Jamie. I didn't know Cleo and Lucasz were inside the building. I would never...' Mum's face shifts, the fixed mask of composure cracks in half to reveal genuine, deep sadness. 'I can't lose you and Cleo. I love you, Jamie. I never wanted you to find out the truth about me. Who I am. If you'd known...'

'And who are you?' Jamie's voice comes out almost like a snarl.

Mum pulls the oxygen tube from her nose. 'Antonella.'

Jamie sinks into the chair by the hospital bed, her legs weak. The name on the bedroom wall in that damp, crippled house. 'You're Tony Kerr?'

She nods. 'My dad insisted I was named Antonella. Mum hated it, so she registered me as Tony. Dad never knew, said forms and certificates were women's business. A small victory.' She shrugs. 'I became Ella when they died.'

'Tony.' She remembers the child in the family photograph,

their face blurred as the camera caught their movement. Not a boy, but a little girl with an androgynous bob haircut, standing with her parents at the Moorburn Bay bandstand. Just a year or two before the arsonist burned it down. Jamie can hardly breathe. 'So the child from The Old Manor did set the fire which killed their parents. Cleo was right. The only thing she got wrong was the identity. You're an arsonist.'

Mum flinches, then gives a little smile as if accepting it. 'That's the first time anyone's ever said it to me. It's the first time I've heard it out loud, even if I've known it since I first lit a match and watched the flame creep down the wood. But it's amazing what you can force yourself to get used to.'

'You killed someone. The woman in the theatre.'

She closes her eyes, nods. 'Even horrors start to feel normal if you carry them inside you long enough. I was very young, though, Jamie. Younger than Cleo.'

'That's not an excuse.'

'I was a victim too. No one heard my calls for help, or my mother's. Deep in those woods, in that cursed house. So I spoke long and loud with every fire. It was the only communication I knew after years of being told to shut up, keep quiet, cope and don't complain.' She reaches out to Jamie, but Jamie shakes her head. She can't go near her, not now.

Mum shrugs, carries on: it's as if now she's started talking, she has to keep going until she's said it all. 'It burned inside me, bright and hot until it burst out and set things alight around me. And then it was out of my control. I had a voice and I made it heard, just not in the way society wanted to hear it.'

'You're dangerous. You need help.' Jamie's voice cracks.

'I just…' She sighs. 'You're right, Jamie. Since I first saw my dad hit my mum in front of me, I feel like I've been screaming for help. I begged at the top of my lungs. No one heard me.'

Exhausted, Jamie sinks to the floor, her back against the wall. She shakes her head. 'You had a choice.' Something glimmers at the edge of Jamie's consciousness. 'Spider and I made a list in our shared drive of local fires from the 1980s from old police reports and newspaper articles. It took us months. Why wasn't The Old Manor on there? It's impossible we missed it.'

'You left your laptop open one day and I saw your list. You were too close. I deleted The Old Manor file.'

Jamie's breath catches, almost choking her. 'You sent me threats. A horse's hoof. You told me I would *die* if I kept filming.' She spits out the last sentence like it's poison.

'At first I thought it would fizzle out. That you'd film for a week or two and then move onto something else. But then Ant got involved and started pushing you to film more, to investigate more—'

'Of course he pushed. Of course he wanted us to investigate. He wanted us to catch the arsonist, to bring them to justice for what they did to his mother.' Jamie's voice gets higher. She hears a conversation falter across the corridor. She lowers her voice, climbs back into the chair. 'Didn't you know who he was?'

Mum's forehead creases. 'He tried to tell me, earlier today. It was too much. I couldn't process it.' Her eyes twinkle with tears. 'I'm sorrier than you know. Than he could ever know.'

Jamie swears under her breath. She thinks of Catherine, shuffling through the ashes of her stables, picking up a horseshoe from the wreckage and sobbing at the memory of the creature who used to wear it, reduced to dust. 'I can't do this.' She covers her ears and closes her eyes, unable to hear any more. Maybe no one's listened to Mum, but the first person to hear her cannot be Jamie. 'You need professional help. Cleo, too.'

As if she heard her name, the curtain opens and Cleo walks through, a big grin on her face and a Krispy Kreme doughnut in her hand. She has a black eye threatening to form, and dried blood clotted in her eyebrow, with fresh butterfly clips holding the wound together. Her clothes and skin look so clean compared to Mum and Jamie's blackened faces.

Mum gives a breathy groan from deep in her chest. 'Poor Cleo.' She holds out an arm and Cleo nestles into her side, sitting together on the hospital bed.

Jamie almost screams. 'Poor Cleo? What are you talking about?' She controls her volume, aware of the nurses bustling around outside the curtain. 'She's dangerous,' she whispers.

Mum nuzzles Cleo's hair. 'Terrible things happen when people don't listen. Cleo sets things on fire in a different way. She's inherited all my rage, the poor thing. She needs help, like I do. She just has a different way of showing it. A healthier way, I think.'

Cleo nods, nestling into their mum.

'I'm so sorry, Cleo. This whole mess was manageable when it affected me alone.'

Jamie interrupts with a sarcastic, fed up, angry laugh. 'Affected you alone?' she chokes out. 'Catherine lost her livelihood. Ant lost his mum, his family.'

Mum closes her eyes and continues as if Jamie never spoke. 'But now I've seen it's transferred to Cleo, I can't let any of this carry on. We need to get help.'

'And what about Ant? What happens to him? They have no evidence he did anything wrong. They'll release him. He's coming back to our house. It's his home.'

'He can't come back there; they wouldn't let him. Not after what I accused him of?' Cleo looks to Mum for confirmation.

Jamie tugs at her hair. 'You burned yourself on the oven that day and you blamed him. The police will see that in the footage.'

'There wasn't enough proof on the tape. I never handed it in. They would have just laughed at me.'

'Then why…?'

'I needed you to believe me about him.'

'Did he burn you?'

Cleo doesn't answer.

'She maybe had to twist the truth a little.' Mum frowns and pats Cleo's shoulder. 'But Cleo was more right than she knew.'

Cleo nods. 'I didn't make it all up. Just some of it.'

'What do you mean, "more right than she knew"?' Jamie asks Mum. She feels like her head is exploding.

'He wasn't physically abusive, not yet. But he did damage. He pushed me to marry him too fast, isolated me from friends, from people like Tina. And you.' She nudges Cleo. 'He made me think I was happy, but really I was on a rollercoaster all the time: the highest highs, or the lowest lows. He gave me no time to think, to realise the difference between reality and what he wanted me to believe. I didn't know how to get out, and Cleo showed me the way.'

Jamie pulls at her own hair. 'She made it all up!' she shrieks. 'You mean it's fine he got arrested, because he MIGHT eventually have done the things she accused him of?'

Cleo wipes powdered sugar from her mouth with a napkin. 'No one listens until there's violence. But *Happily Ever After* says emotional abuse is just as destructive. I needed something to happen, for people to see what Ant really is.'

'That's not the right way to do things, Cleo.' Jamie's mouth fills with saliva. She looks around for one of those cardboard bowls in case she needs to vomit.

'I agree. People should see emotional abuse as just as significant. But they don't.'

'And what about the message from his ex-wife's daughter?' Mum tilts her head, remembering. 'I'm stumped on that one.'

Cleo shrugs. 'Sent it to myself. Stole the text from Reddit. It's not original, what Ant's doing. He's a specific type of person, and there's a lot like him out there. It wasn't hard to find someone talking about it. More people should talk about it.'

Jamie feels a sudden panic. Her stomach roils, full of acid. 'This is a cycle, you know that? Your dad, you, Cleo. You need to break the pattern, or it'll just carry on.'

Mum nods, pulls Cleo in closer.

'The type of person he is… Ant doesn't like to lose. His ego is too fragile. He'll try to persuade you to come back. If he does, you need to say no. You're strong enough, I know you can.'

But Mum's not listening, her nose buried in Cleo's hair.

Jamie stands up slowly, feeling the ache in her ribs spread through her whole body when she feels just how tired today has made her. She picks up her bag and turns to leave, looking back at her mum and Cleo one last time.

'I'm done. I've had enough of this fucked-up family.'

Epilogue

One Year Later

The Theatre Royal looks almost glitzy in the dusk, with strings of fairy lights flanking the red carpet that rolls up to the entrance. Alone in her car, Jamie takes a moment to gather her thoughts. Her car bonnet points out over the cliff, and through the windscreen she can see lights bobbing far out to sea: an oil tanker.

She takes a deep breath, and another. She's waited for this so long and now it's finally here.

She flips down the mirror and takes one last check of her lipstick. There's a faint shadow on her cheek, a reminder of her broken jaw. But the bruises are long gone and the surgery scar is a faint silver now. She grabs her handbag and swings her legs out of the car, making sure to steady herself on her heels before she stands.

No crowds clap at her as she walks towards the entrance, but two people wait by the door. A couple, holding hands, stand under the overhanging roof. Above their heads, the white sign with red lettering reads: 'PREMIERE: A PORTRAIT OF FEMALE RAGE, A FILM BY JAMIE DAVIDSON'.

'Your name's up in lights, J,' a familiar voice calls.

She shivers in the cold night air.

'Bloody well done,' he shouts.

He steps forward and the light catches his face. He's still handsome, still beardy.

She pulls a smile to her face and raises a hand in a wave. 'Hey, Spider.' She steps towards him and air-kisses him on both cheeks, careful not to touch her lips to his skin. 'It's nice to see you.'

The woman steps from the shadows and reaches towards her, her head turned sideways for a kiss. Her hair is longer now, her face softer as time distances her from the brutality of the loss of her stable.

'And lovely to see you too, Catherine. Thank you for coming.'

Catherine grabs Spider's hand again and they turn towards the theatre. 'Are you ready?' he asks Jamie, and she nods, following them into the theatre.

It should be strange to see Spider with someone else, but in a way it's a relief. She'll never forget the cold feeling in her stomach when she saw his spy camera blinking at her while she lay in that hospital bed. She swallows the memory, fakes a smile as she enters the foyer.

The smell of popcorn reminds her of her days working at the cinema. There's a good crowd inside, local people and press milling around, drinking wine, buying snacks from the kiosk, and reading the programme, which Jamie knows by heart:

A portrait of female rage: the power of speaking up and the manifestation of unexpressed anger.

Behind the words on the front cover is a bright collage of faces: all women, all angry. None ashamed. The women she interviewed for the documentary. Somewhere in those faces are Mum's and Cleo's.

'I'm excited to finally see this,' Catherine nudges her and whispers.

Jamie grins at her. 'I couldn't have done it without you. You gave me the idea. You and my mum.'

She greets a few friendly faces and Spider and Catherine melt off into the crowd, Jamie glad to see them go. She orders a Diet Coke from Pamela Dunning, the theatre manager they interviewed what feels like a lifetime ago. Pamela doesn't seem to remember Jamie, but she may get a reminder soon: Spider's finished the arson documentary with Catherine, and Jamie's heard a rumour that Netflix is interested. She feels only relief that she finally let go of that project, relinquished the control she once fought so hard to retain.

'Ms Davidson?'

A man pulls out the barstool next to her and sits down. 'Mind if I join you?'

She shrugs, her answer not important when he didn't wait to hear it.

'Glenn Tyler.' He holds out a hand. 'From the *Moorburn Bay Gazette.*'

She smiles and shakes his hand. A reviewer. She must be nice. 'I hope you enjoy the film.'

'Thank you, I'm looking forward to it.' His smile tilts. He glances at Pamela behind the bar, checking she's out of earshot as she serves some other people further along. 'I'd like to ask you about your mum and sister. How are they doing?'

Her heart beats faster. Not a reviewer. He's sniffing around for a story. She grabs for her handbag on the bar.

'Don't go, Jamie. I just want to know they're all right. I heard your mum's seeing a psychiatrist in prison.'

She tries to climb down from the stool without falling off her heels.

'And your sister?'

'Please leave me alone.' She gets to the ground and straightens her dress. She thought this had ended months ago, the hounding by the press, the intrusive questions: if she knew, if she could forgive, does she visit Mum in prison, are Mum and Ant still married... she can't answer any of their questions yet. Not even to herself. At least he doesn't seem to know anything about Cleo.

'Ant Gardiner sends his regards. He had a lucky escape, it sounds like.'

Ant. Once a stranger, briefly a stepfather, and now what? A stranger again.

So he's still in the area. A sniff of domestic abuse arrest – even with no charges filed – and he lost his job in television, but the local paper didn't have so many scruples about their employees. The insurance money paid for repairs on the house and he sold it soon after Mum's sentencing. Cleo was right: Mum did sign the house over to him.

His lip curls with frustration and he reaches into his pocket to check his phone. 'Well, I'd love to chat more and stay for your little film screening, but it looks like I'll have to head off. Suspected arson over in New Grange. Looks like your mum's not the only firestarter in the area.'

She trips but manages to get away without falling flat on her face. She's straightening her hair and catching her breath when someone calls her name. She closes her eyes. Not another one.

But when she turns, she sees it's Dad and Sahara, their

smiles wide and happy. Sahara's massively pregnant, her hair even wilder than usual as it's piled up on her head in huge curls. Dad looks tired but happy. They both hug her and whisper, 'Congratulations' in her ear.

'I'm so proud of you, Jamie.' Sahara's eyes sparkle in the theatre lights. 'You took all this trauma and used it to create something amazing.'

Jamie smiles, swallowing her nausea. 'My therapist is more cautious. But thank you.'

The bell rings three times: the show is about to start.

They take their seats in the auditorium, Dad next to Jamie and Sahara next to him. Spider and Catherine slide in behind her with a whispered greeting.

Dad leans towards her. 'Cleo wanted me to say hi. Her psychiatrist says she's improved a lot. She's allowed out into the local town sometimes.'

Jamie smiles at Dad and gives a nod. 'I've got a birthday card for her. Can you give me her address?'

As the lights drop and the fire curtain rises, Dad hands her a piece of paper covered with his scratchy handwriting. 'Cleo's school,' he whispers.

The town written on the paper catches her eye, illuminated by the dim light of the nearby emergency exit sign. She frowns, runs her finger over the text, and her heart stops.

Cleo Davidson
New Grange Hall Behavioural Unit
New Grange
North Yorkshire
YO65 7LT

Her hands shake as she stands from her seat. She peers into

the dark, frantically searching the cinema, looking for the beige of the journalist's tweed jacket, the auburn tinge to his hair.

Suspected arson over in New Grange.

'Sit down!' a voice grumbles behind her. Her cheeks burn. He's gone.

Next to her, Dad gazes at the screen with a proud smile on his face, his brow unwrinkled. He has no idea.

Barely supressing a sob, she folds the paper, slides it into her handbag.

The crowd hushes as the music begins: the whole soundtrack is angry, loud feminist protest punk.

And the dedication appears on the screen:

To women who cry, who shout, who scream, who complain.
To women who refuse to stay quiet.
To women who burn to be heard.
We are listening.

Author's Note

This book is a work of fiction, but coercive control like we see in *The House Fire* is sadly a very real part of daily life for many. When there is no physical violence, it is easy to deny, deflect or ignore the elements of a relationship which feel uncomfortable; to brush off the insidious creep of small yet destructive actions. Coercive and controlling behaviour is not easy to identify or prove, as we see in *The House Fire*, but in 2015 this pattern of behaviour became recognised as an offence in UK law, marking great progress in the UK justice system's response to survivors' experiences.

While prosecution rates remain low, we are seeing an increase in public and professional awareness of what a controlling relationship looks like. You can help by understanding coercive and controlling behaviour, and how subtle it can be. Check in with your family and friends. And if you or someone you know is in an emotionally or physically abusive relationship, please seek help through a local support network.

Acknowledgments

Even though my name is on the cover of *The House Fire*, it is thanks to so many people that you can hold this book in your hands today.

First I need to thank Colm Boyd and Suzy Pope. The best friends in the world are the ones who see you at your worst and still love you, no matter what. And the best *writing* friends are the ones who offer to read your first drafts and still speak to you afterwards, even though you both know that:

a) you should *never* inflict a first draft on anyone, and
b) first drafts are always total garbage.

Suzy and Colm both battled through this novel in its earliest forms, helped me dig through all the terrible parts to find the scraps worth keeping for subsequent drafts, and gave me the motivation I needed to get to 'The End'. I couldn't write anything without these two amazing humans. Thank you both so much.

My literary agent, Charlotte Robertson: I could not ask for a better agent. She knows the publishing industry inside-out and always makes time to talk things through, give me advice, and help me navigate my way through this crazy book-writing world! I know my books are in the best possible hands with Charlotte, and I hope that the last couple of years are just the start of a long career together.

Thank you so much to the team at One More Chapter: Jennie Rothwell for her enthusiasm and support throughout the publication process, Hannah Todd who was on hand with guidance and encouragement while I was writing, and Charlotte Ledger for fostering an open, exciting and dynamic imprint by which I am proud to be published. Thank you also to Bethan Morgan, who helped shape *The House Fire* right from the start with her thoughtful and engaged assessment of the first gems of an idea. Thanks to copyeditor Tony Russell and proofreader Laura Burge for your brilliant attention to detail, and to Lucy Bennett for such a striking book cover. And finally, a big thanks to Emma Petfield and Sara Roberts, whose tireless marketing skills will ensure that *The House Fire* will find its way into the hands of readers around the world.

I was lucky enough to chat with a number of helpful experts on various topics while I was writing *The House Fire*. Many thanks to Louis Kitchen and Luka Vukosavljevic: two excellent multimedia producers who talked me through the technicalities of documentary film-making. Thank you to Keith Derrick, who outlined what it's like to work in a cinema. And big thanks also to Natalie Birdsall-Charnock, who talked so eloquently about horses, riding schools and horseback riding. I'm sorry that the fictional horses in my book didn't fare very well! Any factual errors are my own.

To the readers who write reviews, who recommend my books, who send messages to say they enjoy my writing:

thank you. Book reviews make a huge difference, and hearing from readers always puts a massive smile on my face.

Thank you to family and friends who bought my first book, *Secrets of a Serial Killer*, and got in touch when it was published. Even though it came out in the middle of a pandemic when bookshops were closed, I felt so supported and loved; not to mention how delightful it was to catch up with old friends who I haven't spoken to in years! Thank you so much for being there, for saying hello, and for telling people about my book. Your support means so much.

And to Kevin and Chris, who arranged a surprise 'Zoom' launch party for *Secrets of a Serial Killer* on publication day: you guys are brilliant. I had the best time that day, and seeing all your faces on that screen will stay in my heart forever: Ann, Jim, Chris, Dave, Gazelle, Denise, Conrad, Genevieve, Emily, Mum, Fraser, Colm, Lauren, Suzy, Laura and Kevin King. Hopefully the next gathering can be in person with lots of drinks, dancing and fun.

I want to make a special mention to my parents and sister for their amazing support over the last couple of years: Mum, who emailed practically everyone she has ever met when my debut was published; Emily, who offered to wear a sign on her forehead to advertise my book; and Dad, who re-joined social media just to tell people about my novel. All three of them read an early draft of this book to check I hadn't gone mad, and I'm so grateful for their insight and support, for my whole life — not just with writing.

Thank you to my husband Kevin, who talks through plot knots tirelessly on daily dog walks with Bella, pays as much attention to my novels as if they were his own, always asks 'can I get you anything?' while I'm hunched over my laptop, and rarely complains that half of my brain is off gallivanting with fictional characters. Thank you.

And finally to Elsie, who didn't yet exist when I began writing *The House Fire*, and who is now the best, most delightful thing in my whole world. Everything is for you.

YOUR NUMBER ONE STOP

ONE MORE CHAPTER

FOR PAGETURNING BOOKS

One More Chapter is an
award-winning global
division of HarperCollins.

Sign up to our newsletter to get our
latest eBook deals and stay up to date
with our weekly Book Club!
<u>Subscribe here.</u>

Meet the team at
<u>www.onemorechapter.com</u>

Follow us!

 <u>@OneMoreChapter_</u>
 <u>@OneMoreChapter</u>
 <u>@onemorechapterhc</u>

Do you write unputdownable fiction?
We love to hear from new voices.
Find out how to submit your novel at
<u>www.onemorechapter.com/submissions</u>